CW00431381

Blue Rain

Oliver Campbell Series Book 2

JULIA JOHNSTON

Copyright © 2021 Julia Johnston
All Rights Reserved.

ISBN-13:

ALSO BY JULIA JOHNSTON

If Everyone Knew Every Plant and Tree
(Oliver Campbell Series Book 1)

For my parents,
Cecilia and Thomas Johnston

CHAPTER ONE

She's called Jasvandi and she's deaf. He didn't even know he *had* a sister and now my best friend, Kamal, had a sister who was deaf. AND, she was coming all the way from America to Newcastle-upon-Tyne on the train to live with him. Mental. We were going to meet this sister he never knew he had at Newcastle Central Station. Just to be clear, she didn't get the train the entire way, but you know what I mean.

"What will she be like, Ollie? Do you think she'll look like me? A miracle to behold, no doubt."

Kamal is in love with words, which is fine, in fact I love words too, but it can be quite annoying too how he goes on.

"If there exists another person who looks like you, it *will* be a weird miracle," I said, my eyes widening.

"Ha! You kill me, you really do," he said.

His expression morphed from sarcasm into seriousness then into hyper-seriousness and he fiddled with his glasses, pushing them right up so they were totally above his eyes before he lowered them again saying,

"I've been meaning to ask you... We've never really talked... I think we need to talk about—"

"Kevin," I said. Which is the name of a book. I mean the book's called, *We need to talk about Kevin.* I knew what he was talking about really.

"No."

"What, then?" I said.

"Lily."

As we sat on tree stumps in the lowest section of my favourite place—the garden at my house in Newcastle—rehearsing *Othello* by William Shakespeare, the thought of Lily sucked the air from my lungs then dragged burning pressure from my throat to my stomach. My eyes fell to the mound of damp dead grass in the corner and I imagined it as a rotting heap of doubled-over, wilted forget-me-nots. They always made me think of Lily. She had helped me plant some once. It was as if the wind whispered, 'Remember me'.

Since my little sister had died last July, I had never talked about 'it', about *her* to anyone much, let alone my best mate. Mam had begged me to go to counselling, but I didn't want to. They offered it to all the family at the place where she died—the hospice. Apologies if you already know this, but a hospice is a peaceful place with exceptionally caring people who look after other people who are going to die. I didn't even know that till near the end, I mean that they were places in which to die.

It was September, so it had been over a year. She should have been at my sixteenth birthday party (which I didn't have in the end) and she should have been nearly seven years old. I have to say, though, 'a year' is totally meaningless to me. A year, a decade—who cares? No amount of time could alter the truth: my little sister, Lily Ethel Campbell, was dead. Time stretched ahead of me like a dirty swirling mist.

"You can't just say, 'We need to talk about Lily.' We don't *need* to do *any*thing," I said, leaning forward, stamping down the grass with my new black baseball boots as if it were on fire. They weren't actually new but my brother, Nathan, had given me them so they were new to me. Come to think of it, they were pretty shabby.

"What about when Jasvandi comes? It might be difficult for you, meeting her?" Kamal said.

I stayed bent over, staring at the grass. "Cool name isn't it? Are we going to call her that or shall we give her a nickname?" I said.

"In the first instance," said Kamal, "but after a while, we should call her—"

"Jaz" we said at the same time. Though my face had felt like smiling for a second, to be honest, the thought of meeting Kamal's sister for the first time made me feel physically sick.

"I did that list by the way," I said.

"What? Oh, the goal list for school? We can compare notes later," he said. "Jasvandi. Mellifluous isn't it?"

I'd looked up that word at some point but couldn't remember what it meant. Kamal saw my puzzling eyes and said,

"Like honey. Flows off the tongue and melts the air with its sweetness."

"Like the French for honey, 'miel'," I said, sitting back up straight. Couldn't believe I'd remembered that and felt a tinge of smugness.

"You learnèd chap!" he said shoving me hard so that I nearly fell off the tree stump. That was the sort of thing that got Kamal excited. Anything to do with words.

"Surely that didn't come into our French lessons?" he said.

"No. Grandpa once gave me the music to a jazz song called 'Lune de Miel'. Who's it by again? Gipsy or Gipsy Project or something. It means—" and we both said, "honeymoon". In synch. We were like that. At least during that time in our lives, we were like that. You couldn't imagine things would change. But they do... like, loads, like more than you could ever think possible.

"I don't need to look at notes. I remember what I wrote on my goal list. Do you want to hear?" I said.

"If you want," he said, apparently irritated by my enthusiasm but patient too. "Fire away then."

3

"Right let's see if I can list them all..." I looked up into the changing sky to focus:

Design a garden for sick children

Play saxophone in a band and perform in London

Go to America, and maybe Australia and Costa Rica

Make Mam proud of me

What else? We had to think of at least five, didn't we? Um?"

I reached for my paper which was in my right-hand back pocket.

"Oh yeah:

Discover a cure for Lily's illness, Alper's Disease, and you'll like this last one,

Find out how to make dhal."

"No. Ha. Dhal, seriously? I don't believe you. Let me see," Kamal said as he snatched my list. He always went on about this lentil curry dish called dhal and cooked it often during that time, so I thought it would be cool to solve the mystery and learn how to make it myself. Not that I was any good whatsoever at anything like that, but that was the point of the list I suppose.

"Hang on, what's this one crossed out here?" kamal said. "Oooh— Mary what? No, 'Marry', 'Marry Poppy Teasdale'! Hilarious."

"Give me that back."

Every time I went to grab the paper, he jumped up to keep it out of my reach. I grew tired of stressing over it; a calm came over me and I didn't care. I didn't care about the list, about Kamal being a dick, about anything. As soon as I stopped trying to get it, he handed it back anyway. I didn't take it, though. Instead I wafted it away saying, "It's all crap anyway. I don't care."

"Hey, it's not crap."

I sat back down, and my head fell into my hands.

"It isn't crap, Ollie. It's interesting in a way. Though it's probably best not to have a 'maybe' on a goal list. And the order's a bit ropey if you think about it, isn't it? You could consider placing the lentil dish second last then perhaps finishing with the cure for the fatal disease?"

Without looking up or moving, I said, "Interesting? In a way? That's kind."

"Well then I apologise. Come on, I know you're in love with Poppy. It's no secret."

I whipped my head up to look straight at him.

"I'm not," I said. "It's Mr Robinson's fault. He said we should include a jokey goal."

"Okay," Kamal said folding his arms. "If the dhal one wasn't a joke, I could easily teach you to cook it. That way, you could make a good start on your list. You could always add your own twist and make one even better than mine. Sorry, no... no, that's an impossibility."

If there's such a thing as half-heartedly raising one's eyes to heaven, that's what I did after he said that I reckon.

"So what's on *your* list, then, smart arse?"

He told me that he didn't even bother to write his out yet because he knew his goals already. He said he wasn't ruling out tweaking, but that in fact he had finalised his list at the age of ten.

"PPE degree at Oxford or Cambridge University, PHD, Write a book on Shakespeare, Find my parents' graves, and Learn to forgive. Oh and I have a jokey one on a reserve list because you'll say mine are all too serious—Play chess on every pier in the United Kingdom."

Smiles and sudden flinching. It was like my body wouldn't let me laugh or smile for any length of time before I lurched into some sort of toxic spasm. A cross between being conscious and unconscious. Like I'd had some *Brugmansia* poison blown into my face. *Brugmansia's* a flower, by the way, also known as 'Angels' Trumpet'.

"Who do you need to forgive?" I asked Kamal. "Your parents? But they died. Or you mean the bastards who bullied us? Thought you didn't give a shit about them?"

"These are life-long goals, you know?" Kamal said, putting his palms forward and facing up, like he was The Pope or something. "I'm thinking ahead. I'll have racked up a list of folk to forgive by the time I'm older no doubt so it would be good to make a start. Plus I wanted to include something spiritual."

He went back into the house to go to the loo, probably thinking he'd be giving me time to mull over his profound and clever goals. I didn't even know what PPE was though I looked it up later and found it meant 'Philosophy, Politics, and Economics.' Better him than me, I thought. He was so clever. How did he know exactly what he wanted to do? My mind didn't dwell on his words of wisdom at all but drifted back to *Brugmansia*.

I used to think these flowers were sweet and innocent in their shy South American droopiness, but they pack a powerful punch of toxins. The flowers contain atropine, hyoscyamine, and scopolamine. Don't know what they mean, but I'll tell you for nothing, I love those long words, daring you to pronounce them, poking you with a stick—"Go on then, try to say me!" Oh, I should say I know quite a lot about plants and flowers and trees. Not massively about words—that's Kamal's territory—but I'm improving.

I had seen this insane documentary where criminals in Colombia extracted scopolamine and used it as a drug that makes victims unaware of what they're doing even though they're totally conscious. Imagine that. These crazy men blow the powdery poison in a person's face and it's absorbed, probably through the nose. One time, a man got powdered and moved all of his possessions out of his apartment and handed them over to robbers, without remembering any of it. 'Colombian Devil's Breath' they called it I think, this magic powder. How can 'Angel's Trumpet' become 'Devil's Breath' I ask you? An angel becoming a devil... or is it the other way around?

I fancied growing some *Brugmansia*. Maybe I would. I could be like Amy Stewart. I found a book she wrote called, *Wicked Plants: A Book of*

Botanical Atrocities. She made this wacky garden of about thirty species of poisonous plants. Pretty handy if she ever wants to do someone in. Or herself.

When Kamal got back from the toilet he said,

"That song was on the sax, you mean?"

"What?"

"Did your grandpa give you the music to play on your saxophone? *Lune de Miel.* I wouldn't know, would I?"

Kamal had been sitting back on his tree stump, but he got up, flung his script onto the grass, and put his hands on his hips facing me.

"Now that we're on it, why is it that you won't ever let us listen to you play? I know you don't like showing off, but I can never fathom it. It's just us, you know?"

By the way, his 'us' meant him and Poppy. Poppy Teasdale. I can't believe she insisted on haunting me when she knew it was all over (not that anything had happened as such). I mean I suppose I did really want her to haunt me... hard to explain how it felt. I'd need my imaginary Emotion Library to 'look up' that particular one. Woman at the library: 'Don't leave that jar open for too long, son, or it'll do your head in. A serious concoction that wrings out your heart till it's a twisted limp vessel incapable of feeling.'

"It's something I do on my own, that's all."

I got up from the stump too, then turned to stand up on it. I didn't really even want to talk about it, but I kept thinking about meeting Kamal's sister.

"What are you going to wear anyway? At the train station. When Jasvandi enters your life, like an angel from heaven or a devil from hell."

Slightly loopy thing to say, I realize. I'll blame the *Brugmansia.* Wasn't worth worrying about though because Kamal, in all his unpredictableness, loved it.

7

"Yes indeed! Who knows how she might tilt and bend my life! Arsenal top and cool jeans I reckon."

"Eh? She won't have a clue that Arsenal's even a football team, man. And, *you've* got *cool jeans*?"

"The stunning pair with the stripes down the sides, you know? From Primod."

"As long as they weren't manufactured using cheap labour from India, otherwise, it could turn out that it was your sister who made them!" I jumped onto the ground and stretched my arms right back so that all my hair fell back onto my shoulders and I helped it by sweeping it back further before returning to an upright position.

"You're so funny," said Kamal, sitting back down on his stump. "Jasvandi didn't work in a sweat shop—she went to school, in the United States of America, as you know, and therefore knows shit. And as for Primod, they're an ethical trader; I've read their code of conduct."

I splayed my hands over my ears, like they needed protecting from his lunacy.

"Oh my God, you read their code of conduct? You're truly amazing..."

"That said, I may well plump for formal attire in the end since it's a momentous occasion. And yes, I know I'm amazing."

I was about to say, 'Not in a good way', but I was still feeling sorry for him, so I just shook my head with a half-smile and took to my stump once more. When I say I was sorry for him, I mean I couldn't believe his aunt and uncle, with whom he had lived most of his life, had never told him he had a sister. We could have looked for her. In fact, we didn't need to look for her because they knew where she was all along. Turned out it wasn't even India where she'd been adopted after Kamal's parents died in a car accident, but Los Angeles in America. That was somehow worse, I thought. Not the Los Angeles bit, but that they knew where she was. Turned out he'd been a baby at the time; she'd been two or three years old.

He had no memory at all of her, never mind a memory of being adopted and separated from a sister.

Kamal put his up-pointed finger across his mouth then pointed with it at the tree stumps. He flopped his head to the left.

"These weren't here before, were they? Have you been cutting down trees?"

Dad had got them chopped down ages before. I couldn't believe Kamal was that unobservant. Of course, I hadn't been cutting down trees—that is something I could never do. Planting trees, yes, but chopping down...? He knew how much I loved plants and trees, so I don't know why he said something like that. Poor stumps. Poor trees denied their lives, their remainders paraded there on the grass like stags' heads nailed to a wall.

'You honestly think I'd kill a tree?" I said.

"I suppose it *is* killing. But can you ascribe feelings to plants?" Kamal said. "Do you think stumps like this had tree friends and family who've been mourning their loss since the execution?" He fiddled with his glasses (he always did this when he was talking serious). "Or is it our loss? Are we all connected? All one? Am I this stump upon which I am on the verge of sitting again?"

"Is this stump in fact your rump?" I said.

"This world is indeed full of poetry," Kamal said without cracking a smile. He patted the side of his tree stump with his right hand and gave it a bit of a stroke. "Farewell! Thou art too dear for my possessing."

"Shakespeare?"

"Sonnet 87," he said, with one nod and a slow blink. He suggested that, talking of playwrights, we ought to get on with our scene rehearsal. Kamal and I had just started Year Eleven and not only had we already been in two Shakespeare plays, *Hamlet* and *A Midsummer Night's Dream*, he had persuaded me to get involved in the next school play, *Othello*. I was cast as Iago, and Kamal was Othello. Thing is, I had only wanted to be a clown or a sailor or a tree or something, so I'd nearly fallen out with Kamal as he had told Miss Pratt that I was becoming 'distracted' (whatever that meant) and desperately needed a big part on which to focus. Kamal struggled with the fact that he wasn't black like Othello was supposed to be, but I kept reminding him that there was no one black who wanted to take the part and that a lot of Kamal's family had emigrated from India to Tanzania, so he was sort of from Africa. He wasn't even that good at acting but he was brilliant at learning lines and taking direction, so the teacher loved him.

I won't go on and on, but I'll tell you a bit about the play... Othello was an important military leader in Venice, Italy, but he was from North Africa, so he was perceived as an outsider. In case you're interested, Shakespeare's plays have crossovers, like with the themes and that, but they fall into three main categories: comedies, histories, and tragedies. *Othello* is a tragedy, which basically means a large dose of loss and suffering type stuff and a body count to rival a massacre. But even though you notice these themes of death and destruction, the audience is supposed to somehow feel better after the play's over.

Kamal and I were practising a famous scene from the play that day. I said to him,

"How come the audience is supposed to feel better after watching loads of suffering and murders and things?"

"Catharsis is the word you're looking for, dear boy. From the Greek meaning 'purification' or 'cleansing'."

"Oh? Go on."

He got up and started pacing about.

"'A purging of the soul' is another definition of which I'm fond."

"Go on."

"If you think of us poor mortals as being addicted to pity and fear, an audience, experiencing a tragedy on stage, is able to feel compassion and go some way to restore their own emotional balance."

"Go on."

He paused his pacing for a second then continued,

"Are you getting any of this, Ollie? Honestly, 'Go on, go on'. I'll fin-ish with this: the audience learns how to bring these emotions back onto a more correct level."

"More correct? Can you even say that?"

"Is that your only comment?" He came over and shoved me off the stump. I hoiked myself back onto it. "At least you've stopped saying, 'Go on.' More balanced, then."

I picked up my script from the grass and flicked through the scene we had to rehearse.

"Is any of this registering, Ollie? Are you even attending or am I talking into the wind here?"

I let the script fall back to the grass, pushed myself up from the stump, raked my hair backwards off my face and started pacing the patch of gar-den as Kamal had done, hands behind back, like a philosopher, mulling over the mysteries of life.

"Is it like when you talk about something bad that's happened and you feel better, like you've got it out of your system instead of trapping it in?"

"Hmmm. Well, yes that's all linked." He pushed his glasses up from his nose with his right index finger and stroked his hand down either side of his chin like he was feeling his beard. He had more to say, it seemed clear.

I stopped pacing and swivelled to face Kamal.

"Should we do the actual acting now instead of talking about it?" I said.

"You started it."

"No, Kamal, you did with your big word—what was it?"

"Catharsis. Watching the play can be a cathartic experience. It can make you feel better, as you put it."

"Go on... Joking! Okay, okay, let's get on with it."

I got my script and handed Kamal's to him.

"I wonder who'll come to watch the play? Maybe Jasvandi, eh?" I mustered up as much mock-interest in the play, the sister, our life, as I could. "Funny talking about her seeing the play when we haven't even met her yet. I can't believe we're going to meet your... Jasvandi tomorrow."

He smiled a mix of excitement and terror. "Ah yes, about that..." he said. "Her train gets into Newcastle Central Station from London at mid-day, so we'll pick you and Poppy up at 11:30, okay?

"Okay," I said.

"Now, let's get on, this scene isn't going to rehearse itself," Kamal said. "And I won't be needing that." He flung the script next to his stump. "I've learnt all my lines."

JASVANDI'S JOURNAL 1

Dear Journal,

Can't remember when I was this afraid! Here goes. Meeting my kid brother for the first time. I know I have Avin and Keri, but Kamal is different. I still can't get my head round all those wasted years. I've decided to call them 'The Lying Years'. Betrayal is the cruellest weapon. I wrote this last night:

> So that whole life was what, then, as you kept me in your home?
> Was not I worth a dot of froth scooped from life's scruffy foam?
> That truth would be a useless friend to such a flimsy soul
> That honesty would swift repel a heart as dark as coal

I'm guessing Kamal would think I was nuts trying to write poetry. Avin and Keri do. Mom pretends, but I see her face. Anyways, I wouldn't let her see stuff like *this*.

Now that I know what really happened, I blame myself. Maybe Kamal would blame himself too, but I sure don't want him to ever feel what I do. If I hadn't gotten meningitis and lost my hearing, my birth mother would maybe have coped, I guess. Maybe she would have kept me and wouldn't have spiralled downwards? There was the other one too—Kamal's twin brother. I don't even know his name. Mom and Dad never found that out. Would have been nice to know of my brothers' existence, thanks Mom and Dad. "I promised I would tell you the truth when you were sixteen." Promised who? Promised my mother—a drunken mixed up mess who should never have had kids in the first place?? I much preferred the car accident story: both my parents, in love, with their little girl and baby boys, on an idyllic family road trip, when tragedy struck.

Will I be able to tell Kamal the truth? Should I tell him about what really happened and about his twin brother? Mom says it's my duty to tell him. It's what my birth mother wanted before she died. Why did she even take the time to write a goddam note?? 'Tell my kids everything when they're old enough at sixteen. Please God they won't be separated. Make certain the three of them know that it is the drink to blame and not them. I wouldn't do this if they weren't taken away from me. If I still had them, I'd get help and get better. I can't go on alone like this with everything I love taken from me.'

Do you agree, journal, with what my mom said about it all? That it could be my genes from my mother why I mess around with guys all the time? And even maybe why I had to face that hell when I was only twelve? I hope you don't agree because, for the record, I still don't think it was my fault. Can you even remember what that teacher said?? "A pretty girl like you should know better than to take a ride from a stranger." What an asshole. He wasn't a goddam stranger! You know he wasn't. I refuse to go into all that again. I will at some stage I reckon... I won't let him get away with it... I'll deal with it. Just not now.

I'm sooo excited about meeting my baby brother! He does kinda look like me in the photo. How cool is that? But I just want to get this trip over with and go back home to Los Angeles at Christmas like I planned. I hope I can get Kamal to come back with me. He's sixteen now, though, and sounds real bright, so I guess he has plans for school here in England. I'll find all that out and so much more after we meet in... let me see the time... one tiny little hour!

So long for now, dear journal. Wish me luck!

CHAPTER TWO

I know I've said this already, but almost to get my own head round it—Jasvandi was coming to England to live with Kamal. I should explain a bit more... His aunt and uncle hadn't been able to take her as well as Kamal after their parents died in the car accident, so she was adopted by a couple in the United States and brought up there. She wore hearing aids, we were told, and could speak a bit since she lost her hearing after acquiring speech, but had learned American Sign Language, which is different from the one they use here, British Sign Language. Kamal was learning up about hearing loss, hearing aids and loads of other stuff about being deaf. He told me I had to make sure I wasn't covering my mouth when I spoke and to speak clearly so she could try to lip read and not to shout. He said not to be embarrassed as she would no doubt make very keen eye contact in order to pick up as much as she could and would probably be able to read our minds through our eyes and body language. I hoped he wouldn't be giving me constant instructions while I was communicating with her. I hoped more that it wasn't true about her being able to read our minds. Anyway, I'd find out soon.

Poppy was coming to my house at half past eleven to go to the station. I didn't see why Poppy had to be in on everything, but as soon as I thought anything negative about her, the image of her at my little sister's funeral smashed into my head—the mascara tears splatting black marks on her pale dress, me being cruel to her for not contacting me for so long—and it passed quickly.

She arrived fifteen minutes early, so I asked her if she wanted to come in.

"You look five star," Poppy said at the door. "All in black though, eh? We're not going to a funeral, you know."

She flung her hand to her mouth like she'd said the worst thing ever and apologised, but it didn't matter. I didn't mind. I didn't mind about much at all, to be honest. I opened my mouth to tell her I didn't care and that she looked good too, but I didn't manage to form words. Her hair was different—it had been in a bob shape, but she must have had it done as it was in layers and all messy. It wasn't massively warm whatsoever and was unusually gusty, but she was wearing a thin summer dress. It had these skinny straps and was kind of short and brown and had a cute pattern of daisies. I'd been reading up on flower meanings since a teacher at The Tate Britain art gallery in London, where I'd been on a school trip, had got me interested in the symbolism of John Millais' painting, 'Ophelia'. Daisy meant innocence, beauty, loyal love and patience. Poppy's make-up looked like she was going to a night club, so it didn't seem that good a fit; I'd say she'd over done it, in fact, but she looked... well, 'hot' I suppose they'd say in America.

"Bellis perennis," was what came out of my mouth.

"What's that?"

"Daisy in Latin." I looked at her hard, checking for her reaction. She didn't say anything.

"Your dress is like a lawn," I said, as if that somehow added a deep and meaningful slant on things.

The way she smiled at me sent a flutter through my whole body, like a pebbly wave washing up the sand. It flowed all the way to my throat so that I had to take a deep breath. I could feel my eyes starting to glaze into a daze, so I said,

"A lawn taken over by weeds."

She ran her fingers up the back of her neck through her hair and clamped her mouth closed so tightly that her lips totally disappeared. She looked down before flicking her head up and opened her mouth, staring at me, and said,

"But you like weeds, don't you?"

I couldn't stop a smile forcing itself on me and when she laughed, I had to take another very slow and deep breath in and out as she said,

"Let's sit on the wall till Kamal arrives."

"Sure," I said. "You can use daisies to treat bruises, you know? And other stuff like coughs and asthma."

She lifted her chin in recognition of my revelation. I wasn't some sort of hippy herbalist, but I'd learnt a few bits of information like that over the previous year. My aunt had thought it was cool that I was growing mint (three different kinds actually), lemon verbena and rosemary and had got me a book called *Herbs and Flowers for Healthy Living*. Poppy turned to walk down the three steps to the low mossy wall which ran in front of our house and I noticed how smooth and brown her legs looked. I sat down first, and she sat next to me—too close. Her right bare leg pressed against mine and I couldn't do anything about the return of the wave. I was the tide myself, surging and frothing forward over smooth brown sand. I put my hands on my knees. The feel of the black denim gave way to silky skin. It was only the outer edge of my little finger which brushed against her leg, but it seemed that all life was concentrated there. She took a sharp breath in as if I'd given her an electric shock but didn't move away. It was as if we spread into each other like the gentle violence of two waters meeting. She said, "Kamal told me you're going to start growing food. What's that mean? Burger trees and pasta plants?"

It's odd because if a guy in my class had said that, I would have thought he was a right twit, but coming from Poppy's mouth, it just sounded sweet.

"Vegetables and more herbs."

"Isn't that what retired people do?" she said, now trapping her leg against my finger and tapping her right sandal on the ground, sending pulses through me. I glanced down at her foot—she was wearing brown leather sandal things with ankle straps and those high rope heels that are flat at the bottom.

"Retired people and me. That's your thing is it—bracketing people together? Stereotyping? I suppose you think men shouldn't wear pink and women shouldn't work and should stay at home and have babies?"

"Don't be a turnip." She pulled her leg away from me and stood up, straightening her necklace—a gold chain with a dolphin on the end. By the way, it was me who started using 'turnip' as a mild insult, so I only have myself to blame for that one. "I'm not like that. I didn't say anything like that. You think I'm stupid, don't you?"

She looked left along the street as if she wanted Kamal to arrive with his aunt and uncle. Just when I thought she didn't want to be with me, she swung round to the right, her ropey foot spinning her 180 degrees, so that she was now facing me, looking down at me. Seeing her glowing skin inches away from my face and her daisy dress tickling her thighs, I thought how easy it would be to pull her forward and have her sit astride my lap. I embarrassed myself with the thought. I wondered if other people imagined stuff like that which would be so easy to do but which they'd definitely never actually do, like throwing someone's birthday cake out of a window or tripping up a toddler or pushing someone over a cliff. Only I shouldn't say things like that because there are bound to be people who have really carried out such deeds.

"Anyway, I'd like to help you with the planting and growing," she said. "Will you let me?"

"I'll have to think about it."

And I couldn't help a slight smirk sneaking itself onto my face just for a millisecond. She pushed her knees forward so hard that I started to topple backwards over the wall. Just as I was swinging my right arm back to stop myself falling, Poppy grabbed it and pulled me back to a sitting position. Then she took my other arm in her right hand. That was it—I was under her spell. Her face went into neutral. Mystery and promise nestled behind thick black eyelashes. She stared at me.

"Why do you keep being horrible to me?"

Time froze and we held each other's gaze for about ten hours. I didn't exactly know I *was* being horrible, so I knew even less 'why'. It felt like a huge sacrifice, not telling her that maybe it was because I was falling in love with her and how much I thought about her and how much I longed to be with her. I couldn't properly truly fall for her as I'd never get up, if you see what I mean, so there was no point in saying anything. I remembered one of my dad's friends told me he didn't want to be ruined by alcohol anymore and that the only way to prevent it, he decided, was to get rid of absolutely all of it from the house. He had to minimise temptation. Yeah, those were his words— 'minimise temptation'. Does that make any sense? I mean in terms of Poppy?

Holding my arms now, she pulled me towards her. She tempted me to find the word, the words to tell her who I was. Which word would say 'mixed up, but also somewhere, alive and throbbing with vague possibilities'? Words are just not that clever – quite sorry things at times. Eyes speak better; they stir all those words and serve them out in one spoonful-look. I wondered if Jasvandi would be skilled at eye-language, relying less on words than hearing people do. Alive and throbbing with vague possibilities: that was the bit of me Poppy saw, perhaps. She spoke again.

"I don't get it. I don't get you. I thought I did, but I don't—not anymore."

I thought of saying sorry. I thought of saying, Be patient. I thought of saying I love you. Nothing came out except, "Conundrums are cool, though, aren't they?" Someone rescue me, I thought.

Loud beeping and shouting ripped the moment away, ripped my chance to say something meaningful to Poppy, instead of coded bullshit. My arms still in Poppy's grasp, we both snapped our heads sideways to see Kamal hanging out of the window of his uncle's car. As if finger-clicked into another plane of existence, Poppy broke connection with me and we both segued into Kamal-world.

"The earth did bestow on me a sister!" Kamal shouted out of the window as the car slowed to a halt. "Ten syllables. It's the start of a sonnet I'm writing. The day hath come, my pretties. Enter Jasvandi, stage right!"

Thank God for Kamal. Aunt Colette (the one who gave me the herb book) once told me that we each have an angel looking over us in heaven and an angel on earth too. Yeah, right. Except that's what jumped into my head at that moment. Kamal, at least during that brief snippet of time, was my angel on earth, rescuing me.

"Loony-pants!" I shouted back, as Kamal hurried the car door open, scrambled out and started pogoing like a punk rocker in front of our house. As I watched him, I saw him pogoing into a new phase of his life—the part where his sister miraculously appears like a genie out of a bottle. I saw he was wearing a three-piece suit, which made the pogoing look even more crazy. It was his auntie's turn to shout then; the engine was still going as she lowered the front window and bent over her husband who was in the driver's seat to say,

"Calm down Kamal. Your shirt's coming out after I've just straightened you up. Everyone, get in or we won't ever meet this sister the earth has bistoed."

She said it like 'Bisto' the gravy, and the three of us over-laughed, me standing up from the wall only to crease over. I imagined a massive gravy jug being poured from the sky and a sister glooping into Kamal's arms. It wasn't long before my laughter turned into a now familiar twitch because my mind managed to gloop out *my* sister, Lily, from the same gravy jug. In my mind I ran and ran faster than I ever had in my whole life and caught

20

her just in time, right on the precipice of a treacherous cliff. She wasn't alive though. She wasn't alive, but I loved the feeling of holding her in my arms. This is what it must have felt like when Mam and Dad held her in the hospice, Rachel house, that day. I hadn't wanted to—hold her I mean. But I wanted to now. Just then, I couldn't think of anything I would ever want more.

"Get in, come on!" Kamal's auntie called.

We piled into the back of the car. It was like 'take two': I sat to Poppy's right, her bare leg pressed even harder up against me. We seemed to have our own communication system—she tried to pull her leg away from me, but there was no space, so I found my left hand on my left thigh again, brushing her skin and sending a telepathic message: 'Sorry if I'm horrible to you. Let's just chill.' She put her hand over mine this time so that she touched my leg too, as if to say, 'It's okay. Yeah, let's start again.' If I could have bottled that feeling, that moment... Emotion Librarian – 'Hardly even take the lid off that jar, love, or you could turn to jelly.'

"Uncle's getting the bus back so that Jasvandi can go in the front," Kamal said. "Best she has her own space in the initial stages."

"Initial stages?" I said. "You'd think we were collecting an animal in a wooden box sent from Africa."

The laughing distracted from any awkwardness. I wondered if Kamal had spotted Poppy's and my weird body, or should I say hand, language, what with his comment about having your own space. Thing is, Kamal misses stuff like that; he's the opposite of most people—sees the bigger picture and not the details.

"I shouldn't have come," said Poppy.

"Nonsense," said Kamal, "Jasvandi will feel much more at ease with another girl there. Everyone feels more at ease when you're around, Poppy. Isn't that right, Ollie?"

He didn't feel like my angel now. Anyhow, I surprised myself by moving my hand further to the left and squeezing Poppy's skin and saying,

"On the contrary, *I'd* say she makes everyone *nervous*."

Poppy slapped my hand—the one on her leg—which was exquisitely painful. I added, "I mean in a good way." She turned towards me and gave me the cutest smile I've ever seen and when our eyes met, there was a momentary connection, a look, which encompassed a world of unchartered waters, of untold sensuality. To dilute the intensity, she shoved me with her shoulder and said,

"Like you get nervous before you're going to perform, you mean?"

"Exactly that," I said.

"Hey, less of these sexual remarks in front of my folks, if you don't mind!" said Kamal. His aunt and uncle were very strict, so I couldn't believe he'd even said that.

"Stop that talk right away, Kamal!" said his aunt. "Jasvandi is a very delicate girl. I don't want her sullied by that sort of disgusting talk."

Ah, okay, that's what she was like, this auntie. I'd known Kamal for ages but had only been to his house a few times coz there wasn't really anywhere to hang out (sounds rude but his bedroom was like a postage stamp, oh and he had no garden to speak of). What she had said didn't surprise me one bit—Kamal told me she was always serious. What did surprise me was Kamal's response:

"How do you know she's delicate? Have you been in regular secret contact with her all these years? Or is she delicate because it is the case that you've had *no* contact whatsoever all these years?" An awkward pause stretched out as we all went quiet in anticipation of a mood-lightener...

"She was brought up in America," Aunt Gopi said (as you will find out, Gopi was about to figure more in our lives, so I will mostly refer to her by her Christian name from now, I mean Hindi name, well, you know, first name.) "They have high morals over there and they don't put up with cursing and dirty talk."

I smiled inwardly at the prospect of how Kamal would respond to that, but he just said,

"No shit."

At that, Gopi leant backwards and hit Kamal on the legs with a teddy bear.

"How come you've got a teddy bear, Gopi?" Poppy said.

"It's for Jasvandi."

No one said anything so I offered,

"That's sweet of you. She'll like it, I'm sure."

"How did they make that?" I asked Kamal. I marvelled at the structures made of iron and glass as we stood on platform nine at Newcastle Central Station, just the two of us, Poppy having been told to stay in the car. Three curved arched spans roofed their way over the railways, air and people rushing through. Kamal began, "It was designed by local architect John Dobson and opened in—" but I zoned out as I began to visualize Jasvandi getting off the London train. My heart quickened. Were we standing in the right place? Would she recognise us? What if she missed the stop? Would Kamal cry? Should I take her bag from her or would she think I was a stranger stealing it and anyway shouldn't Kamal be on his own and—

"Here it is! The train's coming in," Kamal shouted in a manner I'd never heard before—a cross between terror and rapture. The Emotion Library jar would need a warning on it like 'Stand well back when opening'. I swung my head round to check the time on the monster clock suspended up high with its Roman numerals, like an old stern but trusty uncle willing you to stop dallying and catch your train. Twelve o'clock noon precisely. A new afternoon about to begin. A new era. A new life.

The train's yellow frontage inched towards us, its precious cargo about to chug us into the unknown. My older brother, Nathan, who was good at art, had made us a sign saying, 'Welcome to Newcastle Jasvinda' instead of 'Jasvandi' and I hadn't even noticed the spelling mistake, or the missing comma. I had bought some bright pink and red gladioli from Poppy's mam's shop, 'The Fuchsia's Bright'. I knew these flowers were sometimes called 'sword lilies' but I couldn't remember why, so I'd looked them up in my horticultural dictionary and it's from the Latin word 'gladius' meaning 'a sword'. I remembered this as the train squeaked and screeched and squealed itself still. I imagined everything around me freezing except for one carriage door slowly opening, thick steam evaporating to reveal Lily standing there. I would rush up to her and she would spring onto me with such fervour that we'd crush the delicate flowers between us, and she would say, 'I've killed them Oliber' and I would say, 'No, Lily, they've killed us—they're swords.' And we'd crumple to the ground, pierced by the fierce flowers and then lie in each other's arms surrounded by the deadly red and pink spikes.

Kamal started waving the sign, jumping up and down and shouting, "She's here! My sister's here!"

Then everything went quiet. I looked to my left to see him dropping the sign, dropping his jaw, and just standing there staring out. My eyes moved to the object of his gaze. Jasvandi. I dropped the flowers and dropped my jaw too and watched as a girl holding an old-fashioned tan leather suitcase took a few steps then stopped and lowered it to the ground. She stood up straight and reached with her right silver-ringed hand for something in her leather jacket's inside left pocket. Her unruly short black satin hair was half bunged into a grey beanie hat and half sticking out, pressed to her neck and face. Her sunglasses looked too big for her; transferring the paper to her left hand, she eased the glasses off with her right, to look at the paper, all done with substantial poise. One word came to my head— 'cool'. She looked down at the paper, up at Kamal, down at it, up at Kamal, before lowering it so that it became obvious it was a photograph.

She hooked her shades onto her tee-shirt—a worn out Mick Jagger's mouth with sparkly bits on—put the photo in her black jean's pocket and clomped her green Doctor Martin boots towards us, one arm raised in a wave, as a soldier surrendering to the enemy. She had picked up her case as if to say, 'Well, here I am, I'm all yours. Do with me what you will.'

"Are you wearing your hearing aids?"

Can you Adam and Eve it?? That's the first thing Kamal ever said to his long-lost sister. I was worried she'd be upset or that she might not have understood what he'd said, but not only were my fears misguided, it seemed to Jasvandi like it was the most natural thing in the world to ask. She said,

"Yes, but it's difficult to hear in this environment, this noisy station."

I thought, 'environment', eh? This girl can talk more than just a bit. And her voice was as cool as she was—gorgeous flowing American drawl which always sounds so sensual. I couldn't tell she was deaf.

Kamal said, "I can imagine. I don't suppose that hat helps though. God knows what the reverberation time is in this echoey railway station."

Blood and sand, was he going to carry on talking like this, like he'd met someone off the train for an interview on acoustics and was keen to make a start? I was compelled to alter the course of this riveting conversation, steer it onto a more welcoming path. I said,

"I like your hat, Jasvandi."

"Oh, sorry," said Kamal, "This is my best friend, Oliver. We call him Ollie."

As I went to shake her hand, saying hi, she put down her case again, and instead of taking my hand, held my shoulders as she kissed me on my left cheek. She smelt of liquorice and jasmine. Then she said,

"Choob."

I so didn't understand what she was trying to say and thought it must be a deaf way of saying something. I didn't want to ask her to say it again, so I just smiled inanely, but Kamal said,

"She means it's not a hat, it's a choob. Get with the vernacular, man. I had to buy one for that moped course I did. A choob twists into an assortment of shapes for an assortment of uses and styles."

I decided not to show him up by letting it slip that he only just made it through moped lesson number one. He'd annoyed the instructor so much by correcting his English that he got kicked off the course. I seem to remember that when the teacher was going over some points at the end, he warned the students, saying, "I've larned yuz not to ova-rev, so divvent dee it!" which means in Geordie, "I've taught you not to over-use the accelerator, so don't do it." By the way, Geordie is what people are called and also the name of their accent if they come from Newcastle-upon-Tyne, in the northeast of England (near to the border to Scotland) like we do. Except we don't sound like proper Geordies or at least Kamal doesn't because he speaks the 'Queen's English' which basically means quite posh and sophisticated, though he doesn't say grarss and barth, but grass and bath with a hard 'a' and I have what you might call a mild accent. Anyway, Kamal had said to the instructor, "Is that Urdu you're speaking?" I bet I know which choob-use the instructor fancied trying out...

"And who are you with the fine suit?" Jasvandi asked, looking at Kamal. For once, he was lost for words, until her poker face melted into a smiling one, like time-lapse photography. Then it happened. They stood about a metre apart. Kamal started to shuffle, pull weird faces, and push his glasses up his nose with his right index finger, then a calmness came over him. Their eyes fixed on each other and there was this bam like an explosion and the whole station shook and everyone was flung backwards with the force of it. "My sister," he said, followed by the next line of the play spoken by Jasvandi: "My brother."

They stretched out their arms and moved to cling onto each other, rocking from side to side, their synchronised feet alternately lifting from the ground, like some mental Indian dance. While they were holding each other, Kamal said,

"This is an historic day," and then, "We'd better go to the car. Auntie and Uncle are waiting."

When they pulled apart, Jasvandi said,

"What did you say?" and I added in,

"She has to see your face to lip read you told me, and you were crushing her hearing aids."

I gathered up the flowers, picked up her suitcase and said, "Follow me," overcome by an urge to 'get on with it' and get back to Poppy.

Jasvandi took Kamal's hand which was pretty bizarre to say the least.

CHAPTER THREE

By the time we got back to the car, Kamal's uncle had gone to get the bus, but was going to a Spanish class, not home. I couldn't believe he hadn't waited to meet Jasvandi, but Gopi said too many people would be overwhelming and that they'd decided to stagger the introductions. Poppy and Gopi stood leaning on the car, watching us approach. It looked like a still from a film I saw with my mam called *Thelma and Louise*. They both looked defiant for no apparent reason. Maybe they were trying hard not to look nervous. Poppy was linking Gopi in a sort of, 'In case you were wondering, Jasvandi, I am very much part of this group, this 'family'. I'd never seen her do such a thing. Certainly, Gopi was not at all a touchy-feely person. Poppy reminded me of Geena Davis's character, Thelma, who was naïve and fun-loving with a bit of a rebellious streak. I wondered if Poppy would still be as pretty when she was older, which reminded me that mam had told me Geena Davis, who was brilliant, was in tons of movies till she was forty, then she was suddenly in hardly anything. I thought it was odd, but Mam said that unfortunately she hoped it would change, but it wasn't odd at all and simply 'how Hollywood works.'

"You look very much like your mother," Gopi said as she pulled away from Jasvandi, whom she'd been wrapped around. She placed her arms on her shoulders studying her face, as if checking it was the correct model she'd ordered. "My word, yes, what a resemblance."

She didn't seem to have a clue that her words could possibly seem slightly inappropriate. Then something strange happened—Kamal's and Jasvandi's eyes met and they both made the same face at each other like they were sending out comfort and surprise and glee all at the same time. It's hard to imagine, but I'll tell you, it was the exact same look on both their faces, like they'd gone to the same facial expression classes. I suppose they *were* brother and sister after all.

"I like your hat, Jasvandi," said Poppy, still leaning on the car.

Kamal and I blurted out, "Choob," and everyone laughed, Gopi more than anyone, even though I don't think she had any clue what we were talking about but was glad of a lighter ice-breaker than she had come up with.

Kamal said to Jasvandi, "This is Poppy. She's our best friend," and they went first to shake hands but then held each other like long lost cousins. Jasvandi said,

"Pleased to meet you. Your daisy dress is real neat."

Poppy looked down at the top of her own dress and started fiddling with her necklace saying, "Weed-dress". Then quite a lot of time passed before Jasvandi said,

"I'm sorry. What did you say?"

"Weeds instead of daisies. That's what Ollie called them," Poppy said, now starting to blush.

"I'm not sure what that is," Jasvandi said.

Kamal then gave us a mini lecture on how hearing impairment can affect language development:

"There will be swathes of vocabulary which may seem commonplace to us but which Jasvandi will have simply missed because she doesn't over-hear conversations, radio, television, that sort of thing, never mind the fact she was raised in a different country. We live in a soundscape in which language is emitted from multifarious sources and we pick up new words without even realising it sometimes. So here we have an example with the word, 'weeds'."

"Weeds are annoying plants which grow really quickly where you don't want them to and take over," I said, "and people like to pull them out of the ground and throw them away, but I don't, well not very often... coz I'm weird."

"That will have cleared things up no end," said Kamal shaking his head. But I could see Jasvandi smiling as she itched the hair above her right ear under her hat.

Poppy said, "And is like talking about someone while they're standing right next to you part of it all?"

"Thank you for that definition, Ollie," said Jasvandi. "But I know what weeds are. I didn't hear Poppy, that's all. Shall I drive?" and everybody did a mental double-take then laughed, except me.

It turned out that Jasvandi wanted to sit in the back and it also turned out that Kamal was relieved to sit in the front as he gets car sick (first I'd heard of it), so yours truly sat in the back between the two girls.

Two girls' thighs frotted up against mine. By the way, I'm not sure that's a real word, but it sounds right and maybe you can get the idea of how it felt. I couldn't make myself thinner, so I had to make the most of the situation and settle into this odd threesome. That sounds terrible, but you know what I mean.

"I'm like a common ragweed pushing up between two daffodils," I said.

"He's always on about flowers and plants, Jasvandi. Take no notice," said Poppy.

These, it turned out, were interactions that were too difficult for Jasvandi to understand or I suppose just hear properly in a noisy car and where she couldn't easily see our faces. Gopi, who you've probably worked out, was now in the driving seat, changed the subject by nudging Kamal to pass Jasvandi the teddy bear, which was in the footwell. He took his seatbelt off and twisted right round, getting onto his knees, facing backwards, so he could hand the bear over the top of his seat and so that Jasvandi could see his face to lip read.

"A token of our welcome and love!"

"Oh, how sweet. I'll call it Geordie," she said. Kamal, who was still facing the wrong way and whose aunt was now slapping the back of his legs and pulling at his suit jacket to sit back down, scrunched his face up and said:

"You're sure about that?"

"I love that word. It's what you're all called, right? We are in 'Geordieland', I believe, yeah? Or shall I call it Oliver?

"And why would you do that?" Kamal said.

"Good name for a bear," she said. "The real Oliver is sweet like a teddy bear too—he brought flowers for me. And he's a good teacher."

Blimey, all I'd said was something about her hat and something about weeds. When Kamal suggested she call the bear my middle name, she had asked what that was and Poppy had said, in my opinion quite a bit louder than she needed to, "Timothy." It was agreed, the bear was to be called Timothy. I tell you, the day was most definitely on the bizarre side, but, believe me, it wouldn't be long before it got quite a lot weirder...

Once back at Kamal's house, I had got roped into helping him make dhal which I couldn't complain about since it was on my goal list. Though the Indian dish is made mainly of lentils, Kamal said you could make it with loads of different kinds of beans. Cooking was one of his new things. He'd been so mortified at how badly his dinner date had gone the year before with Becky Bailey, that he decided he needed an extra string to his bow in case, as had happened that fateful evening, his charm might, once again, go utterly unnoticed. I had made it with him before with a similar assignment of roles, in other words, me - peeler, chopper and sweater, him - sprinkler and stir-rer. I hadn't wanted to taste dhal at first, but he convinced me I was leading a sort of slug-like existence if I wasn't ready and willing to try new foods and eat something as 'clearly nutritious, simple and beautiful as dhal'. He said it would be like him acting grossed out by the thought of tinned baked beans. He does tend to say it as it is. He convinced me too that if I were to be a successful grower of food, I would have to become more in touch with basic foodstuffs like lentils. It was delicious, I have to say, in a mushy yellowy way. He made it the way his aunt taught him which apparently was how her mother made it, so Kamal worked out that his own mother, who died in the fatal car crash, might well have made the exact same dish, so he felt a connection with her every time he made it. It was blinkin' tasty, I'll tell you.

I was asked to do the boring, labour-intensive stuff again like chop-ping onions, ginger, garlic and tomatoes (which apparently not everyone puts in dhal but he does—tomatoes that is), and doing constant washing up, while Kamal did his magic, bunging it all together and making noises of ecstasy as he wafted his steamy mixture from the wooden spoon into his nostrils. He even said,

"One of the many delights of this dish is the little effort required to make it in relation to the results it yields."

I swear he saw zero irony in his comment. I didn't like to ask why we weren't using one of those little whizzing machines my mam has, where you just chuck everything in and it gets chopped and mulched in seconds. I think he's one of these people who scorns new inventions.

"Effort is important in cooking, no matter how quick the recipe. Put the love in and you get the love out," he said.

I thought, 'But what if someone *else* has put the love in, then you serve it as if you have put the love in? Does the love come through or does it become a bitter dish?'

Kamal prepared the rice to cook and asked for the jar of cloves. He totally overreacted when I took three cloves out to put in the pot. He assured me that one clove was quite sufficient and that the rice would absorb its essence and result in a wonderful aromatic yet delicate flavour. He told me he had counted them out the week before and had calculated that they should last about five years. I questioned whether they would not lose their potency over time. He went on about correct storage, ignoring the sell by date etc. He was certainly 'careful' with money, it has to be said. Actually, it doesn't have to be said, but well, I've said it now.

"Trust your sense of smell," he said. "The nose is not to be sniffed at; the olfactory system is highly sophisticated. Did you know that the nose is superior to the mouth?"

"What makes you say that?"

"Latin"

"Okaaaay?" I said.

"'Super', in Latin, means 'above.'"

He couldn't contain himself and did an insane little jig around the kitchen, using the wooden spoon as some sort of waving baton.

"Haha, above the mouth. See what you're saying, you clever old goat," I said, joining in the dance for a moment.

Jasvandi had asked if Poppy wanted to help her sort her room out, so they were both in her new bedroom, the door to which was more or less opposite the kitchen. It was usually Kamal's room but he was to sleep on a camp bed in a room I would class as a broom cupboard which was normally used to store food. When I went into the corridor with onion eyes to leave Kamal to his stirring and wafting, I could see a blurred Jasvandi holding up a red swimsuit and laughing that she probably wouldn't get to wear it in cold old England. I began to feel like a spy, subtly shifting along the wall so there was less chance of being spotted.

"Do you think I'll be able to put up some pictures? This place seems kind of dreary, huh?" Jasvandi said. "Kamal said he took down the ones he'd put up. I see he still has one there on the wardrobe. William Shakespeare. How sweet."

Poppy asked Jasvandi how she'd heard of him and was amazed to discover that kids learnt about Shakespeare all the way over in the USA.

I knew what she meant. The house had an old-fashioned feel, for sure. I surveyed the hallway. The faded pale floral green and white wallpaper and the clashing patterned carpet led my eyes to an ornate console table next to the front door, which displayed dusty plastic flowers in a vase and a pair of ancient-looking men's leather slippers on the shelf below. Combined with the four or five formal portrait paintings hanging in the hallway (as in the kind of stuff you might see in a palace or a stately home except much smaller), the scene called to mind the set of a horror film.

"You mean big posters? Or photographs?" said Poppy.

"Like this," she said, flinging the swimsuit onto the bed, pulling out a poster from her suitcase and unrolling it to show Poppy.

"Wow, five star."

"I'm sorry?"

"I mean very good. It's pretty. I thought you'd like more kind of dramatic art though, like shocking or unusual."

I was dying to see what the painting was, but I didn't want to make it obvious I'd been listening in. That would be a great early impression for Jasvandi—Ollie the stalker. The doorframe was a painting in itself to me: 'Two Girls and a Poster'. Poppy now barefoot, was balanced like a stork, in a yoga pose, her right foot clamped to her left ankle. She scraped her painted finger nails up and down her left thigh, over the same silky patch of weed dress. With the other hand she held the bottom left corner of the art print, helping Jasvandi to open it out. How nice she was to make her feel so welcome, I thought. Jasvandi still wore her clumpy boots and hat, but her now sparkly eyes were new, as she gazed upon the artwork. Couldn't I knock on the door and go and have a look at it myself?

"You mean edgy?"

The way Jasvandi pronounced 'edgy' I could tell she was deaf. Her speech was mostly so clear, it was easy to forget that without her hearing aids, she wouldn't have been able to have this conversation at all. Kamal said she was 'post-lingually deafened' which meant she had crucially learned to speak before she lost her hearing at around three. She had learnt enough to carry on developing her spoken language with the help of speech and language therapy, he told me. It was 'just' that she couldn't hear, as in hardly anything at all, even with hearing aids on. She could hear something but not speech as hearing people perceive it. I couldn't imagine it. Kamal told me that hearing aids were nothing like glasses in that they did not restore hearing. He said that if your hearing was damaged, like you had a cochlea which was not normal, hearing aids would make everything louder, but it would be a distorted sound. He read in a book that it was like turning up a radio which wasn't tuned in properly. He played me a recording he'd found of what speech might sound like through hearing aids for someone with a profound hearing loss: I felt my eyes and throat starting to hurt as I struggled to make any sense at all of the crackly quacking scratchy tune. I say 'tune' as it was more like an unpleasant melody than speech—I could not make out one word. Kamal said that's why it helps so much if people who are deaf can see your face and why they have to work so hard to try and match the strange noises with movements of the mouth, facial expressions and body language. I had asked Kamal if it was hard to learn to lipread; he thought it was more or less impossible and that 'lip guessing' would be a better term. He pointed out that loads of mouth shapes and lip patterns could be confused saying,

"You see 'm', 'p', and 'b' look more or less the same on the lips."

He even made me block my ears and look at him whispering either 'mat', 'pat' or 'bat': I had no way of discriminating between them until he put them into sentences like 'I want a new mat for the living room floor'. I managed to detect 'living room', so worked out it must be 'mat'. He explained,

"A person with a hearing loss trying to 'lipread' has to make intelligent guesses linked with the context of the conversation. And if something is said out of context, it goes back to being bloody hard."

"Yeah, 'edgy', that's a good word," said Poppy. "I don't mean that in a bad way. It's just you dress pretty cool and alternative so, you know..."

"I like a lot of different art, but there's something about this painting which speaks to me. Look at the woman's face and how the water's painted."

"Kind of gentle but focused. All those colours in the water!" said Poppy.

"Those colours *are* the water. That's how comes it's so beautiful."

My heart skipped a beat as it occurred to me that it must be John Everett Millais's 'Ophelia', the painting which had so affected *me* and so reminded me of Lily. Just as I was imagining this earth-shattering bolt of connectedness with Jasvandi, she said,

"It's called 'Summertime'. That's how the light is so amazing on the water."

I couldn't believe my ears and eyes with the conversation that came next... Poppy said,

"Ollie might like that. It reminds me of a painting he loves."

"Wow, that guy gets more appealing as the day goes on!"

The look on Poppy's face. Lady in the Emotion Library would be ages scratching her head, trying for the life of her to remember where she had seen that particular emotion labelled on one of the shelves. We're so good at face-reading, us humans, but that facial expression at that moment—I had no idea, but it seemed to mean something. I was now watching a TV drama and I think my jaw literally fell open as the pause which hung in the air swelled by the nano second, pregnant with possibilities, as Shakespeare might say. It was Jasvandi who broke the silence, Poppy's expression lingering.

"I'm so excited about getting to know him better. He's so my type of guy. Tell me more about him. Like does he have a girlfriend?"

With that she turned to look at Poppy, both of them still stretching out 'Summertime'. "Oh no! I'm so sorry. I didn't realise you and he were... Kamal said you were *friends*."

The painting sprung out of their hands and bounced across the bed. Jasvandi took a step back. Poppy said,

"It's okay. We *are*... we're just friends. Yeah, don't worry, we're not... together, you know."

"Oh wow. I was so worried there for a minute."

"But he's going out with someone else," Poppy said.

"He is? Are you friends with her?" Jasvandi said.

"I don't actually know who she is. He's very secretive. Who's it by, the painting?"

"What? Oh right. Yeah, it's by Mary Cassatt. She was an impressionist painter. You know The Impressionists?"

I couldn't believe my ears. Poppy was slicker than I thought, casually dropping in a lie then swiftly moving on. I contemplated bursting in then and there, so Poppy knew I'd heard her.

"I thought they were all men?" Poppy said.

Jasvandi laughed and told Poppy that it was unfair that you only hear about the male impressionists like Renoir and that Mary Cassatt was just as good or better, but that women never seemed to receive the same attention because of sexist attitudes. I was impressed she got her tongue round the words, "Systematic underrepresentation of female artists."

She added that Mary Cassatt had promoted the work of Degas, helping him to succeed and that he went on to be massively famous, mostly with his depiction of ballerinas. The moment had passed in terms of making an entrance.

"I've heard of René."

"Renoir," said Jasvandi.

"Yeah—him. And there's that Monet bloke as well," Poppy said. "That is sooo wrong she wasn't as famous as them. How could that even happen if she was really good?"

This was surely my second cue to appear at the doorway and join in the conversation, so I inched forward as I was summoning up the courage to make my presence known. At that moment, though, Kamal sprang out of the kitchen more or less onto my back, pushing me forward, to announce that dinner was nearly ready and did anyone want a 'mocktail'. I remembered the revolting layered dessert he'd told me about—the one he'd rustled up for Becky Bailey— and my face must have looked weird because Poppy asked me if I was all right and if I'd got a sudden pain. I smiled and said that a scrawny chef on my back was my sudden pain.

"Mango, coconut and lime you said earlier, yeah?" said Jasvandi. "That sounds like a fun cocktail, Kamal, though some rum in there would have been nice. We have similar taste, huh?"

"Well you are my dear sister, are you not?" and as an afterthought he smiled at me, I suppose seeking my blessing for mentioning that dreaded word. Would it be for the rest of my life, I wondered, that people would be pussyfooting around me, scared of upsetting me, of bringing painful stuff up that ought to be forgotten about. I smiled back. There wasn't a word for what I felt. Poor words again unable to cut it. Let me try to... Imagine your heart sitting on a cold scruffy counter, singed and ridged, freshly flicked from a waffle machine.

Gopi had made a chicken dish that morning and chapatis, which are flat circular bread things like little 'wraps' but much nicer, so we were in for a right feast, though I didn't at all fancy the chicken curry. It would be the first time we were all to sit down to dinner together. I hoped we'd all get on and that Jasvandi could keep up with the conversation because it must be hard around a table to work out who's talking and hard to eat at the same time as watching people's faces. Maybe we would find out more about Kamal's family. Whatever was to follow, I hoped that Gopi wouldn't say anything annoying or put her foot in it, which I was learning was one of her fortes.

CHAPTER FOUR

"I'm vegetarian," said Jasvandi. "Sorry to be a pain."

Gopi said, "You should have told us" at the same time as Jasvandi said, "I should have told you." Then Gopi said, "I might have knocked up an aloo gobi if I'd known."

"Sorry, I don't understand what you are saying."

So that was a good start to the meal.

By the way, aloo gobi is a dish of potato (aloo) and cauliflower (gobi). All I could think of was 'Aloo Gopi' which would be a dish of potato mixed with Aunt Gopi. I worked hard to exorcise the image of Gopi smeared in spicy spuds.

The dining table was circular, which I realised was useful for Jasvandi as she would be able to see people's faces more easily to 'lip guess'. Kamal's uncle wasn't back as his Spanish club had gone for a Rioja-tasting evening, so there were five of us; I had found myself with Poppy to my right, Jasvandi to my left, Kamal was to the left of her and then Gopi, between Kamal and Poppy. I marvelled at the crisp white tablecloth and how it could be so clean after surely years of stainey spice splattering. Or was it new, especially for the long-lost niece? The table was at the window in the living room and looked out onto a titsy witsy front garden which could win a competition entitled 'Most flowers crammed into a tiny garden'. I was facing the garden, so it was easy to stare out. I'm not sure if the row of three hanging baskets was to act as a privacy barrier, but if it was, it wasn't doing a very good job—every passer-by had a good gander at the garden and through the plants at us. I spotted some multi-coloured *Viola* in the middle container, boldly posing despite being half-strangled by some dangling *Hedera*. I smiled to myself when I remembered suggesting the *Viola* to Gopi and buying the seeds for her from Poppy's mam's flower shop, The Fuchsia's Bright. I had wandered round and chosen a packet, but had decided to ask Poppy directly, as I thought the name was cute. "I'm after Irish Molly," I had said. She tilted her head to the right, smiling with a tight mouth and fiddling with her necklace, as she often did when she knew I was being funny but didn't quite know what about. "Sorry, she only comes in on a Thursday," Poppy had said, which I thought was pretty quick-witted. Not that Poppy's stupid, gosh, anything but, just well, naïve I suppose, gullible maybe. I glanced at Poppy, as if somehow she was telepathically thinking of the same thing. And at that moment she seemed just like a *Viola* Irish Molly herself—yellow, dark brown, and browny red with a strong centre and delicate wafery wiggly edges. Neat and bold, but fragile and graceful with exquisite soft edges. Oh, by the way, I forgot to say that *Hedera* is Latin for Ivy.

The garden seemed proud of its titchiness. Garden: "Yes, I'm the teeniest garden in the world. What ya gonna do about it? Look as long as you like." I spotted Jasvandi's purple ear moulds, the rubbery bits that are pressed into the outer ear, each one attached with a little tube to the hearing aid; they were proud of themselves too and maybe saying the same thing (not the bit about teeniest garden of course). Ear mould: "Yes, she's deaf and proud. What you gonna do about it? Look as long as you like."

Despite the pungent curry hanging in the air, you could still detect a perfumey odour. I can tell you that it was the smell of patchouli. Not that I'm an expert in that sort of thing, but it was my mam's favourite and she often lit those long sticks that fill the room with scented smoke and drop ash everywhere except into the holder intended for the purpose. 'Joss sticks' she called them.

Once we were all squeezed around the table, I thought to myself that it would have made more sense for us all to sit on the floor, it was that cramped. It made sense, too, that Jasvandi couldn't be adopted as well as Kamal because there really wasn't much space at all in this house. In fact, I'd say the table was meant for four people maximum, so you couldn't help but brush up against the person next to you. We each had a table mat with country scenes of hunting, which seemed particularly inappropriate now we knew Jasvandi didn't eat meat, and the weirdest coasters you've ever seen which in no way blended with the mats. I said,

"Where did you get these, Gopi?" holding one of the coasters up. They featured small hamsters wearing sombreros. Jasvandi threw her hand to her mouth to stifle a laugh, but Poppy let it all out, so to speak. Kamal said,

"Auntie's dear sister left them to her. She was only thirty-six when she died of a brain tumour. Auntie had started with two sisters but was left with none."

Rrrrrright, thanks... Silence. Lots of fiddling and avoiding eye contact, but no words were spoken. 'Left them to her,' he had said about the drink mats, as if they were a pair of diamond earrings. I imagined the grave gathering, all ears at the reading of the will. "And the set of beverage coasters illustrated with Chinese rodents sporting Mexican headgear goes to..." everyone on the edge of their seats, teeth clamping knuckles, before Gopi, the announced recipient, faints with shock and elation. When Jasvandi said,

"She must have been such a fun sister," I thought, 'This girl is good at teasing out social knots'. Poppy and I glanced sideways at each other without moving our heads and took in deep breaths before slowly releasing the air.

"She was the most fun sister you could have wished for. She was always making me laugh." Gopi shifted herself on her seat and pulled her long hair backwards with both hands, so that it all hung behind her shoulders. Of course, Jinisha, my other sister [Kamal and Jasvandi's mother, I worked out], was dear, but she wasn't funny at all. In fact, she was very very serious."

She brought her white serviette to her eyes and just as Poppy was twisting to the right to put her arm around her, Kamal gesticulated to leave her alone and a split second later, Gopi brought the cloth down to her knees, snapping back to normal, saying,

"Mad was vegetarian too, but Father would still serve her meat; she scraped it into a small tin she had on her knee when he wasn't looking."

"Mad?" Jasvandi said.

"Her name was Madhubala, after a famous film star, but I called her Mad which got me into trouble plenty times." We all laughed and waited, even though there was a long pause, as you could tell more was coming. "Would you believe it, she died at thirty-six, too, this film star. I wonder what date it was the actress died? Couldn't you ask your phone, Kamal?"

Kamal reached into his pocket.

"Not now though, not at the table—that is most vulgar," Gopi said. "Yes, they both died. Terrible. Should never have named her after an actress. Thirty-six. Half a life... only half a life. A *third* even in this day and age."

The exact same ritual was repeated: serviette to the face, Poppy leaning towards her, Kamal with his gesturing and Gopi's sudden throwing of the serviette to her knees. We waited again.

"One hundred and eight, Auntie."

Everyone slowly turned their heads towards Kamal.

"Three times thirty-six. By your calculations, my auntie Mad might have lived to the ripe old age of a hundred and eight."

We let out a collective sigh and I feared Gopi would get upset again, but she said,

"What a thought, Kamal, what a thought indeed. We should call you Jaz. Can we do that, Jasvandi?" As Jasvandi smiled and nodded, Gopi said, "Religious reasons, is it? You're a strict Hindu, are you? Is that why you're vegetarian? That is refreshing to hear. Young people are so indulgent these days."

"Meat can cause disease," said Jasvandi. "Like for instance diabetes. But my reasons are of nonviolence, Aunt Gopi."

"I see. Very good," Gopi said awkwardly scratching the back of her head, her face, screwed up as if she'd been hit. "It's difficult to keep it up, though, I bet, going to school and what not; you don't want folk thinking you're odd just when you are desperate to fit in. Not very good that you say it causes disease; you can't say that without proof."

A flurry of shuffling went round the table.

"It's quite common these days, being vegetarian or vegan. And gee, there's like tons and tons of proof," Jasvandi said. "How long have you got?" She leaned forward in her chair and picked up her Mexican hamster coaster. She began using her thumbs and fingers to twirl it round and round in front of her with nervous intention. It was like a new age method of flicking away objection and criticism, not that the technique worked for very long...

"I met this amazing guy called Dau in Thailand who taught me that humans weren't designed to eat meat. It made perfect sense. He said our digestive systems were utterly and completely set up to be herbivores, like apes to eat stacks of fruit." She continued spinning (the coaster, I mean, not her).

"I saw this documentary—people were cured of diabetes by switching to a plant-based diet. This one guy was taking like a whole heap of meds and at the end of the experiment—"

"No time. I've got no time for that sort of nonsense." Gopi flicked her napkin about. "As if everyone wouldn't become vegan if it cured disease? There's so much bloody hype around food these—"

"With all respect, you don't know what you're talking about," Jaz said. "So please please stop—"

Poppy was overcome by a coughing fit and I patted her back, probably more dramatically than I needed to in an attempt to shift the focus away from the heated talk.

"Giving me commands in my own house?!" She threw her napkin onto the table, the corner of it lapping into the pot of dhal. My instinct was to pull it out, but another instinct was that Gopi might slap my hand, so I did nothing. "How old do you think you are, young lady? You young frothy rebels who've lived a second and think you know everything."

"Whoa!" said Kamal. "Let's leave this till my sister's been here more than less than a day!"

"More than less than a day? Can you even say that?" I said.

"Don't you start, Ollie," Kamal said. "Or 'Stop starting' as I heard a woman say to her kid on the bus the other day."

Welcome mirth. The snuffing out of fiery words by the skilled Kamal. He was good at that. He was a master of mood manipulation, that lad. And perhaps Jasvandi, not so, as previously and seemingly 'erroneously surmised', as Kamal put it later.

Gopi recovered some ground by telling us that in India, at the time she was born, people ate very little meat and that it made their immune systems stonger. Jasvandi, or should I say Jaz, said they ate loads of meat in America and maybe had weaker immune systems because of it, but she didn't know if it had always been like that, at which point Kamal started reading from his phone despite Gopi's protestations:

"In 1961 in India, meat consumption was 3.7kg per person while the US consumption was 89.2 kg per person," which he converted into pounds—8.2 pounds versus 197 pounds. Gopi whacked Kamal's left arm and told him to put his phone away at the table and to serve the rice and dhal while she served the chicken. But he couldn't resist reading more:

"Ooh listen. This is from a divine text called *Bhagavata Purana*: 'Those sinful persons who consider themselves to be completely pious, without compunction commit violence against innocent animals who are fully trusting in them. In their next lives, such sinful persons will be eaten by the same creatures they have killed in this world.' Ha!"

"Please no! Not the giant chicken with the gnashing teeth!" I said, and Kamal took on the role of the chicken, leaning across the table with his hands towards my throat, saying, "Your time has come, loser. Shouldn't have messed with the homicidal hen!". The girls laughed their heads off, but Gopi was not amused. She was pretty unpredictable, I'll tell you.

"You're the one who has blood on her hands, Auntie, it's you who'll be devoured by the giant chicken," Kamal said. "The clucking and chuck-ling lingering and weakening in your fading ears." And he started clucking in her ears. She finally saw the funny side of it and cracked a reluctant smile before she gathered herself together and grabbed Kamal's phone from him.

"Hey!"

"I'll give it back when we've eaten. Let's get serving."

Once we were well on our way through the meal, Jaz said,

"What did your sister do with the box of meat?"

You must be kidding. I asked myself why she would have brought the subject up again when it had caused Gopi distress just before? But then I thought of Lily and how I would love to tell everybody how even at two years old, she would give her lettuce to the rabbit while Mam wasn't look-ing or how she scraped marmite off her toast with her fingers and pretend-ed it was something else. Gopi surprised me again by answering without emotion this time. Her sister, Mad, would take the meat to a boy at school who was very poor. We all made pained faces, I suspect not out of pity for the boy, but at the prospect of cold curry in a dirty metal tin, but Gopi banged her fist on the table and we all jerked up straight.

"You're a spoilt lot these days. You think you're entitled to anything and everything. You haven't got a bloody clue. The little boy's face when he saw the food would break your heart. Life is so easy for you all. Do you think of the suffering of others? Some have not even a roof over their head, you know? Have you any compassion? Pah." She started speaking down into her lap in a whisper, like a lunatic. "Very self-absorbed, self-obsessed, all of you. Think the world owes you a favour. Sad if you ask me. Something huge will happen, I bet, and you'll all see. There'll be a day of reckoning if you ask me."

She kept you on your toes, that's for sure. I was dying to say, 'I'd rather it didn't fall to me to say, but, fyi, no one did actually ask you.'

"The big bloody chicken will come back to get you all for certain," she said. "It's called Karma. Reap what you sow."

Jaz said, "*Jesus* would have been safe from the big chicken—he was vegetarian."

'Oh God. Here we go again,' I thought and focused on my plate of food.

"Who on earth told you that?' said Gopi. "Do you believe everything you read or see on commercial television? You ought to question things more."

"Hmmm yes, that would make sense," Kamal said, scratching his chin, fiddling with his specs, and shuffling in his seat which he always did before launching into a monologue. "Jesus did oppose animal sacrifice and his ethical teaching about showing mercy to the powerless, oppressed, and weak would surely encompass animals. [I know what you're thinking but, incredibly, no, he wasn't reading this from his phone.] And in his day, they didn't grind live baby chicks at an egg hatchery either."

"That is dark," said Poppy. "And you shouldn't make up stuff like that."

"It's true, Poppy," I said, chewing up a mouthful of chapati. "Did your year not see those documentaries called 'Hungry for change' and 'Food Inc' at school? It *is* dark—the way animals are processed for food in some places. Doesn't happen in the UK I don't think, but it does happen, or it *did*."

"You're right, Ollie," said Jaz. "You know a lot too. The people who aren't questioning are the greedy idiots who cram their mouths with tortured beings. What about pigs kept in cages, yeah, cages so small their bodies rub against them and they develop sores?" Now she started to shuffle on her chair. "They don't have room to turn around. The piglets feed, then they're taken away after only a couple of weeks."

"Then the sow's impregnated again," I said, "and that cycle continues for three or four years before she's slaughtered for meat." It sounds daft now to say it but I started shuffling myself at that point, I presume out of nerves or excitement or fear or all three. "Did you know that when the stun gun doesn't work, some of them are still alive when they're flung into scalding water to soften their skin and get rid of hairs? Imagine the squealing in some of those slaughter houses..."

Gopi was making all the right noises of horror, Poppy was silent, and Kamal was doing some speedy shuffling.

"It makes one shudder. What would Jesus think of that?" said Kamal.

"What would anyone think, Kamal?" said Gopi. "It's a wonder we're not all bloody vegetarian," she said between mouthfuls of chicken curry.

Talking of squealing, Poppy's face looked like she was about to do something similar. She started to look a bit pale and excused herself to go to the bathroom. Jaz laughed and implied Poppy was a wimp. She even said that she was a hypocrite if she couldn't bear to hear how animals were treated in intensive confinement and with cruelty, but was happy to stuff her face with the resulting dead flesh. I was about to stick up for Poppy and tell her the chicken was organic, when Gopi said,

"These are good lessons for all of us. We are all ignorant and lazy. We shouldn't have opinions about bloody anything unless we know what we're talking about."

That was rich coming from her, I thought. I was just thinking how Gopi cursed quite a lot for someone who often picked Kamal up for his foul language and that she was quite harsh and insensitive when she said,

"How are your grandparents, Ollie? I hear they're looking after you at the moment?"

There was silence again as we all bundled our animal thoughts back into our heads, consigned, by Gopi, to our individual vaults called, 'Unfinished Conversations I Have Had'.

"No, they aren't. Well yes they're staying at our house while Mam and Dad are away,' I said scooping up some dahl into a chapati, "but they're not really looking after us."

Gopi picked up her coaster and started using it as a fan. She said, "So they're not cooking for you or doing your washing or giving you lifts and such like?"

"Well, yes" I said, now with a mouthful, "but—"

Jaz laughed.

I was on the point of saying something rudish to Jaz but instead I found myself gulping down the food and heard myself saying, "Stunning Lobelia," pointing to a hanging basket at the window. I had marvelled at them in my head earlier, but hadn't said anything.

"The purple ones?" Kamal said, taking a swig of his water. "What do you know about them?"

"Lobelia Inflata variety, Gopi, right?"

She shrugged her shoulders, still fanning her face.

"Means Indian tobacco," I said. "Native American Indians used to smoke it as a cure for asthma." I hadn't noticed Poppy coming back into the room as I added, "It was also known as Pukeweed—doctors would prescribe it to induce vomiting."

"Nice one, Ollie," Kamal said, pointing his thumb to the living room door. I turned just in time to see Poppy running out of the room again.

Gopi said, "Very interesting, Oliver, but I was asking about your family. Have you heard from Anna and Ben?" Then the phone started ringing. Gopi pushed herself and her chair away from the table, wiped her mouth with her napkin before throwing her now stained napkin onto the chair and running into the hallway to pick up the telephone receiver, even though there was a handset in the room we were in.

"Speak of the devil!" Gopi shouted back to us with food still in her mouth, even before she had said hello. I couldn't believe it was Mam phoning—and I was right not to because it wasn't Mam, it was Grandma. That was strange...

Jaz asked how old my brothers were and before I'd opened my mouth to answer, Kamal clarified that they were my half-brothers, which I thought was pointless and kind of rude. He saw my face and apologized, immediately qualified by the reasoning that it was best Jaz was given the full picture in case she "put her foot in it" at a later date. Now I was bemused, and Kamal saw that too, but he was at a loss to explain what he meant, so I'll never know.

When I told Jaz that Nathan was eighteen and Sam was twenty-two, she laughed again and questioned why our grandparents needed to be there at all. I was the one doing shuffling in my seat again now, but Kamal came to my rescue, suggesting that since our little sister or *my* sister, as he put it, had died, my parents were over-protective. Which is a bit funny since they'd buggered off to Australia. He told her she'd love my grandparents and called my grandpa 'cool', which he'd never said to me. When he painted this picture of a whacky grandpa listening to jazz music, driving a VW camper van and making hilarious jokes, Jaz used the word again and by the time Kamal had explained how well I got on with my grandparents, that I "used to live with them" (which was only slightly true as in it wasn't for that long) and how we simply enjoyed spending time together, she let up with her line of questioning.

As she deftly dragged her chapati across her plate, to mop up the last of her sauce, she said she'd like to meet them, so we arranged then and there that she could come round the next evening to my house. As she finished her food, Jaz told us she'd never met any of her own grandparents and how lucky I was. Just then, Poppy, in her daisy dress and bare feet, floated back to the table, still looking pale but in a sort of pure way.

"You okay?" I said and Poppy half-smiled and nodded as she sat back down to my right, picked up her coaster, and pretended to look at the picture on it. I couldn't quite believe that Jaz immediately yanked us all back into the animal conversation:

"These so-called 'free range' chickens, as in not crammed in cages stacked one on top of the other, live in sheds with no windows—"

I looked at Poppy.

"Hey, Jaz, come on, we know all this. We're finished with that," I said, but she insisted,

"That's a pity, but I'm not done...'

I picked up the two coasters nearest me and started tapping them together like a percussion accompaniment to Jaz's speech which must have been reeeeeally annoying.

"The chickens are stuffed with food and can barely move so they grow fast and fat."

She adjusted her left hearing aid.

"Sometimes they can't stand, or their legs break with the weight of their bodies or their hearts and lungs can't keep up. They can take as little as six weeks to reach processing weight."

She pushed her chair back as if to give her more of 'the floor'.

"Nine billion are raised in the US each year to be killed for meat. Okay, now I'm done, but you know, you're wrong," she said looking at me, "not everyone does know about this shit."

I did want to join in and learn more, but Poppy was getting upset again: "You mean me? You mean *I* don't know?" she said, by now looking like she was going to cry and placing the coaster back down, so she was free to fold her arms.

Jaz said she didn't want to apologize for slightly upsetting someone because that was nothing compared to billions of suffering animals around the globe.

I felt an ache of disappointment in my throat as it struck me how badly things had turned out between Jaz and Poppy. I wondered if Jaz was so vociferous because she was disabled. That sounds terrible. What I mean is, she had probably suffered discrimination at some point so had no doubt developed one of those discriminated against back bones, so that when there's any talk of ill treatment of anything, her back straightens and tingles and sets her in defense mode. Or maybe she was just vegetarian for reasons of non-violence, like she said.

Poppy said she understood, and I couldn't help myself putting my arm round her, more out of relief than anything else, I think. Then Kamal put his arm around Jaz and told her well done and that she was right to stand up for her beliefs. I was about to say that everyone had been totally accepting of her beliefs, but I just said, "You okay?" again to Poppy. I wasn't expecting her to put her arm round me too, so that when Gopi walked back into the room, she said,

"What's going on in here – has somebody died?" No one answered. She said, "That was your grandmother, Ollie. Your grandfather has been taken into hospital. He's in Newcastle Infirmary. She's coming now with Sam and Nathan to pick you up."

CHAPTER FIVE

No one said anything in the van on the way to the hospital. Nathan sat in the front biting his nails. Sam sat behind him, on his phone. I sat with my face pressed against the window. It was weird Grandma driving the camper van instead of Grandpa. As I recognised the well-worn route to the hospital, having made the journey many times to see Lily the year before, my horticultural Tourette's clicked in— 'Dizygotheca Elegantissima' chanting itself in my head. It's the Latin name of a plant called False Aralia, which has masses of very dark green serrated leaves. As I started counting the chant syllables on my fingers, Lily kept flashing before me. I mostly liked seeing her face in my head as I feared a day might come when I couldn't conjure her up, but seeing her face on the way to the hospital was different. And now my grandpa... I felt my breathing speed up.

Déjà vu. "There's never any space to park," Grandma said, just as Mam used to say every hospital visit. "How can that happen in a place like this?"

"We'll find somewhere," said Sam.

Text from Poppy— 'Let me know how it all goes. x'

"There!" Nathan said, so we parked up and made our way in to find Grandpa.

As we walked into the ward, déjà vu number two—Nurse Celia! Lily's special nurse. It didn't feel in the least out of the ordinary to run up to her and give her a hug. She had put a hand through my hair before I'd spoken and my first instinct was to pull away until she reminded me that I shouldn't be surprised as it had been me who'd once said, "Nurses are very bodyish." I asked her how she was and before she had time to answer, I asked how Grandpa was.

"It's so wonderful to see you again. He's not too bad at all, but he has to have an operation, so he'll need to stay in."

"Operation? Really? Is it his heart?" I said.

"His foot."

"His foot?" we all said together, like a rehearsed scene in a farce. Grandma had told us he had collapsed and was unconscious when he had been taken away in the ambulance. That's all we knew. I thought he'd had a stroke or a heart attack.

"He was dancing barefoot and tripped on a plant of all things," Celia said. "He took a nasty knock to his head, bless him, but his main injury was to his foot. He fell so awkwardly that he put a lot of pressure on his right foot."

"What kind of plant was it?" I couldn't believe I'd said that out loud. Needless to say, Sam and Nathan called me selfish and stupid and Sam clipped me round the head. Grandma said,

"Boys, leave him. He's just feeling guilty. In fact, I know exactly what it was—it was a box of three little cacti."

"That would make sense," Celia said, trying to train threads of brown hair back into her bun. "There's lots of scratching to the ankle as well as the protruding bone."

"Err. Gross, man. Can we see it?" said Nathan.

"You're sensitive and thoughtful, aren't you?" said Sam, flicking the peak of Nathan's backwards cap.

"I thought you said you'd put that box on the kitchen table for me, Nathan?" I said. "Mam's friend was delivering it this afternoon and you agreed you would—"

"Yeah well, sorry, but I had to finish a film I was watching in the living room. Big deal."

"It is not the tiniest of deals," said Grandma, pointing at Nathan, "Your eighty-year-old grandpa lying in a hospital bed with concussion and an exploded foot is a big bloody deal."

I thought Grandma was going to cry. The tension was broken by Celia who physically took her hand and said, "Follow me".

Just seeing Grandpa in the bed sent shards through my heart. I stood still as the others went to sit with him. I looked around the ward. Every bed occupied. They all looked like shocked hostages. Beeping, flashing, clicking. Monitors, tubes, tanks, wires. Harsh chemicals and sweet gravy. Everything came flooding back. Celia walked to where I was standing; her hand rested on my back and rubbed up and down. She had a sixth sense about people. She always seemed to know what to do. I couldn't have predicted her next utterance, though. She asked me,

"Hey, do you want some cake?"

I hadn't eaten much at Kamal's once the talk of crushed baby chickens had kicked off, so cake would have been appealing in theory, only I felt sick, so I shook my head.

"Cake?" said Nathan. "Did someone say 'cake'?"

"Is there no end to your greed?" Sam said, folding his arms like a third parent. He then turned to Grandpa. "The nurse said you were dancing, you devil. What disc were you cranking out when you took a tumble?"

Grandpa beckoned me,

"Come here Ollie."

Celia gave me a nudge and I pushed past Nathan to get next to Grandpa who waved for me to go close to his face. This was my clever, cool, highly independent grandpa. His whitey wisps were all over the place (they must have removed the grubby but loved cap he always wore indoors and outdoors), his lips looked as dark as a bruise and his grey eyes bloodshot. 'But he just fell down. How come his face has changed this much?' I thought. Impossible to maintain any dignity I suppose, trapped in a hospital bed.

Grandpa whispered in my ear, "On Green Dolphin Street."

That was the tune he'd been dancing to. I whispered back to him, "Miles Davis and John Coltrane."

He patted my hand, his deep purple Midnight Calla Lily lips trying to smile and said,

"Good lad."

"Guess we'll never know," Grandma said, properly smiling and winking at no-one in particular.

"Did someone mention cake?" Grandpa said, but Celia told him he'd have to wait till after his operation. Grandma asked if that was usual, to have cake on the ward after which Celia explained that it had been a birthday cake, but that the birthday boy had passed away and the cake left by the family.

"One of the perks of working on a geriatric ward," Celia had said, followed by the 'Oops' gesture of a swift hand to the mouth and just as I was screwing up my face, thinking the comment was a bit distasteful, Grandma added,

"I suppose a lot of people leave the ward feet first?"

Nathan objected to this talk, which I agreed was unsavoury, so neither of us would eat cake, even though I wasn't going to have any anyway. Grandma took Sam and Nathan to buy some coffee and Celia was called away, so it was just me and Grandpa. I told him about Kamal's house and Jaz and her strong ideas about animal welfare. I told him she seemed like a tough cookie and that even though she came over as quite powerful, I liked her a lot.

"Girlfriend material, is she?"

"No. I mean... no. Kamal's sister?"

"It's how you feel that matters. You're keen on Poppy too, though, aren't you?"

I didn't say anything. Grandpa ruffled my hair then winced and I couldn't believe I was being all pathetic talking about me when he was the one in hospital, in severe pain.

"Poor thing," came out of my mouth even though I had only planned to think it.

"Suffering is very normal, Ollie. If I accept mine, will you accept yours?"

I laughed, as it sounded like some sort of childish truce. But he was being serious.

"Is it as easy as that, do you think?" I said, sitting down on the grey armchair next to his bed.

"Yes. Yes, it is. And don't restrict your impulses to go for something just because you think you may not succeed, or you may lose something."

I think he was talking about Jasvandi, but I didn't ask for clarification.

"That's all normal too. You like the way Charlie Parker plays the sax, don't you?"

I nodded.

"And John Coltrane and Sonny Rollins?"

I nodded again.

"What makes them sound amazing is taking risks."

I think I was still nodding from the last time.

"You got to be dangerous, Ollie."

Then I centred my head.

"Dave Brubeck—I've played his music to you—wonderful pianist, said, 'There's a way of playing safe, there's a way of using tricks and there's the way I like to play, which is dangerously, where you're going to take a chance on making mistakes in order to create something you haven't created before.'"

"That's cool," I said. "Yeah. I see that."

I could see that discussing musicians had taken him away from his discomfort momentarily, but then it was the return of the winces. I felt he might be better listening to me rather than talking. Thing is, I seemed to be addicted to seeking his advice.

"So then I should go out with Poppy *and* Jaz at the same time and see which one I prefer? Is that what you think?"

Grandpa laughed. I felt my heart warm up.

"Is that how you interpret it?" he said. "There's being dangerous, then there's being plain barmy."

We both laughed this time as Nurse Celia approached us. Just so you know, I hadn't meant what I said, I mean about going out with Poppy and Jaz at the same time.

"You've perked your grandpa up no end," she said, hitching up her tights. "He's a good lad, isn't he?" she said to him.

"You *know* each other?" Grandpa said.

"I used to work in a children's ward. I knew his little sister... sorry, I'm sorry, your granddaughter."

Grandpa's eyes lowered.

"I looked after Lily," Celia said. "I'll never forget how pretty she was. Looked so much like Ollie too, didn't she? Those long curly eyelashes... So sad."

Then Grandpa 'perked down'.

"Oh, I *am* sorry," said Celia. "I shouldn't have—"

"No, I should have recognized you," he said. "Only, we didn't make it in as often as we'd have liked. Too upsetting. Nightmare time, wasn't it?"

Grandpa seemed to lie further back in the pillow and tilted his head to the left, to look away, to look at nothing, to remember, to forget. "Was a real tragedy. Poor Anna." Then he turned back to face Celia. "Sorry, Anna's my daught—"

"I know. I know her," she said, tucking hair behind her ear even though it didn't need tucking. "Yes, sweetheart, I know who she is."

"I don't know what I'm thinking. Of course, you know who she is if you know Ollie," Grandpa said turning towards me. "Sorry."

"It's fine," Celia said mustering up the most massive grin. I imagined she had a facial expression remote control in her pocket. Let's face it, things must turn on a sixpence in a hospital ward. "Stop apologizing," she said. You're concussed. You should be resting."

As close as I was to Grandpa, he'd never said anything like this before. I mean 'nightmare time' and 'didn't make it in' and all that. He looked like he wanted to walk away, but he was stuck there in the bed, regret and painkillers pulsing through his veins. How sad, how normal, he might say, to switch from strong to weak in a split second. How roles reverse in the blink of an eye.

Celia told us that she'd stopped working as a nurse for a while but had come back part time, but not on children's wards. Grandpa said he quite understood. Roles switching around again.

Grandma, Sam and Nathan got back to the ward just as Grandpa was about to be taken to have his foot operation. Celia suggested we leave and come back the next day, so we wished him luck, and left after a long round of hugs. Grandma had decided not to tell Mam and Dad about the fall. There was no worry of them finding out through someone else since they weren't in the country. They weren't even in the continent. They were in Australia.

It had seemed such a long day as I lay on my back contemplating the last twelve hours. A huge abstract canvas unfolded in front of me made up of millions of different bits of legs. The day had featured limbs, let's face it—Poppy's leg up against mine, chickens' legs deformed from cruelty, Grandpa's exploded foot. I surprised myself, considering all that had gone on, by dwelling on Poppy's leg. I don't mean just her leg, as in like a false leg unattached to a body, but the touching part. I tried to feel again what I had felt when my one little finger had brushed against her thigh, but it was so physically linked with that particular moment in time, it was impossible to experience it again. I could see now why people went back and back for more of this physical stuff because what I did sense was the craving to feel whatever it was I felt again. So that must be the cycle—the craving and the satisfying of it... just that, going round and round, the craver never tiring of the perpetual desire and the temporary relief. And did I feel that stuff because it was Poppy? Or would I feel like that about any leg? I mean, you know, within reason. Not a chicken leg, for instance. Chickens... and all that horrible talk of how badly they're treated. Broken legs. Perhaps I would become vegetarian. Broken feet. Poor Grandpa. Suffering is normal, he had said. Is cruelty normal as well then? Thing is, people have vastly differing ideas of what cruelty is.

Text from Jaz: 'So cool to meet you. I heard it was an accident and your grandpa is gonna be ok. I guess I'm not meeting him tomorrow? Or should I come to your place anyway?'

So she was quite pushy as well. She's being dangerous, I thought, or was it that she was being normal and I had lost touch with what normal was? I had to text Poppy back. I wondered where it would be stored in the Emotion Library, my jar full of whatever it was I was feeling. What would be marked on the front? Why had she lied and said I had a girlfriend? I didn't think Poppy was capable of telling lies. I should have been more angry. I should have texted her saying, 'So I've got a girlfriend, have I?' but I sent her: 'All okay. Grandpa's foot broken, but he'll be fine.' She wrote back instantly: 'Okay so not so bad. Still, poor Gramps. How you?'

'Yeah all is well with me. Hope Jaz didn't upset you too much. I've got chickens on the brain!'

Can't believe I was all jolly when she'd betrayed me. Was I that desperate for her approval?

'Ha ha. No, I'm fine too. May become vegetarian!'

'Know what you mean. We can start by organising my vegetable patch. You said you'd help, yeah?' And now I was inviting her to help me. What a loon.

'I'd love to. Shall I come round tomorrow and we can make a plan?'

So, they were both dangerous... The question stopped me in my tracks. I hadn't even answered Jaz's text and here was Poppy asking the same thing. They couldn't both come round. Could they?

'Yeah sure, come round and meet Grandma,' I texted Jaz.

'Jaz is already coming round as she wants to meet Grandma,' I texted Poppy.

'Another time then.' Poppy wrote.

I remembered Grandpa with his wretched foot in hospital and his wise words. It was like an out-of-body experience when my thumbs texted to Poppy,

'Come round.'

'Great!' Jaz wrote.

'Great x,' Poppy wrote.

Was I insane? I would have to ask Kamal too; it would only be Jaz's second night ever since he'd met her. How would I behave with both Jaz and Poppy, having heard what I'd heard?

I decided to look up 'Catharsis' in my Chambers dictionary – It was quite long, but it finally made sense, what Kamal had been on about: '**catharsis** noun **1** relief that results either from allowing repressed thoughts and feelings to surface, as in psychoanalysis, or from an intensely dramatic experience. **2** the cleansing of the emotions through the elicitation of acute fear and pity in spectators of drama, especially tragedy. **3** medicine-the process of clearing out or purging the bowels.

Etymology: 19c: Latin, from Greek kathairein to purify.

Blimey, that was a shocker, the bowel bit. Literally getting rid of stuff. Ha. I was more interested in the emotions aspect, though. Interesting idea, I reckoned, 'cleansing' emotions. If I had expressed that to Auntie Colette, she would have recommended a crystal to use or would be telling me my 'chakras' were out of balance. I'm never quite sure what chakras are. I always meant to look into that.

I still couldn't get Poppy and Jaz out of my head. And now they were both coming over. How would it be—the three of us together at my house??

CHAPTER SIX

I opened my curtainless window and looked out onto the waning morning garden. Not much colour any more, but for September, it was amazingly warm, so it would make complete sense to have a meeting about gardening in the garden in the afternoon, I thought. It was a Sunday, so Grandma said she'd make some lunch and then a dinner to have after our meeting. She told me that Sam and Nathan would be there too, but that Sam was going out at nine o'clock. Chicken casserole. I decided not to tell her that Jaz was a vegetarian. I don't know why. Maybe I didn't want to spoil her cooking plan.

The steps Dad had built which ran down the side of the steep garden were weedy. He had asked me to do a bit of weeding every week, but I hadn't done any. I enjoyed watching the wild weeds grow in their bushiness, spikiness, and utter unpredicatableness. It was a work of art I was letting develop. Every fresh push of green felt like a defiant move. I complied with my urge to disobey his wish for me to keep everything neat, however tiny a rebellion it was. "Those steps are getting pretty damned out of hand, Dad. What you gonna do about it?" I actually said out loud.

Mam and Dad had already been away for three weeks and wouldn't be back for ages— "I hope you'll give us your blessing to do this trip to Australia and New Zealand?" Dad had said. Like I had any say in it whatsoever. Like I had any say in anything. It didn't bother me that they hadn't been there for my birthday on 25th September—but I couldn't believe they'd be away on Lily's birthday, 7th November. What were we supposed to do? I didn't want to do the cake thing like last year and the singing and the crying. *I* would go away too maybe... and not tell anyone.

The forget-me-nots Lily had planted were flourishing, but I'd never moved them to the bottom tier of the garden like I'd suggested to Dad. We hadn't started up the meadow either. I didn't want to move them. Anyway, I could have planted some more but that wasn't the point. New ones wouldn't be the same. Lily had planted them when she was five, you see. I could see her sprinkling the seeds with Poppy. I could see her face telling me not to prune the pink roses she'd chosen—the polyanthus. "Don't poon it," she'd said. "Don't let it die," she'd said. She would have been nearly seven years old. I felt my headache coming back. I never told anyone, but I started to get headaches, like throbbing fiery headaches all the time after Lily died. I quite enjoyed them, to be honest. Yeah, I know that's weird, but it's hard to explain. I couldn't sleep properly either, so I was in a daze a lot of the time. I got into trouble at school for not concentrating, which made me hate school even more. She would have been nearly seven. She never even saw the flowers bloom—the tiny precious sweet delicate flowers. How could I sever their roots and wrench them from the earth? Would I think this same thing every year? She would have been ten, she would have been fifteen, she would have been twenty-one, she would have been eighty? Well she wasn't anything. She used to be five and now she was nothing. How are you supposed to do it? Looking back at time with my sister was like flinging me against a wall till I was black and blue; looking ahead at the time devoid of her was like sitting in a dark corner, rocking back and forwards. It's the first time I 'got' that rocking back and forwards thing, like a monkey trapped in a cage, agonising over where his family is and when the next experiment will be.

"Oliver!" Grandma shouted up the stairs. "Will you come down now, please, pet? I've made boiled eggs and soldiers."

I sat at the kitchen table, looking out onto the patio and Grandma served me my egg and bready dip things—soldiers, as she called them. She'd put some forget-me-nots in a plastic cup in the middle of the table, without asking me. "Myosotis," I could hear Lily saying, which is the Latin name I'd taught her to say. She used to say it so well. Grandma took her 'pinny' off and flopped it over the back of a chair (she always wore a pinafore, or a pinny as she called it whenever she was in the kitchen. It means apron.)

Grandpa had to stay in hospital after his operation, she told me. He had to have a plate put into his foot (not a plate you eat from. God forbid. It would encourage bugs to live as parasites in his leg and eat off the plate). A chunk of some sort of metal, apparently. Grandma said he was very drowsy and in pain and that no one was to visit that day apart from her.

"That'll be nice having your friends over, Oliver, won't it?" She straightened her blouse and leaned one hand on the pinny chair.

I didn't feel in the mood anymore, so I just nodded.

"Your mam's ringing later; will you have a word with her?"

"No. I mean, she won't want to anyway."

"Of course she'll want to."

Grandma pulled out the pinny chair and sat on it. Her face was kind but serious as she looked at me.

"She's missing you all. She worries about you, you know?"

I didn't look up from my egg, and poked the yokey goo with a soldier. "Does she?"

I pulled out the yellow-headed soldier and held it still.

"She worries about everything these days I suppose," I said.

"Your parents have talked about visiting relations out there for years. Are you going to eat that? They missed two weddings last year because they were stuck here. Eat your egg, darling, please."

"Stuck here? Coz of Lily you mean?" I lay the soldier to rest on the plate. "How annoying for them."

"Yes, Ollie, because of Lily. I wish you would—"

She stopped mid-sentence so I'll never know if she was going to say, 'I wish you would snap out of your annoying teenage moan' or 'I wish you would eat your egg.'

Either way, I couldn't stay moping around all day, so I forced myself to perk up and totally change the subject. I turned to look at Grandma and surprised myself by saying,

"What would you do if you liked two girls and they both liked you?"

Her eyes brightened along with the mood and she got up and put her apron back on. Perhaps she tended to take it off only for serious conversations, not that the present one was frivolous or anything.

"Do you mean *specially* like? Are we talking fancying here?"

"Yes, I suppose I am," I said, waiting for my red face to make an appearance, but it didn't have a chance because Grandma said,

"I'd have to accept that not only was I a lesbian or bi-sexual, but that I was spoilt for choice and would probably have to consider a ménage à trois."

"What's that—no wait, I can guess. You're gross, I mean, no, sorry, Grandma, just rude, no that's the wrong word too. You messin' wit' my head, lady!" We both laughed. She sat down next to me again and wiped her hands on her Princess Diana apron—didn't seem right somehow, wiping dirt on Diana.

Turned out she knew exactly who I was talking about and gave me a very long squeezy hug which practically winded me. When she'd got up again to make two cups of tea and had brought them back to the table in smiley face mugs, stained tea-brown in the exact spot you drink from (Mam was not an obsessive cleaner), she said she reckoned Poppy had lied about me having a girlfriend because she didn't want me to go out with Jaz. I don't know how she worked that out, but it did make some sense to me. She told me there was no urgency with anything and that a solution might present itself to me in the course of time. I was so glad she'd said that as I really couldn't be bothered to fuzz my head up any more than it already was.

Jaz was the first to arrive at about midday.

"You look nice," she said (I definitely didn't).

"So do you." (She definitely did.)

She wore a grey trilby hat with a black ribbon around, which she doffed as I opened the door. And I noticed she had millions of rings on including one thumb. She kind of scared me, truth be told, she was *that* cool. She had on a cap sleeve black hooded tee-shirt with a denim waistcoat on top, blue jeans and her green Doctor Martin boots. I was glad I'd put on my best trainers, but wished I'd worn something other than the t shirt Kamal had given me as a birthday present, which said on the front, 'Life's A Garden. Dig it!' and on the back, 'Give peas a chance. Make your own.' At least he hadn't given me his second choice which he'd told me was a top with the slogan 'I believe in gnomes.' To my astonishment, my next utterance was,

"Do you have any tattoos?" I think I must have thought that she looked so cool, she probably did.

"Excuse me?" she said.

"What for?" I said and I wasn't trying to be funny either.

"I mean what did you say?" she said.

"Oh nothing."

"I hate it when people do that. I'm like deaf, not stupid, I just need repetition sometimes. Is that okay? Can you do that for me?"

So this was going well, and she wasn't even in the door yet.

"Come in. I'm sorry."

After she'd stepped inside and we were standing in the hallway, I made sure she could see my face and I said,

"I was asking if you had any tattoos on your body."

She still didn't look like she was 100% getting it, so I said,

"You know, like a snake on your arm or somebody's name here?" sweeping my right hand down my upper then lower left arm."

She turned around and lifted up her t shirt and waistcoat.

"Yin yang. Nice," I said. When she turned back, I repeated the same words in case she'd missed them and added "Is it recent?" I immediately thought that was quite a hard sentence to lipread, so I added, "When did you get it? How old were you?"

"When I turned eighteen in April. I'd wanted one since I was fifteen, but I decided to wait, you know, until I was older, so I'd like know if I really really wanted it."

I have to tell you, she was pretty stunning-looking and now she was lifting her clothes up. I felt my headache easing and some of those exquisite warm wavy surges pulsing through me. It wasn't like with Poppy though—I didn't feel nervous or anything. She said,

"So, have *you* got anything interesting under your fun outfit?"

And you won't believe it, but she lifted up my t shirt. I held in my stomach and made fists to harden my arms, trying to look buff, but she started tickling me and I couldn't help laughing—what a great mood shifter she was. The next mood shift—Poppy comes in the open door and sees Jasvandi with her hands up my shirt and me giggling like a love-struck hyena.

"Am I interrupting something?" Poppy said, while closing the door behind her.

"We're just playing. I was showing Ollie my tattoo. What do you think?" Jasvandi said, turning round and lifting her t shirt up again except this time a lot higher so I could see her smooth brown stomach. Her belly button was pierced. I found myself remembering that Poppy had lied about me having a girlfriend, so I reached out and brushed the back of my right hand over her piercing. She immediately jerked her head away from Poppy and round to me saying,

"Hey!"

"You're done on both sides. No stone left unturned," I said.

"Excuse me?" She said, looking angry.

"You've done everything. I mean you've done lots of... stuff. Tattoo. Belly Button." I shouldn't have touched her. I was no good at being dangerous, I decided. "That's a lot. Isn't it?"

"I've done more than you I'm guessing."

And she smiled with this look in her eye that was like, 'Wouldn't you like to know what I've done or maybe even show you?' I suppose... I did to be honest.

"What is it anyway?" Poppy said. Jaz pulled her shirt back down and turned around properly towards her. "Did you design it yourself?"

"It's a yin yang," Jaz and I said together.

"Oh. What's that?"

"It's a symbol," I said, being vague to annoy her.

"Are you trying to annoy me? I can see it's a symbol. I'm not thick."

"It's Chinese," said Jaz. "Yin is feminine and yang is masculine. It's kind of like a balance thing. It represents balance."

"Meaning what? Like you're bisexual?" Poppy said, slumping her weight emphatically onto one leg.

I was just thinking, 'Yeah, you *are* a bit thick, Poppy,' when Jaz actually said quite emphatically that maybe she *was* bisexual. I gave my comment on the yin yang symbol, saying,

"Opposite forces but connected."

There was a whiff of a pregnant pause and Poppy and I were exchanging an awkward glance, when Kamal popped his head round the front door. He was wearing the gnome t shirt and immediately spun round to show us the slogan on the back. What was it about that day—all the spinning and showing of backs?

'Hangin' with my gnomies!' it said on the back of his t shirt.

Jasvandi had made me promise that Kamal and I would show them a scene from *Othello* after we'd finished some planting, but first we all went into the kitchen as Grandma had made some soup for lunch.

"Leek and potato," Grandma said, as she beckoned for us all to sit round the kitchen table placing a basket of French bread inbetween two flower arrangements. Jaz gave me an approving smile, which I computed to mean she thought I'd told Grandma she was vegetarian. A pang of guilt shot through my body.

"My favourite," I heard myself saying.

"Mine too," Jaz said. "Us veggies should stick together." She smiled and came to sit next to me.

Grandma had filled two little home-made vases with more of Lily's forget-me-nots—one had short coloured pencils, points facing upwards, stuck all around what was probably a plastic container and the other one had four or five layers of different coloured wool wrapped tightly round another pot of some sort. While Grandma served up the soup, passing round ready-filled pink bowls, Poppy admired the vases and the flowers. It won't surprise you to hear that I couldn't stop myself saying,

"Myosotis."

Kamal commented that I would have to tame my use of Latin and my 'non sequiturs' as he called them, since it must be frustrating for a person who is deaf. I would have to look the word up later or the lunch would have been one long round of puzzling over each other's utterances, but I could tell non sequitur sounded Latin, so I said,

"Oh, I can't use Latin, but you can?"

"Touché," said Kamal.

"Oh, French now, is it?!" I said, but realised we were being boring, so decided to tell Jaz that my grandma was always making things because she used to be a primary school teacher.

"Special Needs it used to be called or maybe it still is," I added.

Kamal to the rescue—

"She used to teach in a school where the children had what they call 'learning difficulties' which means problems that affect ability to learn. What sort of IQ did they have? Under 70 maybe?"

Grandma laughed and with a pained expression said,

"We didn't work like that. No one thought... thinks in those terms, Kamal."

She sat down next to the only free remaining space between Kamal and me, swept her left hand from the front to the back of her hair as if to flatten it, even though it was already flattened in a bun and picked up her soup spoon with her right. Turning to face Kamal, she said,

"Our children were normal people who happened to find certain things challenging, like walking or concentrating for long periods or getting along easily with others. It wasn't about intelligence. It isn't all about intelligence, I hope you realise?"

She slurped a spoonful of soup before placing her spoon down onto the table to the right of the bowl and this time moving her head from left to right to show she was talking to all of us, said,

"I had my happiest years with those children. Not always having an awareness of what you're supposed to do, say or look like made for a very happy bunch of people a lot of the time. You didn't get jealousy or bullying. They weren't constantly competing for attention and admiration. The laughs we had!"

Poppy asked Grandma,

"So, did you teach anyone deaf like Jasvandi?"

I couldn't quite believe she'd said that. I think all of us were ready to jump in with a response, but it was Grandma who got there first. She picked up her spoon again, and before taking another mouthful of soup, said,

"The children had quite significant learning difficulties—I suppose you could say disabilities, so no, children with hearing loss wouldn't go to that sort of school."

She continued with her lunch as her words lingered, and it occurred to me that Poppy possibly knew exactly what she was doing. She seemed to be playing out an urge to put Jasvandi down for some reason. It was so unique and potentially joyful really for this group of five quite different people to be having lunch together on this bright, warm Sunday, yet I wasn't 'feeling' it. An atmosphere was seeping into the room, swerving its way in and out of the spaces between our bodies, misting our vision and muddying our minds. Through the mud and mist, Jaz spoke out—

"I must be normal then because I was bullied real bad at high school."

I would bet that everyone's mouths opened slightly and there may even have been dribbling of soup...

"And no, I don't think of deafness as a disability—I am capable of pretty much anything. I went to a regular high school, but I sometimes wished I'd gone to a school for deaf students. My best friend did, and she was much happier than I was."

All I knew was I wasn't going to be the one who picked up on any of her comments. I wasn't going to stoke any fire. Kamal started shuffling in his chair, which, as you know by now, meant he was about to say something meaningful.

"Ollie and I were bullied at school too, weren't we Ollie?"

Whaaaaaat? I hadn't just heard that. I never talked about that. I didn't want to talk about it. I hoped Kamal wasn't going to tell everyone too many details. Surely he wouldn't tell them that we kind of studied bullying together to try to avoid being affected by it? We really did do that, by the way. I needed to say something to stop him coming out with all that…

My mind misted over again as I struggled to form a useful or interesting response. I clocked Jaz's expression—one of comfort and hope maybe. Then an awkward silence pervaded our space. I was thinking that compared to being beaten up or mocked for a disability, I don't know if what happened to us could be classed as bullying and was about to say, 'Not really', but that would have thrown a spanner in the already clogged up works, so I just nodded, accompanied by a weird forced smile. Kamal carried on—

"We were lucky having each other in the end as we self-counselled."

'Here he goes,' I thought.

"By that I mean we read books and studied websites on the psychology of bullying and did what we could to take charge of our emotional safety."

His elbows on the table, he pushed his glasses up his nose before joining his hands to make an arch, then rested his chin on his hands. He'd rock the arch to help him tilt his head from left to right, shifting his gaze, so he could make eye contact with everyone in turn.

"If Darren Cragley said to me, 'You stupid stinking ugly stick-man', which he genuinely did verbatim, I would say, 'On the contrary, I emit, from my finely featured visage and slender frame, a rather refined fragrance to match my considerable wit and charm.'"

Brilliant—everyone laughed, Grandma so hard that she had to get up and leave the table to get a glass of water.

"You're the oddest boy, Kamal!" she said as she gulped down her drink, to which he answered,

"I take that to mean a rare and exceptional specimen, so I thank you kindly, ma'am."

She spluttered her water down her apron and blouse and Poppy and Jaz caught each other's eyes and sniggered too. I think Jaz was just generally joining in the lightened mood. It was Poppy who spoke next—

"I'm sorry everyone if I said something stupid before."

She wiped her mouth with her hand though there was nothing to wipe.

"I wasn't thinking, Jaz, when I said about, you know—"

"It's okay," Jaz said without looking at Poppy, so it probably wasn't. "It's tough for hearing people to get the idea that deafness is not necessarily seen as a disability. Julie, my bf, calls hearing folk 'deaf-impaired'; put that in your pipe and smoke it!"

I sensed I wasn't the only one with an opening mouth. 'Deaf-impaired'? What was she on about? Then she comes out with the clever pipe phrase?

"I love that technique, Kamal," she said, "—taking the sting out of an insult by turning it on its head, into something positive."

Grandma sat back down even though she'd finished her soup and asked Jaz if she'd asked for help when she was bullied. It saddened me that she said she hadn't. I watched her as she related some of the incidents. It occurred to me that, like Kamal, she radiated strength despite a heart-rending past. How she acted, held herself, spoke, was so commanding, you couldn't help but admire her. She told us that though she'd been taught that being included in a regular educational setup was to be favoured, her friend, Julie, who went to a school for pupils with hearing impairments, gained a lot from having specialist teachers, small classes, speech and language therapy, state of the art listening equipment and most of all, likeminded people who understood deafness and who could use sign language. She said Julie had a higher self-esteem. I found it hard to believe that she was implying her self-esteem was low; I found her to be incredibly confident and self-assured. Maybe it was a front, but she was doing a bloody convincing job.

I found myself mesmerised by her persona: her words, facial expressions, hand gestures, body language, dynamic charm and authority. I could have watched her all day, but felt Poppy's eyes burning into me, so much so that I turned towards her and in that instant, she found a gap in Jaz's narrative and sort of interrupted, saying,

"Well that was five-star soup, thank you, but should we not be getting on with some gardening now?" She knew how to get my attention.

"I'm glad you liked it. This time next year, we might all be lunching on Ollie's home-grown leeks and potatoes! Yes, off you go and I'll clear this lot up."

Poppy insisted on staying to stack the dishwasher and while Kamal, Jaz and I hovered on the patio outside the kitchen, I saw, through the picture window which adorned the back of the house, Poppy kissing Grandma on the cheek and then Grandma taking Poppy's hands, saying something intense to her, then giving her a hug. Perhaps Grandma had sensed an uneasiness in Poppy, or perhaps she was advising her to be nice to Jaz, or perhaps they were just being normal loving people. As she came to join us on the patio, I took a deep breath in, huffed it out, then slowly breathed in the outside air and the promise of a gratifying gardening session. I hoped Jaz and Poppy would connect more over the seeds and soil...

CHAPTER SEVEN

Having spent about two hours planting broad beans, peas, spinach, Brussel sprouts, leeks, parsnips, lettuce and garlic in my section of the garden, everyone's moods were high. I had been in my element apparently, as Poppy had said how much she liked seeing me happy. She said I looked 'alive', implying, I suppose, that most of the time I looked dead. But it was true, I don't know what it was about the seeds and the soil, but I did feel connected and grounded and real.

I told them my handwriting was rubbish and asked Poppy to write on the labels and stab them into the ground to mark our vegetable lines. I leaned against the side wall, arms folded, and pushed my hair up and back off my now sweaty face, watching the scene in front of me: Kamal was play fighting with Jasvandi as he grappled to see her tattoo which Poppy had mentioned, but which Jaz had decided she didn't want to show him; Poppy, her hair clamped up off her face with straggly bits sticking out, knelt on the ground, wearing one of my over-sized rappers t shirts to protect her dress, filling out the label sticks with red felt-tip; a tiny bird (goldcrest... no a wren) with long legs, singing with an astoundingly loud voice for its size, flitted around Lily's polyanthus. Lily herself, I then imagined, twirling around, smiling and chanting the names of the vegetables, rhyming the sounds in her squeaky voice: 'Pisum sativum, Pisum fatty bum'. Just as I began to dwell on Lily's no-longer-thereness, Poppy, as if telepathically, raised her eyes from her task, found mine, allowed a gentle smile onto her face and slow-blinked like she was saying, 'I know, I know.' I smiled too as she looked back down, and I felt my throat hurting and pressure building behind my eyes. Odd how pain can so swiftly follow joy or maybe they can dance together, a weird free and thrashy sort of dance involving both kissing of and battering the earth, perhaps accompanied by vegetable and flower juggling.

"Come on then let's see how well you act! Ollie, let me see you and Kamal doing some of your *Othello*!" Jaz was in high spirits, so I forced another smile to support her enthusiasm. Kamal was thrilled that Jaz liked Shakespeare and said they were 'cut from the same cloth' (Kamal and Jaz). I announced that I wasn't in the mood and that anyway I was probably going to give up my part as it was taking away my music and gardening time. Everyone sighed like I was James McAvoy throwing in the towel half way through a film.

Sam sat on the patio for a while, drinking a beer and he offered bottles to us, before going out. I was worried Grandma would disapprove, but she had let us drink it, saying it was a treat after our gardening. Amazingly, Grandma had decided to make tomato and mushroom pasta for dinner, so another awkward chicken scene was avoided. The whole meal was spent listening to Nathan describe how brilliant the new skate park was. We were all a bit tired so it suited us fine. I commented to Grandma that it was cool she hadn't objected to us drinking beer. She explained that she thought it was better for her to know what we were doing than to be shut away in a bedroom 'getting up to who knows what.' Talking of being shut away in bedrooms getting up to who knows what, I did find myself in something of a related predicament later that evening...

You know those weird times when lots of different factors all gang up and pounce on you, when a series of coincidences lead to a happening? They can be amazing or pretty shitty. 'Synchronicity' Kamal says these meaningful coincidences are called. Well, that's what went down that night and I'd say the happening fell into the first category i.e. amazing...

For the first time ever, the four of us, Kamal, Poppy, Jasvandi and I had drunk alcohol together, so, truth be told, we weren't 100% our normal selves ('coincidence number **1** we'll call it, though I suppose it could be **1B**, as it only happened because of coincidence number **1A**— Grandma was looking after us in my parents' absence). Poppy had felt sick after more talk of chicken torture and had walked up the road back to hers, to have an early night ('coincidence number **2**'). I reckon it was more the beer and the teasing really that had made her feel uncomfortable and ill, which was sad because she had been so lovely that afternoon.

Two hours later, "I'm not getting my trilby wet," was Jaz's response to the pouring rain which greeted her and Kamal on opening the front door (rain was 'coincidence number **3**'). Kamal reckoned he definitely needed a walk, so asked if Jaz could borrow a waterproof coat. As I was looking for one, Nathan came to get *his* jacket and said that Grandma was giving him a ride to his mate's house.

"I'm off to Arjun's—lives near Kamal. We can take Jaz home in the car and Kamal can have his walk." (coincidence number **4**).

So, Kamal stumbled off for his 'rejuvenating stroll' as he called it. Jaz put on the cagoul I'd found her, and we hung around in the hallway.

"They're so lame, don't you think, Ollie?" Jaz said. "I could carry on drinking. I could stay up half the night. You?"

I just nodded, but had scary visions of her stripped off and gyrating her tattoo and piercing and was secretly pleased she was being whisked away. But... you'll never guess... the van wouldn't start (coincidence number **5**). Grandma went to get some money for a taxi to give Nathan and Jaz. "Can you believe that?!" I could hear Grandma shouting from the kitchen. "Grandpa's taken all my cash again! I bet it was for his jazz night that he ended up missing anyway!" (coincidence number **6**).

Nathan decided to stay in and Grandma suggested that Jaz stay and sleep in Sam's room as he wasn't coming back that night (final and MOST SIGNIFICANT coincidence, magic number 7).

I sat on my bed in disbelief that Jasvandi (Kamal's. Sister. Whom. I'd. Only. Known. For. Two. Days) was staying the night in our house. There was a knock at the bedroom door. I jumped up. Jaz with an open bottle of beer in each hand.

"Grabbed these from downstairs," she said.

I must have been standing there, frozen, for some time, because Jaz said,

"Is this okay? Do you want me to leave?"

"Yes, I mean no, I mean come in quickly."

"Why quickly?" she said, by now leaning on the doorframe and starting to drink one of the beers. "You afraid? Are girls not allowed in your room? You *are* sixteen, aren't you?"

"Yes. So?" I said. She didn't answer.

After lingering at the doorway for what seemed like half an hour, she clomped into my room.

"So?" she said, then laughed.

She'd taken her waistcoat and hat off and was somehow wearing her Mick Jagger mouth top and not the black one she'd had on earlier. I looked at the big mouth—I was in danger of being swallowed whole, I thought. She passed me the beer and asked if she could sit on my bed. I felt like saying, 'There's a perfectly good chair at my desk,' but I heard myself telling her yes, that would be fine.

She sat on the bed, pushing her back right up to the wall. 'She's put her boots on my new saxophone duvet cover,' I thought.

"This is funky," she said, rubbing her right hand over the cover, her left lifting her bottle to take a swig. Then she patted the bed. "Come keep me company then... actually no, could you help me take my DMs off—they're like so tight? And why don't you put on that desk lamp—the lighting's real harsh in here."

I switched on the lamp then put the ceiling light out and put on some music without her even asking me to. Except it hadn't been the best of ideas.

"I can't hear too well with music on in the background."

"Shall I put it off?"

"Just keep it low if you don't mind."

I stood directly in front of her, looking down at her lounged on my bed. She ran her right hand through her gorgeous gleaming, now hatless hair and took another swig of beer. I reached back to the desk for *my* beer and proceeded to down about half of it in several gulps. I put it down and looked back at her. I looked down at her Doctor Martin boots. They didn't look tight to *me*. The laces were not even done. I lowered myself down, so I was kneeling on the floor. I uncrossed her legs and held one boot in each hand. My head still down, facing her boots, my eyes slowly swivelled up to study her face again; I'll tell you she was what you would call exceptionally good looking. She had a tiny scar running up the left point of the cupid's bow on her lips. I wondered if she had actually been in her parents' car accident. Either way, her mouth was just how you'd draw one, you know, symmetrical with a natural brown line running all the way around. It was slightly open as if she was going to say something, but she didn't. Her nose was small and pointy, but not in a witchy way—much smaller than that. But her eyes... it was her eyes with their extra-long lashes. I thought of moist soil, daring to be clawed at, and tree trunks tempting palms to press and caress. Her eyes weren't lined and filled in with make up like Poppy's always were—and they smiled without her mouth moving. My eyes still entranced by hers, I tugged at the laces on her left boot to loosen the grip on her ankle, which was warmed by a thick woollen sock. Rocking the heel back and forth, the boot eased off with minimum yanking. The right boot responded in the same way and now I found myself holding her socked feet, the heat from which seemed to radiate all the way through me.

Without her asking, I slid her left sock down her ankle, over her heel and all the way down her foot to her toes. All this time, we were still looking at each other, but her eyes looked sort of serious now, like suddenly it was me who was in charge. There was something about her eyes transforming that sparked a shift in me. Electricity crackled through my jaw and zapped down the middle of me, through my throat, nearly choking me, through my stomach, to my groin. I didn't fling the sock, like I usually did with mine, but placed it on the desk behind me and only at that point did I turn my head away from her, to the right, to take my beer off the desk. A thirst came over me and I took several more mouthfuls before placing it back down. When I looked back at Jaz's face it was like she was thinking, 'Go on then. Do what you want. I'm waiting.' The surge running through my face to my stomach started to come back the other way and I felt pressure rising to my throat like it was going to explode. I began taking deeper and deeper breaths before I turned properly back to Jaz and kind of jerked her right sock off at about fifty miles per hour quicker than the first one had come off.

I was in a film and I was somebody else; this boy in the film crossed his arms to pull his tee shirt off and flung it behind him straight onto the lamp, so that the lighting magically dimmed. He held both of the girl's feet and pulled them either side of his hips as he kneeled up so that she was forced to move to a lying position. He crawled up onto the bed, in between her legs, like a lion and lowered his upper body down over her chest, bringing his lips closer and closer to hers. As his breathing slowed, it became more and more intense, so that by the time he looked into the deep pools, the surging and panting had reached aching point, so that when his mouth lowered onto hers, the lion was devouring its prey.

When he pulled away after kissing for about ten hours, it wasn't a film any more, but me, in my murky stale bedroom, desperate for air and light and privacy. I was struck by panic and wanted her to leave. "I think you'd better—" but she grabbed my bare shoulders and dragged me back so that our lips met again. I was lying next to her this time. The kiss knocked me about now in waves of such force that I thought I'd drown, so that the next bit was more like a frenzied grappling for air than making love. But I cannot lie—making love was what happened that night. She undressed herself and me like she was a trained escape artist, deftly wriggling, shedding and discarding. There was no time for me to plan a move or try anything out—it was a dance of animal desire. My hands easily slid around her body, stroking and squeezing and my mouth moved smoothly over her skin too. When the culmination came, the most powerful wave in the world cocooned me and spun me in all directions, finally laying me, like a baby into a goose-down crib, safe and warm and satiated.

My head lay on her bare chest and she stroked my hair, teasing strands from my sweaty brow and neck. The warm stream of her breath anointed the top of my head and her quickened heartbeat was in sync with my own. I noticed a beer bottle on the bed, its frothy contents spilled out, the outcome of our fervour. I saw the woman in the emotion library— 'You'll need to be strapped in when you open this jar. And make sure there are no sharp edges near you; you'll need to flop down somewhere soft and supportive.'

I had gone from feeling as bold and strong as a cactus to a wilted drooping tulip, bent double over the edge of its vase. I was in what must have been a state of bliss and it was only the beginning. I never thought my first proper girlfriend would be so stunning and sexy and clever and strong. It felt so powerful too that I agonised over how we'd be able to keep it a secret. Or perhaps, I thought, everyone would see how perfect we were together and give us their blessing.

"Was that your first time?" she said. I crashed back down to earth and mustered a yes. It was stupid to ask her the same thing as I could guess the answer, but I asked anyway, and she laughed a 'no'.

"I don't think we should—" but she interrupted me,

"Do it again?"

"No, I mean yes, you know. Tell anyone." She must have known what I meant, but the hot damp moments ticked by and she didn't respond, so I said, "I don't want Poppy and your—Kamal to find out."

"You know how to spoil things, don't you? Why don't you want to say 'brother' anyway?"

"It's still weird for me. It's hard to—"

"Get your head round it all?"

"Yes."

"I know," she said, then silence for quite some time. She stroked my head softly and sensuously, but she didn't say, 'Of course not. They'll never know' or 'I swear I won't tell them' or 'It'll be exciting, we'll have a secret love affair.' In fact, her response made me shudder—

"Don't worry, I won't make a point of telling them, but these things have a tendency to come out eventually..."

JASVANDI'S JOURNAL 2

Dear Journal,

Wow, what a night with Ollie! I feel bad like I kinda seduced him, but hey, he went along with everything and let's face it, it was all legal. First time? Yeah, maybe I could tell, but what a kisser. I could so get used to that. I like him so much, but I have to be real careful. I don't want to hurt him, but I know I can't get close to him and I'm not going to be living here either so it's not fair to string him along. I'll have to fight myself to keep away from him as much as I can coz I could see this thing getting real deep. Anyway, it was amazing and so fun but also so definitely, as always, a one off. You know I can't get attached to ANYONE.

I've decided I'm not going to tell anyone that I don't intend to come back to the UK after the Christmas vacation. I do so love it here and I can't get over just how much affection I feel for Kamal. We're so alike in certain ways, but everything is so different here and nobody knows American Sign Language. I miss my deaf club. You know I don't see my deafness as a disability but throw in a foreign accent and a whole lot of cultural differences and all my problems are intensified.

They all seem to talk so fast and come out with such complicated language. If I had grown up with Kamal here in England, I could have learned British Sign Language and maybe gotten to a real cool level of 'hearing' British English, but it just all feels too late now. I'm used to a certain level of isolation just from missing shit constantly, but why would I put myself in a situation where I am further isolated? I love life and I want it to be a breeze, not a hurricane. Also, bad stuff is coming back to me being here.

I think Gopi might know about what happened to me. Just some stuff she's come out with.

My opportunities to tell Kamal about his brother have been a big fat zero. I truly cannot imagine ever finding the right moment. I'm more likely to find the moment to tell Ollie then he can pass it all on. That could soften the blow actually. Or I may have to write Kamal when I'm back home. No that would be soooo lame. I think I'll tell him when we're out in LA. I'm so excited that Gopi is paying for him to come for a vacation.

I reckon I just need to keep Ollie at arm's length now and make sure nothing comes out. If Poppy knew, it would kill her. The girl is so into him. Just a shame Ollie isn't into her. But I mean she could have him if she wanted, she's just so kinda slow with everything. She's missing her chance. Anyways, I took mine and it was all good. Very good! I'm a lucky girl.

Good night, sweet journal.

CHAPTER EIGHT

"You'll have to tell her, Ollie," my grandpa said. He was back at our house and had crutches to help him walk as he couldn't put any weight on his healing foot for six weeks. Grandma was out food shopping with Nathan.

It sounds mental, but he had worked out what had happened from how I was being and some of the things I'd said. I say, 'what had happened', but I imagine he thought it was only kissing. We were sitting on the bench in front of the kitchen window one evening after school. The air was still, as if listening out for secrets to be divulged. I had made us both a coffee. I gave Grandpa his favourite mug which he kept at our house; it was actually half a mug. It sometimes looked a bit wobbly as it was literally half a cup down the middle. I'd spotted it years before and knew he'd like it since he was known for requesting "just half a cup" when offered coffee. I did one of those 'thhh' laughs on seeing his familiar reaction to it—an eye-smile swivelled up sideways to me then back to the cup without moving his head.

He had been asking me how my saxophone playing was coming along. I'd told him it had fallen by the wayside a bit as I'd been distracted with the play even though I was not going to do the play and with life and relationships. And so, the conversation moved on from music to relationships. Was anything clearer in terms of Poppy and Jasvandi, he'd asked me. That's when he came out with,

"You'll have to tell her, Ollie," before I'd responded to the first bit.

I was about to say, 'Who?' 'What?' but then he said,

"Poppy thinks a lot of you. You wouldn't want her finding out from someone else."

He leant over to ruffle my hair, patted my head and said,

"You know what'll clear your head? Music. Music always takes you out of yourself. Why don't you get your saxophone and we'll go up and have a bit of a jam? I can't think when I last heard you."

I waited to come up with an excuse not to get my sax—I hadn't got it out for a while and really only liked playing on my own. I told Grandpa that he must have forgotten we didn't even have a piano, but he said Dad's keyboard would do fine.

In no time, Grandpa had done amazingly well to hobble up the stairs from the kitchen, gone into the front room, and sat on the stool at the keyboard and switched it on. He started playing all these cool chord progressions. I followed him into the room. He reached for a book of songs perched on the edge of the desk to his right which he'd bought me when I'd passed grade three, but which I confess I hadn't opened myself. With his left hand, he alternately flicked the pages of the song book he'd set on the music stand in front of him and swept back to the keys, joining his right, to try out sections of songs, humming tunes. He was so talented that he was adding extra chords and flourishes which you knew weren't actually in the music. He must have played for decades. I wondered if people carried on getting better and better or whether everyone reached their limit. He told me he played every day for years even when he had children. I didn't quite know what he meant by 'even when I had children.' Did having children preclude music or hobbies?

"Great sound, eh, for an electronic piano?" he said over the too loud playing. His hearing wasn't what it used to be, and he must have needed it that loud, so I didn't say anything, but sat on the little sofa and listened for a while. He was right—it did take you out of yourself. I leaned back and pulled one of the fluffy pale blue cushions onto my knee. As I ran my hands over it, I fell into the music and my eyes closed. I imagined I was stroking a sheep and I think I even whispered, "Shhh" to calm it. But there was no breath, no heart. I remembered Jasvandi's breath and heart, her arms and stomach, and my breathing became heavy and slow. Even though it had been over a week now since 'it' happened, everything was so vivid in my mind; I was transported to that time and space, to Jaz and her hair and her eyes, to the intensity of it all. It all came back—the heady leather giving way to rough chunky socks, then the silk of her skin underneath. At that moment I desired her more than anything. I imagined being at Gopi's and finding a moment to grab her and push her into the bathroom, press her up against the wall. Her heightened passion would match mine as our mouths slimed and licked frantically together. I wouldn't be able to stop myself feeling under her top and pushing my hand down the front of her trousers and finding her all ready for me. I'd watch her face panting and moaning as we moved together. I needed a sharp breath in and with the gush of out-air, I opened my eyes, continuing to breathe as if it had been real.

But the reality was, although I had seen Jaz at Kamal's house, she hadn't mentioned anything or even looked at me in a way you'd expect. I don't really know what that means, but you'd think you'd be able to sense something, you know, a gesture, a look, body language. Perhaps fantasies would be all I'd have to live on. It's so crazy that I couldn't say, "Hey, it seems like you really really like and desire me so can I ask if I'm right about that and if we're going to do something about it?" I was never going to ask her of course but I still figured Jaz and I were going out together after what had happened, though maybe she'd decided she had to play it cool since obviously the whole thing would have to be kept secret. My mind faded into the present—the soothing music, the sitting, the musky lingerings of mam's patchouli incense sticks, the atmosphere of calm and sort of nothingness. I noticed that the room seemed *particularly* nothingy that day.

Yet, I *knew* this room, I mean I got where it was coming from; it couldn't decide what its function, its purpose was, whom it was supposed to welcome and for what purpose. We were lucky enough to have two living rooms and this was the secondary one (it used to be the kitchen).

Grandpa sat at the 'piano' which looked out onto the front garden, though it couldn't really be called a garden. Steps led down to the street from the front door to the left of the window, but the space directly in front of the window was a bit of a dumping ground—bins, broken gardening tools, a bag of rubble that no one knew what to do with. I sat on the sofa looking at Grandpa's back and thought how young he looked from behind. He wore jeans and one blue canvas deck shoe. By the way, he never wore slippers. I had once bought him a pair for his birthday and he said sorry, but he would have to take them back, saying something grand like, "I fiercely and tirelessly embrace adventure over comfort." He wore a t shirt with an orange VW camper van on the front, though I could only see its khaki-coloured back, and a navy blue shabby cap. He always wore a cap whether inside or outside. I was never sure why—perhaps so he was always ready for the next adventure. Or perhaps he had his secret ways of seeking comfort.

To my right, against the wall, was a desk piled so high with papers, no one could ever work at it. I felt sorry for it. It must have had dreams of essays and memoirs, of novels and business plans. It wanted so much to serve the family, to support it, to provide inspiration and practical solutions and yet it failed at the one thing it was meant to be good at. It aspired to order and ambition but had encouraged chaos and apathy. It had seduced its owner only to be abused.

"What's that, Grandpa? It's lovely."

"From that book I gave you—piano and sax versions of modern classics—only I wouldn't call it a classic at all, it's just a well-written song. Not a bad book, this."

I stayed sitting and looking as the chords and tune softened the walls and stroked the desk. To the right of the desk was Lily's table—a shrine to her, if you like. I had put quite a few things on it over the months: a photo of Lily in the garden (with Kamal and Poppy labelled 'Three Flowers', having found out Kamal meant lotus), the precious unakite stone Auntie Colette had given me at the hospice, Rachel House, the poem Kamal had written for me after Lily had died and some other bits.

"*Think of Laura* it's called, by Christopher Cross. Come on and join in. You can read the music."

I spotted the card depicting John Millais' *Ophelia* from Nurse Celia on the table. It showed her floating in a stream (Ophelia, not Celia), serene-looking, surrounded by flowers. I thought of Lily lying in the bath at the hospice, her hair floating around her face, her bloated body seeking solace in the warm water. I felt a chant coming on. As you know, repeating the Latin names of some plants lifts the darkness for me, like meditating. Grandpa's playing lilted on, then he started singing, "... Hey Laura, where are you now? Are you far away from here? I don't think so, I think you're here, Taking our tears away..."

'Dizygotheca elegantissima, dizygotheca elegantissima, brugmansia sanguinea,' I said in my head over and over.

"Think of Laura but laugh don't cry..." I could hear Grandpa singing above my chanting. "I know she'd want it that way."

Grandpa, with his sixth sense, stopped playing and spun clockwise on his stool to face me. He pointed for me to get his crutches for him, got up and came to sit next to me. It was too late—I hadn't been able to stop the spillage from my eyes and lifted the baby blue cushion to my face. I felt his arm rest on my back.

"No patting see?" he said to me. We had once talked about men being embarrassed to be in an emotional moment and so couldn't hug someone without patting their back to take away from the intensity of the connection. I managed to sniff out a laugh. He said,

"Daft old Grandpa. Sorry. Shall I make some tea? Do you want to be on your own?"

Without moving the cushion, I said, "I want to play the sax now."

"It's not a winning combination—speaking through a cushion and someone with a hearing impairment," Grandpa said.

"I'll get my sax," this time said with no sound muffler. I grabbed my sax from under the desk and Grandpa got himself back onto the stool, removing then replacing his cap as if to mean 'Take two'. He said he would play *Sailing* instead, but it sounded really sad too, so I asked him to do something different.

He pulled a Beatles book from a pile on the floor and we played through loads of them together... well, about five I suppose and he couldn't stop himself singing the lyrics every now and then. We started with 'Don't Let me Down' which apparently was the B-side of the single, 'Get Back' and although I easily got into it, I wondered if he was choosing depressing songs on purpose, with a view to catharsis, but then we did one called, 'Can't buy me love' which was much more upbeat. It had a cool blues feel to it. I told him I thought that was a powerful message, you know, that love is more important than money, but he told me that Paul McCartney had said at some point that the song should have been called '*Can* buy me love' when reflecting on the perks that money and fame had brought him.

I told him I liked the Beatles, but did we have to do any more love songs? He explained that there were very few of their hundreds of songs which *weren't* love songs. "In fact," he said, "Most songs ever written are love songs of one sort or another. They fall into four basic categories: happy with who you've got, not happy with who you've got, in love, or breaking up. There are sub categories of course like being in love with someone you can't have, not being in—"

"Okay, I get the idea." Grandpa chuckled. "Anyway, sounds correct, what you're saying."

94

He made his point about love songs by choosing to play *If I fell* (which should strictly have the words 'in love' afterwards), plus *And I love her*. We finished with *All my loving*: "Close your eyes and I'll kiss you, Tomorrow I'll miss you," he sang, while bobbing up and down. At the end of the song after, "All my loving, I will send to you," he finished with an amazing chord. He swivelled round to his right, where I was standing and said,

"You definitely are."

"What? In love?"

He adjusted the front of his cap before putting his hands in his lap and laughing, saying,

"No, better, much better than you were on the sax. You're getting good, boyo." And he stood up, all his weight on his good leg, and messed my hair. A fleeting hint of smugness dared itself onto my face before I said,

"I don't know about that."

"Well that's a pretty good tone you've got already and a hell of a glissando. I told you you'd play like Courtney Pine one day. Bit of a way to go but..."

I was surprised he even knew what glissando meant, but I suppose Grandpa never failed to amaze me with all the stuff he knew. He started tickling me when I asked him if all old people had picked up as much useless information as he had or whether he was unusual. He had me laughing which lifted me so high. I'd seen something on TV about laughing therapy and at that moment I got exactly what they were on about. Oh, by the way, just to bore those of you who don't know (and why should you?) glissando is an Italian musical term—actually I think all musical terms are in Italian—sometimes called a 'fall off' meaning gliding or sliding. On the sax, you kind of change the pitch of the note to slide to another one by using your tongue and lips.

"If you want to know, I've been working on my 'growling' as it happens," I said, to which Grandpa started mimicking a bear, grabbed his crutches and hobble-chased me out of the room (I was going to tell you what the technique, 'growling' means, but it's pretty obvious I think.) Grandpa said he was going for a rest in the living room, at the back of the house. That was the primary room which was nice and big with a huge window bit which looked out onto a valley.

"Shall I get you a cup of tea and a ginger biscuit, Gramps?"

"Good lad, Oliver, yes, yes please. Only make it coffee, will you? Just weak, mind you."

I stood still watching him limp his way along the passageway to the living room and this time, from the back, he didn't look young any more. Though he was the brightest and most positive person I knew, there was no getting away from the fact he was getting old, as in really old. His no-remainder-of-stiffness jeans and his faded t-shirt looked too big for him, hanging off his bony body, and the white hair sprouting in wisps from under his washed-out cap no longer pulled off the meant-to-be-unkempt look and said rather, 'What's the point in being combed?' His extra sensory perception evident once more, he looked back over his shoulder as he turned left to go into the living room. Our eyes met and he blew me a kiss with a crutch in his hand, accompanied by a hilarious face and noise, like something you'd expect a teenager to do. Only he wasn't a teenager. He was eighty. His brain was sparking and flashing and dancing in his head, ready to throw another brilliant pitch, but his body would not play ball and couldn't keep up. I imagined his finger wagging back and forth— 'Game's up. No can do.'

I ran to help him get settled in a chair before going back into the passageway, but instead of going directly down to the kitchen (as you'll have gathered, we had a bit of an upside down house), I stopped.

I stood there for a good few minutes, words and notes swirling in my head. I imagined taking Grandpa his coffee and finding him sprawled backwards in the armchair, arms dangling either side of it, his jaw dropped open. As his body lay stiff, I imagined his sparky brain instructing his soul to get a move on. A vaporous orange camper van would emerge directly from his heart, music streaming from its open windows, swerving its way out of the house, up and up and up till it was a tiny sun. The salt water returned to my cheeks and I leaned against the wall. My body shook at the thought of this faulty dam controlling me, of deciding to break its walls with no consultation and no warning. Just as I contemplated running into the living room to check Grandpa was all right, I heard, "Only half a cup. And I'm down to one sugar, remember, Ollibags!" My hands flung up to my mouth and nose and I let out a single huffed laugh behind them, before running my fingers under my eyes, so that they cradled my temples and my hands cupped my jaw.

"Sure thing," I shouted back, not moving.

After getting on with my task and setting Grandpa up with his coffee and biscuit, I told him I was going up to do my homework. He offered to help me as it was science, but I said I'd nearly finished it at lunch time anyway. He asked if I was part of a homework club and looked disappointed when I told him no and that I usually went off on my own at break and lunch times.

"You're spending a fair bit of time on your own," he said, picking up his book on Egyptology from the side table. "Get me that little foot stool, would you, please?"

I helped him get his legs up onto it. He looked down at his book and removed the Christmas card which had been acting as a bookmark.

"Why don't you go and see Kamal later if you've nearly finished your homework?"

He was pleased when I agreed I would go to Kamal's, then he ruined it by saying,

"If Poppy's there, you could tell her about you-know-what..."

I had to face the music at some point, I suppose, especially if something had got out. I longed to see Jaz again. Her words, "These things usually come out eventually" tapped at my skull, giving me another headache. 'It's a secret,' I thought. 'Surely she wouldn't have told anyone?'

CHAPTER NINE

"You know which side your bread's buttered, Oliver—turning up at dinner time." Gopi had opened the door to me. That was odd as Kamal knew I was coming and was always the one to come to the front door.

"Naan," I said, forcing a smile.

"Are you speaking French to me?"

"No. Naan, you know, instead of bread, 'bread's buttered?'"

"Oh. You should have been a comedian, Oliver... not."

As I was stepping inside, she said,

"As luck would have it, Kamal and Jasvandi have made way too much food, so you're most welcome. Marinated lamb chops and aloo gobi. Enough aloo gobi for a herd of elephants."

"Food sounds lovely," feeling sick at the thought of eating anything at all, never mind rich spicy food.

"Shoes off!" Gopi said as I attempted to spread my street germs along the passageway, into her pristine (about fifty years old and totally washed out and thread bare) carpet. "I hear your grandpa's recovering well. That's good. They're in the kitchen." As I removed my trainers and put them down next to the consul table, Gopi went back into the living room and closed the door.

As I approached the closed kitchen door, I could hear laughing. If anything was 'out', I risked seriously ruining the atmosphere, so I lingered outside for a bit. Had Kamal not heard the doorbell?

I stood there, waiting for clues to the mood behind the door. Deep notes of Indian spices filled the air. I thought how like Jasvandi those fragrances were: pungent, floral, intense, earthy, sensuous, seductive. Music mingled with the aromas. It was Kamal's favourite—a band based in Brighton called Demob Happy. He was willing Jasvandi to appreciate it even though she couldn't really hear it. He implored her to try to 'get a feel for it' but she wasn't having any of it. She said it was like her reading out a poem in Arabic and asking how wonderful he thought it was.

"I would sense the music of it," he said. "The rhythm and flow, the crescendos and diminuendos. It would evoke a feeling in you even without the ability to encode the language."

"What? Never mind. So, okay, I'm getting a loud rumble like a truck going by and like someone jumping up and down on a pile of broken glass," Jaz said.

Her voice sent tingles of delight through me. I was a Christmas tree, twinkling lights spiralling around me, an angel hovering over me. I used my right hand to prop me up on the doorframe.

"What a striking image. You are indeed a poet," Kamal said, turning the music down so that you could hardly hear it.

A piece of cutlery pinged and clattered on the slate floor. I think Jaz had pushed Kamal.

"I don't mean to tease you. I'm sorry that you can't enjoy music, but I realise that's my perspective. It is in my experience. You might pity me for not embracing vegetarianism. Ollie might pity us both for not revering plants."

Sudden pressure in my head and a sharp breath in. I held it, awaiting Jaz's response. My hand clapped on my mouth, my eyes screwed up as the silence stretched wider and wider.

"What plants? What was that word?" Jaz said.

I craned my neck forward, not knowing what was next...

"Revering, from the verb to revere meaning to regard something with respect but tinged with awe. Maybe you've heard of reverent or Reverend?"

"He does rever plants—"

"Revere," Kamal said.

"He does revere plants for sure. Do you think he likes them more than people?"

My hand now clamped round the entire lower half of my face. It all felt wrong now, listening at the door. I wondered if I could creep along the passageway and out of the house. My heart quickened even more. I wished I was back home with Grandpa or on my own in my room. I wished nothing had ever happened.

Kamal said,

"They're a source of pure joy for him. Plants don't inflict disappointment and pain."

"So, you think he *does* like them more than people?"

"Why would you cogitate in this way? Sorry, why are you thinking like this?" Kamal said.

"What? You mean why am I saying that? Because he gets excited about plants but not about people. Poppy clearly likes him, but he can be so cold with her, for instance."

Jesus, why were they bringing Poppy into it?

"That's because he's secretly in love with her," Kamal said.

'You're bloody joking...?' I thought.

"Uh, I don't think so. He doesn't act that way at all. He acts with me like he doesn't care about her," Jaz said.

"What do you mean?" Kamal said.

This was it, I thought—not only is our secret about to be revealed, but in this warped reality, this mental play I was in, I was to overhear it.

I looked at the living room door and willed Gopi to come out or for the phone to ring or for an earthquake.

"You know that night I stayed at Ollie's when my ride fell through?"

Noooooooooooo! I couldn't move, my mouth now open wide.

"Yes," Kamal said. "I walked back and you stayed. Did Ollie talk to you about Poppy that night? Shit, the rice!"

Kamal shouted at Jaz to pass him a cloth, then dragged the pan across the metal.

"I think we've saved it. We'll leave the lid on and let it sit for a while."

Then I drew a huge breath in, my heart battering my chest as if I were about to do a bungee jump. The talk went on with me still firmly in the centre of it. Kamal said,

"Ollie's going through a bereavement, you know? His sister died."

"My God, why didn't you let me know?"

"It's why he wants to be on his own so much."

There was quiet and I wondered if they were embracing or if Jaz was crying or if they just felt awkward and were busying themselves with some culinary task.

"It's why he can't commit to things I think," Kamal said. "That's why he's giving up his part in the play, *Othello*. I thought Iago would be a wonderful role for him. I imagined playing a villain would bring him out of himself and have a cathartic effect. Oh sorry, I mean—"

I heard Jaz laughing and saying, "I'm not dumb! I know what cathartic means. What sort of villain is Iago then?"

I was relieved the conversation was lightening up a bit, so I sighed out a breath of calm but still didn't make my entrance. Kamal answerd Jaz saying,

"Iago has a reputation for being loyal and honest and Othello, my character, utterly trusts him, but Iago betrays him."

Jaz sounded intrigued and Kamal went on,

"Iago makes Othello believe that his wife is having an affair. Othello eventually kills his wife, Desdemona, out of jealousy. In the end Ollie's character, Iago, is imprisoned and tortured and poor me, Othello, commits suicide. By that look, I see you consider such goings-on to be unrealistic, but I assure you, Shakespeare so knew of life. Jealousy, betrayal, spoiled relationships, tragedy—all part of this web we weave."

My hovering in the hallway seemed ridiculous by now, but I finally found my moment to enter the kitchen. Jaz said,

"Would you see it as a betrayal if I fell in love with Ollie and—"

I pressed on the handle so firmly I thought the door might snap off its hinges. I swung the door open, saying,

"What's all the racket in here then?"

I felt like I'd leapt from behind a curtain in a farcical play.

"Aha, speak of the devil, it's wonderboy himself," Kamal said and patted my shoulder, asking how I'd managed to get into the house without him hearing. Jaz fiddled with her assorted silver bracelets which I imagined must surely make an unpleasant noise through her hearing aids. She seemed a bit embarrassed, which pleased me. I told him the reason I got inside without him knowing was because there had been loud music playing.

"There'll be the four of us for dinner," he said.

I had succeeded in perverting the course of the conversation with flying colours, it seemed. I apologized for dropping by and that it was because I hadn't seen them for a while. Kamal said he knew I was coming and that it was no problem. Jasvandi had apparently (oddly?) told Kamal that I wanted some time on my own because my grandpa needed help and time to recuperate and that I was preparing for the Kew Gardens Seed lecture. I glanced at Jaz, trying to work out why she'd said that, why she wanted to stay away from me, but could read nothing. I mean I couldn't tell if she was glad I'd turned up or wished I'd leave, if she was falling in love with me or regretted the whole thing. Perhaps she wanted to cool it for a bit so no one would suspect. She had come so close to telling Kamal about us.

'These things have a tendency to come out'. No shit, especially if the perpetrator blurts it out! It didn't change how I felt about her though.

I felt her looking at me, but I couldn't meet her eyes. Her gaze burned into the side of my face causing it to redden at once. I longed to look at her properly, but if I had, my private feelings would've been written on me for Kamal to see. I'd have been a billboard with the words, 'I slept with Jasvandi and I fancy her like hell' scrawled on it. Exposed. Pushed onto the stage with a stick, in rags, with my hands tied behind my back. Kamal seemed thrilled that I would be joining them for dinner and said something about there being nothing as satisfying as an intimate evening—yeah, he definitely used that word—and that triggered a head-turn to glance again at Jaz. This time I held the stare for an extra beat. She did exactly the same thing so that electricity zapped between us. I felt the heat of passion throb in me and I fought to keep my automatic deep breathing silent. At that swollen moment, our secret seemed anything but shameful; it seemed the most vital and pleasurable reality ever known.

Can you believe that when Kamal said there'd be four of us for dinner, he meant Poppy would be there not his aunt? Gopi was going out for a sitar lesson. Instead of feeling thrilled about the dinner, like Kamal, I wondered why I had been left out of the evening. I suppose Jaz had made out I wasn't up for any socializing. Why was Poppy coming though? I'd have to be careful not to even *look* at Jaz in case I gave something away. How would Poppy react if she suspected something or found something out? I began to concoct excuses for leaving early. I'd say I had to go and help Grandpa. Perhaps I would pretend I'd received a text and would leave right away.

Too late.

I was sent to open the door to Poppy as Kamal and Jaz were still doing stuff in the kitchen. The faded passageway carpet leading to the front door was like a pathway to doom as I imagined seeing Poppy's livid face and her pushing me with violence. The reality couldn't have been more different. She reacted like she'd been told she'd won the lottery, throwing her arms around me and kissing my cheek. She didn't know I'd be there, just as I hadn't known she'd be. I had a sense of 'getting away with it' and a perverse smugness came over me. That gave way to worry within seconds when, after apologizing for leaving my house in a hurry and that she'd thoroughly enjoyed the gardening day, she asked me what was up, that there was something different about me. So, it was true, we are open books, all of us. You have to be careful what you think. Thoughts are very powerful. They affect everything.

She wore jeans and a brown top with a zip down the middle and her hair was carefully tousled. Her make-up was perfect, like she was ready for anything, for life. Throw anything at her and she'd be fine because she had her protection, her extra layer. She was always ready, I'd say. She had to be as she wasn't very good at predicting life. When she kissed me on the cheek, I wanted to grab her and keep her there, to drink in her clean scented hair and her perfume, sweet with the tiniest hint of danger. She felt safe and loyal. She felt like 'coming home'. I was desperate to hear her say it was okay and I was forgiven, but she cut short my imaginings by asking again what was up and how come I was there.

I told her I hadn't expected to see her, that was all and that it was purely by chance I'd dropped round, not having seen Kamal for a while.

"And Jaz," she said.

"What?"

"You haven't seen Jaz either, so it's nice to see them both, especially with her leaving again soon."

"What?"

I had learned that everything writes itself on my face and whatever it looked like at that moment would not have pleased Poppy, so I ushered her inside and past me. That way, I was behind her.

"She's going back to Los Angeles early December for three weeks. Did Kamal not tell you?"

Never mind Kamal, why had Jaz not told me? I felt like a massive spoon was stirring up my brain. I didn't want to be there. All through dinner, they'd be asking me, 'What's wrong?' 'You look weird' 'Are you feeling unwell?' This is maybe why people turn to alcohol and drugs, I thought to myself, because the alternative—scary mind-messing harsh reality—is not an attractive option. My grandpa's words that it is totally normal to suffer played across my brain as if on an electronic notice board and acted like a very mild sedative. I heard myself saying to Poppy that I couldn't stay for long as Grandpa needed my help. Kamal and Jaz had come out of the kitchen, so they heard me too.

"But you've been stuck at your place for like ages now, helping him. You need a night off," Jaz said.

So, she wanted me to stay, this strange but magical being, knocking me about like a skittle. I said something inane like 'we'll see'. I expected it to be awkward city once we were all sitting down to eat, so I was at least being completely honest when I said we'll see.

I sat opposite Jaz, and Poppy was to my right. I was glad it was that way round as it was easier for Jaz to read me and I had nothing to hide with *her*. I decided to go vegetarian and forego the lamb chops, so Jaz and I had the same—aloo gobi, rice and dhal. I mean it wasn't that much different as the others had exactly the same but with spicy lamb. Even though Jaz's talk of animal welfare had led me to read about intensive farming like about crop spraying and shoving heaps of animals, which should be outside, into huge sheds with no light and diseases, I hoped that whole topic would not come up again. I hoped that Jaz and I could one day soon have amazing talks and enlighten each other about all that, but not that night, not with Poppy there. I wondered if Jaz even knew how closely linked plants and animals were.

I was dying to tell her about Chairman Mau and the sparrows. It was a mental thing I'd read a few days earlier. Chairman Mau in communist China decided that sparrows were eating too much grain which reduced the food available, so he initiated the 'Kill a Sparrow Campaign' in 1958 (I swear, this is not a joke). Various methods were used to kill them: banging pans to scare the birds from landing so they plummeted to their death, too exhausted to fly; nests torn down and baby birds killed; shooting them out of the sky. Hundreds of millions of tree sparrows were wiped out. So, sparrows became nearly extinct in China. But, guess what? As well as grain seeds, sparrows ate insects, as in a LOT of insects. So, insects, particularly locusts, swarmed the countryside with no sparrows to worry about. The effect was far worse than if the birds had been left alone. Result—the insect rampage, oh and the overuse of pesticides, ruined crops and led to a famine. About thirty million people died of starvation. I had to tell you that because I couldn't believe it. I mean, could you get a more dramatic example of how we're all connected? I don't even know if we've learnt our lesson. You keep hearing about the next mental idea. I wish us people didn't mess with nature so much. I wondered if Jaz knew about this sparrow campaign. I so wanted to tell her.

Gopi had made chapatis, which I truly love because you can scoop up as much or as little food as you want in the round flat bread. If the flavour or strength of the food is powerful, as was the aloo gobi (I am quite pathetic with spicy food), you could use a biggish chunk of chapati and a teeny bit of spicy food to lessen the impact. Jaz said,

"I love this bread. I've never tried it back home."

"Yeah. It's partly the texture, isn't it and its floppiness?" I said. I felt the urge to shout to release some of the tension which had built up in me, but instead a giddiness came over me... "I sometimes feel like flinging it up in the air, like you see chefs do with pizza dough and letting it plut itself onto my face."

Poppy and Kamal made coughy laughs as they were both eating and Jaz spluttered food into her hand, which warmed my heart (the laughing not the spluttering). I was on a roll now,

"If I were a chef making chapatis, I'd press the odd one into my eyes like this and mold it round my nose and just mushle it round and round, gradually working my tongue through the middle." [In case you're wondering, I did actually put an actual chapati on my actual face.] They all put their cutlery down as they watched me doing all the actions to go with the words.

"I'd have a game with myself to see if I could devour the whole thing whilst it was still on my face—like this."

Kamal said the circle of bread was getting smaller and smaller so that it looked like a weird creature making its way into my body.

It was adorable to see Jaz staring at me, everyone dancing to my tune.

"You were covering your face, so I didn't get most of that, but you are like so funny," Jaz said.

"Oh, I'm sorry Jaz," I said.

"I've told you," said Kamal, "Jaz needs to see your face to optimize her lip reading. Jaz, you didn't miss much—half the words were made up. 'Plut'? 'Mushle'? I particularly like plut. Perfect onomatopoeia."

"Matty what?" Jaz said.

"Oh God, Kamal, please don't—" I said.

"Onomatopoeia is a linguistic device [too late]."

He clasped his hands together in front of him, like a priest about to give a sermon,

"It's when a word sounds like its meaning, like 'boom' or 'splash'. So, the word means nothing more than the sound it makes. It comes from the Greek—"

"Honestly, Kamal," Poppy said, raising her left shoulder and sweeping it back to get hair off her face and about to gnaw on a chop she'd picked up, "give the girl a break."

We all laughed again.

"I don't mind. I find all this pretty interesting. I don't know people like you back home. I mean, you're all what, sixteen? And we're sitting round having dinner which we cooked ourselves, discussing exotic food and literary language."

I took the opportunity to bring up Los Angeles and her trip back there at Christmas. She told us that her parents were paying for Kamal to go with her. Why didn't Poppy and I join them, she asked. I think I kind of froze and I did actually feel my bottom lip drop down in surprise or confusion or whatever it was. Of course, there was no way I could afford to go and would I want to go anyway? and how long would you have to be on a plane? and where would we stay? and there's certainly no way Poppy would be able to go etc etc...

"My uncle has a house in Hollywood Hills. We could all stay there for a couple weeks. He won't be there; he's away a lot."

I was about to thank her but explain how utterly impossible the notion was, when Poppy said,

"Wow that would be amazing! I was just saying to Mam last weekend that I wanted to spend some of my inheritance from my gran on a holiday. Are you serious, Jaz?"

"For real. I'd love you guys to come over. My mom even said I should do this. It would be awesome, you guys—so fun. Don't you think?"

I decided to stay quiet; I didn't want to spoil the mood by telling Jaz there's no way I could go. And what about that? Poppy—safe, predictable Poppy—said yes. Straight away, without a second thought. And there was me thinking Jaz might not even like the idea of Poppy being around us at all, never mind a full-on vacation together. I dipped my chapati into the sunny smooth dhal and nibbled the soggy bread, zoning out from the new animated talk of LA and all it promised. It wasn't long before everyone was telling me, 'there must be a way' and 'we won't go without you' and 'at least say you want to come'.

I told them yes, I wanted to go (lying), but that I/my family would never be able to afford it. They started to annoy me by suggesting selling stuff like my saxophone and exotic plants and it made me realize how little they understood me. And how little I understood.

Let's face it, what did I know about anything? I had feared the secret coming out, causing hurt and angst and I had feared heated discussions on caged pigs and obese chickens, but no, we were planning a vacation to the United States of America. Correction, *they* were planning a trip to the United States of America.

JASVANDI'S JOURNAL 3

Dear journal,

What a day! I just came right out with it. I invited Ollie and Poppy to LA. Poppy said yes right away, but Ollie was pretty vague. I couldn't say if he was into the idea and genuinely saw the cost as a major problem or whether he was kinda freaked out by the invitation. If I'm honest with myself, I'm not sure I even want him to come. He's so sweet and boy do I lust after him, but the way he was looking at me, I got the impression he's into me big time, like on a deep level, and you and I know that nothing can ever come of what happened that night. Plus, what Kamal told me about Ollie's sister dying makes me even more convinced that I must do my utmost to avoid adding any more pain into his life. I meant to mention it at dinner, but Ollie was in such a good mood.

I like Poppy a lot, so I'm real happy she's into the trip to the states. She's just adorable. Her English accent is cute as hell and she seems like pure but real strong at the same time.

I must tell you this, journal. IMPORTANT FACT – Aunt Gopi knows about what happened to me when I was twelve. I don't know how she found out, but that didn't seem important once she held me and started to cry. What was important was that she didn't seem to think it was my fault. She must have known that the charges were dropped and that it never went to court. She thought I should tell Kamal, but there is absolutely and seriously no way I will ever tell him. She was comforted that I had gotten some counselling. She was pushing me to tell her if I was still affected by it. It was real tough to answer as I truly do not know if I am. She asked me if I had a good friend who knew about it or a boyfriend. I just said yeah, I had great friends. I didn't tell her that I'd never had a boyfriend or that no, all the friends I had before it happened just disappeared afterwards. It was a good early lesson that you can't trust anyone, which has been confirmed through other stuff. Like all of this.

She found it difficult, but she tried to ask me if it had put me off 'being with' a boy. I didn't dare tell her how many guys I'd been with, and girls.

When she cried, I felt nothing much at all at first, but something snapped inside me with no warning and it all came flooding back. I said I was tired and went to my room. As you know, I always cry too loud coz of my hearing coz I can't monitor the loudness of my own voice very well sometimes, so Kamal called me on the flashing intercom he'd set up to ask if I was OK. I was soooo embarrassed. I said I was fine, but I felt like a liar. I felt stupid too and ashamed and I mean ashamed of everything, of me, of my whole life. I closed my mouth tight shut when I cried again to be sure no noise could come out. Instead streams ran down my cheeks so that I had to turn over the pillow and then that side was wet too so I threw it on the floor, sat up and shook and dripped into my tee shirt instead.

Just now I've decided I don't want Ollie to come to the states. It would be whack. I wouldn't be able to resist him. Things could only get more complicated. It's a blessing in disguise he can't afford to come. I guess, from how he reacted, he's not into coming anyways. BUT I've also decided I'll tell him the truth about our family's history so he'll have time to digest it and work out how to tell Kamal when he gets back from LA. OR, if I do find the right moment to tell Kamal myself, he'll have his bff Ollie to understand and support him back home.

CHAPTER TEN

So, what the heck was going on with this trip to Los Angeles? There's no way I could face the intensity of being with other people for that long and yet the delightful cool-as-a-cucumber Jaz clearly wanted me to go, which was the most amazing feeling. I could tell the way our eyes met in the kitchen and over dinner what a definite thing we had going. What a relief as well that it was much easier than I thought to keep our secret. Kamal and Poppy would never find out. And what a relief in general to feel wanted. I felt like someone had plugged me in. I had forgotten what a rush it was to feel alive. Even if I couldn't go to LA, Jaz would probably miss me while she was out there, and things would really hot up when she got back. No doubt Kamal would feed back the things Jaz had said about me.

The relationship Jaz and I had was perfect up to now. The thought of trusting someone fully or getting into all that needy crap was not at all something I wanted, so the fact that Jaz was cool and laid back made our whole thing even more attractive. We were both playing it cool. That was good. We were both protected. And Poppy was protected because we were going to make sure she never found out and she was bound to meet someone and fall in love herself before too long.

There was the trip to London to look forward to now when the four of us would be together again. I started to get excited about my little talk I was going to give at Kew Gardens and the thought of Kamal and Poppy and Jaz watching me and listening. I'd have to practise so much to make sure I felt confident and didn't mess up. The last thing I wanted to do was put Jaz off me, just when things were progressing nicely. I would practise with Grandma and she could give me some tips on my presentation. She used to give a lot of talks on teaching children with special needs.

"I know it seems a bit daft," Grandma said, "but if you stand up on the chair, you'll get used to the idea of being exposed. You must feel nervous, but so familiar with your material, that it doesn't show."

So, I agreed to clamber up onto the kitchen chair and Grandma sat about five feet in front of me, her back to the picture window, ready to listen to my speech. I was about to start, when she began tapping her hand loudly on the kitchen table and I asked her if she was going crazy and to please stop it.

"I'm testing you. You mustn't be distracted by noise." She was really into the 'lesson' and was gesticulating much more than usual. "You have to zone into your speech. It's like acting. People will cough and talk to each other and make annoying sounds, but you mustn't be put off," she said.

I wondered if she was going to start throwing rotten fruit at me or start singing. I could feel the confidence draining out of my pores, but Grandma convinced me that it was unthinkable to change my mind about the gardening competition. I did feel daft standing on the chair, but I trusted my grandma.

The competition was to design a garden for a place called Sunshine Hospice as it had been left a substantial sum of money from a benefactor. I hadn't told anyone about it, even when I was chosen for the long list (about twenty people), but then I made it onto what is called the short list, which consisted of five people who were invited to present their ideas at a special evening at Kew Gardens. I adored Kew Gardens and was going to attend two lectures while I was there entitled, 'Poisonous Plants—the Dark Side of Beauty' and 'Introduction to Garden Design' which you may think was a bit late, given that I was there to show my garden design. By the way, Kew's full name is Royal Botanic Gardens Kew (Kew is a town) and I nearly forgot to mention that it's two hundred and fifty years old—can you believe it? You would love it. Well, unless you're not fond of plants and trees and stuff. You still might like the massive Victorian glasshouses (biggest in the world) which are amazing buildings in themselves, never mind the plants inside, or the really high up tree top walkway. If you don't like plants and trees OR glass structures OR heights, well you might still love the generally beautiful landscape or the delicious food they serve across several cafés and restaurants. You'd think I worked there and was trying to sell tickets! I wish I did work there, to be honest. Maybe you've already been, in which case you'll know what I'm jabbering on about.

"Get on with it then," she said, clamping down her folded arms.

I reached with my right hand to pull the sheet of paper from my jean's back pocket and began to unfold it.

"You're not going to read your speech, are you? I thought you had acting skills—you need to learn it. You can use the paper this first time, then we'll lose it."

I started off explaining that my meadow garden would make wonderful use of the space outside Sunshine Hospice, and that it would cater for a wide range of ages. I went on to describe the features: a viewing mound accessible by wheelchairs on which would be fixed outdoor speakers playing *Kind of Blue* by Miles Davis and *A Love Supreme* by John Coltrane; a stream water feature in which the children could safely wheel or paddle or even lie down; a stone circle; a bird hide; a small table piled with crystals; fruit trees and raspberry canes; animal feeding stations to observe and enjoy the wildlife.

"The whole space will be a vision of blues, yellows and reds with its annual and perennial wildflowers," I said, "encircled by a sort of low hedge of pink polyanthas otherwise known as fairy roses."

Grandma unfolded her arms and moved her fists to her hips. "You can't say 'sort of'—you're selling your design, for Pete's sake. And I'm not sure you should be that specific with the music, pet. And you're missing something—you do need to include the section on what inspired you. It's stipulated in the guidelines."

I got down from the chair and questioned whether the inspiration bit was really essential because I would be going into quite a bit of detail about the actual garden.

"Yes. Essential," she said dropping her head to face the floor, hands still on hips, like she wasn't interested in a comeback.

To be honest, I hadn't written anything for that part of the presentation. I didn't want to get into all that in front of strangers. Grandpa had just hobbled into the kitchen to join us when Grandma told me to make something up and see how it came out. She told Grandpa to sit down and be part of the audience. I had forgotten to mention that Kamal had written a short poem to be put on a plaque for the garden, so I told them about that. Grandma motioned for me to get back up on the chair. I didn't really want them to be staring at my face, so I looked up to the ceiling and spoke:

"I have always loved being with plants and trees and flowers for as long as I can remember, but my best memories of my whole life are being with plants and trees and flowers with my sister. We bought a pink polyantha together. We dug a hole in our garden and gave it to the earth. It grows wild now, as Lily was adamant it should never be pruned or 'pooned' as she put it. And so, branches have continued to fill yet more space, though now all of physical space is lacking the special being who planted it—my sister, Lily. There is endless soul space, however, and it would fill my heart with joy if she were to dance forever with all the other children, in this garden at Sunshine Hospice, embraced by the ring of fairy roses."

I thought I had got this dreadfully wrong as when I looked down, Grandpa had his head in his left hand. He had his cloth hanky out, which he kept on him at all times and was wiping his face with it as he raised his head and told me he actually thought it was just right. Grandma said that all I had to do now was remember everything I'd written and said. She asked me if I had a copy of Kamal's poem, so I said no, and she made me go and fetch one.

I came back with the poem and sat on the chair ready to read it out as Grandma had insisted, but she forced me to stand back up on the chair. I told them that Kamal had left a note with it, which I read first:

'The poem is quite simple since it is largely for children, but I've gone a bit loopy with alliteration and assonance.'

"Assy what??" Grandpa said.

"Assonance – when the middle bits of words rhyme – like heat and feel. The vowel bits rhyme but not the ending."

"I know what vowels are," Grandpa said.

"Okay, let's hear it," said Grandma.

So, I carried on and read out the poem. I think it was about the hospice garden even though it didn't exist yet.

"There is a place I long to know Where petals plead with leaves—"

"Aha! There's that assassin rhymey middly thing you were on about," Grandpa said.

"Shhh!" said Grandma.

I let my right hand drop to my thigh, still holding the paper in it.

"Grandpa, I've started. I'm saying a poem. You can't just interrupt, you know?"

"If you get cross every time someone interrupts," he said, "you've no chance of winning. And it's 'reciting' not 'saying.'"

"I'm starting again and don't butt in this time. Anyway, I don't actually think normal people would shout out in the middle of sayi—reciting a poem,"

"Don't get a job in a mental home then, will you?" said Grandpa.

"They're not called 'mental homes' any more," I said. I dropped the paper on the floor this time and Grandma came and scooped it back up and handed it to me, at the same time touching me on the arm with an encouraging pat. I said,

"And thing is, shocking as it sounds, I have no plans to recite poetry at a psychiatric hospital."

"You're lucky," Grandpa said, "I was going to say loony bin. If you did recite it in one of those places, you'd have all sorts throwing snotty hankies, getting up and walking out, pulling their pants down to show their arses, cursing, laughing, groaning, shouting 'Off!!' What was that brilliant film with Jack Nicholson?"

"You're incorrigible," said Grandma, shaking her head.

I jumped down from the chair, threw my paper on the floor again and marched to the steps to go upstairs. Grandpa hobbled after me and squeezed my side. I didn't laugh but when he said, "Patience is a virtue," and I answered, "But I don't have the time," he laughed and I couldn't help smiling. It was a 'private joke' even though it was actually from a song.

"Come on now. Back on the chair. Let's do this," Grandpa said. He stayed standing up this time.

I paused for quite a while to annoy him then I started again,

"There is a place I long to know
Where petals plead with leaves
To taste the shade and share the glow,
The rain, the wind that weaves.
There is a place, beguiles my soul
Where children dance and dare

To hum and buzz and sprinkle soil
And water without care.

There is a place which holds my heart
As softly as a breeze
Where every sense is set apart
Yet with each other sees.

There is a place where joy abounds
A space where life is pure
Oh, that I knew these graceful grounds
Let Nature be my cure."

"One Flew Over the Cuckoo's Nest," Grandpa said.

"What?"

"The name of the film set in a mental institution. Just came to me."

"I don't believe you," Grandma said. "What about the poem?"

"Pleasant enough," he said. "Nice and simple. Yes, I think the tone is appropriate. Not sure about 'cure' though—the children are in the hospice exactly because no cure has been found."

"Don't take it literally," said Grandma. "I think when he writes 'Let Nature be my cure,' he means that everything will seem 'solved' if you like. If you simply put your trust in Nature—you know, succumb to its charm, be entranced by it—it will take your pain away."

"It's the idea that you become fully aware if you immerse yourself in Nature," I said. "And that, in a way, that's all we should ever be looking for. More than that—that we don't need to *do* or *look* for *anything*. All we need is already there," I said.

"I take it all back. I think Kamal's poem is just right," Grandpa said. "Indeed quite lovely. And your interpretation of it was acutely lucid."

"Acutely lucid. Was that a deliberate attempt at assonance?" I said.

"Yes... probably," and Grandma came forward, held out both her hands, beckoning me to jump from the chair. I stepped down, paper still in hand, and Grandma gave me a lovely big hug with no patting. Then Grandpa made it a group hug, flinging his crutches to the floor like he'd been miraculously cured. It went on long enough so that you were forced into your emotions. When we pulled apart, Grandpa held me firmly by the left shoulder saying, "If you don't win, they all need putting in a mental home." I had to wipe my eye at the same time as spluttering a laugh.

As it turned out, Grandma and Grandpa couldn't come to the Hospice Garden Design event. They were supposed to, but Grandpa had to have physiotherapy and had to go to an important appointment at the fracture clinic and to tell the truth was 'not feeling right' in general. By the time the day came, on the Monday of half term at the end of October, I didn't really want anyone else to come and watch me; I hardly wanted to go to London myself.

Everyone (well, mainly Kamal and Nathan) were disappointed that I hadn't wanted a party or anything for my birthday in September and had been pushing me to have one in the half term instead. I had been going on so much to Kamal about how much I didn't want a party, that he had to tell me that Poppy had been planning a late surprise bash for me and that he had felt obliged to put her off. She was part of the reason I didn't want a big celebration. It would have been insane not to be 'with' Jaz at my own party, yet because of Poppy, it was impossible. I started to wonder if I was fooling myself it could ever work. But I was sixteen now and could do anything I wanted—leave school, move to London, move to LA, get married. I'm joking about this last one, by the way. I mean not joking that I could legally; I'm joking that I would ever entertain the crazy notion of getting hitched at such a young age. I know some people do and in certain countries they do but it doesn't seem that sensible to me.

They had all insisted on coming to Kew Gardens for the design competition final. Even Sam and Nathan decided to accompany Kamal, Poppy, Jaz and me on the train. It was a kind thing to do.

"Mam and Dad aren't here, bro, so we're your family support," Sam had said. All I can remember Nathan saying is,

"There's got to be a decent skate park near Kew or Putney, yeh?"

Sam, Nathan and I were going to stay a few nights at one of Mam's friend's, Kathy, in Putney; Kamal and Jaz were going to stay with a friend of Gopi's in Earlsfield, but Poppy was not staying the night and going back up to Newcastle. I appreciated Poppy coming as the train wasn't cheap, though now I knew she'd inherited money from her gran, it wasn't like the fare had broken the bank. Still, she had made the effort. I partly wished she hadn't—I mean without her presence, I could have been more comfortable and honest with Jaz. Who knew what the outcome of the competition would be? Jaz might even decide to come with us to Kathy's house afterwards.

I surprised myself by staying focused while on the train. I put on my headphones and listened to calming music. I sat on my own behind the table seat where Kamal, Nathan, Poppy and Jaz sat. Sam had work to do so wanted to be on his own too, across the other side. I was facing backwards, but I didn't care. I quite liked it. Sitting backwards, I always think there's a chance of seeing something that everyone else has missed. Looking back, but whizzing along with no time to dwell. I loved being in limbo—I'm here, no I'm here, hang on, I'm here now. No cars or people thudding into your vista, only the countryside tickling your eyes.

Bipolar birds stood still as stones, then manically flitted. Sheep, nervous yet uncluttered of mind, hung out with their mates, gregarious, yet on edge, defenseless as they are against prey. Cows were in no rush, grazing and stretching their necks, fully centred and at peace. I clocked the fleeting image of one cow approaching another—"Yeah I'll come over to the meeting in a while. I'll just finish chewing this corner of field and I may need to indulge in a spot of leisurely bowel-emptying on the way, but hey man, no worries, I'll be there when I'm there, okay? You get me?"

Even through my headphones, I could hear the others laughing at Kamal whom I knew had recited the Ogden Nash lines, 'The cow is of the bovine ilk; One end is moo, the other, milk.' I could tell because I could lip read, or should I say, lip guess Jaz asking, "What does 'bovine ilk' mean?" She was facing me. I could spy her through the velvety gap between the seats in front of me. I allowed myself a smile, though my head was in serious mode, in mental preparation for my talk. Sneaking peaks at Jaz and the rest pleased me immensely. Was this what it was like if you were dead? Tranquil as you observed the space which normally held you, bereft of you, voices mingling minus yours, minds melding yet yours apart. Unconscious joy at the connection with those on the other side. A flash as one of the group is zapped into the other side, a vague invitation to a second world, a momentary glimpse of a quickly-vanished realm, like the scenes snatched from the train window.

Watching Jaz lose herself through the window, blurring into the green film, led my own eyes back to the changing landscape and my misty music. I was listening to Eric Whitacre which Mam had put me on to. From Reno, Nevada (Eric, not Mam), and I'll tell you for nothing, this guy is TA-LEN-TED. He's a composer and a conductor. I was listening to outlandishly lovely voices. He writes impressive, complex works for choirs. 'Water Night' was the piece I was losing myself in.

As a wave of anxiety flooded my stomach, I closed my eyes and took deep breaths. My attempt at focusing in order to go through my presentation in my head went slightly awry as the lyrics of 'Water Night' washed over me and I fell asleep.

'...And if you close your eyes,

A river, a silent and beautiful current,

fills you from within.

Flows forward, forward, darkens you:

Night brings its wetness to beaches in your soul.'

"Get your backpack down, Ollie!" as Nathan shook me awake. We'd arrived at King's Cross railway station in London.

"And don't forget that massive coat you've brought for some reason."

It was a super warm day for October, but I had put on my best coat,
a trench coat. It made me feel important. I had worn the one suit I had
too—a grey one my mam had got me for an auntie's wedding.

"Wow, a tie too!" Jaz had said "It's not a job interview for a bank,
dude," and laughed.

"You look five-star, Ollie. So handsome," Poppy had said. "And don't
listen to Jaz—I mean who wears a tie with trees on for a job at a bank?"

She actually winked her cute black eye. I say black eye because of
the lashings of mascara she always wore. It accentuated her gorgeous blue
eyes—sky blue, like all the sky was in them.

It was true I was overworking the layered look, so I decided to carry
my big coat. Now for the tube to Kew Gardens on the dark blue Piccadilly Line and the green District Line. My heart started going funny as I
pulled myself up from my seat to reach up into the rack for my bag. 'In
four hours' time I will know my fate,' I thought. 'Will my entourage be
carrying me through the streets with my trophy later on, cheering? Will Jaz
fall so in love with me that she follows me to Putney, unable to be parted
from me as I hover in the heady heights of success?'

"We'll have to change at Earls Court," said Sam. "And we have to take
the Richmond branch of the District Line, not the Wimbledon or Ealing
Broadway ones. Follow me."

I had looked it up myself and found out that you could stay on the tube till Hammersmith and make an easier change to the District Line there, but I didn't say anything. Sam loved being right. Or maybe he just loved being a leader. He led us off the train, walking too fast, so he kept having to stop and usher us forward with his arm, like a scout leader.

"If you slow down, you won't have to keep waving like a dipstick!" said Nathan.

"We don't want to be late," Kamal said, "This is an historic day! A crucial crossroads!"

Pressure or what...?

CHAPTER ELEVEN

There's no doubt that the chair-performing with Grandma and Grandpa helped. You had to stand on a slight platform in front of a podium. There was a microphone and a place to prop your notes, only I didn't have any since Grandma had convinced me I needed to learn my presentation off by heart. I was the only one who didn't use notes, it turned out, though I had images of my plans to show.

The other competitors were three girls and one boy. The other boy had millions of fancy slides and videos and hardly talked at all. It was a pretty slick presentation, so I thought he stood a good chance of winning, though his garden was very hi-tech with lots of complicated machinery. The person I thought would definitely win was a girl called Semhar. She wore hearing aids like Jaz and spoke well too. She had constructed these stunning models and had made meticulous botanical drawings that were jaw-droppingly impressive. I realized I didn't stand a chance.

I had so wanted everyone to be proud of me, for me to actually excel at something. I imagined Sam saying, 'So you're not just a squirt who knows Latin names of plants.' And Nathan saying, 'Hey, you aced that, man. Now you know what it feels like to win.' He had won loads of skateboarding competitions, you see. My thoughts were interrupted by the announcement of the winner.

"In second place... Oliver Timothy Campbell."

They spoke at some length after that, but I more or less blanked out after I heard 'second'. The five contestants were standing in a row at the front. Someone came up to me and handed me a piece of rolled up paper. I felt so exposed up there. My head dropped as I noticed the row of my five guests clapping. I felt like a slave on sale.

Looking back, I should have felt happy and honoured and all that for coming second, but I was sick of coming second. I didn't care who was going to come with me to the herb garden now—I just wanted to get out of that lecture theatre. In fact, I soon had it in my mind that I would go alone.

My plan was scuppered: all the attendees were asked to make their way to the Orangery. Everyone who had got to the first and second rounds of the competition and their families were invited for drinks and food. I hadn't even mentioned this bit to my lot as you were only allowed three guests and I had five. Nathan was in consternation that I was going to pass up free grub, so Sam went to speak to one of the organizers who told him a fair few folk hadn't turned up and especially since I was the runner up, we were all welcome to go to the 'reception'.

The stunning Royal Botanic Gardens at Kew is one of the most famous examples of gardens in the whole world and it wasn't hard to see why. Even this building, 'The Orangery' was magnificent though it didn't particularly have loads of plants in it. Like I said before, there's something here for everyone even if you're not into horticulture.

As we all approached the glasshouse, I was in awe of its structure. Over the next few hours, everyone in turn came up to me to tell me well done with the competition. I appreciated it but wondered if they were all really thinking 'loser'. Kamal walked alongside me as we left the lecture room and put his hand on my shoulder. He was the only other one in our group apart from me who'd dressed up smartly for the event. He had on a brown suit, a white shirt and.... wait for it... a cravat—a fawn cravat with pink spots. He was so convinced I was going to win that he'd even prepared a speech. I felt I'd let him down, but he didn't seem too upset.

"Felicitations, old chum," he said. My hurt pride was soon swallowed up by Kamal's wittering.

"Though I abhor the expression, I'll say it anyway—you did yourself proud or should I say, being in London, you 'done' yourself proud. How does our great language become so bastardised? I heard someone on the underground saying to her kid, 'You done good,' instead of 'You did well.' I mean what hope is there for that child? Not even 'you done well' but 'you done good'. Have you noticed, as well as starting sentences with 'soooo' even when it doesn't follow on from anything, we've adopted another Americanism—saying 'I'm good'?"

"You mean when someone asks how you are?"

"Yes," he said, patting my back, like I was a pupil who'd answered a question correctly. "We have always said, "I'm well, thank you" because the implication of the question is, 'How are you *doing*?' and therefore the answer must be 'I am doing *well*'. It's an adverb, it describes a verb—I sing well, she draws well, they're doing well in their match. 'I'm doin' good'. Just shitty bloody English." He pulled his arm away from me like he was suddenly angry at everything, including me, which sent a flash of a smile across my face.

"Perhaps you have to accept that language doesn't always evolve in ways you like," I said. "What's important is understanding each other, not the intricacies of English grammar." That got him going even more.

"Oh, let's go back to grunting at each other then shall we?" by now gesticulating. "It seemed to work well enough in Neanderthal times. Or should I say, 'it seemed to work good in them days'."

I was relieved we were nearly at the Orangery entrance and chose to totally change the subject.

"Gorgeous glass building isn't it? My mam would love it. Actually, she's been before, I remember now, and she does love all the glass houses here. Do you know anything about it?" Asking that sort of question to Kamal is the equivalent of offering a normal person a box of chocolates.

"Though it's maintained its name as 'Orangery', designed as it was as a hothouse to grow citrus fruits, it was discovered that the levels of light were way too low for this purpose."

I was intrigued. I was fascinated by the history of the building and despite initially wanting to make a quick getaway, was now excited to be attending an event there, having adored the place for so long. So, I chose to step to the side of the pathway and let others pass as we reached the entrance so that I could hear more from Kamal. I asked him when it was built (whenever we visited anywhere, Kamal never failed to read up about it first; though he didn't even know we were coming to this particular building, it didn't surprise me that his reading of Kew Gardens had included its history.)

"Have you heard of King George III?"

"Yes," I lied.

"His mother, Princess Augusta, the founder of Kew, hired a chap called William Chambers to be her son's tutor. To be clear, her son was the future King George III."

He straightened his cravat as if *he* was giving a talk now... Thing is, I suppose he was.

"William Chambers was also an architect who was employed to design the gardens. He completed work on the Orangery in 1761."

"But you say it was never used as an Orangery? That's weird," I said.

"No, they did try. It was only established that the glasshouse was not fit for purpose when the orange trees failed to grow." More cravat-adjusting. "Eventually in 1841, Sir William Hooker, who was the main man at Kew, moved the ailing orange trees to Kensington Palace. He added huge glass doors at either end of the orangery to increase the amount of light and subsequently used the building to house any plants that were too big for any of the other glasshouses."

"Interesting," I said looking to the interior through the glass. "And now it's a café, is it?" Kamal turned to look inside too.

"Converted into a tea room in 1989 and now, a restaurant."

"Cool. Cheers for all that. I'll try to remember it."

I looked at Kamal and smiled. It seemed like we knew everything about each other in that one look, almost as if we *were* each other. Everything felt peaceful and okay at that moment. As if reading my mind, kamal said, "I am proud of you, young Oliver. I hope you know?"

It was too kind for me to bear so I said,

"Shall we go in?"

We snapped away from our connection.

"Yes let's. Where are the others?" Kamal said.

We'd hardly got into the building when a woman started speaking into a microphone. She welcomed everyone and drew our attention to displays all around the room—all five finalists' entries were laid out in the form of huge photos and models. I couldn't believe the work that had gone into them and felt ashamed that I nearly hadn't attended the function. She proposed that everyone spend time looking at them all and pointed out two tables covered with dishes of food for everyone to share. She told us that a lot of the organic ingredients were sourced at the gardens themselves and added,

"Jessica Pernice [pronounced per-neech-ay as it's Italian] will be pleased about that."

She was one of the entrants whose design was based on sustainability and self-sufficiency as in growing your own food. Gentle chuckles could be heard from a corner of the room and a bloke was pointing his index finger down above Jessica's head. She had short blond spikey hair, a pierced nose and wore a turquoise dress down to her knees and, though I couldn't see them now, I remembered from before that she was wearing yellow, flowery clumpy boots. She made a funny, slightly awkward jiggle with her body, her hands wiggling with a wow face. I made a bet with myself that she was vegetarian.

The woman continued with a question; she asked if anyone could tell her to whom the coat of arms belonged, the one above the central bay of the façade. I was thinking it must be the founder and heard myself shouting,

"Princess Augusta!"

It seemed like there was a momentary pause before she said,

"Well done. Oliver Timothy Campbell, isn't it?"

Kamal put his arm on my back—another correct answer— and we looked at each other connecting again and smiling before he whispered,

"You remembered. Not just a pretty face, as they say. I mean as they *would* say if you actually *had* one."

I shoved him and my eyes were drawn back to Jessica Pernice. Maybe I was thinking, 'See, I get attention as well.' She was looking at me. She touched her nose with her right index finger then pointed it directly out at me. It made me smile. I noticed she looked a bit embarrassed after she'd done it. Kamal said,

"Look, there's Jaz. And she's with the others. Did I tell you she was blown away by my poem? She was practically having a fit, telling me that she also wrote poetry. I'll have to take a look."

They were waving madly from the other side of the room and Nathan even shouted,

"Yo!"

They started walking over to where we were as the woman was saying,

"Thank you so much for coming. Congratulations again to Semhar and Oliver. Please do enjoy yourselves. Thank you."

Sam and Nathan grabbed me and lifted me up, Nathan shouting "Ollie Campbell, winner of the Garden Design competition!"

"Okay, okay, lads. Let me down. This is so embarrassing. I'm not the winner anyway."

"You are to us," said Nathan, which just went to prove that not winning was lame and so they'd prefer to pretend I *had* won.

"I thought it went really well, eh Ollie? No stumbling over words and Kamal, that poem was cracking," Sam said.

"No doubt the weakness in the whole scheme," Kamal said.

Jaz said that was nonsense and that she thought it was great. She gave him a big hug and Kamal looked right chuffed. She came up to me and kissed me on the cheek, saying,

"You'll win next time. Come with me to get a drink and we'll look at all the displays."

She grabbed my right hand and started pulling me away. With my left, I beckoned Poppy, whom I saw, with the corner of my eye, was about to come up to me. She followed us to the drinks table.

Jaz took a glass of red wine and offered me some, but I said,

"I'll just get two lemonades for Poppy and me."

Jaz's response was, "Oh," as she noticed that Poppy had come with us. She then walked off telling us she was keen to see the displays and seemingly dropping the idea of taking me along. As I turned away from the table to pass Poppy her drink, she looked straight into my eyes and said,

"You were incredible. You're so clever."

It didn't happen very often, but I was lost for words. Her facial expression was such a gorgeous mix of joy and awe and pride and love. I'm actually quite sure she truly meant it. Can you believe she honestly utterly meant that she thought I was incredible. She hadn't even said 'the design was incredible,' she had said 'you'. I couldn't take away from the moment and say, 'No, I'm not,' so I just stood there holding two plastic cups of lemonade. She spoke again,

"What you said about your sister was lovely."

I thought, at that moment, how lovely *she* was. I handed her the drink and believe it or not, opened my mouth to say thank you, but ended up saying nothing at all. I hope she could see my eyes saying it instead... and more, other stuff I didn't really understand myself.

We all got the tube back to Earls Court: My brothers and I changed to the Wimbledon branch of the District Line to get back down to Putney, Kamal and Jaz came with us as far as Putney Bridge station then got on a bus to Earlsfield (Kamal had researched buses of course) and Poppy changed to the Piccadilly Line to go back to King's Cross train station. I did say thank you this time. We hugged on the platform and it felt so comfortable, I wanted to say, 'Why don't you stay a few nights? You can come with us?' but I just said,

"Thank you," and she smiled saying,

"I wouldn't have missed it for the world." Such a sweet thing to say.

Kamal told me that Earlsfield was quite near Putney and that we should get together, but I didn't see the point. I only wanted to see Jaz on her own or nothing. And I had my lectures to go to at Kew Gardens.

Sam and Nathan shared a room at Kathy's house and I took the sofa. As I lay there, head nestled in a Spider Man pillow, body covered with a Spider Man duvet, I reflected on the day.

Why had Nathan pretended I'd won? It was stupid and patronizing. But I didn't care. My prize of Jaz hadn't worked out either. She was so hot and cold with me, I couldn't suss her out. Poppy was lovely. I wished I'd asked her to stay. What was wrong with me? I knew. Of course, I knew. I'd blown it with Poppy because even though she could never find out about Jaz, I couldn't be with her, that dirty secret lurking in the murky background. It was crystal clear at that moment—I couldn't have Jaz and

I couldn't have Poppy. I visualized two massive iron doors, like you see on moats or in prisons, crashing and clanging closed in front of me.

There was no point in going back to Newcastle. What was there for me? Okay well yes, Grandma and Grandpa, Kamal, Sam and Nathan, Mam and Dad, but wasn't I adding to their life burdens? And now I had let Grandpa down ("If you don't *win*..."). I should have phoned him, but I couldn't bear to listen to the silence when I told him I had failed to win. I would ring him the next day. Why had I built myself up to think I could win? How dumb.

I would ask Kathy if I could stay in London with her for a while. I had saved up enough to pay a bit of rent and maybe she would let me help her in her music studio? Perhaps there was a teeny-weeny job I could get at Kew Gardens? I could ask the next day. I knew Mam and Dad would let me stay in London. Actually, let's face it, they didn't care a hoot about what I did at all. They didn't even *know* what I was doing most of the time.

CHAPTER TWELVE

'No' was the answer. Kathy said she would need my parents' permission for me to stay with her for an extended period. I didn't want to phone them. I would get out my savings from the bank, go to the Kew lectures, then go off on my own. I remembered my Auntie Colette telling me once that if you trusted in The Universe, it would lead you to your dreams, even in terms of the smallest detail. As long as your wishes were honourable, she'd said, and for the good of humankind, things would unfold as desired. I wasn't entirely sure about the humankind bit, but I decided my not going home would solve quite a few people's problems, including my own, so I'd give it a go. I would trust that something would turn up. Of course, I immediately questioned whether I truly did, you know, TRUST the Universe. But you're not supposed to think like that. Apparently, you welcome the negative thought, let it go, then return to your resolve to have faith. Auntie Colette even suggested saying something whacky like, 'Thank you, thought, but I no longer need you; I release you with love.' I remember she closed her eyes while saying it at the same time as mine stretched open, my eyebrows touching the roof.

Even though I was supposed to be just going off for the day by myself, and meeting up with them later, I must have said goodbye to Sam and Nathan in a somewhat dramatic way. I hadn't realized it was unusual, but Nathan had said,

"You all right? You look well odd."

And Sam said,

"Hey, you're not up to something are you? I can read you like a book."

How I longed not to be read any more. If I didn't understand myself, I sure as hell didn't want other people constantly 'reading' me.

I was lucky there was a branch of my bank in Putney and I was surprised how easy it was to draw all my money out—**£643**. I was ready to start a new life. I'd have to eat frugally and maybe sleep rough, but if I could get work somewhere, that would last me till then. I'd probably have to lie and say I was eighteen to get a good job, though I was told I even looked young for sixteen. I had tried growing a beard, but it looked like I'd stuck on bits of fluff with glue. Maybe I would buy a false one. I was glad to have brought my suit as I felt it would open up a lot more doors in terms of work. I wondered if Kathy would at least let me shower at her place. Where would I live? I released the thoughts (with love).

It felt good being on my own at Kew Gardens. I had got there early so I could wander around. I wanted to see the herb garden since I was growing my own and I thought to go up onto the tree top walkway and pay a visit to The Temperate House which is boiling hot so that tropical plants like banana trees and such like can flourish there.

I enjoyed The Temperate House most of all. I think I had a permanent grin on my face. What would Sam 'read' into that? That I was insane, possibly.

The Temperate House was built at a similar time to The Orangery and was also a Grade I listed building and was a showcase for Kew's largest plants. It's rectangular with pitched roofs and its pillars support wrought iron rib-like beams. I read that it was the largest surviving Victorian green-house in the entire world, and you won't believe it, but it took forty years to build, so that tells you something. I chose to go there because it was about to be closed for about five years while it was under restoration. It felt special to be one of the very last people to experience the whole thing as it was then... By the way, when I said Grade I listed building, that means a building or monument or something of special architectural or historic interest (Kamal told me that in Ireland, the term used is 'Protected Structure' which is easier to understand) and you can't do anything to it without Government permission. People also have to look after the building properly or they are punished and taken off the list, a bit like if you don't look after children properly. There are three grades and hardly any buildings or structures obtain the top status of grade I, so that also shows you how brilliant these glass buildings at Kew Gardens are. To give you a comparison, you might have heard of or even seen The Tower Bridge in London, well that is also Grade I.

How it makes you feel when you're in there is out of this world (The Temperate House not Tower Bridge). Four thousand plants from all over the world. Emotion Library Lady: "That's it, stay sitting and just breathe, dear. Allow the electricity to charge your body and let those neurons have their festival in your brain. Allow everything to permeate all of you, then let it glow outwards, so that you become part of it. That's it. Connect and glow. And... breeeeeeathe."

Trochetiopsis ebenus. I'd have to think of a way of remembering that one. It was a charming little flower with a fine personality. It was both delicate and robust. I read that it was an endangered species. In fact, on the scale of 'Vulnerable', 'Endangered' and 'Critically Endangered', it falls into the worst category. Get this—it was thought to be extinct then, in 1980, specimens were found clinging to a cliff in Saint Helena, which is a tiny island in the South Atlantic. Clinging on, they were, refusing to die. What stamina this flower had for such a graceful, fragile thing. I thought of Poppy. The St Helena Ebony, as it's known in English, with its silky white petals and red and yellow stamens, had only two left growing in the wild in the world. There's only one of Poppy, I thought—she's in an even rarer category. I suppose, by that token, we *all* are. All of us. We're all more than critically endangered. We ought to look after ourselves. Take care of each other.

I saw trees in The Temperate House which were totally extinct in the wild. Saved by Kew. Captive, yet thriving. But now everything was to be moved because the beautiful building itself was now ailing and needed some tender loving care. Can't wait to see it once it's been restored and redesigned. What an undertaking—moving thousands of plants without damaging them and keeping them perfectly alive.

I had been to a talk on seed conservation with my Dad at Kew and it struck me what a great and crucial idea it was—to save plants.

'Poisonous Plants – the Dark Side of Beauty' was the name of the lecture I attended. I had to go to the Jodrell Lecture Theatre, the same one I'd been to the day before for the competition results. I walked in with my head low and made my way to the back of the raked seating. Once settled, I had a good look round. Green flip-up seats were fitting, I thought (the colour, that is). Rectangles of plastic, emitting white light, spaced themselves out on the ceiling—they looked like they'd been stolen from a vet's operating theatre, then again, this was a science talk I was at. The speaker stood at the front behind a solid dark wooden benchy desk thing about eight feet long. She had a laptop to her left on the table and a guy wearing a white coat and a fretful face was madly fiddling with wires attached to it. She was flanked by two six-feet-long cloth banners on long sections of sloped-in wall, so that she looked like she was on stage. I took the wall hangings to be pictures of poisonous plants. Behind her was a white wall lit up in the middle with a projection of her first slide with the title of the lecture, plant photos, and her name at the bottom.

I wonder if you've ever thought about how powerful plants are? You hear people talk about 'natural remedies' like it's the soft option, but blimey, you've got to be careful and not underestimate the strength of some of the chemicals in plants. Now then, my dad makes a scrummy rhubarb crumble, but little did I know, he could easily adjust the recipe slightly and kill us all. Dr Elizabeth Dauncey, who was giving the lecture, told us that eating a stack of the leaf blades (actually quite a mega amount of them, like five kilogrammes) either raw or cooked up, causes convulsions, coma "rapidly followed by death." So, the leaves of the dear ruddy sticks, masquerading as a fruit, but in fact a vegetable, which Dad grows and picks every year, are fatal. Rhubarb was also used as a laxative in Chinese Medicine, I learnt. I made a note to mention that to Kamal as he seemed to have trouble in that department and had a joke where he used to say, "Slow motion time" when he was about to go to the loo.

As much as I loved immersing myself in plant-talk, it wasn't long before people started leaking into my mood. Mention of Atropa belladonna (Deadly nightshade) sprung Poppy into my mind once more—we used to use the name for a boy who harassed her. The lecturer told us that bella donna meant beautiful lady in Latin and Italian (I'm not being cocky, but I did know this already, okay maybe I *am* being cocky, I mean I didn't have to tell you, did I?). Hundreds of years ago, women in Italy used Atropa belladonna to enlarge their pupils, which was thought to be alluring. The same plant has many other medicinal uses, we were taught. It is even used to treat conditions as serious as Parkinson's Disease.

Apart from its alternative sinister name of deadly nightshade, its dark berries are known as 'murderer's berries' or 'devil's berries'. It was suggested that these berries were the cause of Juliet's poisoning in William Shakespeare's *Romeo and Juliet*.

I marvelled over opposites—that so many opposites existed side by side in nature, in life. The same plant that attracts lovers poisons you. The same herb that heals you makes you sick. The same person you adore causes you unbearable pain.

And now the turn of Zantedeschia (Calla Lily). I'm betting you know who showed up in my mind when this flower was mentioned. It seems that the roots of the plant are the most dangerous part. Apart from vomiting and diarrhea, ingesting it can cause blistering and swelling in your mouth and if it's really bad, you can't speak or swallow. Oh, and it can make your eyes burn and lead to possible damage to the cornea.

Dr Elizabeth pointed out that poisonous plants rarely caused harm and that they became harmful only if they looked attractive, like Atropa belladonna. She reminded us that a lot of ugly weeds do not entice you to eat them, but that the beautiful shiny black berries of deadly nightshade appealed to the eye so were much more alluring and therefore risky. Even then, most poisonous berries are bitter and unpleasant to taste, so you wouldn't be tempted to eat a fatal amount. There are always exceptions in nature though and the plump black shiny devil's berries which appear on the deadly nightshade bush, are very juicy and slightly sweet. For a small child, just a few berries could be enough to kill them.

When my familiar friend, Brugmansia (Angel's trumpet) came up, I heard myself chanting the word in my head, as I often did. I slipped into a sort of trance, like I was feeling the effects of its poison, so that I had to slightly shake my head to realize the lecture was over and people were starting to file out.

After visiting the herb garden and cactus house, then buying a poster of poisonous plants in the shop at Kew, I realized it was a bit of a daft thing to do since I didn't have a room or anywhere to live (I mean, I know I did really, but taking my plan seriously, I was about *not* to have). Just as I was thinking about where to go, I remembered that Sam, Nathan and I were all due to stay at Kathy's again that night and since I had told nobody of my intention to run away, I decided I may as well stay one more night at her place in Putney. It would give me a bit more time to make important decisions and I could leave the poster there. I would go to the second lecture on the Wednesday, then stay in London after that. Sam and Nathan would be off the scent because, despite their suspicions, I will have shown up as expected after the first lecture.

I stopped on Putney Bridge with its wide sweeping spans so low down in the water that it looked like most of the bridge was submerged, but I think it was meant to look like that. I was on my way from Putney Bridge tube station (which was actually in Fulham) over to Putney on the other side of The River Thames. I stood next to an ornate Victorian light. There were two rows of them carefully positioned on either side of the bridge. Each light had three lamps in a triangular formation above fancy iron supports. I leaned my forearms on the stone and granite wall and turning my head one way then the other, noticed that there were two ancient churches, one at each end of the bridge. It made me think it must be protected, you know, in a spiritual way, but the thought had hardly entered my mind when I saw a cyclist being knocked off her bike by a bus driver. It didn't look like anyone was harmed, but there was a right old round of swearing and gesticulating. At the Fulham end of the bridge, it looked like there was a park with gardens; it could be somewhere I could sleep rough if the worst came to the worst, I thought.

As I officially arrived in Putney, I saw a poster near the church saying that the famous Boat Race between Oxford and Cambridge Universities (which always started at Putney and had done since 1845) was to include women for the first time. How crazy that it had only been men up to that point, I thought. It seems like it takes yonks for 'traditions' to change, even if they're mental. Like just because something's a tradition, it makes it okay? You could do anything, if that were the case, and get away scot free. 'Oh, I'm sorry if it offends you, it's our tradition to stuff a leek up our dog's arse on the first full moon after Easter'. Anyway, at least these boating folk had wised up, even if it *had* taken nearly two hundred years.

I was happy to turn left just before the main street with its shops and shoppers. I was even happier to find no-one in when I got to Kathy's house (she had given me a spare key).

I lay my backpack on the mushy sofa, made myself a cup of tea in the adjoining kitchen and went through the door at the side to sit outside the back, at a round metal table. There were just two chairs in matching lime green. I say just two chairs like she was a cheapskate or something, but she lived on her own, so there was no need to have more. From what I heard from Mam, it was on the hopeful side even having a *second* chair. She was a bit of a loner and a spinster and 'always would be' according to my mam. She had nephews but no nieces. Horrible word isn't it—'spinster'? Sounds like a wizened, pointy-nosed mean thin person who wears ragged dark clothes and hates people, not just men, and who twitches the curtains to check no-one's about before she hobbles outside to buy whatever gross food she eats. How come the word 'bachelor' has connotations of adventure, excitement, freedom and even wealth? I know why—coz of films and stuff. Well, actually, just like the boat race, possibly the whole of History. What was that film again...? Ah yes *Spinster Party* (not) and didn't my mam and her friend receive Spinster of Arts degrees? Ha ha. Anyway, they'd gone to university together and Mam said that Kathy had failed relationship after failed relationship, never settled and never had children. I wondered if she had *wanted* children or not. I wondered how similar to Mam she was.

If you believe you can tell about people by looking at their belongings and how they've arranged them, I would say we had an interesting case on our hands here with Kathy. Bang in the centre of the little round table was a plant so dead I couldn't begin to identify it. How long had it been there?

I picked it up in an attempt to inspect the roots underneath, but it had become one with the ceramic pot. One of the two suns decorating the pot was badly chipped too. Two candles protruding from multi-coloured glass mosaic holders flanked the pot. Though the holders were pretty manky and half-filled with rainwater, I picked up the one on the right, poured out the rain, and sniffed it—a combination of citronella and sandalwood. I knew these odours because of Mam and I knew people used citrus smells to repel insects, but surely sandalwood would attract them? Opposites again. Here was someone who didn't know what they wanted maybe, never mind how to get it. The only other item on the table was a plain glass ashtray, full to the brim of cigarette ends.

In the back right corner of the yard was a broken swing. I wondered why she had it since she was childless; perhaps it was there when she moved in. Behind the swing were two matching folded broken camping chairs. It was such a small area, they cluttered the place up. Why hadn't she thrown them out? At the back of the yard in the middle of the wall was a water feature... I should say a defunct water feature. It consisted of an old-fashioned tap positioned to pour water into a rectangular stone trough about a foot square, but it didn't look like it had worked for a while, green water having spread out across the thick stone brim and trickled slimy trails down the mossy sides. It seemed that this person wanted to create a calm uplifting atmosphere but hadn't quite pulled it off. She had wanted her yard to appeal to the senses, but it had been a failed mission.

In contrast, leaning on the fence at the side of the table was a bright bicycle. It was purple and looked new. I took a sip of my tea and got up to have a closer look. I rode Nathan's bike occasionally, but unlike a lot of lads my age, I didn't have my own. I unleant it and wrapped my hands around the handles and breaks.

"Fancy a ride, do you, Oliver?"

I jumped so violently, my knee jerked towards the bike, which sent it tumbling to the ground resulting in the loudest ding I've ever heard as the massive bell did its thing. Before I could open my mouth, arms dived to pick it up and reprop it against the fence.

Soap and shampoo and deodorant wafted into my face.

Kathy.

"I didn't hear you come in. I was in the shower," she said.

I could see that as her hair was in a towel and she wore a flimsy Buddha tee shirt, which stopped way above the knees and nothing much else by the look of things. I said,

"Hi. Sorry. I mean I thought the place was empty. I thought you were out."

"Sorry to disappoint you," she said, rubbing the towel into her hair with both hands so that the tee shirt rode up even more, revealing red knickers. I darted my gaze away.

"Oh. No. I mean you just gave me a fright, that's all."

"Sit down and I'll come and join you with a coffee."

She went back in and re-emerged, flip-flopping her way to the table with a Virgo mug and some rolling tobacco. I noticed she hadn't seen fit to add another item of clothing to her get-up even though she knew there was a boy she hardly knew in her house. She was comfortable with her body. She was earthy and exuded a certain sensuality. 'Bit of a waste,' I thought, since she was single, then it occurred to me that being single didn't mean she was a stranger to passion and pleasures of the flesh. I ran my left hand through my hair and gazed down at the dead plant while she rolled up a cigarette.

"What a clever boy, getting through your presentation for the Kew thing and being runner up," she said, ruffling my hair then patting my back. "Such a shame Anna and Ben couldn't be there. Your mum would have been so proud of you. You spoken to her since yesterday?"

Spoken to Mam? I hadn't spoken to her at all since they'd left for Australia, apart from a few words one time. It wasn't that I was making a huge point of not speaking to her when she called... well, maybe something of a point, but it wasn't like she insisted on me speaking with her. Kathy read my mind:

"She's not going to force you to talk to her, Oliver, but I know she's desperate to. She wants to know how you are."

She took a long drag from her cigarette and tilted her head as she streamed smoke back out, like she really wanted me to listen or like she could sense that I didn't really want to listen.

"I know because I'm in regular email contact with her. Is there a reason... are you angry with her?" She took another much quicker drag. "I would understand if you *were*."

This person whom I'd met a handful of times was venturing into some sort of pseudo-therapy bollocks.

"Why?" I said, scraping my mug back and forth across the metal table. "Why would I understand?"

I didn't answer. It was obvious what I meant. She could say what she wanted, but she didn't have any right to push me into talking about something I didn't even care about.

"You've been through so much. You were so close to your sister, honey, and it was an utter tragedy that you lost her."

She put her cigarette into the ash tray and leant forward so that her chest touched the table.

"But you must stop ever thinking it should have been you or that your mother wished it had been you who'd died."

My scraping mug came to a standstill of its own accord. Blimey, she didn't waste any time. Part of me wanted to stand up, go and get my backpack and walk right out of the house, but it was so rare for anyone to face things full on and talk to me about it all, that my buttocks cleaved to the green ironwork and I was compelled to respond:

"How do you...?"

I shuffled in the seat in an attempt to affect my frame of mind, so that I could better express myself.

"I *don't* think that." I said. "I did at one point. You're wrong when you say my mother is desperate to know how I am. She's the one who decided to leave me for God knows how long and—"

"You're sixteen, Oliver," she said, springing back to an upright position.

"Is that the age when you stop being hurt?"

We both took a breath and reassessed where this conversation might go. I took a drink.

"Yes, I know they've been wanting to make this trip for years," I said. "But they've got each other, haven't they?"

"Mothers do not act in predictable ways when their little girl fades away and dies in their arms," she said.

Something about her brutal line was crushing but agonizingly refreshing as nobody had ever spoken like that. I had felt like I was on a roll, but now I was stumped. She said,

"Fair enough, it's nothing to do with being sixteen years old." She leaned forward again. "I know I told you the other day that you couldn't stay here without your parents' permission, so I'm not being very clear, am I?"

She leaned even more and ruffled my hair again only this time I pulled away. She took a drag of the rollie before reperching it in the cigarette cemetery and using the same hand she took hold of my chin and twisted my head towards her. Her brown eyes searched into my soul. She willed me, by her look, to fully absorb what she was about to say. It was all too intense, so I lowered my gaze.

"Look at me... Suffering is what makes us human."

I had heard this before. I can't say that it was an enormous comfort to hear it again. She carried on.

"If we think we're entitled to a life of comfort, any pain is going to seem unfair. If you accept that life is about growing and changing, you won't think you're getting a raw deal when pain and suffering are laid at your door."

She knew she could take her hand away now—she had my attention.

"It's all about balance, Oliver. Think of those crazy mountain climbers who embrace hardship and risk their lives to know something of profound satisfaction in reaching the summit."

"But I didn't choose to climb a mountain," I said looking down again. "I chose none of it."

"Feeling sorry for yourself is the most futile exercise."

She readjusted the towel on her hair and shifted in her chair.

"There is neither rhyme nor reason to life sometimes," she said. "You have to accept that cruel people can seem comfortable while people like you suffer."

She then placed her hand on top of mine.

"Don't bother trying to find the logic there: it will drive you insane. We should be searching for balance and peace not embracing craziness."

She wobbled my hand for this last bit, then pulled it away.

"But what if the pain doesn't go away?" I said.

"Are you saying you never feel happy any more?"

I finally turned completely away from her and swigged off some by now tepid tea. I looked back at her face and the question hadn't gone away. But I didn't answer it. She got up, walked to me, and took my face in her hands again but it was different this time—more like stroking.

"If you're feeling depressed—"

"I didn't say—"

"If you are very sad all the time or most of the time, you need to work on yourself or you need to get some help from somebody else."

I continued to look at her, despite the burning in my eyes and hoping she might come out with a clearer solution than 'work on yourself' or 'get help from somebody.' She properly had my attention now. She unwrapped the scratchy-looking dye-stained towel from her head, all the while keeping her eyes locked on mine, saying,

"I know you refused counselling last year, but it can really help, you know? Are you not ready to think about that again?"

My heart sank with the useless suggestion. I completely wasn't ready. Any solution that involved other people did not speak to me. My head started to hurt. As I looked at her face more carefully—short, red hair, two hoops and one star-shaped stud in her left ear, deep crescent moon lines in each cheek, she told me she would telephone my grandma and suggest they helped me book some therapy. I really did appreciate Kathy trying to read me, to 'get' me, trying to help me, but with her sentence, "I'll give her a ring this evening," I knew I definitely wasn't going back to Newcastle. I knew I had to ring Grandma and Grandpa to give news of the competition, which I did that evening, but I wasn't going back. I would write a note for Sam and Nathan the next morning before leaving for my lecture at Kew Gardens; I would pretend I'd met someone at the poisonous plants talk from the garden competition and that he'd invited me to stay at his house for a while.

I had been right about Kathy in a way. She had good ideas and a gentle heart, but her best-intentioned plans always turned against her, the latest being my 'rescue'.

CHAPTER THIRTEEN

It felt like coming home, approaching the Victoria Gate at The Royal Botanic Gardens, Kew. I had been distracted on the tube and had missed my stop. I was dwelling on what Kathy had been saying. Grandpa had given me similar advice. He had got even deeper, though, saying that feeling happy is a state of mind and you could only reach it by developing personally and trying to be good to others and to yourself. Compassion and Forgiveness, he said, were the keys. I didn't know who I was supposed to care about or who I was supposed to forgive, but it felt like it was good for others that I wasn't going back to Newcastle. Grandpa had said something weird about wolves too. What was it? Ah yes. He believed there were two wolves fighting in my heart: one was full of peace, serenity, love, forgiveness and acceptance and the other was full of anger and fear. It turned out I followed that up with the exactly right question saying, "Yeah but which one wins?" He came back with, "The one you feed." It was frustrating because I did know what he was getting at, but how the heck did you switch your feeding permanently from one to the other? Perhaps it doesn't have to be only feeding one; even feeding one a bit more than the other may have significant consequences.

I had gone to Richmond, the station at the end of the line, by accident, and had to travel the one stop back to Kew Gardens Station. Now at my intended destination, I found a place to stand at the right of the exit to put my bag down and gather my thoughts. The clatter of metal chairs scraping on concrete jagged the cool air and distracted me. I looked to the right—a girl pulling, tipping and dragging chairs outside a pub. Was she trying her best to make as much noise as possible, like it was her best chance at attracting even a scrap of attention that day? One of those fleeting moments of connection, like she knew I was looking at her, as she raised her head from her bent body and mouthed "sorry" to me, stretching the sides of her mouth down in an exaggerated frown. Another person 'reading' me. I smiled and shook my head as if to say, no, it doesn't matter, you're all right.'

I felt someone approaching me from the left, so snapped my head round.

"You lost, son? I live round here if you need directions."

I must have looked lost. Before I'd answered she said,

"If you're after a drink there, the pub doesn't open till 11."

I heard myself saying,

"It's quarter past now."

"Is it? What do you know, I'm an hour behind!? I normally come in for my paper at 10 but... it's been an unusual day. Have you been to that pub before?" I didn't respond. "Do you know, Kew is the only station on the underground network to have a pub attached to it?"

"Is it?" I said. That was it now. I must have had the air of someone who had all day to talk.

"It's got a lot about it. It's a unique station in more ways than one," she said. "It's a Grade II-listed building, but I'm betting that probably doesn't mean anything to you."

"Like the buildings at Kew Gardens," I said, "and even bridges like Putney Bridge."

"A man after my own heart," she said tapping my back with what seemed like the ends of her fingers instead of her whole hand. So, this woman was boldish in her approach to life, but a bit apologetic and unassertive at the same time. I love that expression—someone 'after my own heart'; it's so warm and touching an idiom in its honesty. It wore its heart on its sleeve, you might say. Or maybe it was a lie because how could there be hearty things like love between strangers. Could there be?

I turned to look at her properly. She must have been at least eighty-five, maybe even ninety-five, with little round smiling eyes and apparently no eyelashes, though she had penciled in her eyebrows. Old fashioned little dark lines. Probably the same way she'd done them the last sixty or seventy years. She had on a well-worn hat that was too fancy for her outfit and I wondered if she was a ghost from the Victorian era.

"The footbridge is Grade II listed as well," she said, waving a pointed finger to her left without looking. She seemed thrilled to be telling me all this.

"The train track used to split Kew in two until they built that in 1912," she said. "A pioneering technique was used—reinforced concrete. It was a French fellow who devised it... François... François... can't remember his surname. What was it? Blast."

"They went to a lot of trouble making it a covered bridge," I said. "You wouldn't think they'd spend all that money just to keep the rain off."

"No, you see, it wasn't for rain," she said touching her hat then shaking her index finger at me like she was telling me off.

"The high walls and roof there were to protect people from smoke and steam. The trains weren't electric like they are now."

I needed to get away. I was going to be late for my lecture.

"Ah, right. Interesting... Thank you. I'm looking for Kew Gardens."

I don't know why I made out I didn't know where I was going. She seemed pleased to have some purpose that day and tapped me on the back again and pointed down to the parade of shops.

"Go down there and cross Sandycombe Road at the zebra crossing, then walk down Lichfield Road opposite and you'll get to the Victoria

Gate entrance. You enjoy yourself now. Best gardens in the world we have there."

I looked at her and nodded.

Once over the zebra crossing, I looked back up to where I'd been standing. The woman was still there, waving. I knew she would be. Sometimes you just know, don't you? She looked even more like a ghost than before, her too-long pale mac floating around her, her see-through wrist. I waved back and blew her a kiss by accident. As I walked on, I imagined her going home with her paper and instead of reading it as she usually did, sitting in her favourite chair, a cup of tea on the rickety side table, she'd write her diary instead, out of sequence, in case she forgot about the strange boy she'd helped at the station. The tea-cosy would be snuggled around the pot in the kitchen, keeping it warm, even though she never had a second cup—she always made enough for two, just in case. She always got the crocheted cover from the top drawer which didn't close properly anymore and slipped it over the pot which her husband used to say was a 'good pourer'. 'What do you know,' she'd write, 'the boy (blast, I wish I'd got his name) even blew me a kiss before he turned to walk away!'

And I hadn't even meant to. Or maybe I had.

There were only a few places remaining, so late was I for the lecture; I was forced to take a seat in the front row.

I focused on the speaker straight away. I knew the layout of the room by now. The only difference from the day before was the slide in the middle showing the title of the lecture and the name of the lecturer. Maybe the plants on the drapes were always there and weren't in fact poisonous ones as I'd assumed the day before.

I hadn't recognized the speaker, but she had apparently attended my competition event as, about half way through the talk, she mentioned my name and pointed me out. My ears rang and I could feel warmth building in my cheeks, like someone had switched on a sun lamp right in front of me.

"Our own competition to design a hospice garden was open to all ages, but we were delighted that it attracted mostly young people. Oliver here, in the front row [pointing at me] was a finalist, as was Jessica, sitting up there in the back."

I turned around to see who and where she was. It was the girl with the spiky blond hair and the clumpy boots. Her eyes immediately met mine, like she already knew where I was sitting. When she saw me looking at her, she made the same funny gesture she'd made at the Orangery evening— right index to nose then out to point at me. I smiled and gave a wave that wasn't really a wave, just an index-finger-in-the-air. I tried to work out if I had waved or whether I'd pointed as an animalistic mirror of *her* pointing.

Just as I was getting over my embarrassment of being mentioned and the excitement of seeing the girl, my phone buzzed. I didn't look at the text till after the lecture, when I was outside the theatre. It was from Jasvandi. She addressed me as 'Mr. Second Prize'. I was so annoyed with her that when the garden designer girl, Jessica, came up to me, I was actually saying, "Horrible person," out loud.

"That's a nice welcome," she said.

"Oh, hi. Sorry," I said, forcing a laugh. "My friend's being a pain in the rump. Apologies for the crudeness."

"Hey don't mind me. You can say anything you want. I'm not delicate," she said in a really delicate way. She had those same boots on matched with a yellow dress and she wore a lilac woollen coat on top, "Say anything you want about him."

"Her," I heard myself saying. What was that about? Why did I have to say, '*her*' like I was showing off that all my friends weren't blokes. Then again, it was true, so maybe it wasn't so bonkers, and I was simply overthinking everything at that time.

"The girlfriend then. I know what that's like."

"No, she's not my girlfriend," I said, luckily stopping short of adding, 'though I *have* had sex with her.' Honestly there was no shutting me up.

"I don't have a girlfriend. You do, were you saying? Have a girlfriend I mean?"

She didn't answer. Putting my phone back in my pocket I said,

"It's just that you said, 'I know what it's like.'"

"Do you want to grab a cup of coffee or something?" she said.

I thought it was so cool that she hadn't answered me. I loved intrigue. She was enigmatic. Great.

"Yes! I mean, yes, yes definitely," I said. "Let's go and have a coffee."

"Shall we walk into Kew village?" she said. "The café here's a bit utilitarian... What you laughing about?"

I loved the fact that she knew 'big' words and I think I was laughing out of relief. It was refreshing to be talking to someone new who seemed life-enhancing. I personally quite liked that industrial type way of designing interiors, but I said,

"Nothing. Yeah, let's go."

She took me to a cute café, which was also a bookshop and we sat outside even though the weather had cooled. I noticed she had on lemon-coloured fingerless gloves. When I said I liked them, I even touched one of them. She was just like that, you know, easy to be with, easy to be near.

"You'll be all right in that overcoat," she said. "Is that what they wear all year round in the freezing north of England. I adore your accent by the way. What is it? Liverpool?"

"No, Newcastle, well Geordie," I said, rethinking her level of intelligence. "Liverpool accent's called Scouse," I said while actually thinking, 'God, London is like a different country to the rest of England.' "You can't tell the difference, then, can you not?"

She looked slightly embarrassed which I found attractive. She said,

"I know, it's ridiculous, I have a real block when it comes to accents, which is strange because music is my thing, so you'd think I'd have a good ear for accents."

Aha, something else we had in common.

"Your accent isn't very strong anyway," she said, which was true enough. "That's a point, you don't have a thick accent," she said pulling her gloves further up her hands, "so maybe I can be forgiven for not working it out?"

I liked the way she moved, this Jessica, and I mean physically moved as well as intellectually. She was very watchable. I wanted to sit back and say, 'You carry on being yourself and I'll watch you for about an hour,' but she didn't give me the chance. She kept asking me questions. I must say, it did please me that she didn't talk about herself constantly.

"Are *you* into music?" she said, before I'd answered the 'forgiven question', unless that one was rhetorical and didn't require an answer. She added,

"That's a daft question, sorry, everyone's into music."

She fiddled with her left earlobe, twisting her body and sort of constantly readjusting the position of her head as if she wasn't entirely sure if she was supposed to be there. And I mean 'there' as in 'on this planet.' You know some people have an apologetic aura, like they're apologizing for actually being alive? Well she was like that only it wasn't irritating, it was endearing. Every head movement was punctuated with brief flicks and suggestions of smiles, like she had a whole repertoire of smiles and used several in one sentence. I'm making out she had a nervous manner with twitching and that, but I don't mean that at all—it was all executed in a flow, like a beautiful slow specialist dance. She was one of those amazing garlic plants known as serpent garlic whose stems twist round and round and point in all different directions—Allium sativum ophioscorodon. There was a hint of my favourite flower from the same family too—the whimsical wonderful purple allium, all bold and bright in its sphericalness. She said,

"I meant do you play anything?"

"Do you?" I don't know why I didn't answer her straight. It was like she awoke the playful side in me and it was hard to talk to her in a serious way. I was playing with a mouse. I had this awareness that I was being flirty. I felt like I'd been on a flirting course and was doing my practical exam. But it seemed the most natural thing in the world. I wondered if she had this effect on all guys or if we had what they call 'chemistry'. It certainly seemed to be a day of connecting up with people.

I'll tell you what, talking of connections and being in touch with the universe and all that, what happened next was well-spooky... I told her about playing the saxophone and she was only... learning the trumpet. And not just that, but this is the bit I was just talking about—this is what she said:

"Hey, we should jam together. How cool would that be? I live near here, in Richmond. Why don't you come back? You've probably got other plans."

So, there you go—from being (in theory) homeless, I was now being invited to this lovely girl's house! I must have been crazy to risk her going back on the offer by saying, "I don't have my sax with me," but she jumped in with, "We have tons of instruments at our house; my parents are both in an orchestra and my brothers play brass instruments."

I must have looked weird for a bit because she asked me if I was all right. It just felt a bit mystical, this synchronicity thing playing out just when I needed it to. I had decided to trust in the universe and it had offered up an exquisite gift. To be honest, it didn't really matter what was real and what was freaky because the reality was that I needed somewhere to stay that night and here was an invitation to a kind stranger's dwelling. I wasn't sure how I'd feel later on, but I decided that if it seemed proper, it would be easy to pretend there was a problem with where I was staying that night and I could then accept her offer. I'd play it by ear and try out a bonus dose of universe-trusting.

CHAPTER FOURTEEN

Not that I was impressed or anything, but I'll tell you for nothing, this girl was rich. I mean her family was rich. You could tell from the house. I wondered what her parents would think of their daughter bringing back a stranger. At least we had the garden connection. We had the music connection too, it seemed. What else would we find in common?

Can you believe, it turned out her parents weren't even there? They were on a concert tour in Germany and Austria and wouldn't be back for three weeks. Things were looking up big time.

We didn't even get round to playing music because after watching a film by my favourite director, Wes Anderson, who, she told me, was her favourite too (I am aware that she may have been making some stuff up, by the way, but how well we were getting on seemed amazing and brilliant at the time), her younger brother arrived home and sat on the sofa opposite us. He was called Miles and he was sound. Even though he looked smartly dressed in cream trousers and a work-type shirt in pale blue, he had long fair hair tied back in a pony tail. When he put on *Empire of the Sun*, a really good Australian electronic music duo from Sydney, I started to wonder if this was my long-lost family.

Miles was telling us about his planned trip to Australia and New Zealand when he finished his A-levels the next summer and it made me think of my parents. We'd been talking for ages before he asked me anything. I had felt a deep satisfaction (happiness?) just being me and not constantly feeling like an experiment. It made me think how great it would be to go off to a totally new country, where nobody knew me, and I could make a fresh start. I told him about Mam and Dad being in Australia and New Zealand. While I was telling him exactly where they were going, his phone rang, and I heard him talking to a girl who was going to bring pizzas back. Miles had asked me what I wanted except he didn't actually say, 'Would you like a pizza? What type?' He just said one word, "Pepperoni?" with an open-eyed expectation of a 'Yes of course' so instead of saying, 'Marguerita' which was always my preference, I simply nodded, to which I got a thumbs-up.

When he got off the phone, he said that Maisy was bringing pizza back in an hour. "Beer?" he said to me. I responded with two of our signs (Miles' and my new communication system)—a nod accompanied by a thumb's up. And I can tell you that I liked beer even less than pepperoni pizza. Jessica, who'd been out of the living room for a while and had reappeared wearing a black and red jump suit thing said to Miles,

"And me! Beer here s'il te plait!"

"Hmmm. And how old do you think you are??" Miles said, fondling his pony tail.

"Hmmm. Two minutes younger than you!" she said.

They both made the exact same funny noise—a twin-laugh, which they must have developed over many years. When you're drawn to people, there's something innocent and beautiful about the early hours, when you don't know some of the most basic facts about each other. As sweet a moment as it was, and as little as I knew Jessica, now I thought, 'Oh right, she's a twin', so whatever vague possibilities hung in the air only a moment before, I now knew I could never be truly special to her, or rather, I could never be as special and close to her as her twin brother was. The closeness a brother and sister could have.

Jessica curled up on the sofa next to her brother, facing me. I felt like I was at some weird interview. I noticed she was barefoot now and that her feet were well proportioned with dinky toes and looked manicured. I didn't think she'd be the kind of girl who'd bother about toes. Or maybe it was just nail varnish and she hadn't done all that filing and poking around I've seen my mam do. As I looked over at her, and swilled down more beer, I felt like a lion stalking its prey. I studied her feet more. I felt the desire to rub and stroke the skin. I studied her delicate hands that grappled with her brother's. Every move she made, even her twisty, flitty hand movements, were graceful. I drank more and my beery brain imagined those waxy hands on me—resting on my shoulders, pulling me towards her, stroking my chest, dancing over my jeans' belt. I imagined her whole body spiralling itself around me. Curling garlic. Allium sativum ophioscorodon.

"Let Ollie choose!" came out of Jessica's mouth, mid-grapple.

I liked those words. I loved those words. If only choices were that straight-forward. Feet were all I saw again. They were so much smaller than Jasvandi's. The last time I'd drunk beer was on the night with Jasvandi's feet. When I took the golden chilled bottle of beer from Miles and took a swig, that night flashed back—her skin and her face and the intense fervour I'd experienced. I took in a deep breath. Jessica was looking at the iPad, play-squabbling with her twin about what music to put on next through the sound system. I wished I'd been more experienced when Jaz had come to me that night. Perhaps that's why things weren't turning out how I'd imagined. I needed more experience.

The twin-tussle was beginning to bore me. I wasn't part of anything during those moments. Watching life from the wings. I wanted so much to be in the scene. I got lost in some artwork instead. The mock-bickering faded as my eyes were drawn to three prints on the wall behind them. I recognized the artist but couldn't remember his name. It was the one who'd done that famous romantic painting of a man kissing a woman, gold spangly flowing robes enveloping the pair. My mam had a postcard of it on the noticeboard in the kitchen. In fact, I think the painting is called 'The Kiss'. I remembered it. I saw the empty kitchen. I saw the noticeboard. I saw the mini painting—gleaming globes and oblongs, patch-blended like a celestial duvet cover, a couple floating underneath, buoyed up by a magic carpet of pink and gold petals. Yes, this was the same hand.

The three pictures were in the same style. The middle print was of six swirling females, all intertwined. The flowers surrounding them made me think of John Everett Millais' 'Ophelia'. Spirals and waves of multiple colours, mosaiced with woman-shapes. Looked like they could be in water, as Ophelia. The two either side were of trees, kind of abstract with similar patterns to the middle one. They both seemed to be set in a forest; the left depicted completely vertical reddy, orangey, greeny trees, reaching for the unseen sky, more trees at the sides than the centre, leading the eye into a warm flowery glade, painted in the same hues; the one on the right was not cathedral-columny like the first, but more zoomed in, a forest floor and fat tree trunks. This second was equally light and equally calm—none of the eerie darkness you might expect of a forest. Surely the painter loved the woods. He must have felt peaceful in a forest. You could just tell. He must have loved trees. This was a guy 'after my own heart'.

My trance was broken by a second beer plonked on the coffee table. The music now was of another Australian band called *Vertical Horizon*. A track came on which hit me in more places than my ears. Poppy had played it to me on her return from Australia.

"Vertical Horizon," I said.

"This one's a keeper," Miles said pinning first me then Jessica with his eyes.

I'd been really impressed by the song when Poppy had put it on, but I'd only said it was 'not bad'. I don't know why I didn't tell her the truth. I hadn't played it ever again and here it was—Poppy's song. "Oh God," I had even said to her, "Is this what your Ozzie boyfriend put you onto then?" and she had looked hurt and told me no, but I didn't believe her.

I wondered if Poppy had got home all right and why I cared if she had or hadn't. I started focusing on the lyrics. Is this why she had played it to me...? When it came to the last chorus, I felt a pain in my throat, the back of my nose and my eyes:

'I am everything you want
I am everything you need
I am everything inside of you
That you wish you could be
I say all the right things
At exactly the right time
But I mean nothing to you and I don't know why
And I don't know why'

I was seduced by the pizza aroma well before the living room door opened. When it did open, I was seduced anew, but not by the food. Poppy flung from me like a spirit being exorcised. The most gorgeous girl I'd ever seen, Miles's 'girlfriend', emerged from the doorway, a stack of pizzas in her arms. She may as well have flung them all up in the air to land on the soft grey sofas and the fluffy carpet for all I cared about eating, now that this wondrous being was in my midst. I brought the beer bottle to my lips and just kept on pouring the honey down my throat as my eyes glued to this girl's face. Maisy. Wow.

She glided into the room and after saying, "Grub's up," in a deep husky voice to Miles, her gaze swooped down to me. I prized the bottle out of my mouth. I must have looked like I was anticipating an exotic dance or something because as I watched her, she kept looking at me, lowering the pile of pizzas onto the glass coffee table between the two sofas. She did actually start this sensual dance, executing a full twirl in the process. Her eyes stayed on me the whole time and even when her head turned, she did that thing when you keep your eyes fixed on a single spot till your head can't keep that twisted any more, then you flick it the other way to catch the same spot again as your body moves round, like ballerinas do. In this instance, the spot was me. "So, this is the handsome stranger you told me about, Miles?"

"I don't think Miles used those exact words," said Jessica, "but he is rather dishy isn't he?"

The alcohol and the compliments were going to my head. Waves of dopamine and adrenalin raged through me and I took a deep breath again. She was being a bit saucy, I thought, considering her boyfriend was in the same room. I still hadn't spoken when Maisy said, "Yes, he *is* dishy, Jess. Where did you pick him up again?"

It struck me then that these people could be anyone and the snippets that you only found out gradually, like being twins, could include being kidnappers or Satan worshippers or murderers. I was fired up, though, and didn't care what they had in store for me. It all seemed exciting and desirable.

Maisy slinked over and sat next to me on the sofa opposite Jessica and Miles (and when I say 'next to' I mean more next to than you'd expect a total stranger to sit)—I felt an urge to move away, but was enjoying the blatant flirting, the overt body language and the enticing wafts of amber from her perfume with hints of thyme and I'm pretty sure, coriander. She wore denim shorts, navy high tops and an oversized white tee-shirt with a huge number on the front. I can't remember the number, but remember thinking it was quite a classy look, you know, showing a lot of leg, but no top, if you know what I mean. I had read that in one of Poppy's magazine's once at her mam's flower shop, 'The Fuschia's Bright'. 'Boobs or Butt, not Both!' the article was called. It recommended showcasing (their word!) one or the other and it went on to talk about men being either breast or leg men. It didn't even mention which parts of the body women like, even though the magazine was aimed at girls, which I thought was interesting. As for breast or leg, I felt like there was something wrong with me because I was neither or both or something more, well, something better than that. Don't people notice faces more than anything? And even then, the face doesn't have to be beautiful in the sense of symmetrical and all that. And you would hope to see some intelligence or a look of compassion or something, wouldn't you? And you need to feel some sort of indefinable connection, surely? I mean can it be only about physical stuff?? Maybe it is at first. Anyway, I'll shut up because all I can say is that Maisy was appealing to me in a big way and who knows what was at play there?

"Hand the pizzas out then, sis," said Miles.

'Sis,' he'd said... I could hear myself having an excited conversation with myself in my head but trying not to show anything on my face. *Not his girlfriend.*

She leant forward, reached for the top box and frisbeed it to her brother. He caught it, springing the lid open in one smooth move. He and Jessica then made a twin noise to convey the message, 'We love the smell emanating from this box'. As they were dangling their first pieces above their mouths, Maisy said,

"I suddenly don't feel hungry anymore."

I looked at her face. Striking features framed by silky long curls. I looked over to Jessica's face for the interpretation of what Maisy had said. Jessica smiled at her older sister and said,

"Other things on your mind now?" to which Maisy picked up a small remote control from the coffee table and threw it at her, narrowly missing her pizza hand, I think on purpose (the missing).

"Hand Oliver his pizza then," Jessica added. "I bet he's ravenous. Aren't you, Oliver?" she asked me, but I couldn't 'read' her. She still seemed in playful mood and not at all annoyed at my obvious flirting with her sister. Perhaps it wasn't obvious. Perhaps I wasn't even flirting, and it was all in my head?

"Cheers, Jessica," I said. "Yeah, I'll have some, thanks, but I think I'll finish my beer first."

"Beer's lame. I'll make some proper drinks," Maisy said, sliding her bottom to the edge of the sofa and dramatically springing to a stand. I watched her walk over to a drinks cabinet in the corner of the room. It had glass doors and Maisy scanned its contents, ready to pounce on her victim. "Aha, there you are," and she opened both doors and reached in with her right hand for a bottle of brown liquid and pretended to swig it down with the lid still on. Miles started singing a song and the other two joined in. It ended with them shouting the word, 'Tequila!' and laughing hard and dangerously.

"Bugger it, there's no triple sec. You can use Cointreau, can't you?" Maisy asked to the cupboard, but Miles answered,

"Yes, sure you can. Margueritas. Yay!"

I'd heard of that drink but had no clue what it was. I considered how old they all were. I mean how old Maisy was, I suppose. It seemed like a very adult sort of drink she was making.

"Do you like margueritas, Oliver?" Jessica asked me. "M had them all the time when she lived in LA for a year and now she can't stop making them for us."

"You lived in LA?" I said. "I might be going there soon... to stay with a friend."

It seemed like I was pretty unadventurous and inexperienced compared to this family and I was glad to sound a bit like a man of the world.

"Oh, cool. Whereabouts?" Maisy asked.

Before I responded, it jumped into my head that Kamal had once made me a marguerchita and said it was a mocktail which was a fake marguerita in other words with no alcohol. I remembered him making a huge fuss about squeezing loads of limes. So, I brushed over the fact that I didn't know which part of Los Angeles Jaz lived in. I'd seen a programme on TV where people were working out on the beach and I'd laughed at the time because the place was called 'Muscle Beach'. I said, "Muscle Beach. You've got fresh limes, I hope?"

They all laughed, and I felt like a right idiot.

"You can't live on Muscle Beach," Miles said.

"He means behind Muscle Beach, stupid," Maisy turned to me, "Like off North Venice Boulevard, yeah?"

"Yeah," I said. "That's right."

She came back up to the coffee table, put down the bottle of Tequila, put her hands on her hips and said,

"That's too weird. I lived on Pacific Avenue, right near there, overlooking the canal. What street does he live on?"

"I haven't been there yet, so I don't know. I can't remember."

"I'm going back to visit at Easter." Maisy said. "When you going?"

"Nothing's fixed yet. And stop avoiding the crucial lime question," I said. It occurred to me I was 'playing' these people. How did they know *I* wasn't a murderer? Perhaps you could just tell I wasn't.

"Ask your friend where he lives," Maisy said. "That would be so fun if it's near Pacific Avenue."

Maisy sounded so interested in me. It puzzled me. How did she know she liked me? She was making this vague plan to meet up in a different country... different continent actually and we'd known each other for precisely half an hour. Don't get me wrong, it felt exciting and daring and appealing, but all the while, a tad crazy to talk like that. Maybe I was just a dork who could only pretend to be cool. Isn't that what happens though? You pretend to be cool for so long that it becomes automatic and then you seamlessly transition into being genuinely cool?

"He's right," said Jessica. "We need limes."

"I *will* ask her when I see her tomorrow." I threw in 'her' like a sack of the juiciest limes ever. I saw Maisy's face alter so minutely that only the keenest observer would have detected it. If her expression was verbalized, it would be something like, 'Oh right, so you're not some curious creature which has landed on my lap to play with, but a real person with a life outside this house and a history and friends... some of whom are actually *girls*. That is mildly disappointing and irritating—that you're only a human boy.' It was that phenomenon reoccurring—the state of innocence and dislocation from the real world stripped away in a moment. But she didn't say that. Instead she said,

"Nice one. So yes indeed, limes. No limes. Hmmm. I'll have to use cordial." She picked the tequila bottle up from the table and walked back to the cupboard to reach for the cointreau, saying, "I'll do my thing in the kitchen. Wanna join me Oliver? I can teach you."

The beers had already gone to my head and I became slightly concerned that not only would I topple over if I got up, but that I would lose my mind if I drunk a cocktail.

"You go ahead," I said. "I've got to respond to a text."

"Playing hard to get, eh, Ollie?" Jessica said.

Were they trying to pair me up with Maisy? Why? Thing is, it was amazing that everything was conspiring for me to get it on with Maisy, but even in my tipsy state, it did seem whacky. I ought not to drink any more, I thought. I'd pretend to drink the marguerita but tip it into one of the many plants in the room maybe. I wasn't used to drinking. If I took even a sip, I'd be screwed, I thought—they hadn't asked me to stay the night yet and I wasn't going... or very possibly *couldn't get myself* back to Kathy's. I heard crushed ice clattering and crunching into a jug and thought, 'Oh God, this is it'.

I shouldn't have worried—Maisy brought a tray of four cocktails but in two different types of glasses. *She* had a proper (pink) cocktail glass, but she handed me, then Jessica, then Miles, taller fuller glasses and told us she'd added sparkling water to ours. So, *she* wasn't what *I* thought either. The wild creature turned out to be a big sister who was responsible. Not *that* responsible though, it turned out...

CHAPTER FIFTEEN

Maisy was twenty-one. I know because I looked inside her passport in her bedroom.

I didn't get that drunk on the margueritas with sparkling water, but they certainly loosened me up.

I couldn't believe it when Maisy and I went for it. It's weird how it all works—we spent several hours talking and alternating between being coy to being suggestive, then as soon as Jessica and Miles went to bed, it was all gut-level honesty and straightforward lust that played out.

Jessica started to say a few things that made me realize she was gay, so it didn't seem the worst thing in the world to maybe get off with her sister. Having just met them all hours before and having been invited into their home, I would never have actually made a move on Maisy, but it all seemed to happen naturally. However weak they were, I had downed three margueritas and though I didn't even feel drunk, I was definitely 'something' because I seemed to have zero inhibitions. I didn't feel self-conscious at all and was making Maisy laugh a lot. I don't really know if I was ignoring Miles and Jessica, I mean I didn't actively not pay them attention or anything, but when I look back, I can only remember fully focusing on Maisy. I think that's what you do, though, if you fancy someone. I remember at Kamal's house a few weeks before, talking to him in the kitchen and having a chat to Gopi about my grandparents and all the time being utterly aware of exactly where Jaz was and what she was doing and saying, even how she was standing. It was like I was feigning being present with Kamal and then Gopi but was actually completely elsewhere mentally and emotionally. I did feel bad about that even at the time.

When I opened my eyes in the morning, I experienced that amazing feeling for just a second or two when you don't know where you are—you're just in the present moment and completely and simply yourself; you're so light you hardly exist in time or space because you have no clue where you are or how you got there. If you make an effort, you can actually enjoy it. Except I didn't. It was more or less plain old anxiety that flooded in at high speed.

I couldn't remember exactly what had happened the night before. I knew I had been in Maisy's bedroom, but was now on one of the sofas in the living room—the same one I'd sat on in the evening, facing the other one with the window behind. I had meant to switch my phone off but had forgotten and I had loads of texts. I saw Nathan and Sam had texted, but I didn't catch any other names. I didn't want to think about them or anybody else just then, so I didn't read them. I couldn't help thinking about what might happen with Maisy. I had to accept that I had blown it with Jaz as well as Poppy, so somebody totally new, separate from everybody else, would be perfect. And Maisy... she was more than just somebody separate, she was phenomenal. She was what I've heard people call 'a catch'. A sudden exciting stab in my throat—that's what *she* had said to *me*. That's what Maisy had said about *me*.

My bottom lip drooped down as the events of the night before came back to me. I was lying on Maisy's bed with her and she'd said,

"You're a bit of a catch then aren't you, handsome boy."

She had actually called me that. I'm pretty sure she wasn't being sarcastic. Gobsmacking or what? Me—a 'catch'? A sweet river of possibilities ran from my belly to my head and washed back down all over me. Was *she* the girl for me? She was older, but I could learn from her. A lot of stuff was now coming back to me as I lay on my back, flicking the pink blanket off me and dangling one leg to the floor. I ran my hands through my hair then put them behind my head before sinking back into the pillow. I *had* learnt from her. Yes, I remembered now. I started smiling as I recalled what we'd got up to. I felt older. I felt like I was twenty, not sixteen. Could we be together, Maisy and I? Could I maybe even live in that house? The parents seemed cool. Jessica was great and she hadn't minded me flirting with her sister. But I was getting ahead of myself. I wanted a period, however brief, of being in the here and now, not dwelling on the past *or* the future. I turned my head to the bay window behind the sofa.

Teal and grey to-the-ground curtains hadn't been closed and rays of light splayed through two matching plants which I renoticed either side of the window. I say renoticed because at one point or another, I'd spotted all the plants in the room. 'Blue Rain'. That was the English name for these stunning flowering plants—Aechmea del mar. How was it possible that nature could concoct such a specimen? I couldn't help a smile stretching itself out on my face again. Another smile of sensual pleasure. I properly flung off the scratchy blanket and got up to walk over to the window to closer inspect one of these staggeringly beautiful plants. I slung my bag out of the way, round the side of the sofa.

I had never seen an Aechmea del mar that close up—only at Kew Gardens and on a TV programme during Chelsea Flower Show, but not that close. I had taken a photo from the telly hoping to find an app on my phone that could identify flowers and plants from photos. I had hundreds I needed identifying. A fair few of them I had found out about anyway, including this beauty. The plant is from the Bromeliad family and has purply blue, white and red stripes on its rubbery flower spikes, with bright green glossy leaves. I knelt down and looked at the flowers. Mind-blowing. I might as well have taken a psychedelic drug—it was how I imagined you'd feel if you'd taken some. How life might dance and dazzle in front of you. I touched a flower and felt like crushing it, but not in a weird way, just in the same way that an adult might say, 'Oooh, I could eat him up' about a baby.

I realized I was hidden behind the couch when I heard Jessica's voice crescendoing into the living room and she didn't see me. She was talking to Miles.

"I told you he'd have left. That's our spunky sister, Maisy, scaring him off. At least he obviously slept down here. I thought at one crazy point that they were going to get it together."

I froze. I didn't exactly decide to remain unseen, but I was compelled to stay put so I could hear more. I needed to know what had happened.

"Oh yeah, as if she'd do that," Miles said, "now that she's engaged to Rupert? No, I'd say he's all yours if you want him. In the unlikely event that they did get it on, and Rupert found out, well, I'd forget Ollie because he'll be dead anyway! Ha! No, I reckon he's there for the taking. No question."

"What, so you think I want to ensnare him?"

She must have pushed him or hit him as he said,

"Hey, less of that, thanks. Ensnare? He's not a wild creature, Jessica."

Her response made me double-freeze if there is such a thing.

"That's funny—I *do* see him as something of a wild creature," she said.

"Do I think you've got your sights on him? Let's see..." Miles said. "It's the first time you've ever brought a boy back here apart from that bloke, Max, who turned out to be a douche bag. Correction, he was a douche bag to begin with." I could hear her flinging a cushion at him. "So, I'd say yes, you have the very hots for him. You *have* got his number, I take it?"

"I can easily contact him coz of our Kew Gardens connection. He did say he might have to meet his brothers today. Hope he's not too hungover. I think we corrupted him slightly. How's your head?" she said while collecting glasses from the table. "Mine's throbbing. I can't even remember going to bed."

"Well you still managed to be the perfect host, Jess, setting Ollie up with a pillow and blanket."

I could hear him fumbling the empty pizza boxes into his arms.

"I went up then too and Maisy was getting him a glass of water. Trusty old sis. She made him feel at home all right. Why didn't *you* set yourself up next to him during the evening if you like him that much?"

This was insane. I wanted to be zapped out of the house, zapped into a different realm. I felt like I was hardly breathing now.

"You know me—I'm like a kid," Jessica said. "The more I like someone, the more I play hard to get or even try to put them off me. Come on, let's take these into the kitchen."

As they left the room, Jessica was saying,

"I think I even managed to imply I was a lesbian at one point!" and her brother's response was,

"You're perverse. No wonder you've never had a boyfriend. And you never will at this rate."

I was now in a film. Wearing only my boxer shorts and socks, I crawled along the back of the sofa. Establishing, by listening, that they had definitely left the living room and were now in the kitchen, I got up and walked to the door and leant my back against the wall next to it, like a spy.

"Come on then, you're good at analyzing situations—do you think *he* likes *me*?" Jessica was saying, clinking glasses into the dishwasher.

"Uhhh, he goes to have coffee with you, tick, which is like a date within ten minutes of meeting you, tick." I hear a chair scrape on the wooden floor and Miles asking Jessica to pass him a can of lemonade from the fridge. The can is plonked on the work top as Miles goes on, "He wants to come back to your house so he can spend more time with you, tick. No matter what other plans he had, he wants to stay the night at your house, tick. It's not rocket science..."

My only plans for the future now were how to get out of the house without ever looking at or talking to anyone who lived there ever again. I stopped eavesdropping and slipped into survival mode. 'Make a plan. Clothes on, grab bag, get to the door, run for it,' I thought. First hitch—clothes not in living room. Crap—they were obviously in Maisy's bedroom. I had no choice but to hope the stairs didn't creak, hope Maisy was still sleeping and hope I could get changed, back downstairs and out of the house without being seen. Blood pulsed through me like a fire hose through a narrow corridor. I was afraid it would spurt from my ears.

I speed-crept to the side of the sofa to get my bag, looked on the table to check I had all my stuff and with only a moment's freeze at the living room door, clambered up the stairs on all fours, like a wild creature, bag over my right shoulder. Reaching the landing, oh please no, I had no clue which bedroom was Maisy's. Jessica and Miles were both downstairs, though, so it didn't matter if I went into the wrong rooms initially.

First door half open—saxophone, bed hanging from rope, empty cans of beer. Miles.

Second door, properly closed. I open it. This must be it. Posters of flowers. Trumpet. Model of garden. No. Jessica.

Three more rooms, two of which had doors wide open with light beaming through. No point checking those.

Last bedroom. Duh—actually says MAISY on the door...

Locked.

Please, no.

I'd have to come clean. My breath quickened and my face made a crying expression even though I wasn't crying. I was about to go downstairs and explain everything when, as mental as it sounds, Grandpa jumped into my head and his words about being daring. Within a second, I was knocking on Maisy's door.

No answer.

Was she zonked out by the alcohol? I knocked again a little louder.

No answer.

Too hard to believe.

I have to knock even louder, and this time have to call her name.

Too late. I hear Miles' voice at the bottom of the stairs,

"Hey, is that you Ollie?" He sounded thrilled. That wasn't to last for long.

"Yes... I need... I've been to the toilet and... and I was wondering if I could have a shower. I heard you both downstairs, so I'm knocking at Maisy's door to ask for a towel."

I don't even know why I'd said that. I was biding time. All I needed now was for Maisy to come to the door, I could whisper and gesticulate madly and she could throw my clothes to me.

It wasn't to be.

Miles spoke back to me. He said three words, but it sounded like one long evil cursed sentence,

"Maisysatwork."

He even said it a second time,

"Maisy's at work."

Then he gave me a ten-minute gift—

"Use one of the towels in the airing cupboard, next to the bathroom," he said.

"Oh, cheers, Miles." It was getting too weird calling from the landing without showing my face, so I poked my head over the banister to say hi. He told me he and Jessica had thought that I had left and how great it was that I was still there and how it was a fine day and how we could all put coats on and have breakfast on the patio at the back. Yeah, right.

"Nice one," I said as I walked backwards to lean on the nearest wall. My bare back slid down it so that I was sitting on the beige carpet. I stared forwards through the bannister bars, my arms balanced on my bent knees.

"See you in ten," were Miles' last civil words to me. First my elbows propped themselves on my knees, so I could drop my head into my hands, then my head dropped to my knees. Emotion library lady—'Sit down and try to hold onto something with this one; the pain can knock you backwards and the fear can knock you forwards. Imagine you're on a see-saw with a devil. How he will harness all his might to jolt you off balance. You'll crash if you're not strong enough.'

I didn't move. I stayed there, my eyes giving way and my shoulders shaking till Jessica came up to find me.

"Ollie, what's happened? Are you okay? Have you had bad news?"

I didn't look up. "Can I talk to Miles, please, Jessica?"

I told him everything, but not that I'd been spying on them from behind the sofa. I couldn't say I knew about the engagement, but I told him what had happened between Maisy and me. He changed towards me. He went to his room, came back and threw some clothes at me as I sat, still bent and crooked and broken, on the carpet.

I decided I was not really worthy of speaking to him after that, so I didn't even say thank you. Before he went back downstairs, he said,

"Just get out. Get out as soon as you're dressed, you scumbag piece of shit."

I was about to drag myself up when he said his second last words to me from the top stair—

"Jessica said you were 'troubled'. Some tragic past, is it? Well, spiral your troubled ass into a hole, well away from my sisters and this house."

When I shook my way into the clothes and shook my bag onto my shoulder and down the stairs, this time clinging to the hand rail, like a very tame and frail old man, I opened the door. The light and the water blinded me. And there were more words—Miles' last ones.

"Your clothes were behind the sofa. Here." He threw a plastic carrier bag at my back. I turned and caught his eye. He sort of half sniff-laughed and said, "Get out of my clothes and put your rags on. You really are tragic, aren't you?"

At least he hadn't physically attacked me. That was something for which I was grateful. I had managed to avoid being beaten up. Up until that point in my life anyway...

CHAPTER SIXTEEN

Miles had left me at the door and slammed the kitchen door. There was no way I was hanging round changing clothes.

An extra change of clothes was some comfort to me. Plus, I had all my money. I had to face facts and move on. I wanted to go somewhere nobody would find me. I headed to Richmond station in a daze. You could get either an underground train (even though it wasn't underground in that section of the network) or a normal train from there, so I had plenty of options. I decided on the underground, otherwise known as the tube and got off at the first stop, which was Kew. I was parched, so decided to go and get a drink from one of the shops outside the station.

I checked my phone and it was just after 10am. Perhaps I'd see the woman getting her paper. Perhaps she could help me even more than she had the day before. Or perhaps it was another unusual day for her. Perhaps it was an unusual day all round.

It wasn't to be. I never saw her again.

I got on the next tube into London and looked up the engineer François something who devised the pioneering method of using reinforced concrete in structures such as bridges. Hennebique was his surname it turned out to be. François Hennebique. He had certainly achieved something, and it said he'd had 'a hard life' and was self-taught. I wanted to find out more about him. I wanted to tell the lady that I had genuinely been interested in what she was telling me, that I had looked it up, that I wasn't a good-for-nothing liar and cheat.

Bits of the Richmond episode played back in my mind. I had so enjoyed myself during most of it and yet I'd remember it as one of the worst nights of my life. Opposites together again. This universe 'working for you' had gone more than slightly off course. Unless it was overall for my good? I mustn't have been pure enough in my longings... or maybe the whole thing was a load of shit. I looked up 'The Kiss' and several people looked at me when I said, "Oh, yeah," out loud when I found the artist's name, Gustav Klimt. I was interested to look at more of his paintings—all the plants and flowers and trees in his work. Kamal would think it was namby pamby nonsense. He only liked massive landscape stuff, battles and serious old portraits. I remembered going to The Tate Britain art gallery with Kamal on our school trip. I'd go back there, I decided. I wondered if I'd see any Klimt trees there... I wondered if I'd ever see Kamal again. I'd had a text from him... and Jaz... and Poppy. And a missed call from Grandpa (I'd ring him later). The unanswered messages were mounting up, but I didn't want to read them. Not reading them was a crucial element in the success of my escape. I mean my escape from them, from 'the situation'. That world. My old world. Everything.

There was that lovely park at the back of the Tate Britain building, where I'd met Thomas Diamond the year before, the homeless man who helped me when I got lost, well ran away really. I could go there. I wouldn't be seeing him this time for sure—he had died. I knew this because a card I gave him with a seascape by John Brett was found in his pocket; I had written my address on the back of it, so he had contacted me from hospital when he was very ill. I say 'he' had contacted me, but someone else wrote for him (I don't think he could write at all). He wrote me the nicest letter I've ever received. He would be disappointed to know I was running away again, so although I'd have truly loved to have surprised him, I was relieved he was dead. I felt bad for thinking that and imagined I'd somehow got it wrong and would actually meet him—"It's me, Thomas! Oliver. Oliver Campbell. Oliver Timothy Campbell!" "It's never you, little feller, is it?! Come 'ere ya daft sod!" and I would have felt his frail boniness under his cardboard coat again as I went to hug him, but I would have been so elated to see him that it would have felt like holding jillions of precious jewels in raw silk. I never found out what had happened to him, you know, how he'd ended up on the streets. I do know that he would think I'd been mostly very lucky indeed, the cards that I'd been dealt. It made me appreciate having Grandpa and Grandma and guilty for being unfair to the folk who *were* alive. I needed to ring them.

Before switching to the Victoria line to get to Pimlico where the Tate Art Gallery stood, watching over the River Thames, I did one of those meditations on the universe to wish Thomas Diamond was still alive. I didn't have much time before my stop, so I don't think I did it long enough—like for about forty seconds I think.

Once at Pimlico station, I called home and Grandma answered. I did that thing they do on films where they make a funny noise and say, "You're breaking up" then hang up. I told Grandma I was fine and was still staying with friends. All I remember her saying was, "You're making your grandpa ill." Those words still haunt me today.

'Poor Man's Picture Gallery', the room was called. I figured I would soon be very poor myself and wanted to see and feel what that might be like. I felt like I was signing up for the army that day except more like signing up for Poverty Duty. I pretended to myself that it was a normal thing to do and that it was an expected part of life in Britain that you had to go off and have nothing for let's say a year, so you could learn the value of having stuff. The value of *not* having stuff. You could learn how to love people instead of how to kill them. I did personally already feel sorry for people living on the streets, but maybe other people need first-hand experience to feel empathy so I would accept my year's 'service'. And maybe poor people would have to have a year's service of Rich Duty. Not quite sure what that would entail or teach.

Kamal would have said I was being an idealistic idiot—I mean the bit I said about learning to love, not to kill. We did once talk about it (war) when we were studying the First World War in History. I had said, "Those poor boys joining up to fight in the war, thinking it was going to be fun. They started calling it The Great War before it had even begun. I prefer The Great Lie." Kamal told me not to be naïve and that no one denied the vast human tragedy of it all but that it resulted in freedom. He dragged out the old, 'We'd all be speaking German if...''

Our teacher projected an advert onto the board at the front of the class, encouraging people to enlist —'Come and travel to pastures new, learn new skills, meet people your own age, get fit, enjoy the great outdoors!' We had to invent alternative posters. It was one of the few times I had to stand up and read aloud to the class (I hated doing that). Mine got chosen and read, 'Make death your constant companion! Enjoy rat-infested mud, have a good ol' lice-itch, feel the fungus on your feet, excite your nasal passages with the sweet odours of dried sweat, stagnant mud, overflowing latrines and your mate's rotting flesh exploded in front of your very eyes!'

The rest of the lesson was cool. Some of us had to pretend we were 'conscientious objectors', CO's, which meant you refused to go to war for moral or religious reasons and we had to write a sentence expressing our stance. Kamal was asked to read his and in true flamboyant style, he went to the front of the classroom and stood on the teacher's chair (he didn't bat an eyelid—the teacher). Everyone laughed till Kamal said, "Shhh!" and waited a few moments after the space had already fallen silent. His line was, "I'm a person in a play of peace, not a twirler in a dance of war." And everybody cheered. He had to be coaxed down from the chair. Then someone shouted, "Conchie coward!" and so the roleplay went on. "Am I a coward to leave my wife and family, like the soldiers do, and wilt in prison like they don't? Or even be sentenced to death? Am I a coward because of my principles? It is to Britain's credit that I am permitted to exercise my right not to kill another human being."

"Your stupid fault if you go to prison! Be brave and fight for freedom!" Alex Beaumont cried. Some people clapped and shouted. The teacher, Mr. Courtney, loosened his tie and nodded his head. He seemed to like this and made a 'Go on, go on...' hand gesture. "Is it brave to bow to bullies?" Kamal said. "This war is for land not people—capitalists who seek wealth and global domination. No glory in war! Nought about the people, all about the pocket!" And he did actually say, "nought". Then this hilarious thing happened where a group of us started chanting, "Nought about the people! All about the pocket! Nought about the people! All about the pocket!" and Matthew Murray got up and started stamping his feet, so the rest of us joined in. You could see Mr Courtney's face spasming in ecstasy and fear.

One of the deputy heads was passing the room. He pressed his deeply lined forehead to the glass in the classroom door to gain a proper view, then opened the door with such vigour that the teacher's papers gusted into the air, swirling and landing, like leaflets from a biplane. Lizzy Smith grabbed a sheet of paper and waved it, hollering, "Read all about it! Read all about it! Conscientious Kamal causes chaos!" Then everyone howled and the chant became more intense with most of the class joining in, "Nought about the people! All about the pocket!"

It wasn't till Dead Man Walking, the deputy head, slammed a hardback book onto the teacher's desk that we all shut up. The tome was no doubt one of his easy reads. Maybe *The Anatomy of Fascism* or such like. By this time, a few pupils had wrapped their ties round their heads and made caps out of tee shirts à la Che Guevara.

"What a vile racket!" he said. "You should be ashamed of yourselves. In front of your new teacher, too. You're acting like hooligans."

"We *were* acting, sir," Becky Bailey said. There was a stretched-out moment, before he said,

"Is that right?" while looking at the teacher. "Is this part of your lesson?" He took the silence as a yes, shaking his head and stretching his eyes in disbelief. "Would you like to share that with the class?" he directed to Kamal who had just whispered something to me. Darren Cragley said, "I heard him, sir. He said, 'Why don't you slip into something more comfortable, like a coma.'" The class were out of control again and Darren made swaggering movements like it had been *his* joke.

"You'll all stay in over break. None of you will leave this room, do you hear?" Ah, that was the man we'd come to know and love—impeccable sense of justice.

Anyway, what with the war lesson flashback, I thought maybe I should find some horrible battle paintings or dead soldiers or something after the Poor Man's Picture Gallery, just for Kamal's sake, so I could tell him about them, if I were ever to see him again that was.

It turned out that the gallery wasn't at all what I thought—it wasn't full of work depicting poverty. I think the 'poor man's picture' part referred to these special pairs of photos, one taken from a slightly different angle from the other, which would allow a 'poor man' to see a picture/a painting in depth that he wouldn't normally have been able to see at all. In fact, the subtitle of the room was, 'Victorian Art and Stereoscopic Photography' because the exhibition was of paintings and matching stereoscopic pictures. When you look at the little pair of pictures through a stereoscope (binocular things), you could see the painting in 3D because your eyes do their magic of seeing the two separate images and merging them. A man I met in the gallery (more about him in a second...) told me that the process, in terms of science, is exactly the same as seeing 3D movies except in those days, there was no TV or movies, so that these stereoscopic photographs were amazing and 'before their time'. To be honest, they were still amazing because you felt like you were in the painting itself when you looked through and the people seemed real, like you could shake their hands or throw them a ball.

When I entered the room, I wanted to look like I knew what I was doing, so I copied the first person I saw and went to look through my first stereoscope. I had to jump back. There was a boy lying down on a bed, but I felt like I was standing in front of him and it looked like he needed help. I couldn't do anything, so I didn't want to be in the room with him. I hadn't yet seen the actual full-size proper painting which was in the same room on the wall somewhere, so I scanned the room to look for it and there it was. Nobody in front of it, I took my position about four feet before it. It was a mind-blowing painting. It was like light shone through from behind it. My eyes were drawn in through an arched top-of-frame to a tiny attic room, a window in the background, looking out onto London. You could even see a tiny church at the bottom of the window on the right—I mean it looked tiny, but it was a long way away, so it was probably huge. It could have been the famous St Paul's Cathedral, built by the brilliant architect, Sir Christopher Wren. You know I've been on about listed buildings a bit? Well that cathedral should have its own number, like not Grade I-listed but Grade IA* or something. The main focal point of the work was this boy. He looked very ill and was lying face up on a bed with his right arm dangling down the side. I wanted to know who he was, what was wrong. I took a step forward and read the plaque—'Chatterton' by Henry Wallis.

I took a step back to my spot saying to myself, 'Chatterton. Was that the boy's name then?'

"Ooh careful!" said a lady with two teenagers who I'd bumped into. They had taken my spot, so I moved forward again and to the left so as not to mar their view.

"Who was *he* then, Mum? Come on, you're the expert on nineteenth century art," the girl said. This brightly dressed, brightly expressioned woman was keen as mustard to divulge what she knew of this painting.

"Thomas Chatterton. Can you see the bottle on the ground? That's how he killed himself." The two young people made suitable gasping sounds.

"It was arsenic. Poison."

What a dork I was, not even realizing that he was... dead. My mouth opened to turn and ask why he'd—

"Why did he commit suicide?" the son asked, looking less curious and more really quite shocked and sad. I empathized with him.

"He was a writer. A misunderstood poet. He had a hard life, an unlucky life I should say."

We all took in what she said and waited patiently for the next bit.

"He was clever and wrote poetry at a very young age. He didn't fit in where he lived in Bristol."

"Bristol's a totally cool place to live," said the son.

"Well it wasn't then." She put her arm round her son and pulled him to her, the boy nearly toppling over but unfazed. You could tell they were close, this mother and son. What a heart-warming sight to behold.

"It was a noisy smelly industrial port. People didn't believe Chatterton's poetry was his own at first, so he wrote them out on old parchment paper in self-taught script and made out he'd discovered a mediaeval poet."

The boy flicked his head up to look at his mother, surprised and intrigued at what he'd heard.

"He headed off to London to seek fulfilment but could only afford a garret room and barely had enough to eat."

"So, didn't he make money from the poetry?" the girl said.

"Very little." The mother now pulled her daughter in too. It was like they'd finally got to see a portrait of a cherished but deceased family member, not a strange forgotten boy.

"He did work. His writing was eventually taken seriously, but he was exploited really. And he wouldn't have complained because though he was moody, he was introvert."

"So he was doing what he wanted to do," the girl said, "but did he make friends?"

"No, he was very much alone," the mum said.

I gazed upon Thomas' face, drained of dreams as it was.

"So why was he so depressed?" the son asked. He pulled away from his mother then.

"He'd suffered. School life didn't suit him at all—no one recognized his talent either. He was found out too and was known as a forger."

The girl moved forward next to me and, wagging her finger and said, "You shouldn't have killed yourself. You should have waited it out." The brother said to his sister, "You really are tragic."

"He's the one who's tragic," she said.

"Well, romantics like the idea of a tragic tortured artist," the mother said, adjusting a burgundy coloured scarf thing she had wrapped around her head (a choob, maybe??)

"That's why this painting caught the imagination of creative types. They're probably all misunderstood. There's a chance that his death was accidental, too, but that doesn't have the same kudos, does it?" She picked up a multi-coloured cloth bag she'd put on the floor earlier and slipped it onto her right shoulder. "Come on, we need to be going."

I wanted to ask the woman a question since she seemed to know a lot about this boy, Thomas Chatterton. I wanted to ask how old he was, but that word 'tragic' stuck in my throat. The morning's antics smacked into me like a freak wave and dragged me under so that I needed to get myself to a seat.

I sat on the bench and looked up at 'Chatterton'. I stared at it for a long while before going to look at the stereoscope of it again which was in a well-designed wooden unit in the centre of the room, in which all twelve stereoscopic 'scenes' were installed. My eyes pressed up against the rims that you could easily pull out to the position you desired.

I was in the room with Thomas. I imagined talking to him: 'What do you go and do that for, Tommy, mate? I'll come and shake you. Perhaps you're still alive. And you shouldn't have ripped up all that poetry. I'll pick it all up for you and glue it back together. We can get through this. Look, your plant's doing okay. A single rose is it, hanging on? A fairy rose—pink Polyanthus? I see you couldn't afford any more candles, but you've watered your plant. Good lad. I'll take it and look after it for you. So much more blooming to do. So much more blooming.' This time I pulled away slowly and the strain on my eyes was too much.

"Everything all right, young man?"

The day was getting more and more unusual as time went on. This is going to come as something of a surprise to you, but it was only Brian May from Queen! No, I'm not kidding, it 100% was Brian May, the guitarist from a well-famous band you may or may not have heard of called Queen. I snapped out of my mood. I was living in a parallel universe and had no clue what was coming out of my mouth.

"I've lost my bag," were the words that snaked into the room.

"It'll do that to you," Brian May (I know, it sounds mental) said. He'd noticed I was a bit sad. "Your bag's there, by the bench. That's why I came up to you."

I rubbed my hands over my face and swept them through my hair.

"Thank you. My dad loves your music."

Blood and sand, why had I said that? He was just a person. I didn't want him to think he was defined by his music. 'Here we go, another 'fan', another person who loves something they don't understand.' But I know Dad would have gone loopsville if I hadn't mentioned him and that he used to be in the fan club. Not that I went as far as telling him that. In fact, partly why I always wanted to play the drums was because I loved Roger

Meadows-Taylor, Queen's drummer, but I definitely wasn't going to tell him *that*! I needed to add something quickly.

"It's a brilliant idea, this gallery, isn't it? And the pictures make you feel like the people are real. It's the first time I've walked into a painting, for sure, even though I've tried." I managed a small laugh. "That's not true come to think of it. I did once walk into one of my mam's paintings she'd left leaning on the kitchen table." Good God, was there no stopping me? But, guess what? He laughed!

"Well thank you. I don't know if you're aware that it's my exhibition. It's exciting to me, especially seeing young folk like you enjoying it."

"Oh, sorry. I mean thank *you* then. Good. Thank you, Brian."

This day was off its head.

He said to me,

"Would you mind saying what you just said on camera? We're doing a little vox pop today, getting some feedback to use for promotion."

Okay, I know you're dying to know if you didn't already—vox pop is short for vox populis, which is Latin for 'voice of the people'. Incredible stuff this Latin, eh? (sorry, what did you say? I can't hear you—probably just as well...).

I did that thing you see in films where the person's face is motionless apart from the eyes looking to the right then back—one, two—while the mind's thinking, 'Okaaaaaaay...?'

"Oh, really? Sure. I mean yes. Yes, definitely." I gathered myself together and before I knew it, Brian May (you heard right again) had this camera bloke and a man with a boom microphone ushering me back to Henry Wallis' painting. A moment before the filming started, the cameraman said,

"He was around your age—only seventeen."

So, the beginning of the film was my genuine reaction to this new information. From nowhere came the idea, "He was a martyr to society." Then, "He was lost, this seventeen-year-old boy called Thomas. Even though he must have been loved, he felt lost. You feel Henry Wallis, the painter, is perhaps criticizing the treatment of artists..."

Brian May had walked up and nodded with his thumbs up as if to say, 'carry on'.

"Thomas was only seventeen, but he was misunderstood and exploited. He did enjoy some commercial success but was terribly paid. And he was a creative genius type anyway, so it probably mattered more to him to affect people, to change the world, than to make money. But he was unknown. It is not hard to see how he was driven to going loopy and destroying himself."

I was shimmied back to the wooden cabinet in which the stereoscopic image of the same painting was fixed. With no words, Brian May let me know he wanted some verbal feedback on the binocular vision side of things. I obliged and took another look through at the stereoscopic photographs.

"The stereoscopic image brings you bang into the emotional heart of the scene." I said. I felt like a dead art critic was chanelling through me. "You can almost smell the snaking smoke from the candle and you feel that if you blew, the wisps of paper-words torn from his heart to the floor would fill the room like jagged snow. His candle burned out long before his legend ever will... in the words of Elton John. And you feel it all here when you look at this miraculous stereoscope."

When they 'cut' the filming I threw my hands to my head—"Oh my God, cheesey or what? Can't believe I said that. Candle burned out long before—"

"Hey, no, mate, well done. That's just what we wanted," Brian said. "Don't be afraid to speak from your heart, what's your name?"

"Ollie."

"Don't hold back with your self-expression, Ollie." He was so cool. He scratched his head and folded his arms. "We're all experimenting. Nothing's wrong or right."

"Easy for you to say. I mean... I'm sorry. Are you still experimenting? You've fulfilled your dreams, haven't you?" I said. He now started rubbing his chin.

"I very often think, 'Is what I'm doing really worth anything?' or 'What's my motivation?" I screwed my eyes up.

"It's weird *you* saying that."

"Why?"

He sort of crossed his legs even though he was standing up, one white trainer over the other and tilted his head. His hair, like a lawyer's wig on acid, framed the painting which was his famous face.

"When you said about experimenting," I said, "did you mean your dreams never end?" He smiled really an incredibly sweet innocent smile for a man of his skill and experience, saying,

"Yeah. Carry on dreaming."

"Isn't that one of those saucy films they made in Ealing Studios in the seventies?"

"Very possibly," he said, his innocent smile turning into a dirty laugh. "Actually no, I don't think they went down the abstract road with that series. Listen, thanks, Ollie, and if you leave your email address and mobile number with Suzanne over there, we'll send you a link to your interview."

"Oh right, thank you very much. Thanks."

I looked across to where he'd pointed and saw Suzanne sitting on a chair near the entrance with a clip-board. I looked back and as I bent down to pick up my bag, I noticed Brian wore grey suit trousers with his trainers. I liked the look of opposites. All the best things seemed to be full of opposites, I was thinking. Then that Universe thing clicked in and he said,

"You loved that painting, didn't you?"

I knew he wasn't expecting or didn't require an answer. He carried on,

"I do too. Resonates with me actually. There's not much of a jump from despair to prolonged creativity and success, you know." With intelligence in his eyes, he checked to see if I was 'getting' what he was saying, if I was interested.

"That's what I should have said earlier," he said. "Just gotta keep your head down and your eyes up, you know. And questioning everything, questioning yourself is good. We don't have to understand, do we?"

He didn't want an answer to that either but I couldn't stop myself micro-nodding. He finished with,

"Good luck, mate."

And he gave me a high five. Thing is, I wasn't star-struck in the least. I had the sense that day more than any I can remember, of us being connected. All of us. All relentlessly teasing out the same knot.

JASVANDI'S JOURNAL 4

Dear Journal,

Damn and blast.

Why do you always want stuff more when you can't have it? Ollie's playing hard to get now and I find myself thinking about him more than ever. He hasn't even returned my text. I used to get a reply within seconds. I'm bummed he hasn't replied because it was quite a big deal for me, begging him to come to the states. Okay journal, I know it's whack, but I changed my mind. A person's allowed to do that, right?

It's not like everything's changed. I mean you know I don't do relationships, but I find the guy intriguing. I hope we get it on again. I mean I'm pretty sure he would want that.

Shall I send him another text? He obviously needs me to make it clearer how much I want him to come out to LA.

I was hoping we could all meet up in London, but that never happened. It worked out pretty well, though, because I so enjoyed my trip to The Tate Britain Art Gallery. I went on a 'Women Artists' tour, which took twenty minutes. That says it all right there! I feel like crying with frustration when I think of all the superb talented women who have been ignored through history. There must be like heaps and heaps of beautiful art work rotting in lofts that no one ever got to enjoy. Hey, even the female artists who were successful didn't get enough exposure. I've heard of the artist Augustus John, but did you know he had a sister, Gwen John, who was equally gifted? Of course, she struggled for recognition. I read a bit about her and she was part of a group known as 'Bohemians' who lived experimental lifestyles. Imagine that, journal? All those intellectual painters and musicians and writers hanging out, not following convention, not giving a shit about disapproval? I reckon that movie, *Moulin Rouge* is about

Bohemian lifestyles. That was set in Paris, yeah? Oh, how I yearn to go to Paris.

It's lame, but I also yearn to get back to LA. I must follow up that job. I need to persuade them that I could do it without having to take phone calls. You know I still struggle on the phone. Amazing that they literally didn't believe me that I can't hear on the phone as I speak so well! I told them that it's partly because I already had learnt speech before I lost my hearing, but they couldn't seem to get it. Hey, if I can't get work, I'll become a Bohemian! Kamal, Ollie and Poppy could form a new group with me.

No but seriously, I need to get back because I've decided to take up that offer of counselling so I can work out how I'm going to prosecute that guy. You know who I mean. Aunt Gopi made me revisit it all and I got to think real hard about it. I've decided I'm not going to let him get away with it. Am I crazy, choosing to put myself through whatever the hell it will be?? I never ever use deafness as an advantage. Well, I guess I do sometimes pretend not to hear! But I mean this is like so serious. Maybe it could work in my favor that folk feel sorry for the disabled. Not that I think I'm disabled, but lookit, you know what I mean, right?

That evil bastard raped a twelve-year-old deaf girl.

That's the first time I've written that. I mean written that word out like that. I don't believe it myself when I read it back. Okay, I need to drop this for today.

Now then, do I text Ollie again or not? I know, I'll text Nathan to see what they're all up to. I already tried Poppy. She's heard nothing.

Pray for me and pray for Ollie, dear Journal.

CHAPTER SEVENTEEN

I couldn't face battle scenes after the drama in the Poor Man's Picture Room, so I went to the gallery shop to buy a postcard of Chatterton, paid at the till, then stood at the exit. I realized I had no clue where I was going next.

I knew I had to look at my unread texts before too long, so I decided to go to the side entrance of the Tate and walk down Atterbury Street to the park behind the gallery. I reached in my backpack for my sunglasses—don't ask me how I'd thought to pack sunglasses when I hadn't even packed a change of socks. It wasn't sunny, but I felt like disguising myself. By the way, I know I did have a pair of extra socks now from Miles.

As I walked down, I glanced to the left at Chelsea Art College except I could see a sign saying University of the Arts London (UAL), so it must have changed its name. Seemed like every educational establishment was called a 'university' now. Does that mean they're all the same, or are some still better than others? You can't tell. Well, I suppose you could if you read up on them all, but they don't make it easy for you.

I remembered my heart pounding when I'd come this way the year before, attempting to run away, the school coach waiting for me at the front of the gallery on Millbank, Thomas Diamond, the homeless man I'd met in the park, taking me back to it—"They ain't gonna leave a feller like you, is they?" Last time, I saw students sitting on the grass rug in the centre of the bleak-looking college square, but now a massive piece of art (I nearly said something else instead of 'art' then! Not that the art was rubbish) took up all the room on the 'rug'. It was a giant sculpture. I stopped to check it out. No rush this time. The opposite. I crossed Atterbury Street to take a closer look. I pulled my bag off my back. It looked like a gigantic bent rusty comb (the sculpture, not my bag). I took a photo, slipped the phone into my pocket, then leaned on the low glass and metal barrier with my hands, wondering how the heck you could make something that big and if it was the very bigness of it which made it good. I imagined the exact same work done in miniature and crowds of people with binoculars and magnifying glasses surrounding it. The exact same form, but tiny. The same concept of the contrasting curves and iron prongs, the same motivation to construct it, but tiny. I suppose size is often equated with worth. Nature-built stuff as well as manmade stuff. 'Check out the size of my sunflower,' 'Cor, that's some yacht you've got.' People who couldn't get the funds for huge sculptures could make tiny ones, take two similar photos of it, then get Brian May to set up a stereoscopic sculpture gallery.

I felt like going in and having a good feel of it. That was an advantage of being big—more to feel. Instead, I crossed back over and down to the end of the Tate building and went to see, well to touch in fact, the statue of John Everett Millais, hiding behind the building. The last time I was there, I had imagined that he too was escaping something. I mean you normally find statues with loads of space around them like the comb one, so you can admire them from afar and walk around them leaving a good distance, checking it out from different angles. This time he looked like he just fancied getting away from it all for a while so he could paint in peace. Part of the sculpture was a stool behind him. I wondered if he took a sneaky rest when no one was looking in the dead of night. I might even find out if I decided to stay in the park all night. I didn't know where else I was supposed to go. How were you supposed to actually sleep on a hard bench? The grass would be better I supposed, but what if it rained?

And then how would you get dry? These must be every day questions for people who are homeless. I'd have to sit up on Millais' stool and dry off in the wind rushing and swirling round the corner of the Tate. I could close my eyes and imagine I was on a ship sailing to undiscovered lands. I would have plenty time to tell John about everything (I couldn't call him 'Millais' if he was my friend, just like I wouldn't want him calling me 'Campbell'). I could tell him about Lily. I could show him my photo and he could paint her, I thought. Then I could take it to Brian on our return and I could be in a room with her again. He could maybe paint her with her hand out and I could reach in and hold it or pass her a rose.

I had a photo of me with the statue already—Thomas had taken it— but I took another now, with a view to building up a series—one every year for X number of years perhaps. I looked like a nutter on the photo because I had to take it from below to get both John and me in.

I crossed over John Islip Street and walked alongside the park railings. I came to a little green wrought iron gate and saw the wooden sign—'Mill-bank Gardens'. The park was so much more beautiful than I had remembered, situated behind The Tate Britain Art Gallery, tucked away in this secret pocket of Pimlico, one of the many quarters of London. The square comprised three small lawns and an area of paving surrounding each one. I was glad to see that they had built attractive wheelchair ramps too. The paths were lined with wooden benches, one of which I would soon be 'moving in to' well, commandeering.

In many ways it was an idyllic place to be, to stay in. If it was the last place you ever saw, I thought, you'd be lucky. I'd really have to hide in the bushes if I decided to stay, though. I might not be safe in the open air on a bench all night.

I settled on a bench in front of a Rowan Tree. The diversity of plant species surprised me; beech trees, holly bushes, and more exotic planting like bamboo and even palm trees punctuated the park.

Once seated, I saw a man with a book sitting across from me, eating a sandwich. I realized I hadn't eaten anything yet. I took a swig of my water, wanting more than a swig, but needing to ration my supplies. I took my phone out of my pocket. Battery was 90%. I had thought it would be running low, so was puzzled. How could it have retained so much charge? It only took a few moments before the name Maisy came to mind. "I plugged your phone into my charger," she'd said to me as I sat on her bed with her the night before, the night before a mountain of possibilities came thundering down, like tombstone rocks. "You put it on my dresser right next to the charger, so I did you a favour. If you're anything like my bro, your phone's always dying."

"I hope it has long enough to fully charge up," I'd said. She pushed me, moved in to kiss me, then said, "Depends how long you want to stay in my room…"

Wow, she was a good kisser. I never really knew what that meant. I mean how far wrong can you go? Wasn't it something you just got on with? 'She's a good coffee-drinker.' 'He's a good shoe-lacer.' But of course, you couldn't do it on your own, so practice could be incredibly limited. Come to think of it, it was about two separate people doing something their own way, so the combinations could be endless—a whole spectrum from ecstasy to crushing letdown. Yes, on second thoughts, the experience must vary enormously. Kamal had been more than disappointed at *his* first kiss—he'd said, "Put it this way, had I practised solely on dried out, half-rotten squid rings, more pleasure there would I have gleaned than from the offending embrace." Of course, he had to say it using some strange Shakespearean format, and he did say he probably hadn't committed 100% to the snog, but it dampened any hope I had that a kiss could ever be deeply sensual. I now knew otherwise.

I didn't want to look like a loon, sitting on a park bench staring into space, so I made sure I was looking at my phone, well looking *through* it.

A cool breeze swept through my new station. The lullaby of leaves tranced me through my daydream.

Maisy again. Even before she kissed me, her eyes stared hard into mine, and when she brushed the back of her hand down my cheek, her silver ring drawing lust on me, the funny breathing came back.

"As long as you want," I said, "I can pencil you in for all night."

The only light in the room was through a dim tassled orange lamp on her bedside table, so that when she smiled, slowly dragged her tee shirt over her head and pushed me back into a cocoon of satin and velvet cushions, strands of light flickered and danced on her skin, arching over white silk.

Yeah, we'd been drinking, and the moment enveloped me with exquisite intensity, but it wasn't long before I switched from fully fired up mode to too-raw-in-the-moment mode. Self-consciousness visited suddenly. How was I going to get my shirt off now that I was lying down? I would keep it on. The silence was too loud. I had to say something, so I said, "I'm only 75% charged." What a wazzock. I sounded like a corny romantic novel, but the situation was too scary for me not to be funny, if that makes any sense.

She whispered, "We'll have to do something about that," and just as I was visualizing her kicking off her loose high tops, slithering out of her already-undone shorts and crawling toward me in a mystical slink, I jolted back to my senses, feeling rubbing and nudging at my ankles. My delicious reverie was cut dead by a dog who'd come up to the park bench nuzzling at my legs.

Its owner wasn't far behind and told me I was on '*his* bench'. He was scrawny with dirt rubbed into his pointy face and his hair was strands raked from a hundred-year-old carpet stuck on his head with cheap glue. It was hard to tell where his fingerless woollen gloves stopped and his hands began. He wore cardboard trousers of unidentifiable colour and tough battered boots with the laces undone. He could have been a character from a Dickens novel if it hadn't been for the green hooded top and yellow (at some point) smiley face tee shirt underneath (not that I had actually read many novels by Charles dickens, by the way, only *A Christmas Carol* and *David Copperfield* at school, but I'd seen TV versions of *Oliver Twist* and *Great Expectations*).

"Oh, is that your name on the back?' I said, pointing to the dedication plaque on the bench.

"Aye, I'm dead. That's how come folk don't see me."

I marvelled at his poetry. This guy had stuff to say, for sure. How did he end up like that?

"Do you mind if I sit on the end?" I said.

"Haven't ye got a home te go te?"

I could tell from his accent that he was from Scotland. I loved the Scottish accent. Perhaps because Newcastle-upon-Tyne is so near to Scotland.

"No. I mean, yes. It's complicated."

"Ya story's as complicated as ye make it. Ye can get it down te a few words if ye try. That's mine."

He showed me a square of cardboard with writing on it: 'It started when I was ten. He raped me regular. One day I had enough. Ma chose him.'

"Pretty depressing poem," I said.

"S'not a poem."

"'Tis," I said.

"S'not."

"'Tis sort of if you don't mind me saying."

"Ye reckon?"

"Aye."

"Ye Scottish too?"

"No, but I love the accent," I said and told him that I was from Newcastle-upon-Tyne which I suggested was nearly in Scotland, but he said there was no such thing as nearly anywhere. It was only at that point that

I shimmied along the bench and he sat next to me, wheeling his suitcase round to the end of the bench nearest him. His dog curled up by his feet. The gorgeous golden-haired dog was such a contrast to its owner. He wanted a good life for his posh-looking hound. Made me think of poor mothers going hungry so their kids could eat. 'He must even buy shampoo for the dog,' I thought, the coat was so lush and shiny. Funny because usually dogs with homeless folk look as scruffy and scrawny and undernourished as they did. He asked me how old I was and what I was doing there, but I was more interested in *him*.

He told me more than I'd wanted to know. He was called Andrew and his story was stunning in the worst possible way. I thought I'd have to make something up to compete with his, but his retelling (God knows how many times he'd been over the gory details) had sent him into an instant bout of mini depression and he no longer wanted to know me. He told me I could share the bench for the night. I did. I was glad not to be alone. With the help of half a bottle of whiskey (yes, you heard right). I had given the money to Andrew to get it—I hasten to add that it had not been my first choice of beverage. I'm not sure I'd have slept at all without it, though. In fact, I suppose you could say I even 'slept in'.

Andrew and his dog had gone by the time I'd woken up. I'd wanted to give him some money. It occurred to me at that moment that I shouldn't have all my dosh in one wad, so I decided to gather my things and go to the loo in The Tate to rearrange it. Once there, I came up with about ten separate places in which to stash my notes: left sock, right sock, right front jeans pocket, zipped back section of bag, inside of Kew Gardens leaflet etc.

I was going to head to Soho and wander around, but I went through Millbank Gardens again first in case Andrew had reappeared. I spotted a skinny guy with dreadlocks who looked like he spent a lot of time there, so

I approached him. He sat on a different bench, smoking a rollie. He had long hair, but only a bit of a beard – didn't look like he ever shaved though, so the hair on his chin must have decided to play ball and stop growing. He was called Mitch and knew who Andrew was. He told me that Andrew often wandered off and sometimes didn't come back for days. I was grateful for the information and asked him to say thank you to Andrew from me and to send my love to him and the dog. He didn't respond, but as I walked off, heading to central London, he called after me, "Yes, mate, I'll give your best to Andy and Glitter."

I turned back to smile at him and then did one of those double takes. "What did you say?"

"I'll tell him, mate. I'll pass on your message."

"Andy and who?"

"The cockapoo—Glitter."

Bloody hell. That was Thomas Diamond's dog.

Glitter.

It had been Thomas's dog and I hadn't said anything. I hadn't known. It must have been him—people don't call their dogs Glitter. I needed to see Andrew again. He must have been the friend who took Thomas's dog when he died.

"Is Andrew—? Is Glitter his dog, I mean has it always been *his* dog?"

"Far as I know."

I had to find Andrew...

CHAPTER EIGHTEEN

I didn't find him—Andrew I mean. I slept for two more nights in Mill-bank Gardens. I hoped to see him again to tell him that I knew Thomas Diamond and to ask what happened to him.

I say 'slept', but it's not sleeping that you do when you're on the streets or in the parks. What I did those nights is not unusual—a bloke I met told me about a society called Homeless Link and I went online in the university library on Atterbury Street to look it up. I was reading about homelessness in London and I couldn't believe this: over two thousand people slept rough *for the first time* in London alone that year. And re-member, London is only one city in England. I wondered how many had slept rough in Newcastle. I wondered how many cities there actually were in England., and in the UK. So, I looked that up too. There are sixty-nine cities in the United Kingdom: fifty-one in England, seven in Scotland, six in Wales, and five in Northern Ireland. By the way, 'my' city, Newcastle upon Tyne, is the furthest north of those in England. Like I said, you get to Scotland after that.

'Dispossessed' they were referred to, these people sleeping or not sleeping outside, all night, in cities around the country, around the UK, around the world. I looked hard at that word. I remember Kamal once saying, "Connect with people who remind you who you are, Ollie." He said that at a time when I wasn't really 'connecting' with anyone, with any-

thing. Dispossessed? I looked it up and it meant having your possessions or anything that belonged to you taken away. I mean I didn't have my stuff like computer, saxophone, clothes, but it wasn't that; that wasn't a terrible loss. It was people. You can't possess people, though I reckon some folk try to, you know control everything they do but give nothing back. You can't possess people, but they *can* remind you of who you are or maybe start to help you see who you might be. Another meaning was 'having suffered the loss of expectations, prospects, relationships.'

'The loss of expectations'. I didn't feel like I expected anything from anyone or even wanted anything. Vague expectations maybe, linked with fear. Fear of waking up with my throat cut prevented me from ever really sleeping. No wonder the homeless, the 'dispossessed' look a bit vague—I felt like I was in a trance after only three nights. Hardly any sleep will do that to anyone. It occurred to me that must be why street-people drink alcohol. It must provide a chance for the loss and the fear to go away enough so that you could sleep for a few hours.

By the way, my fear was well-founded because I didn't exactly get my throat cut, but it wasn't far off. On my third night in the open air, things went a bit wrong. I had drunk some whiskey and had slumped into a version of sleep unknown to me before, where you're sort of paralyzed even though you're only half asleep, as if someone has blown Brugmansia, devil's dust, in your face. I was awoken by a hand or maybe there were two, around my neck. I'm not sure if they considered me less than human and therefore it didn't matter if they killed me, but it felt like that's what they were trying to do. My 'fight or flight' adrenaline response kicked in. It was like a miracle when the paralysis left me and I threw myself off the bench, shape-shifting like a ninja.

"Bloody hell. He's possessed by the devil!" one guy said, as the other said,

"Hey, look, you're right, he's got cash in his socks. Idiot, hiding it there."

They were actually laughing. Their faces were dimmed by dark hoods, but I breathed in wafts of stale alcohol, fried chicken and cheap aftershave as the first guy yanked my right ankle off the ground with such force to get at the money, that he toppled me backwards onto the ground. The side of my head met the iron arm of my bed-bench on the way down. I heard the thud but felt no pain.

"Nice wad of cash here!" the first guy said.

"That's a lot of blood. Let's scarper. Come on. I'll call an ambulance in a minute," said the second.

"Don't be a twat, they'll trace the call."

Then, instead of buggering off with my money, he kicked me quite a few times while I was on the ground.

Then everything went blank.

I awoke to the sight of ropes and the smell of smoke.

"You're okay, mate."

It was Mitch and his dreadlocks, too close to my face.

"You're in hospital. They've put stitches in your head and your ankle."

"Ankle?"

"Yeah, mate, they messed up your ankle. Lacerated."

"Grandpa." I said. I couldn't see.

"No, it's Mitch. From Millbank, remember?" He shook me but not violently.

"Where's Grandpa?"

"It's Mitch from Millbank." He slapped my face, but not violently.

"You want your grandpa, do you? I'll call him, shall I? Your phone's there in your bag. You was on the end of a miracle not getting that pinched."

"Socks?"

"Your socks are here, mate. Other clothes and your bag—all here, mate. You gotta sleep in the day, man. Safer sleeping in the day, you know?"

Mitch was far too near me, so I turned my face away from him, which sent a shard of pain across the left side of my face and up into my temple and skull. He seemed to get the message and sat back. I'd never been in hospital before. That's a massive lie—I'd been in hospital more times than I could bear, but it was when I used to visit Lily, my little sister, before she died. I'd never been at the other end of things. So many opposites—I felt safe but exposed, glad of the help but guilty for taking up a bed, comforted by Mitch's presence, but wanting him to leave, tumult and fuzz in the head yet a stillness and clarity I hadn't felt for a long while.

"Okay, Oliver, I'm giving you some pain relief and we'll be taking you for a CT scan soon."

"Computerized Tomography," I slurred to the nurse who'd approached my bedside.

"My guess is your injury isn't serious if you can say that. You need to rest now. Is there someone we should call?"

"He was asking for his grandpa," Mitch said.

"Is that something you could do for him, please? Ring the grandfather?"

"No," I heard myself whispering.

"Okay," the nurse said, before walking off. "We'll see if the scan shows up anything. You'll have to leave now, Mitch, I'm afraid."

Mitch came too close to my face again.

"You gotta sleep in the day, mate. Kid like you, man—danger all around. And sleep up, you know, on rooftops and shit. People don't look up. I'm at Millbank at night a lot, but not to sleep. Unless you wanna go to a shelter, but you're not gonna be on your own there, you know?"

I felt like I had died and was fizzling in purgatory.

"I got sick as a dog in one o' them shelters," Mitch explained. "Picked it up, you know, mate? And you were lucky with your bag. Strap it on you. You gotta go to sleep with it strapped on you."

I slurred, "You saved me."

"Gotta watch each other's backs, mate. When you got no-one left, you gotta watch out for the next guy innit."

He bent even nearer my face and kissed my forehead which made me wince with pain. He tripped over something, swearing as he made his way out.

'No-one left'. That wasn't strictly true for me.

For the first time, I could make out the room I was in, where I was. Saved by Mitch. Saved by The National Health Service. Good old NHS. Plucked from a park, bleeding, rescued, cared for, despite it being my own stupid fault. And all for free. I say that because my dad told me that in America you have to pay for health care. I can't imagine it's totally true, I mean how could poor people pay? Were homeless people not allowed to receive treatment in hospitals? I could ask Jasvandi about it. And Kamal would know. When would I see him again? Had I even answered his texts? I needed to contact him.

I couldn't remember getting to the hospital. It felt like another ninja trick, transporting myself there. But of course, I had not. Someone, more than one person no doubt, had taken me, had carried me. How lucky to have been lain on a bed in a clean warm room with stitches and bandages and painkillers, cocooned by expert help and reassuring wires and numbers on screens. I imagined an extra machine, not monitoring heart rate or blood pressure or blood oxygen levels, but feelings and thoughts. The nurse might check the data and say,

"That's nice that you're grateful, young man. Oh, but you're wondering why I've never had my teeth done? And didn't I know there was hair coming out of the mole next to my lip? And how could I be so thoughtless as to have eaten a cheese and onion sandwich for lunch? Something else coming through... you were thrilled to sleep with the older sister, but now you regret it. Why's that? Ah she was engaged! But you didn't know. Hang on who's Poppy? I see, a friend from home, oh, 'more than a friend' you're thinking now. You love her? Wait, you're not sure. And who's Jasvandi?"

God, it would be horrendous. You'd be displaying the constant stream of mind clutter, of sand thoughts washing over the neglected medium stones of quite important stuff and the big stones of stuff that really mattered.

The scan showed some bleeding inside my skull. It puzzled me as I didn't feel like a zombie or anything. I had to have an intercranial pressure monitor fitted. A tiny hole was drilled into my head so that a thin wire could be inserted between my brain and my skull. That wire apparently is attached to a device which alerts hospital staff to changes in pressure. So, I had to stay in hospital. I was told I should call someone.

As if by magic, just as I was going to ring Grandma and Grandpa, a text came through from Kamal. I could just about read it. It said, 'Please will you ring me or if not me at least your grandparents. They are beside themselves with worry about you. Your grandpa has even been ill in bed. I am coming to London today to look for you myself if I don't hear back by 4pm.' I don't know where he got 4pm from or where he thought he'd start looking in a city with a population of nearly nine million people, but I texted straight back.

I say I texted, but I was finding it hard to focus, so I decided to ring instead, only I found it hard to see the phone, so a nurse called for me. She called Kamal's number and was about to pass the phone to me when I was overcome with I don't know what, but I didn't want to speak to him. Emotion Library worker—'Go around this corner with this paper bag to open this jar. You'll be overcome with a nauseating wave of deep shame and embarrassment mixed with remorse and yet a through line of obstinacy and anger, the whole thing wrapped in a veil of pain and confusion.'

I shook my head to say I didn't want to talk, which hurt a great deal and I saw the nurse's eyes dart to the monitors.

"Your friend Oliver Campbell is here in hospital. [I could hear anxious shouting from Kamal and was glad it wasn't directly into my ear.] He's sustained a head injury and will be monitored overnight... St Thomas's Hospital... yes, in London, on the other side of the river to the Houses of Parliament... he has some bleeding, so we have to keep him in for observation."

She told him to contact my grandparents.

"We've got to stop meeting like this."

Grandpa, standing at the end of my bed.

I wanted to cover my face with the sheet, but it covered itself with salty water instead.

"Don't be sorry, Oliver," Grandpa said, and I hadn't even uttered a word. "None of this was your fault." He sat on a chair by my bed and held my hand. I hoped I'd become one of those 'elective mutes' who decides not to speak after a trauma. That happened to a girl in my class when I was six. I certainly didn't know what I could possibly say.

I worked out that Grandpa must have set off from Newcastle in his van within an hour of receiving the phone call from Kamal. It would have taken him five, six, seven hours to drive. What about his foot? Maybe someone else drove?

"Any excuse to come to London. How are you? Or is that a daft question?"

I did another one of those micro nods.

"I wish you'd... we'll talk about things later."

He stroked my head but so very gently that it didn't hurt.

"We've booked into a little hotel near Westminster Bridge. We're not allowed to stay in the hospital for long, but we'll be back tomorrow morning."

He had rushed to see me. In hospital too and I knew he hated hospitals. Maybe he was making up for not visiting Lily all those months because he couldn't bear to see his beautiful perfect grandaugher with the biggest eyes you've ever seen, jerking and twisting and fading away in front of his eyes.

"There's a free concert at St Paul's Cathedral tomorrow morning, then we'll be along."

I wondered what he meant by 'we'. As if he read my mind, he said,

"Grandma and Kamal are here too. We didn't want to overwhelm you."

Grandma had driven because Grandpa's foot was still not properly healed and what's more, he hadn't been feeling himself, he explained. She came in shortly afterwards and sat on a chair at the other side of the bed after kissing my right cheek. She smelt of freesias and coffee. My embarrassment had lifted. I was grateful they had come to see me. I was sad they had to make such a long journey. Wasn't it their turn to be looked after? They'd spent decades nurturing children and grandchildren and now, in their twilight years, they were due other people's effort. And there I was draining them further, squeezing more time, resources, attention, love, life from them.

"I picked you some flowers, love, but I'm not allowed to bring them in. You can get them tomorrow when you get out."

I hoped she knew I was getting out and wasn't just guessing. She placed her hand on my arm and squeezed it.

"Everything's stable for now which is a very good sign," said Grandma. "I think you probably just need a good night's sleep, love."

"Dare I postulate that needing a nice nap may not be the most sophisticated assessment, based purely on the observation of an apparent wire penetrating the patient's skull?"

Kamal!

I took in a loud gasp, like I was seeing a long-loved but never met idol. Meeting his gaze was like falling into a cosy nest after a treachourous fly along the cliff tops.

"You can smile," he said.

He smiled too, as he stood at the end of my bed, shaking his head. I wasn't sure what it meant—the head shaking. A combination of chastisement and forgiveness, I decided. He pulled either side of his black jacket together and folded his arms and said,

"You're looking decidedly pastey. You need a bit of sun. And on that subject, we can talk properly when you're better, but on the way down from Newcastle, we decided—". Grandma interrupted,

"—we decided that you need a holiday, so we've bought you a plane ticket."

"You're coming to Los Angeles with me, Jasvandi and Poppy!" he said, so misguidedly thrilled for me that I felt like screaming at the craziness of everything.

The monitor must surely have shown a dramatic shift in heart rate, blood pressure etc. Kamal said,

"Your smile's gone. You're overcome, I imagine."

Maybe so, but not in the way he thought.

CHAPTER NINETEEN

"Thank God that the bleeding stopped," Grandma said to me standing in the short queue to get into Kew Gardens. "It would have been unbearable for Anna if she had lost another child."

"Blimey. That's very dramatic." It shouldn't have surprised me, Grandma speaking straight. "I wasn't even sure Mam knew what happened till she phoned."

"Of course, sweetheart. We let her know immediately and she'd wanted to fly back from New Zealand, but we told her you were going to be fine and that it wasn't serious. Mind you, I hardly slept, I was so worried. I thought I might have been too optimistic."

I was not fit to travel to Newcastle in the VW camper van, according to the doctors at St Thomas's Hospital, so I spent another week recuperating at Kathy's house in Putney with my grandma. Grandpa had to take Kamal back for school and he managed to drive even though he shouldn't have. School could not have been further from my mind. Well it was on my mind slightly, but only in connection with my decision: I was not going back. Not that I had told anyone.

Grandma and I had taken a trip to The Royal Botanic Gardens, Kew, the day before our train back to Newcastle. It was 7th November which was Grandpa's birthday and my sister Lily's. She would have been seven. I was secretly relieved we weren't going ahead with the party in Newcastle and that I wasn't even there. What better distraction than a trip to my favourite place in the world—the seductive three-hundred-acre oasis of tranquility which is Kew Gardens. Grandma was shocked I had never been to the gallery we were heading to and I couldn't work out how I hadn't heard of it either.

"It's only recently been refurbished. The reason you won't have heard of it is because the artist is a woman," said Grandma.

"You think?"

"Yes, I do think."

"Maybe it's because the gallery's small or she wasn't very famous?"

As Autumn fell into winter, the day was colder than usual for that time of year. The sky was cloudless, so you felt the crisp fresh sting of frost even though the temperature was not quite zero. I took pleasure as the spikey wind pricked my cheeks and my head. Grandma had gone on and on about me wearing a hat, but I knew I wanted my head free and fresh and fizzing with life.

"How lucky we are, darling. Rain was forecast yet look at this beautiful sky."

"And it's hard to hold a candle In the cold November rain," I said.

"What lovely lines, Oliver. Did you just think of them?"

"Guns N' Roses."

"Pardon?"

"The lyrics are from a song by the band, Guns N' Roses called *November Rain*."

"Oh, who could find a dearth of bliss With autumn glory such as this," Grandma said. "Last lines of a poem by Gladys Harp."

We both laughed and I linked Grandma's arm, which I never normally did. It was like we were partners in nature, partners in poetry.

"Oliver, before we go in, you should know that the gallery is the only purpose-built gallery in the whole of the UK where all the work on display is produced by one female artist."

I pushed my hair back off my face with both hands, exposing the bald patch, shaved for the insertion of the wire, before linking Grandma again. I think I was getting myself ready to say I was impressed with the gallery, whatever it was like, just to please her.

We climbed the first flight of steps and stopped before the gallery, still linked and flanked by two matching exotic plants. Before ascending the second short flight to the double front doors, we looked up at the brick building; it appeared to be new and was in a mixture of classical and colonial styles.

"Here we are. The Marianne North Gallery," said Grandma.

I learnt that Marianne North was born in 1830 and had spent her life travelling around the world, painting plants. The gallery had originally opened in 1882, to exhibit only her work, but had been recently restored, so I was excited to go in.

"Wow! You're joking me. It's massive," I said.

"I never said it was small—that was you, dear boy. She is famous too, contrary to your belief. This is the longest permanent solo exhibition by a female artist in the world."

"The whole world? Wow. Can't believe I haven't heard of her."

The place was a marvel—floor-to-ceiling framed paintings of plants. Every inch of wall was covered. Pretty mental, to be honest. You couldn't even see the ones at the top. At floor level were vertical thick strips of loads of different kinds of wood (246 types I read!)—gorgeous mixed colours from around the world like zebra wood from Brazil and tulip wood from Guiana. It was altogether bizarre yet brilliant.

"There is hope for us all, Oliver, because she didn't start painting till she was forty! Mind you, she died when she was only fifty-nine. No doubt the punishing travel contributed to her early death," Grandma said, tightening her scarf. "And she was a real adventurer too. She endangered her life to get as close as she could to specimens, climbing rocks and the likes. Fifty-nine is young. But she produced more than a thousand paintings. Probably over eight hundred here," she said, holding the top of her scarf now in a sort of overwhelmed clench. "She crammed a lot into her life, eh?"

"Yeah, you're not kidding." I said, taking in her words and the wondrous sight. "How come you know all this anyway?"

"You know I come here quite often when I visit my great friend who lives in Kew?"

"No. How come you never told me... or brought me for that matter?" She gave a knowing smile, but kind too.

"We all have our different lives, Oliver. We miss a lot that goes on."

It struck me how true that was. I studied Grandma's face, her eyes squinting, looking up at a painting, her makeup, still applied dutifully but maybe less deftly than decades before. It struck me how beautiful her skin was. It struck me that the face I beheld had lived a whole life I knew hardly anything about. She scratched behind her right ear and got some hair caught in a green ring she wore on her middle finger. As she teased it away, I wondered if any other man apart from Grandpa had touched her hair. Had she ever loved someone she wasn't supposed to? Had she ever cried as she touched her own hair, imagining it was him or her?

"We do," she said.

"What?"

"You're miles away, Oliver. I was saying we do miss such a lot of each other's lives, but that's normal. That's okay. All part of it," she said, now fiddling with the green ring like it held a secret. "Even though sometimes you're shocked by what you learn, eh? We suffer losses from time to time, not just people dying, but because what we thought was there *wasn't* there."

Surely she must be talking about a past love? She carried on,

"Like a great love perceived but not being real. Perhaps we imagine we know more than we do based on our own perspectives, eh?"

I thought of Grandpa saying that suffering is normal. I thought, 'Is Grandma reading my mind?'

"Spose so," I said. "I know someone who lives near here too actually."

"Well, there you go. I didn't know that. *I* didn't take *you* to Kew Gardens and *you* didn't take *me*. We're quits," she said pulling a funny squidgy face. "How do you know someone from London anyway?"

"Long story. Short story to be honest," I said, wishing I hadn't opened my mouth. "It didn't really work out, so I don't know why I bothered to tell you. I mean we fell out."

"What is it with you young folk, always falling out?" she said, tutting. "I blame technology. Text messages and emails can be so misleading, so ambiguous. And then you have these daft expectations of people because of all the misinformation you get on the Internet."

"Grandma, it wasn't technology in this case. It was something, well, very physical, if truth be told."

Her hand went to her mouth and her eyes widened.

"You got into a fight? I really am getting worried about you now, Oliver."

"No, no, no, not a fight."

Now her eyes screwed up small. I said,

"Look, I'm sorry I ever mentioned it. Maybe I'll go travelling around the world like Marianne and that way I can fall out with someone in every town and simply move on."

"Don't be daft. Why are you saying things like that?"

"I didn't mean it. I don't know what I'm saying. Hey, so if Marianne North went travelling all over the globe, did she take her children?"

"She didn't have children, though she had four plants named after her."

Grandma seemed to think this was a hilarious joke. She laughed even harder when she saw that I didn't seem to think it was funny. Her laugh grew and she covered her mouth, her eyes watering. She got me started when she said,

"I'll have to rush to the loo at this rate!"

We were like a pair of school kids, then. We became giddy. Possessed. Every move made us laugh. I tried to use her scarf to wipe my eyes and she nearly fell backwards snatching it away from me which sent us both into howling shrieks. She said,

"Oops, too late for the loo," which had me bending over double, the movement giving me a shooting pain in my head... which made Grandma laugh even more. She told me to get her hankie out of her bag for her as she couldn't see for tears.

People were looking over at us sort of tutting like we were in church and were being irreverent. I think Marianne North would have told them all to get a life and would have laughed with us!

We eventually calmed down and Grandma pushed some of her shimmery white hair into the front of her hat.

"Quite right I'd say since she discovered them," I said.

"Who discovered what?" she said, still panting with sparkly eyes from the laughing fit.

"The plants! Named after Marianne."

"Oh God not that again."

But this time she blocked her mouth properly with two hands and only her eyes laughed. She shook her hands and head as if to realign herself and said,

"Being serious, it was unusual for someone who was not a professional scientist to have a plant named after them. Never married either."

Not again. A throat laugh from Grandma. I stood still and pointed at her like a strict teacher as if to say, 'That's enough of that nonsense', which seemed to work.

"In her autobiography, she famously referred to marriage as 'a terrible experiment' that turned women into 'a sort of upper servant.'"

It was weird as you would have thought this is what we'd both have laughed at, but we just stayed calm and I said,

"She had an interesting point, I'd say."

We smiled.

"Maybe she liked plants more than people. Less complicated," I said.

"Hmmm. I'm not sure how well she really knew plants, for instance she didn't have any proper training. In fact, her real love was for music and in particular, singing."

All this was said while we both surveyed the room and its abundance of art work.

"You wouldn't know it wasn't her first love, looking at all of these," I said. "I wonder if she had her favourites? Look at that tree, twisting itself round to avoid slipping down the rock. It says, '*Juniperus virginiana*', an old Red Cedar, painted near West Manchester, Massachusetts."

The tree was awe-inspiring, the way it clung to its rock.

"You look like a kid in a sweet shop!" said Grandma.

"I *am* a kid, and this *is* a sweet shop."

As we wandered round, I was taken out of myself, drawn to the bright fruits and flowers and leaves. It seemed to be the trees, though, that impressed me most.

"You wouldn't mess with this one, Grandma," I said, pointing at an African Baobab Tree, *Adansonia digitate*. "How long must it take to become that strong? The size of the trunk is unbelievable."

"It looks comical to me," said Grandma, "like the trunk got too wide for its own good or didn't know when to stop growing."

"Ha," I said, then pretended to be the tree talking, "'I'll show you all, not even a giant's giant will be strong enough to uproot me when I've finished growing.' It says it was painted in a princess's garden in India. I wonder how she got to go to somewhere like that?"

"Oh, she was well connected, was Marianne. Her father was a well-known MP, so she probably had many letters of introductions and the like. Come on, we'll watch the film about her—it's all in there."

She pointed to an adjoining smaller room and took my hand, pulling me behind her. We stood in front of the screen for the length of the film.

Turned out she hated school, this Marianne North, which drew me in straight away. She spent a lot of time in her garden at Hastings and was close to her dad who also loved plants and the outdoors. He built three greenhouses in the garden and they often worked inside them together, I'm guessing growing unusual plants. She used to go to Kew Gardens and on one occasion, Sir William Hooker, the first official director of the gardens and friend of Frederick North, Marianne's father, gave her a hanging bunch of Amherstia nobilis which were the first which had bloomed in England and which she found so beautiful, it made her long to see the tropics.

She became addicted to oil painting so merged her two passions, painting flowers, plants and trees all over the world. It was only after her father died that she planned her trips, though—eight in all, visiting seventeen countries in fourteen years. It struck me how independent and strong she was, especially for a woman in Victorian times, and how much humble faith she must have had in other people to travel so far in the days before planes and stuff. She'd written in her diary in 1871,

'In the West Indies at last! Christmas Eve!... I landed entirely alone and friendless, but at once fell into kind helpful hands.'

I started to wonder what some of these places were like myself. How would you know where to start? In 1876, Marianne wrote,

'Java is one magnificent garden of luxuriance, surpassing Brazil, Jamaica, and Sarawak combined, with the grandest volcanoes rising out of it.'

She must have been pretty edgy too: in India in 1877, she wrote,

'Everyone was taking opium, so I followed the fashion...'

She must have had such confidence and verve and will. I so admired that she wasn't afraid to push herself forward.

In 1879, she wrote to Joseph Hooker to ask if he would like to have all the paintings for Kew Gardens and offered to have a gallery built in which to exhibit them. She even added Australia, Tasmania and New Zealand to her travels at the suggestion of Charles Darwin, the world-renowned natural scientist, before finalizing her hoard of paintings for the gallery. After a year of sorting and framing her pictures, the gallery opened on 7th June 1881.

We walked back into the gallery, Grandma rolling her shoulders backwards to avoid stiffness I presume.

"You could say she broke all the rules," she said, scratching the back of her neck, itchy from her hat. "Women hardly even left the house in those days, never mind the continent. A botanical rebel in a big dress." She laughed at her own joke.

"Hardly left the house?' I said. "Are you joking?"

"It's hard to fathom because it's not even a hundred years ago, but women didn't even get the vote till 1918."

"After the first world war?"

"Yep. *She* was scaling a cliff in Borneo while her counterparts were making tea. You know, she wanted to serve tea and coffee here, but Joseph Hooker refused?"

"Refused? Really? Why?"

We walked further into the room, Grandma looking around for somewhere to sit.

"Most people might have just accepted the decision, but not Marianne North. She took her proposal of a refreshments room to the House of Commons."

"Blimey, she sure was feisty, wasn't she?"

"Oh yes. They rejected it too, but she was determined to see her idea through, so she boldly and cheekily decided to paint tea and coffee plants and include them here in the gallery. Look, over that doorway—tea plant. And over there, above that one, coffee."

"Haha. I like her style. Good sense of humour. And all about the people. That's what this whole gallery's for, isn't it? She's sharing. Sharing her love and fascination of nature. Shall we sit down?"

Grandma linked my arm again after squeezing it and led me towards a bench saying,

"Yes, darling. It was a male dominated world, but she fought through and made a name for herself so that we could share all of this. That she was willing and able to capture the flowers and plants is her gift to us."

She pointed to a seat as we carried on walking. "Remember there was no colour photography at this time, so she really was sharing something truly unique with this collection."

We sat on one of the two double-sided benches in the centre of the gallery and I drank in Marianne's mosaic of life which faced us. Grandma took off her hat—a bottle green bobble one she'd knitted herself and wore every winter as long as I could remember—and managed a combination of scratching and straightening up. She shimmied up close to me and put her arm around me.

"How's your head, beautiful?"

"Okay, thanks. Not bad now."

'Beautiful'. Mam had called me that once, or was it twice? It had been around the time that Lily was ill or maybe after she'd died. Mam must miss Lily terribly, I thought. I dropped my head down and moved my eyes left to right through the wooden panels. Was it even possible to miss Lily more than I did? Why did I not miss anyone else? Could I only be close to dead people? I wondered if Mam missed me.

It was like Grandma was reading my mind.

"Imagine this day seven years ago, getting a new sister."

"I can remember."

"And your great grandmother eighty odd years ago getting a new son in the form of Grandpa? Anna was so ecstatic with Lily. Your mam was delirious with joy. I'd say *you* were as well. You were the first to hold her, you know?"

"Was I?"

I remembered it very well.

"Yes, darling."

Grandma pulled me in closer.

"Lily would have loved it here," she said.

I wished she hadn't said that.

"I was supposed to bring her. I promised, you know?" I said as I turned to see Grandma's pretend-happy face. "I broke my promise. Maybe you shouldn't promise anything. Maybe you shouldn't trust anyone. Any*thing*. I was supposed to bring Lily here. I told her I would."

I felt my eyes starting to sting and spill over and said,

"It's like in films when they say, 'Everything's gonna be all right.' Bloody lies."

Grandma reached for the crumpled-up damp hankie from her grey woollen coat and dried my face like I was about three, careful not to jolt my head. She then leaned us both gently back against the tall wooden support. My head dropped further, to face the floor of patchwork terracotta and cream tiles —a magic carpet in this magic room on this magic day.

"We're supposed to do a lot of things," she said, "But life takes you by surprise sometimes. We can be knocked for six in the wink of an eye."

"Is that two metaphors for the price of one?"

You wouldn't have thought it possible, but Grandma squeezed me even tighter than before.

"Wink of an eye's more just a turn of phrase."

"What about knocked for six on a sixpence then," I said.

"Genius—two '*six*' metaphors for the price of one..." There was a beat and I just knew something serious was coming.

"It's tough, but you have to try to live in the present," she said. "It's good and normal to grieve, but don't dwell too long. Regretting and longing are so draining, sweetheart. That's what I loved about my kids: they didn't do that."

"Mam, and my aunties and uncles?"

She pulled away now and looked right up to the highest drawings opposite.

"No. No, my kids at school. My pupils. Beautiful uncluttered beings. They had what we used to describe as 'complex needs,' you know?"

"Oh, yeah. You told me," I said. "Remember those badges you had saying, 'I've been dry all day'?"

"I do," she voiced a tender laugh. "We had loads of stickers and badges. They loved them. Doesn't everybody? When they were upset, they really went for it, I mean howling and throwing chairs across the room."

"Blimey," I said, sitting up, wiping my eyes with the backs of my hands and swivelling my head to listen properly.

"And when they were happy, well, there was nothing like it to keep you in the moment."

She put her arm around me and pulled me to her again.

"You were witness to unadulterated joy in its purest form: swaying, bouncing, clapping and grunting with sheer happiness, wearing the wrong clothes, having the wrong hairstyles, making ugly faces, distorted with delight. And not giving a shit."

"Grandma!"

Then *we* were swaying with delight.

Back at Kathy's in Putney for our last night, as I lay in bed, I thought about what Grandma had said. Desire to affect the future or even go back and change the past were futile. I loved that idea—to live in no time. Kathy had got into a conversation with us about that sort of thing too and she gave me a book by Eckhart Tolle called *The Power of Now* which she urged me to read. The thrust of what she said was that it was okay to set goals and seek out thrilling experiences and adventures, but not to long and yearn for stuff. I must live in the moment, I thought, and be grateful for everything that was there—simple free stuff like people, nature, music, and beauty in general.

Kathy had passed me a framed poem to read which usually hung in her upstairs toilet. She thought I'd like it and I did. It was by John Updike and was entitled, *A Child's Calendar* and went like this,

'The stripped and shapely Maple grieves
The ghosts of her Departed leaves.
The ground is hard, As hard as stone.
The year is old, The birds are flown.
And yet the world, In its distress,
Displays a certain Loveliness."

Learning about Marianne North made me consider the LA trip suddenly thrilling. There would be amazing new plants and trees... and people of course. If my parents were against me leaving school, maybe I could stay out there? Live out there? The thought of a warm climate and being outside all the time sent a chill of excitement through me. I settled into a deep sleep as I remembered the last words I'd read from the amazing inspiring woman I'd 'met' that day:

'Begin now by observing as much as you can of what nature teaches and you will find a new happiness in life.'

CHAPTER TWENTY

Los Angeles.

As I woke up on my first morning, the sheet and the heat reminded me where I was.

Nothing had seemed clear when I returned to Newcastle after London and nothing seemed any clearer when I got to Los Angeles. From the car journey to Newcastle Airport, to the long wait at London Heathrow Airport, to the even longer flight to America, I had said very little.

Kamal and I were sitting together in the departure lounge at Heathrow while the girls went to look for books and to try on perfumes and buy sun tan lotion. Out of the blue (pardon the pun), he said,

"Would you say you were suffering from depression?"

To be honest, it hadn't crossed my mind before Kamal mentioned it even though Kathy had touched on the same subject.

"How would I know?"

"It would be normal not to know. It can creep up on you. I'll tell you what—I'll get a checklist up on my phone and see if we can get you diagnosed."

Had he really said that?

"Really?"

"Yes... right... here we are. You have to answer with one of the following: none of the time, a little of the time, some of the time, most of the time, or all of the time. Okay? One of five responses—none, little, some, most or all? Got it?

"Seriously?"

He pushed his backpack between his legs to prevent it from being stolen while he was giving his counselling session and focused on his phone.

"All these questions pertain to the last four weeks. Ready?

I sighed very very deeply.

"As I'll ever be."

"How often did you feel tired out for no good reason?"

"Some."

"You look tired all the time to me."

I folded my arms and repositioned myself in the chair, saying,

"Why don't you just fill it in *for* me?"

"Sorry. Number two—about how often did you feel hopeless?"

"Most."

"Most of the time, okay. About how often did you feel so sad that nothing could cheer you up?"

"Most."

"About how often did you feel worthless?"

"That's enough now."

I slumped further down the blue plastic seat, stretched my legs out, and crossed them to match my arms. General airport buzz and moods all around of anticipation and maybe apprehension, like we were all already on a massive plane together to an unknown destination. The white noise hustle and bustle was pierced periodically with shrill announcements. Children's voices cut through it all. I turned to the noise of shouting and laughing. A brother and sister. Five and eight? Unable to contain their joy, their excitement. The simplest of games—sitting on the seats then sliding their bottoms off the seats. I had only ever been abroad once with *my* sister. Spain. I pictured her with the straw hat Mam had bought her at the airport the day we were to fly out. I would snatch the hat from her head, she would run after me to get it back. That was our game. Our joy. Our excitement. What I wouldn't have done to feel that again.

"Aha! A smile. You're *pretending* to be depressed then? About how often have quizzes on your mental health caused you irritation?"

"All. All of the time."

"Ha ha."

I caught both their eyes as Poppy and Jasvandi walked towards us laden with carrier bags. Poppy smiled a sort of shy smile before looking at Jasvandi. How could she be shy when I'd known her for so long? Jaz watched me. She side-pouted coolly with twinkly eyes and kept looking at me till she reached us and sat directly opposite me. Poppy sat next to me on my right, started fiddling in her bags and presented me with a book she'd bought for me. She was being ultra-sweet and nice. I wondered if it was possible that she really hadn't picked up anything at all about me and Jaz. It made me convinced nobody knew about it and that, in fact, she was no longer interested in me despite what had happened. Unlike Poppy, *she* was being distant. Did she really even want me to go with them at all? We hadn't spent any time together since I'd got back, apart from one evening at my house when Grandma cooked dinner for us all and I told them about London... well the bit about being on the streets and being beaten up. So, I found it almost rude that instead of having a proper catch up there at the airport lounge, sitting together without adults, she got out her iPad and started typing.

I decided to put on headphones and listen to some music, so I bent forward to rummage in my bag. I put on my laid-back jazzy dance playlist and *Lost* came on by Buschemi. Love that track. Chugs you along on a dreamy train. I found myself closing my eyes.

227

Dear Journal,

Oh my! I can't tell you how good Ollie looks! He has this amazing like drop-dead cool aura about him since he got back from London and I swear he's only worn black and nothing but black and he looks so HOT. He's being real cool and mysterious and saying like very little to keep us all guessing. His head needed stitches, so he has this neat style that's real short all-round the sides then blond floppy hair above. It falls over his face when he leans forward which he's doing now as he looks for something in his bag.

Kamal told me he seduced this older woman who was like thirty or something. Get this, this woman was engaged to some guy and he found out and beat Ollie up real bad! He now has his eyes closed. How cool can you get, like he doesn't care?

Poppy has no clue about the older woman thing or about anything else and I mean like ANYTHING.

I'm thinking I'm going to tell her about it all when we get to LA. I mean, I could do with her advice. Plus, I need to tell someone that I might be pregnant.

Can you believe I asked Kamal if he would come out and live with me after he's finished his exams in the summer, what are they called, GCSEs I think, and he didn't say definitely no?! Get this, he actually said, "It depends how Ollie is and what *he* wants to do." OMG you'd think he was like in love with the guy! Anyways, I can work on him when we're out there. He's gonna love it and wanna come back.

Ooh must dash! Our gate's just been called...!

I sat up in the double bed, noticing myself in the mirrored wardrobe opposite. No one else was awake. Didn't sound like it anyway. I saw my weird hair with the shaved side and tilted it to get a better look. It made me think of London and Mitch and then Maisy. I contemplated the devastation I'd probably left behind me in that house in Richmond. Was I one of those selfish bastards who went around leaching off other people, systematically ruining their lives then moving on?? Messing up folks' possibilities then casually waving, 'Byeeeeee'. And there I was at the next plush venue to destroy someone else's life. I didn't know whose, but it seemed not an outlandish thing to predict.

I computed the pros and cons of flopping back down on the bed and pulling the sheet over my head but mustered the strength to push it down and swung my legs to the right and onto the floor. Cool stone floor and a sharp twinge in my ankle. The room was white, and I mean WHITE: white floor, white walls, white bedding and... wait for it... a white painting. Well, I say 'white' but there was a tiny green tree pushing its way through a mountain in a snowscape—only one.

I put my hands on my knees and noticed the unfamiliar feel of cotton on my bed legs. I normally wore boxers for bed but Grandma had bought me two pairs of pyjama bottoms to take on holiday. I thought of Kew and Marianne North. Was I like her now, the intrepid explorer? It wasn't quite Java, but here I was thousands of miles away from England. It was a good start for a potential world traveller.

Apart from the bed, there was only an armchair in the bedroom. You'll never guess what colour it was... Ha. I bent to drag my case over to it, sat down and opened it up to unpack, not that there was anywhere to put anything. I smiled when I spotted the second pair of pyjama bottoms Aunt Gopi had bought for me. To be precise, there were pyjama tops as well. There had been a 'twofer,' as she called it, at the local supermarket, which means 'two for one,' so she had snapped up matching pjs for kamal and me. They were navy blue and had a slogan on the front saying,

'I'm off to Club Bed featuring DJ Pillo and MC Blanky.' I pulled out my wash bag which reminded me I hadn't brushed my teeth the night before. I thought of Lily. She was so funny. 'It's so neat to brush your teef. Brush your teef to the beat!' I pulled out a tee shirt and shorts. I chose my 'The Who' tee shirt which my dad had bought me the Christmas before. It had an arrow pointing up from the 'o' and the name of one of their albums underneath—'Live at Leeds.' My dad thought it was their best album. I thought of Nathan saying, 'Why would they like actually *tell* people to live at Leeds?' And I said, 'It's *LIve* at Leeds!' as in with an 'I' sound, you know, sounding like 'Lyve' coz they were playing live.

Those days of Mam and Dad and Sam and Nathan and Lily and me living together at home seemed like someone else's life. By the way, there was a trend at that time to wear tee shirts with 'old' bands on which most kids wore because they thought it was cool, but I really did know this band, The Who, because my Dad played their music to me. Not that I have to explain that but well hey I've done it now. I loved a track called 'Who are you?' I really wanna know. I mean that was the next line in the song—I really wanna know. I threw the wash bag, tee shirt and shorts onto the bed and went over to the window.

Sliding one of the pale blue (not white come to think of it!) sheer curtains revealed a garden I hadn't known was there and the realisation that my room was on the ground floor (the other two bedrooms were upstairs I remembered.) 'Wow, a pool!' I thought. Wooden decking all around, three separate seating areas and grounds with tons of plants. I would need to find out what they all were, so many trees and flowers. To be honest there weren't many flowers but loads of exotic trees and bushes.

Jasvandi's uncle was away for a month and had suggested we stayed there at his place in Hollywood Hills for the two weeks. Kamal and I had a room each and Jaz and Poppy shared. They had an ensuite bathroom and a wooden floored balcony which overlooked the pool. Jaz had showed us round the night before, but I had been in a daze and hadn't taken everything in. I remembered that though – a fantastic balcony with two sun loungers. I had imagined she and I lying on them side by side, the others having gone off for the day.

Sliding doors behind the silky curtains meant I had direct access to the garden and the swimming pool. Excellent result.

I rubbed my eyes and slid one of the doors open. Blimey it was hot. It was Christmas time and it felt like summer. "It's like UK summer all the time in LA," Jaz had said. I liked that idea and now the warmth on my face and the flickering and flashing of sunlight on the swimming pool and the beckoning greenery made me smile. "That must be a pool house," I said to myself except out loud. There was a wooden hut to the side of the pool. I stepped onto the decking and walked to it. I imagined I was on a Carribean cruise ship as the smooth wood warmed my feet. The door to the hut or pool house was locked, but I saw through the window that it seemed to have wooden seating fixed around the walls. I continued to the end of the pool, settling on a rattan chair which made up part of a set—a little glass-topped table, a mini sofa and two armchairs.

It was peaceful, but for birds and the small stone fountain at the end of the pool—the trickling of one water into another, daring streams venturing up then, losing their nerve, returning to their source. I looked back towards the house. Wow it was so modern. So much wood and glass. I loved it. I could imagine living there. Even wider sliding doors which would surely open up the whole of that area—the living area with open plan kitchen. It occurred to me that I had done a (somewhat brief) 'Poor Service' in the UK so I could think of this as my 'Rich Service.'

I slumped right down in the chair which wasn't massively comfortable to be honest. 'I could get used to this,' I imagined Grandpa saying as I smiled and felt my eyes falling closed.

A ginormous splash sprung my eyes open. A brown skinny face emerging from the water, chin resting on the poolside, right in front of me said,

"Too much of water hast thou, poor Ophelia—"

"And therefore, I forbid my tears," we both said. We had both acted in the play at school.

"Good old *Hamlet*," said Kamal. "Good old Shakespeare. A quote for everything."

"It's a bit loose, the link, though," I said. " I mean it's about his sister dying, not fun and laughter on an LA poolside."

"Sorry, am I at a party? Strange silent party for one is it?"

I pulled myself up to an upright position and dragged my right ankle onto my left knee. "It's amazing here isn't it?"

"I know. I can't get over it," said Kamal, turning to look right then left. "Have you seen the living room?" He wiped the water from his eyes and crossed his arms in front of him, rested his chin on his hands. I wondered if he could see me without his specs. He said, "Can't get moved for white leather and the size of the TV screen...! We'll have to indulge in some movie nights. There's a kitchen attached, did you see?"

"Yes, Kamal, it's called open plan," I said. "You see the funky lights dangling over the central island? Sooo cool."

"Designer situation we're in, my man. And I dig your designer tee shirt. Remember Nathan saying, 'I can't believe they—"

"Yeah, I was just thinking that before. He'd love it here." I didn't bother telling Kamal that my tee shirt wasn't 'designer'. It was funny that he was so clever but hadn't picked up other obvious stuff.

"A designer pad, for sure," I said. "These seats aren't that high end, mind. Bloody uncomfortable actually."

As if by magic, Jaz appeared at the sliding doors, said hi, then took a few steps to the side, opened a garden chest and grabbed some furniture pads. She walked towards us, bare foot. "Move your ass, Ollie," she said. I got up and she slung the cushions onto the base and back of my chair. Kamal slid his scrawny frame from the water saying, "I'll help you get the rest." Jaz wore denim shorts which looked like a person who couldn't see very well had hacked off too much of the legs of a pair of jeans with scissors which were crap at doing the one job they were supposed to be good at, so that you could see the pockets coming down. To match the ragged piece of material posing as shorts, she wore a white vest which had suffered the same chopping, apparently with the same dodgy scissors. I can't deny, though, that the look worked for me. I had made a pact with myself not to indulge in any fantasies. I was simply observing.

Once the rattan furniture was as it should be, we all sat together—me on my chair and those two on the little sofa. It occurred to me that they must have already got quite close, as it would have been more normal to have spread out, using the other chair.

"Morning all." Poppy, framed by the living room opening. "I'll bring some coffee out. I mean I want to, but I don't know how to do it."

'I don't know how to do it.' Poppy often looked a bit like she didn't know how to do it. How to live. How to get what she wanted. How to work out what it was she wanted. Or maybe she spoke for all of us.

"I'll come and show you," Jaz said.

"I bet it's one of those spluttery machines you see on films and tv shows," Kamal said, attempting to mime a filter coffee machine. I loved that about Kamal – 'no job too big' in terms of getting a message across. "You know those fat jugs that seem to be constantly full of coffee and constantly hot. They fill their cups like there's no tomorrow."

"Yeah," I said.

"Automatic drip brew I'm guessing," said Kamal. "Coffee grounds are placed in a paper funnel, which is set over a coffee pot."

"Yeah, that's right," I said, tickled anew at his commitment to explain something accurately.

"Cold water poured into a separate chamber is then heated up and directed into the funnel."

The explaining continued... I realised I was being a bit of a damp squib, so forced myself to be a bit more jovial.

"Remember that tv series Poppy used to watch?" I said "That woman and her daughter were addicted to coffee. Ridiculous it was. So unrealistic." I noticed Kamal nodding so I carried on. "Like it was supposed to be their thing and cool. Coffee and junk food. Carried cardboard cups of coffee all the time, like kids over-attached to cuddly toys."

I could hardly believe I'd come out with all that, not that it went down well.

"Didn't pay much attention," Kamal said, yet still nodding and swinging his skinny legs up onto the sofa and laying back.

"True," I said. "Your attention will have been on your iPad."

"Someone's got to keep abreast of the news," he said, finding his glasses which he'd left on one of the sofa arms.

"Who'd want to tune into that? It's so depressing."

"Those who tune out are part of the problem," Kamal said. "You don't seem to realise we all need to connect with each other and in my opinion, your disregard for other people is immoral."

He took off his glasses and looked through them, using the sun to assess how badly smeared they were, before wiping them with a towel. Can't imagine that action cleaned them particularly well.

"Bloody hell. I only said I don't follow the news," I said. "That doesn't mean I don't care about people." I changed my mind about trying to be upbeat.

Kamal moved back to a sitting position. He meant business. He started waving his hands about. I truly did not want to hear what was going to come out of his mouth. More intense thinking, more intense talking.

"How can you care if you haven't a clue what's going on?" Kamal said. "It's your duty as an intelligent person. I don't mean watching tv news—that's too manipulative—I mean reading."

He waited. He crossed his legs. He crossed his arms. More waiting.

"How could you know who to vote for?!" he said. "God, that's another topic altogether. Next, you'll be saying, 'But I can't do anything about these tragedies'. You think the scope of your concern should end with your ability to influence?"

I sank further into the chair. I knew Kamal wanted to study politics and history at Oxford or Cambridge, but I had no such aspirations and couldn't match him in this sort of debate. I knew if I carried on, we'd be onto Noam Chomsky's 'Thought Control' and 'Manufacturing Consent'. Not that I wasn't interested, but we'd been through it all before and this was lovely warm laid back, positive, uplifting LA and I wanted to talk about the ocean and the mountains and the birds and the trees.

"Those terracotta pots look great, don't they?" I said.

On the poolhouse side were three huge pots, two at the ends of the pool and one in the middle. Kamal was like a statue after his monologue, petrified into a bent forward position, agog and awaiting a pithy comeback. He came back to life by taking a deep breath, still bent over, knowing I wasn't going to respond to his maybe rhetorical questions. After a few breaths, he leant back again, adjusting his glasses to a new mood, but folding his arms to semi-shut himself away from stupid old me if I didn't want to play ball.

"Dramatic," he said. I was glad he'd 'agreed' to change the subject. "What's in them?"

"Good question," I said, pushing myself up out of the now very comfy rattan chair. I stood studying the middle pot from the other side of the pool.

"You're joking," I said, and ran around to the pot. I squatted down in front of it, the swimming pool behind me. Cupping either side of the earthy container, I took a close look at the plant. "It is. Aechmea Nudicaulis." It was so beautiful. I felt my mouth dropping open. The outer stiff yet arching leaves were banded with silver. Then the precious central stem. "Have you ever seen such a vivid inflorescence?"

"A what?" Kamal said. I laughed. It always seemed odd yet satisfying when I said a word Kamal had never come across.

"The middle bit."

"Must you be so technical?" How glad I was that nature had worked its magic and smoothed things over. The plant had drawn Kamal out of his mood. He got up and plutted his flat feet round to join me. He got down on his honkers too and steadied himself by putting his arm around my shoulders. "I see what you mean. Doesn't look real does it, that red spike?"

"I know. And the yellow flowers on the end... Funny seeing it in a pot. They're epiphytes," I said, "as in live on other plants. They normally dangle with their roots free like on tree or rocks. From South America."

"What a day this is turning out to be," said Kamal. "Two words I've learnt since getting up."

"Smile!" It was Poppy taking a photo on her phone from the other side of the pool. She'd put a tray of drinks on the little table and was now grinning at Kamal and me. "What have you found there?"

"Shell Dance," Jaz said.

Kamal said, "Aechmea Nudicaulis to be more scientific!"

How the heck had he remembered the exact words? I was so impressed with him that I put my arm around him too and squeezed him so tightly that we toppled over and Kamal somehow managed to roll me into the pool, though, I'm glad to say, I dragged him behind me. We messed about splashing and stuff then swam over to the girls.

"Did my brother say something funny?" Jaz said.

Poppy said, "No, he just said the Latin name of the plant—eek... eek something," and they both laughed, and we all laughed. Kamal and I lined ourselves up at the edge of the pool, Kamal somehow managing to be still wearing his glasses. I noticed Poppy's dress. It was short and mostly white with blue parts including a row of elephants around the bottom hem and it had no straps but a stretchy-looking top bit. I'll blame the heat, but the vision flashed in my mind of me pulling the top of her dress down to reveal what was underneath. I had to remind myself of my anti-fantasy pact. Just as I was thinking that, they both sat on the sofa and took their coffee cups.

"Should be in more of a shady position really," I said.

"We can put up the parasol if you'd like?" Jaz said.

"I mean the aechmea." To which Kamal ducked my head under the water followed by us engaging in some sort of ritualistic water fighty dance thing.

Once we were all settled on the sofa and chairs, drinking our coffee (except it turned out Jaz had a herbal tea and told us, like we had asked, that she considered coffee to be poison), we discussed our plans for the next two weeks. I don't think I actually shook my arms in the air with glee, but I was chuffed as hell when Jaz announced that we were going to a garden in a few days. It was somewhere called The Huntington and was in fact a library, botanical gardens and art galleries all rolled into one. She told us there was a free day every month and she had booked the tickets the month before. I remember thinking it was quite gutsy that she had gone ahead and arranged the outing without asking everyone first. And how brilliant this 'free day a month' idea was. Anyone could go if they were so inclined. I loved that. No one was excluded. They should do free days with plays and films and stuff, I thought. And supermarkets. They'd have to have an upper limit or people would hire trailers to get tvs and bbqs and stuff.

"They've got some of those there too," Jaz said, looking at me and pointing at the terracotta pot over the other side of the pool.

"What did you say the common name for it was?" I said. "Shell something was it?"

"Shell Dance. The two at the ends are slightly different though."

I stood up again to look over and saw that they were Aechmea Chantini—the leaves have green and white zig-zag banding and the flowers are yellow and red clustery buds. I told them all and asked Jaz what *their* English name was, but she didn't know.

"My favourite plant ever is a bromeliad too, just like those at the ends of the pool but with purply and red buddy flowers," I said.

"Blue Rain," Poppy said.

I was staggered and sort of honoured that she'd remembered. Yes, I had told them all about the Richmond experience (well some of it anyway...), but I'd forgotten that I'd mentioned the stunning plant I'd discovered at the 'house of horrors'.

"Wow, you remembered," I said to her. "Yeah, Aechmea del Mar. Blue Rain."

I kept looking at Poppy because, though she seemed simple and sweet and predictable, I thought at that moment that she wasn't really. Predictable I mean. Or simple for that matter. I started smiling because I actually loved that she had remembered the name. Except then she slightly ruined it by saying,

"It sounded a bit sad. And it reminded me of you."

After a few beats, I changed the subject and asked Poppy the name of the programme with the mother and daughter where they ate junk food and drank coffee all the time and the mother thought it was cool to never ever cook anything and never to eat anything fresh? She told me it was 'Gilmore Girls' and that it pissed her off too that they ate crap food all the time. I said to Poppy,

"*You're* not that bothered about healthy food, though, are you?"

"It's the fact they're both super slim and sexy with shiny hair and perfect skin!" she said, which I thought was a very good point. "Like they'd look like that if they really ate the junk they piled into their gobs."

Jaz said she had only seen it a couple of times, but that she agreed that it gave a hideous message to young girls. She actually said,

"I'd say it was sinful."

I don't think Jaz was religious but she chose a powerful word on purpose, I guess.

"They're lying," she said. "They're saying it's real important to be slim and look sexy, but it's totally okay if you eat only meaty fatty floury salty sugary poisonous crap! You'll still look like a million dollars... not."

With some vigour, she messed up her black shiny hair. It looked like it hadn't been washed for a few days, so it stayed exactly where she'd put it—very textured and spiky and cool. It was going to be a tall order trying not to fall for this girl. Jaz was so strong and feisty and opinionated. I failed again and imagined a cross between her and Poppy and what a perfect girl that would be. Then I chastised myself for being greedy and desirous, reminding myself that they were both their own perfection already. Jaz carried on mocking the series, 'Gilmore Girls'.

"The kind of food they eat would literally kill you and they're implying it makes you look amazing. Lying ass wipes!"

Ha! I loved her. And as if it was part of the same topic, she then said,

"I'll go get the info sheet thing I have. Tells you about The Huntington."

She said we'd need a whole day and more to get around it.

CHAPTER TWENTY-ONE

"Deaf people can drive?!" I'd said to Jaz. I thought I'd blown it completely. I'd never seen Jaz like that. We were all standing around the island in the kitchen, ready to go off to the Huntington and I was about to ask how we would get there, when she jangled her car keys. Kamal, Poppy and I had taken a cab from the airport when we first arrived, so didn't know that Jaz had driven herself from her flat in Venice. We'd hung out at the house for the last two days, you see, so we hadn't been anywhere. It had been so chilled and cool, and Jaz said we should form a movement called The New Bohemians. It had been like we were all genderless. I saw that it truly was pointless fantasising about Jaz or Poppy and did well at quashing all my feelings. We all just got on, cooking, swimmiming, playing cards, watching movies, lounging around, laughing, like we were all a-sexual. The keys clanged onto the black granite work top. Jaz put her hands on her hips, tilted her head and said,

"Okay you guys, listen up. When I'm next to a car blaring music out, I can feel the music coz it like vibrates my car, but do you think *they* could hear an emergency vehicle...? I don't think so."

Nobody responded. Poppy was annoyed at me for saying something stupid. She took off her sun glasses and looked at me with a semi-scrunched scolding face. And it was clear Jaz had more to say on the subject. She even interrupted Kamal who said,

"Driving is mainly a visual—"

"You might be interested to know," she went on "that studies have proved deaf drivers are not more likely to be in an accident than hearing drivers. In fact, some research suggests that we have *better* peripheral vision than hearing people."

"Sorry, Jaz. I wasn't thinking," I said. "Well I mean I didn't know. I hadn't known what you were just saying."

I shuffled in my black baseball boots (with no socks because amazingly I had forgotten to pack any) and leant lightly on the granite, knowing somehow this wasn't the end of it.

"I was refused a rental car once," Jaz said.

"No, that's awful," Poppy said. "You must have been so upset."

"I was. They had the same attitude as Ollie."

Kamal said, "To be fair—"

"But I'm not stupid. I get it," Jaz said. "Most people think like that. But it's a fundamental right to be able to drive."

"You're so right," Poppy said, slotting her sun glasses onto her head. "You must get fed up when you have to explain things people should know already."

Jaz nodded and slapped the back of her sideways hand underneath her chin. I was thinking it was some sort of nervous reaction, but she said,

"That's the sign for 'fed up'. It's actually from British Sign Language."

Kamal then repeated the words and the action. He made the deaf sign again and pointed at me. Jaz laughed. Then we all did the sign and the mood was properly shifted up a notch.

Once in the car, we soon realised it was really hard to have a conversation with Jaz when she was driving. I had got in the back with Poppy and once we'd set off, I said I loved the rug on the seat, but she didn't answer me. Poppy nudged me and pointed to her ear. I felt sorry then. Again. I mean I felt quite a lot more sorry than before to be honest. For the first time I had a teeny weeny idea of the amount of challenges Jaz had to face not being able to hear. She could work out what you were saying much better when she could see your face, lip-read, lip-guess or whatever, but at the driving wheel she couldn't possibly see you. She had to look at the road, so she wouldn't even be able to make out what Kamal was saying next to her. I thought of maybe writing things down, but the sentences would have to be very short because she would mostly have to keep her eyes on the road. It was as if she read my mind. She said,

"If you're wondering what that extra mirror is for, it's so I can glance across and try to lip-read the front passenger."

"Great idea," I said, before I realised that she probably wouldn't hear that either. I then flung my hand to my mouth as Poppy nudged me again. Kamal repeated what I'd said which seemed to work as she thanked me. We soon got used to this method of Kamal repeating anything worthwhile that Poppy or I had said.

Kamal picked up on the 'right to drive' comment and started telling us that till recently, women were not allowed to drive at all in Saudi Arabia because they would most likely end up in contact with unrelated males "...which went against strict rules about gender segregation," he said. I thought the topic was a bit heavy and maybe hard to lip-read, but Jaz got right in there, adding,

"Can you believe it was only in 2015 that women were even allowed to vote there! They're like stuck in the dark ages!"

She seemed to be speeding up as she got more heated and Poppy and I looked at each other and started clinging onto our seats.

"They need male consent to do anything!" Jaz carried on. "Travelling, even signing a document! It has to end soon. It can't go on. Imagine being a deaf woman there? You probably need male permission to go piss!"

Poppy and I nodded to each other both thinking that it was working out well that Jaz had a lot to say on this as it made communication easier. In fact, she went on so long that I confess I started zoning out. I noticed Poppy had a massive ring on her left hand and I instinctively picked up her hand to have a look, saying, "Wow, where did you get this?" only I didn't actually say it out loud but rather with an exaggerated shocked and questioning face.

Poppy moved right next to my head and whispered that an 'admirer' had bought it for her, swiftly pulling away, but gifting her sweet scent that lingered under my nose. Again instinctively, and I realise now, pretty embarrassingly, I dropped her hand as quickly as I'd picked it up. She persisted in whispering in my ear—was I jealous? —so I started tickling her and she giggled and shouted. That's when Kamal turned around like a cross school teacher, so I zoned back into Jaz who was saying,

"...dipshit of a cleric wanted women to stop even wearing decorations on their abayas which already cover their whole damn bodies! Such oppression. I can't stand it. It cannot go on."

"They can't believe it," said Kamal pointing back to us two, deftly explaining away our noisy antics. "It's an abomination."

I even said,

"Just a bit of decoration on their plain black cloaks? It's not like they're demanding to wear ugly big jewellery or anything." Kamal responded by passing it on to Jaz, and Poppy responded by whacking me on the shoulder.

I had what I thought was another great idea which was to ask Jaz to give us the lowdown on this Huntington place. That way she could continue to do the talking and we'd all be able to hear, and we wouldn't be talking about politics on the gorgeous sunny day.

Jaz said,

"It was founded by this like huge business man called Henry Huntington—"

Kamal asked the question I was about to ask, the answer to which was that no he wasn't fat, just very successful i.e. rich. The driving slowed down as she described the cultural centre which was the Huntington: a world-famous research library, art collections and botanical gardens. When Jaz told us there was a collection of very early editions of Shakespeare's works in the library, Kamal said, "I'm getting palpitations." Then it was my turn to quiver when she threw in that it wasn't just A garden, but about a dozen different gardens. Jaz said,

"Your turn to get excited about the art galleries now Poppy!"

"She said she doesn't know much about art," Kamal passed on.

"Well I'm excited," said Jaz. "Even though I've seen it a heap of times I always feel warm and happy when I'm about to see this painting. Remember that poster I showed you at Kamal's' house, Poppy?"

"Mary Cassat," I said, then flung my hand to my mouth again only mentally this time. I wasn't supposed to know about the poster. I had been eavesdropping. Oops... I must have said it really loudly because Jaz heard me and said,

"I don't get it. Are you like a mind reader, Ollie Campbell? Or did I tell you when we were drunk together that night?"

"Poppy told me about it," I heard myself saying or rather, lying. I couldn't believe it had now become a two-secret scenario, what with the oh-so-not-subtle mention of *the* drunken night... Any more indiscretions and I'd be juggling deception all the way to the Huntington. I had to somehow explain myself to both Poppy and Jasvandi now. Angry possibilities about what they might say chased through my brain: 'When the hell were you drunk with Jaz?!' 'Liar! I didn't tell you. Why are you making stuff up?' 'Oh my God, have you been spying on me?'

But... it was like someone had pressed 'delete' and my words had been heard by no one as Kamal said,

"That's the impressionist painter you told me about, isn't it, Jaz?"

He turned his head to address me and Poppy.

"She was American but was educated in London, Paris and Berlin. She had a painting accepted by the Salon once but didn't have much success after that. She was friends with Degas."

I looked up 'The Salon' a while later and it was the official art exhibition in Paris between 1748 and 1890 and it was considered by many to be the greatest annual art event in the western world.

He turned back to the front. "Jaz, I was saying she didn't have many paintings accepted for exhibitions at first."

"Yeah, because of the sexist male chauvinist dipshits on the selection jury."

We all laughed. Kamal touched the back of Jaz's head in a supportive stroke. The beads of sweat were unnecessary. The spying and secret sex remained undiscovered.

"Little Girl in a Blue Armchair?" Kamal said to Jaz. "Is that the one in the gallery? The one you showed me?"

"No... you'll have to wait."

I liked the sound of that painting. Little girl in a blue armchair. Little sister in a blue armchair. Little dead sister in a blue armchair. Little dead sister in a blue box. I leant back and rested my head, flopping it sideways to face the window. I started feeling a bit sick and looked out. My throat started to hurt. Did the pain swirl around your ankles, I wondered, eager to spread up your body, to your heart, to your eyes, eager to poison you? Did black vapour snake your space, on the prowl, waiting for its moment to leap and spiral around your neck, down your throat?

Jaz was telling Kamal that Degas, who was famous for painting girls doing ballet, had a lot in common with Mary Cassatt; his mother and grandmother had been American like she was. I zoned out. I wanted to look at people, but there weren't any. I mean no one was walking about. I wondered if poisonous gas had been sprayed around the streets and everyone had been told to stay indoors. It was hot though. Maybe nobody was walking because it was hot.

We had been on a busy motorway called Ventura Freeway, so I hadn't expected to see pedestrians there, but now we were on a normal street. I always expected LA to be really sort of crowded, but there was so much space.

So many trees. They had seemed to line the entire freeway. And mountains beyond the green. We even passed a ginormous park on the right called Griffith Park. When I saw the sign, I remembered reading about it in Kamal's travel book. There was an observatory there where you got the best view of Los Angeles, only there is so much smog hanging over the city that you can't see it clearly. Anyway, we'd turned off the motorway, or should I say, freeway, and were on Allen Avenue. So, we were in a residential area now, but, as I said, there were hardly any people out and about. There was space, though, with grass and trees, hedgerows, front lawns, detached houses, and smart-looking three-story apartment blocks. Maybe it was an affluent area. I imagined terraced housing in the UK where you can take one step from the front door and you're on the road. No grass or trees or room to park cars there. They probably did have roads like that in LA where people were crammed together, just not in the part we were in. Flags too. I kept seeing American flags protruding from porches. I didn't get it. What was the point of that? Why did they need to remind themselves and others which country they were in?

"We're here!" Kamal said, pointing ahead to an ornate gated entrance.

What a place! I could go on loads about the blinkin brilliant gardens we saw, but I'll just tell you the highlights. The Japanese Garden was awesome, and I especially wanted to go into the Rose Garden to see if they had any pink Polyanthas, the flowers I planted with my little sister when she was alive.

I can tell you that the high point of the day was both plant-based and Jaz-based. We were all going to go to the library, but there wasn't enough time to do everything, so I said I was going off to The Rose Hills Foundation Conservatory for Botanical Science. It sounded ace— a 16,000 square foot greenhouse comprising three different habitats which were a lowland tropical rainforest, a cloud forest, and a carnivorous plant bog. Plus, there was interactive stuff and experiment stations focusing on various plant parts.

I was saying 'bye' and had started to wander off when Jaz suddenly decided to join me saying she wasn't bothered about seeing the books. I saw Poppy's mouth drop open slightly. She looked like she didn't want Jaz to go with me or she wanted to come with us or she wanted to go with just me. Either way I didn't say anything like, 'Come too if you want.' I just turned to walk away with Jaz while Poppy was still looking at me. It was the first time the group had split up since our arrival, so it did feel a bit strange.

Jaz and I saw aechmeas in the cloud forest, hanging from trees, their roots bravely exposed, drinking moisture from the saturated air. She took a photo of me next to an Aechmea del mar—Blue Rain. "You go together well," she had said.

We were in the rainforest section when it happened. We followed a meandering shadow-patterned path through palms and ferns and stagger-ingly beautiful trees with trunks wider than I'd ever seen. Bamboo stems as wide as tree trunks. It was so hot and humid. Everything seemed to slow down so that when Jaz took my hand, it was like a slow-motion film. Seemed like we needed a sound track, only Jaz probably wouldn't have been able to hear it. I looked over at her. She was wiping the sweat from her face with the hand that wasn't holding mine. It was the first time I'd seen her wearing a dress. It made her look younger. And prettier somehow. It had a low neck on which two of the three buttons were open so that it was flapped open. The sticky air clung the fine cotton to her. I felt my breath-ing change as I looked forward and wandered on. We hadn't walked very far before she pulled me to sit with her on a bench. I stretched my arm out to rest on the wood behind her.

"Look. Over there," she said, pointing ahead and to the right. "It's very sexual, don't you think?"

She was pointing to an impressive plant in a colossal pot. One giant spike in the middle surrounded by a leaf-like structure. And well, she was right, it certainly was pretty phallic.

"It's so sticky hot. I wish I could take my dress off."

I thought but accidentally said out loud, "I wish you could too."

"Maybe later..." She did that half pouty smile thing and that was it. From the resolve to be friends only and 'forget' about what happened that night, this...

I breathed in the earthy air and turned to look at her. I could almost hear reproductive steam from the plants and trees enveloping us. The heavy wetness seeped into our pores. One of those electric moments when your connection is so deeply intense and real. I could feel what was coming. Her damp mouth made me forget where we were, and I lost myself in her. I found my hand, with a will of its own, inside the front of her dress. She didn't say anything, so I carried on. I'd never known a kiss could be so sensuous. It seemed to go on forever. I kept going like it was the last chance ever to kiss her. I wanted to carry her to the soil and roll around there, caressed by leaves and fleshy flowers.

We only pulled apart from each other when a passer-by said,

"Eww. Get a room, you guys." And the wife adding, "Gross. Teens can be so low these days."

Jaz hadn't heard it and I was glad.

"Why do you look so sad?" Jaz said to me.

"I'm happy," I said, but I knew what she meant, and I knew the answer. I couldn't be with her. It would have felt like the most natural thing in the world to go back to Poppy and Kamal, hand in hand, and announce our relationship, but they wouldn't like it. They wouldn't be happy for us. It would have to remain a secret. How do folk do it? *Why* do they do it? Well I had a notion of why because I felt it myself—the strong magnet of one human being to another, the connection, the twin sense of desire, the intense allure of fresh passionate possibilities. And then the thought of love for other people. People who would be so so hurt. Possessive controlling 'love' rears its head, butting in like a stubborn goat. The old solid known worn love, the safe and familiar love.

I knew I cared too much about Kamal to let things go on, let things go further. And I cared too much about Poppy too. I saw clearly, pulling away from the heavy moment with Jaz that I wanted her really badly, but I loved Poppy and Kamal. And that kind of love, boring and steady as it was, was real and was what counted. I had an urge to go straight back and find Kamal and Poppy. I wanted to tell them that Jaz and I had kissed and had made love in England but that it was all over, that I had decided nothing was to come of it. And they would be pleased with me. Pleased that I had done the right thing. I mean I'm not saying part of me knew I could drop everything and be with Jaz. God knows I had mapped out a life for us in my head, but I chose to let my desires float into the wind. At that moment it felt like it was going against nature. It felt like a sacrifice. It felt like grief. It made me want to cry.

I hoped Jaz wouldn't be hurt by my decision either. Probably not, as she was such a strong person. She was a feminist and I loved that. So am I. Maybe so is anyone who cares about equality. Which surely must be nearly everyone? But I didn't fool myself that her being a feminist made her unemotional. I just hoped she'd be okay with it.

"You could have fooled me," said Jaz.

"What?"

"Happy? You do a weird 'happy'. Let's go check out the giant plant, huh?"

It was called Amorphallus titanum and was one of the world's most unusual plants. I've looked it up since that night and it only blooms rarely like once every seven years or something and when it does it stinks like dead bodies. The stench of rotting flesh attracts insect pollinators. And the flower's only there for forty-eight hours. How intense. Waiting that long, going mental, then back to nothing.

Once we'd explored the greenhouse area, Jaz insisted we head to the Rose and Herb Gardens instead of going to find Poppy and Kamal. As it turned out, once we were there, *they* found *us*.

"A rose by any other name would smell as sweet."

Shakespeare. Kamal.

"Hi, you guys," said Jaz, dropping my hand. "What did you say?"

"It's easier with commas," Kamal said. "A rose comma by any other name comma would smell as sweet."

"What? What does that mean?" said Jaz. The answer came from Poppy which I hadn't expected. She looked sweet herself with her hair all messed up from the sweaty day and I saw she had bought something. I loved to see her like that, all natural and content and at one with herself. It felt like coming home. I smiled about my decision re Jaz. No one would be hurt... so I had thought.

"It's like it doesn't matter what your name is," she said. "Like you'd still be lovely even if you weren't called Jasvandi. By any other name, you'd still be sweet."

My lips were still tingling from kissing Jasvandi and now I felt like grabbing Poppy to me. What the H was wrong with me?

"I did Romeo and Juliet at school which is a famous play by William Shakespeare," she said. "It's what Juliet says to Romeo because their family names are stopping them being together. They're madly in love, but nobody else knows about it." She wiped sweat from above her top lip and pushed her hair back. "They have to keep the secret because they both know that nobody else would approve. It's because their families, the Montagues and the Capulets, are enemies."

Kamal started clapping, joined by Jaz, which I thought was patronising even though he meant it, if you know what I mean. He told us that along with *Hamlet*, *Romeo and Juliet* was the most frequently performed play of the thirty-seven Shakespeare wrote. It reminded him that he wanted me to take a photo of him next to a bust of Shakespeare as there was actually a Shakespeare Garden too at The Huntington.

After photographing Kamal in all sorts of funny poses, we all went to have a look at Jaz's painting by Mary Cassatt. Kamal had wanted to see a painting called *Blue Boy* by Thomas Gainsborough which was bought at great expense from England, but we didn't have time.

We all agreed the painting was gorgeous. It was called *Breakfast in Bed* and depicted a mother lying in bed with her young, maybe three-year old, daughter sitting up next to her. The mother looked kind of sad, her eyes glazed over, whereas the girl was present in the space. Maybe the girl had died, and this painting showed the mother imagining her little daughter was still there. It was all whitey blue apart from their limbs.

"You know all her subjects were women, right?" Jaz said.

We all stood in a line, contemplating the work in front of us. Kamal rested his arm on my shoulder and everything felt just right again. I can't tell you how much I wished it could have stayed like that.

"Usually women not in the presence of men too, Jaz said. "All of them look in control. Look at her face. She owns the space. I love that." She shook her shoulders with the thrill she felt. "It wasn't like that with other impressionists. I love Mary Cassatt—so strong and modern. People call it 'feminine', her art, but that's insulting."

"Insulting?" said Kamal, removing his arm from me.

"She was so damn skilled and insightful," Jaz said. "It's not femin*ine*, it's femin*ist*."

She was great, Jasvandi was, there was no getting away from it. I hoped we could still be friends when I told her I didn't want to be in a relationship with her. I would tell her that night, I decided.

CHAPTER TWENTY-TWO

The beer that night was a mistake. A terrible mistake. We had eaten pasta, made by Jaz, and were out by the pool drinking beer. She had laid some tea lights out on the table like she had the previous nights. It was a proper dining table near the back of the house, but outside. I had put on one of my dance playlists which swirled with the warm air. Jaz assured us it was fine to have it on, as long as it wasn't too loud. I mean it didn't ruin her chances of hearing us, though I knew it didn't help.

I was firm in my decision—pursuing anything with Jaz was just too dangerous. I wanted to, oh did I want to, but it wasn't worth it. I knew it had to stop before things got too deep. A few beers would help drown my sorrows I believed.

The lights in the pool were on and lights at each corner of the pool too—like electric candles each about a foot tall. There were fairy lights draped over the pool house and even a lit-up tree. I imagined what the view of us was like from up there. The gentle flickers and flashes of cosy water calmed us all. A track I loved— 'Sure Thing' by St Germain—rocked us further. A hammock of joyous grateful friends, breathing and smiling and swaying to the beat of our hearts. What a vibe. The atmosphere seemed too good to be true.

Freeze frame that moment—four hammock-friends relaxing outside in the warm air, water flickering with mini lightning, candles dancing, tummies full, beers open, stars out. Freeze frame because that was the 'before', that was the 'life is really not that bad at all, is it?', the 'how lucky we all are being in Los Angeles in a cool house, being close, understanding each other, caring about each other'. The 'before...'

Poppy was tipsier than I'd ever seen her. She got up and started dancing, drink in hand. She looked cool, barefoot-twirling. But there was something new about her. She became an animal. Unpredictable. Scary. She spilt her drink. She began bashing into me 'by accident' and making a stupid exaggerated deal of saying sorry. Something was definitely up. Jaz had just fetched ice cream when Poppy said,

"Oooh. Goodie. Something cold. Mind you, we do have coldness round the table already." I felt a pain in my chest. She laughed and nudged me again. "I was going to say to Ollie earlier that he was back to his old self today. We had such a laugh in the car. But now he's gone all cold again."

Nobody said anything. Nobody knew what she was on about. Nobody knew where this was going... and I can tell you for nothing, I wish wish wish it had not been going where it was...

"Were you and Jaz holding hands today?" she said. "Or did my eyes deceive me?"

Shit. No time. No space.

"And what did you mean, Jaz, about 'when we were drunk that night'?"

Double shit.

Nobody said anything. Then, that was it, Poppy went for it.

"Oh my God, are neither of you going to say anything?!" She was pointing her ice cream spoon first at me then at Jaz.

"Poppy," said Kamal. "Why don't you sit down?"

She did sit down but then stood up straight away, still waving the spoon.

"I'm going to get a cigarette," said Jasvandi.

The cool funky laid-back vibe of the music jarred with the now jagged air.

"I can't believe you smoke!" said Kamal.

"I can't believe you give a shit about her smoking when they've been getting it on behind our backs," said Poppy. "Haven't you? Haven't you!" she shouted. "Making fools of us!"

Kamal pushed his half-finished bowl of ice cream to the middle of the table, pushed his glasses up his nose, and folded his arms.

"They've been, you know, finding moments," Poppy said, and her eyes started watering. The anger lifted. Bloody hell I remember how really really hurt she looked. Like her world was collapsing. I mean was it truly really that big of a deal?

"Kissing when we're not there no doubt, Kamal," Poppy said, trying to shake him into some sort of action, get him on her side.

He started shuffling in his seat, glancing at me. Jaz reappeared.

"Is it true that you and Ollie have been physical with each other?" Kamal said to her.

And that's when it happened. That was the end of life as we knew it. Life as I knew it. That was the beginning of the 'after'.

"We only had sex once. It didn't mean anything."

Freeze again. The words hung in the air like hovering hand grenades. Tumbleweed bounced along the pool. Birds closed their beaks. Stars stopped shining. But *she* didn't stop.

"We were like drunk and we were together and it kinda happened naturally. You guys weren't supposed to find out."

And they hadn't needed to find out. "It's bound to come out at some point," Jaz had said all those weeks ago. Jesus not like this though. Please. No.

Poppy now looked like she'd been shot. An anger returned. She threw her spoon into the pool. She picked up her ice cream bowl and flung that into the pool as well. My spoon clattered to the ground as she picked up *my* ice cream bowl and threw *that* into the pool *too*. Poppy stumbled around her chair and staggered to the house. She spun round before climbing the step and said,

"You bastard. I hate you. I so so hate you. I never want to see you again."

More tumbleweed before I looked sideways at Kamal. He wouldn't look at either me or Jaz, but said,

"Was it at Auntie's house?"

"No. Ollie's."

I awaited his verdict. I was in a dock, dressed in rags, pleading for my life, head hung.

"So, having lost your own sister, you tried to steal mine."

"Don't say that," Jaz said, now starting to cry. "He hasn't stolen anything. Don't be dumb."

She then threw her cigarette into the pool saying, "You have to let this go, Kamal."

I wondered what would be thrown into the pool next. Me? Kamal got up slowly with a blank face and Jasvandi followed him into the house.

'Euphorbia tirucalli. Euphorbia tirucalli. Euphorbia tirucalli,' I repeated in my head. I had seen them at The Huntington. 'Sticks on Fire'. My mind went into its 'pause' phase. 'Brugmansia Sanguinea. Brugmansia Sanguinea. Disygotheca elegantissima. Disygotheca elegantissima. Disygotheca elegantissima.'

The Emotion Library had a whole room put aside for this. "This one's big," the librarian would say. "Just close the door, take a quick breath and come straight out. This feeling can kill you if you stay too long."

The swimming pool water was like molten tar. My body floated out of itself and dived into the coffin-shaped black hole to burn and melt and never return.

Tears fizzled onto the candles just before I blew them out. Blew the 'before' out. I sat back down. The cool, laid back self-satisfied song, 'Sure Thing' mocked me.

Weirdly, the spirit of Thomas Diamond, the homeless man I had met in the park the year before, came to 'visit' me. I snuggled into him, lay on his crusty dead coat. "Look after your mam, there's a good lad," I remembered him saying. Then I said out loud, "I want my mam." I didn't even feel embarrassed.

'Euphorbia tirucalli. Brugmansia Sanguinea. Disygotheca elegantissima...'

Jasvandi helped me change my flight and I went back to England the next day. Some days after getting back home, I received a card from Poppy. It's what she had bought while Jaz and I had split up from her and Kamal at The Huntington. She must have written and posted it before everything hit the fan, when they were having tea before they met up with us again. It was of an Aechmea del mar otherwise known as Blue Rain.

'Thought of you, of course, when I saw this. I'm sorry I said 'Blue Rain' reminded me of you. I wanted you to know that I didn't just mean the old you or the blue you. I can see why you love this flower. It does remind me of you. It is beautiful with that brilliant pink spike in the middle ending with purply-blue bracts. I think that word's right. I think the description said they were called that. The plant is very unusual. It is tender but tough. It is perfectly smooth but leathery. You'll be shocked that I looked up the word aechmea and it comes from the Greek and it means 'spear tip'. I read that is because there are very sharp spines on the outside of the leaves, but inside, the plant is incredibly soft. And though a Blue Rain blooms for a very very long time, it is easy to care for. And even though it's easy to care for so you don't have to give it much, it gives a lot back. Blue rain's loveliness is always there even if it hides behind spikey leaves and very important, it never gives up. I think that's the main reason I love it.'

CHAPTER TWENTY-THREE

"You need to enrol on a course," Grandpa said, coughing and spluttering. He still had a nasty chesty thing and he still wasn't walking exactly right. Made me feel selfish, indulging in my own problems, when an old man never complained about anything despite his annoying lingering cough. "Let's go to the library this afternoon and see what's on offer."

I explained that we could look online, and it would be easier, but he decided we were definitely going to the actual library. I didn't mind. It meant getting out of the house. It meant moving. It meant light. It meant imagining something in the future.

I didn't want to do a course. I would have to get qualifications for a start, which meant I would have to finish school. My grandparents said it went against their ideas to suggest I went to sixth form college and not stay on at school when the exams would be over in June. God, even two more terms already loomed like a torture chamber. Grandma went on about signing up for a course too, in fact they both seemed obsessed with education. In the meantime, they said I 'needed to get out'. I told them I'd go the library on my own and do some research into post-sixteen courses.

During that time, Grandma looked at me like she knew. As in everything. It seemed that way anyway.

Grandpa must have told her a few things. Either that or she was psychic. Nobody spoke about it. No one asked details or even seemed surprised I had come back from LA early to be honest.

Jaz had texted and emailed, but I hadn't even opened them. Well the emails anyway. Her texts were basically to tell me about the emails.

I should mention that my brothers Sam and Nathan were both at home when I arrived back. Sam didn't live at home any more, but he seemed to have moved back in. The sudden change had coincided with me flying back from Los Angeles, so I guessed it was to do with me.

"I'm glad you're here," I had said separately to both of them. Neither of them really responded from what I remember. That felt strange at the time. Sam thought he could read me like a book, so maybe he was just managing to stop himself saying, 'I knew this would happen.'

When I say, 'didn't respond', I mean they did ask me what had happened, but they didn't go on about it and I didn't say anything about me or what had happened. But they both told me Mam and Dad were cutting their trip short and coming back at the weekend. I couldn't believe it. They didn't care about me, but had heard, well, something, something bad about me, and had decided to come all the way home. I can't tell you how happy I was about that. I hadn't read some of the emails my mam had sent me. Well most to be honest. The thought of seeing in black and white what she thought of me... To read the explanation of why she didn't want to see me in hospital. I knew she'd wished I'd died instead of Lily. She had three boys then finally got her dream—a baby girl—but she died.

I would have to make amends for not replying, for not keeping in touch. I could buy her some white roses. Yes of course. That's what I'd do. In my book, 'Flower Wisdom' which Auntie Colette bought me, it said they symbolised pure love. And I could make her a card. I could fish out that poem Kamal sent me when Lily was dying. The best lines were:

The rose repays thee all thy smiles –

The stainless lily rears
Dew in the chalice of its wiles,
As sparkling as thy tears.

I imagined Mam cooking my favourite dinner and playing me her music, rocking me like she did that time in the holiday house after we lost Lily. I felt a tropical breeze wrapping round my heart. A little girl holding a broken bird. An old lady firming a fading head to her breast. I found myself trancing through a list of Mam's favourite musicians—Joni Mitchell, Carole King, Judie Tsuke, Janis Joplin, John Martin, Steely Dan, Pat Metheney, Andy Mckee, Eric Whitacre, Keith Jarrett...

I walked to the library on my own. I listened to 'Love me Still' by Bruce Hornsby and Chaka Kahn which my mam loved. I had laughed the time she said she partly hated the song because its instant effect was to make her cry, but I knew what she meant now. The sky was bright grey, and rain came straight down, as in vertical. Grandma had told me to take an umbrella, but I didn't want to. I enjoyed the water trickling down my face. Mam must think of Lily when she listens to this song or *doesn't* listen to this song, it occurred to me. The lyrics prodded every part of my body. 'I need you now, do you love me still?' I thought of Poppy. 'Only you have seeeeeen the hidden part of me.' Waters connecting now, running down the front of my neck. 'Call me foolhardy if you will, I loved you then, do you love me still?' I enjoyed my sodden jeans sticking to my thighs, heavy with rain. 'So many smiles and lies surround me, Empty expectations, faceless fears, Sometimes this life is a bitter pill, I love you now, do you love me still?'

I looked down at the pavement the whole way, lest I should see someone I knew and be expected to say hello. Just me and the song and the water. 'Only you have seeeeeen, the other side of me.'

I pulled one of the glass library doors open and bumped into a woman.

"Oh dear, you're soaked. And not even your hood up?"

How come a stranger thought they could tell me what I should and shouldn't do?

"Why don't you—" I couldn't believe I was about to tell a stranger to shut her mouth. She didn't care about me. She didn't give a shit about me. She was just trying to teach me, set me on a better, more normal road, make me more like her, like everyone who had a clue about how you were supposed to live. Well, I didn't care either. Not even enough to finish my sentence. I took a deep breath and forced a smile at the thought of seeing my parents. They didn't care about *me*, but if I was true to myself, I did still care about *them* and I suppose must have missed them in a way.

I didn't bother asking about courses. I didn't want to talk to anyone. I sat at a computer and enrolled on an online course called 'Horticulture' about gardening and organic food growing. I needed to tend to my vege-tables. I had let it go. I had let everything go. I hadn't planned to sign up for the course but was surprised to learn that those sort of courses even existed. You didn't have to meet anyone at all; it was all from reading and watching videos. My legs were damp and cold and I started to shiver as I looked up and around the room. A few old people. A few young people. Some at computers, some stooped over long wooden tables, one in a soft chair with a magazine. 'New Scientist'. All silent. In their own worlds. Finding out whatever it was they thought they needed to know. To im-prove themselves. To be better versions of themselves. To make people like them. Or maybe to like themselves. In a vain search to take the edge off their self-loathing. It occurred to me it was a good place to come to if you felt you wanted to be near others but didn't want to talk to anyone.

Grandma had made a chicken curry. I wasn't hungry but took a tiny bit. It wasn't 'proper' curry like Dad makes or like Kamal makes with millions of different spices; it was just a jar of some sort poured over fried chicken with tomatoes and curry powder. Nathan was bemoaning his lack of girl-friend and started asking Grandma and Grandpa for advice.

"It's well-annoying. Girls really really like me, but they just think I'm a laugh, you know. It's always just friends. They think I'm funny," he said. "What do you think the secret is, Grandma?"

"Hold back a bit of magic," Sam said. "Don't put all your special offers on the first page."

"What you on about?" Nathan said, stopping chewing for a few seconds.

"Mystery," said Grandpa, wiping yellow rice from the side of his mouth. "If you're like a girl and engage in all sorts of listening and open talking, they'll see you as one of them rather than a possible partner."

"Sexist," I heard myself saying.

"Hear hear," Grandma and Sam echoed. It was nice to smile together.

Grandpa wiped his mouth with his napkin this time before placing it carefully to the right of his plate and saying,

"Hey, I'm saying girls are more open and honest."

He coughed for what seemed like an embarrassing amount of time before continuing.

"Mostly boys struggle with expressing emotions. It's a gift, young man. But, for what it's worth, it was an air of mystery which drew your grandmother to me."

This time Grandma wiped *her* mouth with her napkin, while grabbing her glass of water and gulping some down to prevent choking, like they do in films.

"You were cleaning spittle from your French horn when I first saw you!" (They had met when they played in an orchestra together.)

That got us all going. Even got Grandpa who had to get up and hobble round in a circle to stop himself choking.

"I hardly noticed though, he was so handsome," Grandma added.

"Now we're getting to the truth," said Grandpa, sitting back down.

"He's right really about the mystery," Grandma said. "His good looks couldn't hide the fact that there was a lot there. We didn't get together straight away though. He asked me out and I said no."

Sam, Nathan and I all gasped.

"What if he'd died that night, you know, after you'd turned him down? That's tight, man. Why did you do that??" said Nathan.

Grandma told us that she knew he would ask her out again if he really liked her, which we all thought was crazy. None of this was helping Nathan anyway. I made the mistake of saying I thought Grandma was right to bide her time. Sam said something like, 'Not years like you though, eh, Ollie?' I wasn't entirely sure what he meant by that.

Grandma served herself some more curry (I don't know where she put it—her appetite was voracious, but she was slim as anything.) She said, with her mouth full so you could barely make it out,

"The right person will come along, Nathan, you'll see. Just have to be patient. You may have already met the right person, but the timing has to be right too."

Attention turned to me and my 'course'. Grandpa asked me where it was based and I told a white lie, making out my cheap course was not online. I said it was at Newcastle University which he and Grandma were thrilled about. My life was like a compost heap—set after set of fresh rot on top of old.

It has to be said that Sam really did seem to read me a lot of the time. He put his bent arms behind his head and did a stretchy/breathey thing before saying to me,

"You wanna do a bit of gardening tomorrow?"

"Yeah okay."

Sam had put on Mam's false fur coat and Grandpa's old University scarf and had brought a camping chair to my vegetable patch. I thought he'd wanted to help me, but he must have wanted to just watch me work or talk.

Both, it turned out. Well, all three actually because he did help me a bit too. It was one of those chairs with hanging slots for drinks and he had put a can in each one. He was kind like that. As he opened his and replaced it in its canvas holder, I gestured that I didn't want mine yet.

"What's the plan, my man?" He took a swig from his can—fizzy lemon of some kind I seem to remember.

"The parsnips need harvesting. And the leeks. And I should do some pruning. The acer needs cutting back."

"Acer? Where's that?" Sam said.

I used the trowel in my right hand to point over to where it was.

"There are loads of different varieties. That one's a Beni-kagami."

"Sounds Japanese."

"It is," I said. "They're Japanese maples. They're amazing shrubs."

I dropped the trowel onto the grass so I could go up and feel the leaves.

"They morph into completely different colours through the seasons. There aren't many plants which can have such a massive range of colouring in their foliage."

"Morph through the seasons, eh? A bit like you then."

I didn't really know what he meant, so I ignored it and said,

"There are two pairs of gardening gloves in the greenhouse and another trowel. You gonna help me dig the parsnips out?"

I taught Sam my special technique for removing the parsnips without snapping them and decided we needed kitchen forks instead of trowels, which Sam fetched from the house. I thought of nothing while we harvested the vegetables. I loved the fresh stinging air on my cheeks. I thought of the smoggy heavy hot air in Los Angeles and coughed away the sensation of suffocating. 'Morph through the seasons a bit like you.' The words floated back into my head.

"What do you mean, 'like you'?" I said. "The leaves changing through the seasons. You said, 'A bit—"

"Yeah. Your moods. They kind of vary a lot. Don't you think?" he said.

I accidently snapped a parsnip while pulling it out and flung the fork across the vegetable patch. I sat back with my knees bent and felt pressure in my throat and behind my eyes.

"Is that why Mam and Dad are coming back?" I said, looking at the ground. "Because they think I'm mentally ill?"

Sam gently stabbed his fork into the earth and we both stood up. He told me to sit in the camp chair. I thought he was going to tell me how Mam was going to force me into therapy or that we were going to make a family plan to try to get me on some sort of proper path. I opened my drink can and gulped from it before folding my arms and crossing my legs. I readied myself to hear what had obviously been discussed behind my back and raised my head to face my brother.

Sam slid off his gardening gloves and placed them on the ground beside him as he bent down to my level, steadying himself on the chair. He had the look of someone about to say something serious. Oh God, surely they weren't going to send me away, I thought.

I was wrong. About the sending away. About it being about me. About everything. It's hard to fathom how anyone could have been so wrong about so many things, as I was at that moment.

JASVANDI'S JOURNAL 6

Dear Journal,

Why hasn't Ollie answered any of my emails? For God's sake, it's February now. I am wretched that I have messed up his life.

I told him that I'd explained to Kamal and Poppy that the whole god-damn mess was my fault. I told him that they didn't buy it till I explained everything, like EVERYTHING about my past, I mean our past. Even about Kamal's twin brother. I told Ollie I thought he was probably off the hook. Shit, maybe that sounded too flippant. I only wanted to make him feel better.

In one of the emails, I even decided to tell him that Poppy had been so crestfallen when she found out about us two that she said she'd never speak to him again. I told him that I could tell by how devastated she was that there was no doubt she had been madly in love with him and that my very early hunches about those two had obviously been right. I must say it sure did shock me how much she sobbed, and I mean out loud and for daaaaaays, after it came out that I'd slept with Ollie.

I thought for sure he'd write back after my last email telling him that Poppy had moved in with her new boyfriend. I didn't say much about it, hoping that would spur him on to contact me.

For what it's worth, journal, I don't think it's the real thing between Poppy and Greg. I mean they're like so different. He's five years older than her for a start and he seems much more intense than she is. I'd say he was the possessive, jealous type. I said that to Poppy, but she reckoned it was amazing that someone wanted her that much. Then he persuades her to move in with him after six weeks!

Anyway, I should record that after Ollie left, like the very next day, I mustered all the courage I could to tell Kamal and Poppy about the rape.

Poppy couldn't believe I was only twelve and was visibly upset when I explained that he was a family friend giving me a lift home and that nobody had believed me. Kamal hardly spoke to me afterwards. I was so sad that he decided to change his flight and leave earlier than planned to go back to England. I mean he said something like 'It's terrible,' but nothing much else. I guess he simply didn't know/doesn't know what to say. I wouldn't know what to say. I guess I gave the poor guy too much information. Anyways, he wanted to get back to high school, unlike Poppy, who had transferred to a high school over here and seemed to have plenty of money.

I will admit that it was only when I went to counselling and again when I was telling them about it that I realised it might be why I haven't been careful with myself. At the time, I felt like a piece of meat, so I've kinda acted a bit like one ever since apparently. I learned that my body was disrespected, and my honesty was disrespected so I did this whack thing where instead of fighting everything, I disrespected *myself*. Like I believed I wasn't worth anything.

When my brother went all quiet after I'd disclosed what happened to me, something crazy gripped me and I spouted everything out. I told them of the lie about the car crash and the adoptions. I've never seen anyone fight tears as much as Kamal did that evening. It was like there was an invisible film spilling them back into his eyes. He kept shaking his head like he didn't believe me or he couldn't take it in or he didn't want to take it in.

I know it was all too much. I guess I couldn't bear the thought of everyone going to sleep with the rape on their minds, so I felt compelled to change the subject, but I see now that I just added more upset.

I explained what really happened—that our father had left us, never to be seen again. Kamal shook his head. I described the mess our mother lived in, the alcohol, the drugs, the poverty, the mental illness. He dropped his head but continued to shake it. I told him that me and the babies—him and his twin—were taken away. His head stopped shaking then. I'd say he was in shock. But my mouth kept going.

"Aunt Gopi wouldn't take all of us," I explained. "She only wanted one baby." At this point, head still hung low, he actually started to kind of nod, like it all was suddenly making sense. I related the last bit of the story, that I was adopted and taken to the US and that the other boy was adopted and taken to Canada.

That's when Kamal did whisper something. He looked straight at me like he was begging me to tell him I'd made it up and said,

"My... twin?"

Poppy had covered her mouth and was sobbing by now, but Kamal looked into the distance, adjusted his glasses, and walked away.

Please God Kamal will contact me soon. I know from Gopi that Kamal has gone back to high school but that he has not exchanged one word with Ollie. Gopi told me that Anna, Ollie's mom, said he was in a deep depression and that he was like a zombie, saying very little, but still gardening. He had been not too bad until he had found out about his Grandpa.

Please God Ollie writes back to me soon.

Oh, by the way, I couldn't face ruining three peoples's lives, so I had to make a horrendous decision. You know what I'm talking about, journal, but I cannot ever record it in writing. Plus I cannot ever tell anybody. God forgive me.

CHAPTER TWENTY-FOUR

"It's Grandpa," Sam had said.

COPD. Chronic Obstructive Pulmonary Disease.

That was Grandpa's diagnosis.

"He hasn't got long to go, they think," Sam had said. "Apparently had it for ages."

That's why Mam and Dad came back home.

Life was not all about me. Not at all about me. And it was short. And it should be wonderful but is often a bastard.

I see now that despite how I felt when I heard the news, it was a distraction from myself. For the four months between me getting back from LA and April, the family did their best to avoid talking about problems. Everyone was being as positive as they could be.

I had given the flowers and the poem to Mam when they got back. She had hugged me and kissed me and cried and everything was back to normal. I say 'normal', but nothing really felt normal at that time.

I mention April because that's when things changed.

Nobody knew anything about why I'd come back from Los Angeles apart from Grandpa. And he hadn't told a soul, bless him. Between that December and the following April, Mam kept repeating what a surprise it was that Poppy had stayed in California and how upset her mum was and how everyone at school was shocked because she had always been so, well, reliable and conformist. She kept asking about Kamal too. She was baffled as to why I wasn't seeing him.

That was more than I knew, by the way—that Poppy had stayed in the USA--until Poppy's mother had told mine. In fact, it wasn't till the April that Mam mentioned, in passing, the reason Poppy had stayed out. She must have thought that I knew but that it was a taboo subject.

She'd 'met someone' whatever that meant. Well I'm not daft, I knew what it meant, but I wanted to know who and for how long and why and if she was coming back and if she was in love with him. When was she coming back? It occurred to me that there might be some information in the emails I'd received from Jasvandi. I'd left it so long, but it was time. It was definitely time. I decided to read them.

"Will you come down to eat with us today?" someone or other would be asking me through my bedroom door during those three days after reading the emails.

I needed to reach out to Kamal, but I didn't know what to do. It occurred to me that he might never have been told about his brother if I hadn't cocked everything up. I struggled to work out if it was a good or a bad thing that he knew the truth. And all that stuff about his parents. I felt sick for him. He was lied to sooo badly. And that bastard who violated Jasvandi when she was only twelve. Jesus. I felt like smashing a whole house to pieces. And it occurred to me that Poppy might not have... gosh, even now I can't bring myself to say it. It seemed like people had acted in ways that would probably have life-long consequences.

I kept rereading the postcard Poppy had written to me in LA. I must have read it a thousand times. It became harder and harder to decipher as the water spread the ink out. Just as each of Poppy's words blurred into the next, so each day blurred into the next.

'I think that's the main reason I love it,' she had written about the plant Blue Rain, but in my mind, I read the 'it' as 'you'.

No one knew about me reading the stream of emails and everyone thought I was only upset about Grandpa who'd taken a turn for the worse.

In the end, it was Grandpa himself who got me out of my room.

"You up for a jamming session in a minute?" he had said. It was he who was depressed and for very good reason—he was bloody dying—but there was me, feeling sorry for myself. His mellow voice was all I needed to drag me from my head. His spoken words were like balls of soft squidgy sound floating through the door with all the edges perfectly smoothed off.

His sentence had soothed me and woken me up.

"I'll be right down," I said. I could hear him lingering at the door to make sure I was really going to move. His breathing was shallower than it used to be and was even interspersed with quiet grunts, no doubt triggered by the effort endured to climb the stairs.

Sam and Nathan had moved a single bed to the living room the day I moved into my bedroom. I hadn't quite got it, but Grandpa said it was so he could go to the downstairs loo. And here he was at the top of the stairs.

I opened the door and there he was, leaning on the wall, a grey smiling face and a mouth open like a fledgling bird, gasping as much life into his mouth as would venture in.

"Are you okay?" I said. "You look worn out."

"You don't exactly look the picture of health yourself," he said, and he messed up my hair and pulled me to him for a hug. "See? No patting," he said and when we pulled away, there was a half-hour conversation in one look. The emotion library would have struggled with that one. It would be in the 'still under analysis' room.

I helped Grandpa downstairs, before we settled into the music room.

We talked in between playing. When I told Grandpa how sad he seemed he said,

"It's just because I can't do the things I used to, that's all. It's a strange sadness when you can't go for a walk."

"But you've been out in the wheel chair," I said.

"Yes, and oh I'm so grateful for that, Ollie. Being in nature is wonderful," he said. "But when you're at this stage, each trip feels like you're saying goodbye. Goodbye to every plant and tree you see."

He shuffled on his piano stool and turned away from me, saying,

"I'm trying to say that doesn't feel like joy... you understand?"

I didn't know what to say to that apart from,

"There might be more joy to come though. I mean afterwards, you know?"

He knew exactly what I was saying and swivelled round to face me again, saying,

"A good point, Ollie. A very good point. I'm not afraid of dying, you know?"

He adjusted his shabby cap. He said,

"If there's another world after this, maybe it is one where there is no guilt, hurt or fear. Just pure love. You never know. That would be something, wouldn't it?"

I jumped on this as it was the most uplifted he'd sounded in months.

"Oh, I'm positive that's what it'll be like. It'll be incredibly joyful up there."

I felt a bit stupid saying, 'up there', but Grandpa went on to say that he was inclined to agree and that he would give me a sign if it turned out to be true.

I said, "Nothing scary, please!"

I was sort of hoping that the conversation about death was over, but Grandpa said that if us humans were all capable of reaching this higher level of serenity and pure love in death, we should be able to reach it or get near it on this earth. He said that if we end up in a place where we don't bear grudges and where we care about everything and everybody, then we should start early and be as compassionate and forgiving as we can, now in this world. He added,

"That means forgiving yourself as well, you know?"

I didn't say anything. I wasn't sure how I was expected to answer.

"Guilt will eat you up if you don't release it," he said, actually pointing at me now. He spluttered a cough and said, "Guilt is a very lowly emotion or state. Let it go. Shame, anger, all that bollocks, will keep you trapped. Aim for acceptance, accepting everything. You must take courage, Ollie, do you hear me?"

"Yes."

"You will find it. We all make bad choices sometimes in our lives, but it doesn't mean you're a bad person. You know you're not, don't you...? Look at me."

I raised my eyes to meet his.

"You're not in any way a bad person, Ollie. Trust me."

I carried on looking at him. I couldn't bring myself to agree with him, but I managed to say,

"Can you make *other* people forgive *you*?"

"You can't before they forgive themselves too. You can set the example."

This talk was getting deep and I'm not sure I was even following it. Grandpa must have sensed my confusion.

"If you feel it will help, you can actually let them know that you're sorry," he said. He fiddled with the back of his cap, looked at the floor for a second while he gathered his thoughts and went on, "Or better still, *show* them that you're sorry. Which doesn't necessarily mean doing anything. If you feel it, you'll show it somehow."

I think he was starting to confuse himself by this time. He said,

"Now then, let's play!"

He took off his cap, flung it in the air, caught it, put it on backwards, rubbed his hands together and said,

"I'd say that overall, things aren't going brilliantly well for either of us, so we need to pick ourselves up. Soooo, let's play...—"

"Pick Up the Pieces!" he said and added, "F Minor, yeah?" still rubbing his hands together.

And we were off. We had a right laugh playing, 'Pick up the Pieces' by The Average White Band. The sax part is proper excellent but then the song was actually written by a saxophone player! Grandpa told me that like a lot of great creative works, it nearly didn't make it and that Malcolm 'Molly' Duncan, the songwriter/saxophonist didn't think it should be a single. He apparently thought the band were crazy to suggest such a thing and said, "It's a funk instrumental played by Scotsmen with no lyrics other than a shout!" But he was wrong, I'm glad to say. Grandpa told me that sometimes a creative venture doesn't even come to fruition because the powers that be (whoever they are) decide that it doesn't fit in, that it's too different to sell, BUT that sometimes it's exactly this differentness which becomes the selling point. Interesting stuff.

It didn't take long for us to get back to the subject of death though. After we'd played, Grandpa told me that there was a tragic side to the success of Pick Up the Pieces. The band became well known and started partying like a lot of bands do. Robbie, the drummer, was a real character, it sounded like; everyone loved him, it seemed. He took a drug at a party in Los Angeles and didn't know it was heroin. He must have overdosed as he died of a heart attack the next morning. He didn't live to see the single reach No 1 in America. And can you believe, he was only twenty-four years old?

We needed more picking up.

We were both laughing after playing 'Footprints' by Wayne Shorter as it became obvious that it was just an excuse for Grandpa to show off on the keyboard. It sounded amazing, though! I botched up my bit, but it didn't matter.

When we were trying 'Little Sheri' by Stan 'The Man' Turrentine, Nathan passed the door with his skateboard, must have liked what he was hearing and came in and started playing the skateboard as a drum! He actually started recording it on his phone before he began to join in.

Before the last song, Grandpa said, "Do this for me. Be like Sonny Rollins, will you? He practised every day to master his craft and when there were dark days, he chased them away with delightful tunes. And don't let the gardening drop, will you? You could maybe link the two skills."

I hated that—him talking like we were near the end. I said I wanted to play 'St Thomas' by Sonny Rollins, but Grandpa said no, he wanted 'Theme for Ernie' by John Coltrane. He asked if I'd play it at his funeral and I told him to stop and that I hadn't even played anything in front of anyone, not even my friends and that he shouldn't talk about things like that.

But there was no stopping him. "Oh, and I'd like 'Tenderly' by Ben Webster as the playing in song—you'd swear his saxophone had a voice of its own— and 'O Grande Amor' by Stan Getz as the playing out tune," he said. "Can't beat a bit of Bossa Nova!"

After helping Grandpa to his single downstairs bed as he was tired, I ran straight up to my room to write the names of those songs down before I forgot. We didn't talk at all after leaving the music room. I just gave him a kiss once he was settled in his bed.

As he fell asleep, he repeated the words, "Can't beat a bit of Bossa Nova" but he added my name on the end—"Can't beat a bit of Bossa Nova, Ollie."

Grandpa only woke up when a man came round to the house to deliver oxygen. It had been helpful for Grandpa to have oxygen going up his nose through two rubber see-through tubes, but now apparently, he needed a big ugly mask that covered half his face. The Oxygen Man was amazed Grandpa hadn't been hooked up to the oxygen at all while we'd been jamming.

Mam told me off for exhausting Grandpa. I shouted at her and told her that it was he who'd suggested playing music and that we'd loved it and that he was fine with plenty of energy. That's when Sam said something I'll never forget,

"It's a well-known phenomenon, people having a last spurt of energy before the end."

I wish he hadn't said that. I hated him for saying it. I told him he didn't know anything.

I went to talk to Grandpa after he'd been fitted with the mask and to tell him I was going to say sorry to Poppy and Kamal and Jasvandi, but a nurse had arrived and he was fighting with her, Grandma and Dad. When I say fighting, I mean he was grappling to get the mask off, so the nurse, Grandma and my dad were putting it back on and holding him down. I spun out of the room and leaned against the hall wall. Loud puffs of air started pumping out of my nose every second. I must have sounded like a train slowing down. As I stayed, supported by the wall, my mam appeared from upstairs, rested her hand on my shoulder, and told me that the nurse was going to sedate Grandpa. I didn't even know what that meant, but I shouted no and started crying and Mam held me. "He hasn't eaten for two days, Ollie," she said. "I'm going to sit with him through the night tonight. Do you want to sit with me?"

"No. Yes," I said.

Before I sat with Mam in the living room all night on the sofa, I did what Grandpa had told me to. I decided to try to forgive myself and apologise to my friends for the terrible mess I had caused. I sent this:

'Dear Kamal, Poppy and Jasvandi [it took me about fifteen minutes to decide the order of their names],

Words are cheap, but please accept my heartfelt apologies for spoiling everything. I have ruined the best relationships of my life. I need to write separate words to each of you, but these are for all of you.

I was going to write that part of me loves you all in different ways, but there is no room for half-truths here. All of me loves you all in different ways.

Poppy, thank you so much for the beautiful post card which I have read more than once. I hope you have found the happiness you so deserve with your boyfriend, Greg. **Jasvandi**, thank you for the emails which were both informative and helpful to me. I feel terribly sorry for you about what happened to you.

Kamal, I can't imagine how you must be feeling with the devastating news about your past, never mind as a result of how I have treated you. I hope that one day you will find it in your heart to forgive me.

If I never see any of you again, actually even if I do see any of you again, please can I say thank you for sharing your precious time and your precious souls with me. They will be entwined with mine forever.

Your contrite and humble friend,

Oliver Timothy Campbell'

When I went to sit with Mam and Grandma on the sofa in the same room as Grandpa, they had both fallen asleep. Grandpa was asleep too. He had on the oxygen mask and a bag attached to him, so he didn't need to get up to go to the toilet. It was quite hard to get close enough to give him a proper hug with all that going on, but I did my best. Then I sat down on a little stool which was next to the bed and held his hand and talked to him quietly for a bit. I said quietly,

"You were right, Grandpa. I have written to my friends to say sorry and I have tried to start to stop hating myself and it definitely feels better. That feels better but now watching you here doesn't feel so good. I remember saying this to Lily and I want to say it to you. It's okay if you want to go to the next place, you know, the one we were talking about."

I squeezed his hand harder and put the other on his bony shoulder.

"You know if you think it really is time, you should feel calm and float away. I said this to Lily too... I love you. I know we're not the sort of family who says it much, but I love you, I love you, I love you, Grandpa."

I leant my head on the pillow next to his and heard him gasping and saying something. I knew he wanted me to lift the mask, so I took it off. He whispered, "I love you", then another word after it. I said,

"What?"

And he said really clearly and with a lot of effort,

"Intensely"

And he managed to squeeze my hand.

I made a quarter-hearted attempt to replace the mask but Grandpa managed to show me he didn't want it so I didn't put the mask back on him.

'Intensely' was the last word he spoke. And I'm afraid I have to tell you that I don't mean the last word that night, but rather the last word ever.

I got up and leant over him for one last big hug and kissed his cool maskless cheek which the nurse had shaved that morning (the cheek not the mask). I stayed lying over him, pouring everything I had into the last bit of him. "Don't forget to give me a sign," I said.

"Is everything okay? Your sobs woke me up," Mam said from the sofa.

I didn't want to speak and didn't think I could possibly get words to form, but I managed to say,

"He's gone."

"Oh no. No, Dad," Mam cried, throwing her hand to her mouth and went to hug him. Then she came to hug me. Grandma sat staring into space then toppled sideways on the sofa, her head in her hands. Mam and I stood shaking and weeping next to the bed for a good long while. Eventually Mam pulled away and said,

"Did he say anything?"

I didn't answer.

"Ollie, did he say anything before he passed?"

For some reason I said no. She said she knew he couldn't have as he was too sedated to have been able to speak. Truth be told, I didn't want her to feel bad, you know, that he hadn't said, "Tell my beautiful wife and daughter that I love them very much."

Neither of us wanted to leave the room, so she phoned Dad who came straight down with Sam and Nathan. They all went to Grandpa and said totally different types of things. I mean they expressed themselves in totally different ways. I sat on the sofa and stared in a zombie-type way. Dad said something about missing him and he said thank you at some point. Sam held his hand and told him what a fine man he had been and what a great influence. Nathan kept saying he couldn't believe he was gone, repeating that it couldn't be true and lying his head on him crying out loud. Dad had to pull him off and asked Nathan to let Grandpa go in peace. Sam said he had already gone, which set Nathan off even more. Dad left the room and came back to tell us that he'd made a few phone calls and that a doctor would be coming very soon, then Grandpa would be taken away. The words crushed my heart like a ten-storey house falling on me and sending me spinning down and down through the ground to the middle of the earth.

Grandpa no longer had free will. He would be 'taken away', like a criminal hand-cuffed and escorted off the premises. I suppose his last expression of free will was the decision to die. It did seem like he'd chosen an appropriate moment. He was skilled like that—the way he knew exactly when to say or do something.

We all waited for the doctor, but we had to go out of the room when he arrived. Nathan said that it was unfair and we should be able to spend those last minutes with our beloved grandfather. I was relieved in a way that we had to leave.

I was not relieved however when two men came to carry Grandpa out of the house on a stretcher. I couldn't bear to look. I turned to face the wall in the hallway, leant my head against it, closed my eyes and tapped the side of my right fisted hand over and over on the wall. It wasn't a bashing to create numbness, just gentle drumming as a distraction from the devastating reality. He was leaving. Not going for a walk or going to a jazz concert or going to a lecture on Egyptology or to play the piano in the church hall or to fiddle with his VW camper van but going and really and truly never coming back. No more 'I'm home!' or 'What's cooking? I'm starving!' or 'Hooof it's freezing out there!' Nothing. No more coming home. Never again would his beautiful soul cross the threshold. He was leaving for the last time. Leaving for good.

When I heard the front door close, I ran up to my bedroom, shut the door and went to bed. Well, to be honest, I more or less threw myself onto the bed. I squeezed and rocked the pillow like it was Grandpa and made my throat raw with out-loud sobs which I don't remember ever doing before in my whole life (I mean making quite a significant noise when crying, like they do in films). I can't remember doing that even after Lily. I don't imagine I'll ever do it ever again either.

It's strange what occurs to you at these unreal times. I thought I should let my friends—ex-friends I ought to say—know about the death, but that it would be too embarrassing to write another email to Kamal, Poppy and Jasvandi saying, 'Hi, it's me again. Just thought I'd add that Grandpa died today.'

JASVANDI'S JOURNAL 7

Dear Journal,

It is with a heavy heart that I tell you we all finally heard from Ollie. What a relief, but what weight he has put on himself! And now we find out that his grandfather has died.

So glad that Poppy came to her senses and dropped Greg after hearing about Ollie's grandpa dying from her mom. And even moooooooore glad that she decided to go back to England to attend the funeral and not come back to LA. Ollie's new nightmare ends the one here.

The night before she left, we had dinner together and it all came out: that she had hated me for only a short time because it had been Ollie she'd been mad at and that she was mad at him only because she loved him so incredibly deeply and had done for years and it was like torture seeing us holding hands and imagining us two together.

It was such a relief to hear her finally say it.

Amazingly, she asked me what she should do. I guess I'm older than her. I begged her to go back home and tell him how she felt. I told her that they're not thirteen anymore and that it is actually cool to use words to tell someone the truth instead of playing games.

"What if he doesn't feel the same?" she had said. For sure he didn't necessarily show it, but my hunch was that he was as in love with her just as much as she was with him, so I urged her to forgive him, to go see him, and to claim her prize. I reckoned it would be the perfect time. Geez, the guy needs some comfort after all he's been through and now his grandpa. He so loved that man.

Can't wait to hear how it goes. She promised to call me. She's real sweet, Poppy. She deserves to be with the love of her life and Ollie needs her. I feel so responsible for all the shit that went down too. Please, dear Cosmos, make this work out!

CHAPTER TWENTY-FIVE

Playing the saxophone on the altar was like an out-of-body experience. At least the horror of Grandpa gone for ever, his body lying in a box a few feet away from me and the fear and humiliation of performing in front of hundreds of people cancelled each other out. A detached numbness enveloped me like an anti-depressant cloak.

When everyone in the church clapped, however, when I'd finished playing my version of 'Theme for Ernie' by John Coltrane which I had practised pretty much non-stop for a week, the cloak was tugged off me and flung away. The emotion library would have this feeling in a huge glass case—'Stay well away: person liable to melt into the ether if touched by the faintest of breezes or the lightest of feathers.'

Lucky for me that my grandma is made of something even lighter than the lightest breeze or feather and came to my rescue. Time only existed up to the point of my solo, so I stopped. I just stopped and stood on the altar, still and quiet like dim light-energy hovering, waiting for its next calling. Grandma took my hand and led me to my seat. I floated back and hovered in that space till it was all over.

I remember having to be first with Grandma to walk down the aisle out of the church once the service was over. I can't tell you how exposed it made me feel. I imagined everyone thinking, 'What a pathetic little blob of human suffering' (in a good way). I didn't notice anything or anybody as we walked out. Quivering and sparking with raw electricity, I was snapped back into reality after we'd made our way outside. Sam and Nathan, who'd both been 'pall bearers' (coffin-carriers) patted my back, telling me well done for 'keeping it together' to play my sax and then Mam and Dad, once out of the church, said that Grandpa would have been proud of me. I wanted to say, 'He might still be here, you know, in a different realm? In which case it's okay to say that he *is* proud of me not that he *would* be.' But I only said, "Thanks."

Everyone looked nice, I mean well turned out. Mam looked lovely with her new black coat and the shiny curls of her freshly coloured hair. Her black slightly heeled shoes, polished within an inch of their life, looked equally new, though I'd seen them so many times, I think she must have had them since before I was even born. Grandma shone through her grief with her luminous honest face and her red and green coat with red flat buckled sandally shoes. Dad looked handsome with his hair cut and his new suit.

Us three boys had on the same grey suits we got for Lily's funeral, mine noticeably ill-fitting. The family all stood in a gaggle near the church doors and a constant flow of people came up, all pulling the appropriate faces, making the correct gestures, and saying the right words as they hugged my grandma, mam, and dad. Sam, Nathan and I seemed invisible (not that it bothered me one tiny bit—I was gladly slipping back into my numbing cloak.)

Then it happened.

A skinny Asian guy in a suit and tie was shaking my grandma's hand, but she grabbed him and gave him a swaying rocking nearly-lifting-him-off-the-ground hug.

Kamal.

He said something to my mam and she hugged him too, then she pointed to me. He turned his head and body to the right in slow motion to see who she was pointing at then whipped back to face her. She said something else and I saw him shaking his head. I imagined he was saying that no, he wouldn't be talking to me. But after walking away from Mam and briefly shaking my dad's hand, he looked back over to me. This time it was me who whipped my head away, well down to the ground actually.

I felt him, his energy, moving towards me. I couldn't look up at first. Then he was there. I wanted a trap door to open underneath me and for me to drop down, and for the whole thing to take its course so swiftly that he wouldn't know where I'd gone.

"That was the first time..." he said, but he seemed to halt, to wait to see if I was going to look up. His voice made me want to cry. I felt like I'd spotted a long lost fragile but steadfast ship sailing into the harbour after countless treacherous years at sea. My gaze remained fixed on the ground, but I said,

"Funeral."

"What?"

Then I looked up. Silver threads of pain shimmered and tightened between our eyes, so taut that I had to look down again. But I did respond. I said, without looking at him,

"Grandpa's was your first funeral?"

"No," he said. "It wasn't. It was the first time I've seen you play. Heard you."

"Oh."

I looked up at him briefly without moving my head, before glancing over to my mother who was smiling and nodding at me.

"It took everyone to a different place, like there was a vaporuous drug permeating the air," Kamal said. I had missed Kamal's talk and felt the vague rumblings of a smile which never quite emerged. He said, "Music is the safe king of high."

"Shakespeare?"

"Jimmy Hendrix."

"Oh."

"Did you see who is here?" Kamal asked me.

"Plenty of people; it's comforting. I heard about the secrets coming out. Must have been terrible."

"Yes. Well. I would say I've had my fill of secrets for one lifetime. Turns out you were right all along. You can't trust anyone. You shouldn't."

He was about to say something else when my mother came over to us and said I had to join my brothers to go to the crematorium. She insisted that Kamal come back to the house afterwards for the funeral party, the wake. He made a wriggly awkward protest, fiddling with his glasses and saying he didn't know if it would be appropriate. Mam (quite rightly in my opinion) told him to stop being silly and that he'd better be there. I seem to remember that she did say those very words—"You'd better be there"—because I wanted to say, "Or else what? He would be no longer welcome at the house? You will not permit him to see me ever again?" Such bans would seem entirely meaningless since he hadn't been to the house or wanted to see me for months anyway.

As I made my way out of the church gates, I heard Grandma saying to Sam, "See you at the Crem." People her age must have so many folk die on them that they give the crematorium a nick-name, it being such a regular haunt. Seemed weirdly flippant to me.

It wasn't till I was sitting in the back of the posh black car with Sam and Nathan, my face soothed by the cool glass, that my eyes were drawn to a straggly group of girls at the gates of the church. Hanging back from the group, like a bird who hadn't learned to fly, was a vision that jolted me upright. A pulse of electricity charged through me. The car pulled away and as it crept forward, my head slow-swivelled to the right, my eyes fixed on the apparition. Just when I couldn't move my head any further, my gaze still locked on her, the girl looked up like she'd been tapped on the shoulder and stared straight at me. Her eyes sent stinging wells of water into mine. I suppose everything was just sitting there behind my face, ready to gush out, waiting for the movement of a hair to set it off. And this was not a hair. This was a volcano. The sobs came so loud that the driver, who'd barely set off, put on the brakes. Sam put his arm round me and told the driver to go ahead and that I was all right. I'm glad he said that because I wasn't at all sure myself. I couldn't see, but I felt that Nathan was passing me a full box of tissues. After scraping one after the other from the box, and when it seemed like we must have arrived at the crematorium as the car was slowing right down, my eyesight started to return and I noticed it said, 'Man Size Tissues' on the box. I hadn't realised that men's tears were bigger then women's.

The short service in the crematorium was torture. All I remember is the musical backdrop to the pain—some of my grandpa's favourite tunes and a new stunning but sad piece my uncle Francis had written called 'Be Still'. I left the nearly empty box of tissues on the bench, hoping the next poor sod in that day's grieving queue could make use of them.

"I saw Poppy outside the church," I said to Kamal as we sat on the edge of the bench outside the kitchen. We both held plastic beakers of punch that my mam had made—a fruit punch, not alcoholic, though I wished at that moment that it had been. The plants in pots lining the patio alternated between being perfectly still then bobbing back and forth, unsure of which way they were going.

Kamal pulled the sleeves of his suit down over his hands as if trying to protect himself. Maybe he didn't want to talk about her or maybe he had nothing to say. I said,

"I didn't even know she was here. In England. I wasn't expecting—"

"She was so fond of your grandpa," Kamal said.

"Of course."

He sat upright and moved back saying,

"You didn't think she'd come back for *you*, did you? After everything that happened?"

I stayed on the edge of the bench and leaned forward to create more distance between me and him. I felt knots in my chest and my ears started throbbing. I said,

"I didn't expect her to come back at all. I can't tell you how it makes me feel, though."

"The course of true love never did run smooth," Kamal said.

I turned to look at him and his eyes shone into mine with pain and hope. I said, without averting my gaze,

"Midsummer Night's Dream. Act 1 Scene (i)."

It warmed my heart to know how much that would tickle Kamal— me knowing the exact provenance of the Shakespearean quote. And it warmed further when he added,

"Line 134."

I'll never forget the way we connected then. I don't know if I fed off him or he fed off me. It was as if we'd spent months practising our lines and we'd finally got them right. A beautiful baby emerging at the end of a troubled pregnancy. A tomato plant snapped in the wind, patched together, then miraculously bearing its first fruit. I pushed myself up and walked to the brim of the patio, looking down onto the tiers of garden. I thought of Grandpa telling me to keep it up, keep the gardening going. My eyes panned to the rose bush Lily and I had planted. I was glad she was dead so she didn't have to be upset about Grandpa. Then I changed my mind and imagined how well I could have comforted her and how we'd have talked it through, talked and talked. About everything. I imagined how cross she'd be if she knew Kamal and I had fallen out. It occurred to me that I had hardly anyone left at all to talk to. I took a deep breath, pushed my hair back and turned to ask Kamal if he remembered gardening with Lily. Of course he did. That was only the second time I ever saw Kamal cry. His smile was of regret then.

"How life can slip through your fingers," he said. "How you can lose everything. We should make bloody sure we don't lose people if we can help it."

"I concur," I said.

He laughed through his tears and said,

"You sound like me."

When I told him I took that as a complimnt and I saw his thin face light up with smug love, I knew we were okay. That we would always be okay.

Kamal had received a text to say Gopi had arrived at the house so he made his way back inside. I stood and stared for a bit then I too made my way in and up to my room. I climbed the stairs to the ground floor, passing pictures of me and my brothers, but mostly Lily, turned left to go along the corridor and swung left again, past the living room door to go upstairs to the bedrooms. My right foot was on the bottom step when a certain voice stopped me in my tracks. I turned around a hundred and eighty degrees and sat on the stairs.

"It's so nice being here, even though it's a dead sad time."

Poppy was in the house!

Poppy Teasdale was there, in person, in the room where Grandpa had died a week before, talking to Nathan. Talking to my brother about America and her lover no doubt. My jaw naturally dropped open again. I thought that only happened in books, but here I was, sitting on the stairs, jaw most definitely dropped.

Nathan was never one to beat about the bush—"How come you and Ollie fell out? Did something happen in Los Angeles?"

I put my hands by my sides grasping onto the edge of the stair and leaned a teeny bit forward, wanting to hear, not wanting to hear, still open-mouthed.

"Yes, but I don't want to talk about it," she said.

I leaned back again and let out a long tired breath.

CHAPTER TWENTY-FIVE

"You've spoken to him now though right?"

She didn't answer and I was starting to pull myself up to standing, to continue climbing the stairs, when she said,

"I was thinking that might happen today, but I haven't seen him. Not apart from in the car, you know, the funeral car."

Nathan said,

"He's probably in his room. I think Kamal's here. He'll be chatting with him up there I expect. I'm relieved they're friends again. He's been pretty depressed lately."

As I started up the stairs, he was persuading her to go up and join 'us' and said that he would go with her.

At that, I put on a burst of that quiet secret running-upstairs you sometimes do which always ends in falling over. I picked myself up and scuttled left up the next staircase to my room. Once in, I closed the door and leaned on it, puffing. I locked it. It was easy now. I'd just stay quiet if they came up. Poppy was not scary yet my heart pounded at the thought of seeing her, talking to her, listening to her speak of her new boyfriend. I would leave it for today, I thought, and call her maybe the next day.

It didn't work because as soon as I heard Poppy's voice asking if I was in there, I forgot all logical intentions and opened the door. Nathan had his arms folded, composed, mildly expectant, like he was about to watch two people debating or playing Scrabble.

Nathan and Poppy stood in the corridor waiting to be asked in, but it felt like an unarranged meeting I was being forced into. God, not at all that I didn't want to be with Poppy, even slightly near her. I just couldn't face everything being dredged up that particular day and Nathan's reaction hearing it all for the first time.

"What do you want?" I cringe when I remember saying that.

"I want to talk to you. I'm sorry," Poppy said.

It made my eyes sting that she thought it was she who needed to apologise. I saw her, really saw her that moment, like for the first time properly in my whole life. Sweet, beautiful Poppy Teasdale. I loved her more than anything. She took my breath away. Not as much of that black stuff around her eyes as usual, I noticed, though what was there was slightly smudged. She seemed altogether lighter, more angelic. The blonde hairstyle she'd had in LA had grown out and the tousled look softened her already wildly pretty tanned face. It killed me that this perfect soul was about to tell me that although she forgave me, she wanted to let me know that she'd met someone else and that she was properly moving to LA to be with him.

"Are we coming in or not?" Nathan said. It was like he was the bodyguard or something. Mind you, I had hurt Poppy so much, maybe she did need one.

I didn't want Poppy to feel bad, being forced to sort of reject me in person, so to soften the blow, I thought I'd more or less suggest that I wasn't available anyway.

When we were finally in my room, I asked how Poppy was. She didn't seem to have much to say at all, which made my job easier. She said she was 'fine'. Great. Then she asked how I was.

"I don't feel 100% in my life at the moment, but I'll feel a lot better when [and I honestly swear to you now that I didn't know at that point what was going to come out of my mouth] ..."

"What?" Nathan said, tilting his head and screwing up his mouth.

"I'll feel a lot better when... I move to Leeds to live with Grandma."

There you have it. Instant ticket out for Poppy. And what a bloody good idea it was too—to move in with Grandma. She would be going back to her house in Leeds now and without Grandpa. Nathan, innocent as ever, said,

"Oh wow, I didn't even know you were doing that. Makes sense I suppose. Lovely for Grandma. Nice move bro."

I couldn't quite suss out Poppy's expression. I thought for a moment she looked disappointed, but that wouldn't have made any sense since she didn't even live in England any more, never mind Newcastle. I was on a roll now with my next layer of compost,

"Cheers, Nathan. I've enrolled on a course there starting September too, so that should keep me busy and out of your hair for a couple of years."

He came to hug me saying,

"Enough of that, man. You don't get rid of me that easily. Some awesome skate parks in Leeds. You'll be back here plenty though, eh?"

"I don't feel like there's much here for me anymore."

Poppy turned her head to the right and covered her mouth with her hand. Had I made her cry? I suppose I *was* partly trying to make her feel guilty for 'leaving me'. Nathan, give him his dues, did try to smooth the awkward situation by saying, "But you have friends here?" However, it went more than slightly wrong. I said, "I used to," which was apparently the worst thing I could possibly have said. Poppy made for the door. I ran after her and pulled her shoulder round. I said,

"You haven't even said anything!"

"I said sorry, but that's obviously not enough. You obviously still hate me!"

She pulled away and started running down the stairs, so I shouted after her,

"You're the one who said you hated me! Back in Los Angeles?!" Don't you remember?"

She was out of sight by now, but she shouted up,

"Oh yes, I remember Los Angeles all right! So long, Ollie!"

A frozen moment having passed, a shriek emanated from my mouth which seemed to come through me from the depths of the earth itself,

"Come back! Please come back, Poppy! I love you!"

Nathan said,

"Finally. When or if Poppy leaves, I'm coming back to your room with Sam, and I want to hear the whole bloody LA story. Okay?"

"Okay."

And with that, the being of light in the form of Poppy Teasdale appeared at the top of the stairs. I mouthed the words, 'I'm sorry' and wasn't expecting no sound to come out. Maybe I had made myself mute from the yell. Nathan walked round her as he descended the stairs and he patted her back. Poppy didn't move so I went to her. Life concentrated itself in my hand when I went to take hers. I thought it would melt in mine, her hand was so soft. It made me gasp for air. Poppy closed her eyes. Did she want the ground to swallow her up? Did she want to be beamed up to the sky? Did she want me to kiss her. I decided the last was the most likely so I helped her up the last step, she leaned back onto the bannister and I kissed her. Her eyes remained closed till I pulled away. It was the briefest of things but seemed like the only kiss which had ever happened in the history of the universe. It was as if all my life and everything which had ever happened till that point was leading to this moment. Her lips were as I had always imagined. We surely knew each other from a previous life, so perfectly did we fit together. Everything was exactly as it should be. Intensity and honesty spilled from our eyes. She opened her mouth to speak and I knew she was going to say she was sorry as well, but I shook my head as I took her cheek in my right hand and pressed my left onto her back.

I wanted to say, 'You're so beautiful, so perfect,' but Poppy was the one to shake her head this time. Words were too cluttery for what we were feeling, for what we had, it seemed. I imagined the lady at The Emotion Library—"Ah yes! This euphoric jar! Simply drop your jaw, close your eyes and floooooooat..." I could hear the words and felt my jaw dropping as I moved my head closer and closer to Poppy's. There was wetness there this time and I did find myself floating. We gave ourselves to the swirling warmth of our watery world. We were each other's breath and had no need for air. All time was in that moment. It was still yet stretched forever.

As we moved apart, my hand still on her face, I wiped her tears with my thumb. Rivers and rivers of longing surged through me and without words, I led Poppy into my bedroom. As she floated behind me, we could hear words cutting through our space from another world:

"There you are! I wanted to say how sorry I was. How lovely to see you back from America, dear Poppy! Did I hear you have got engaged?!"

Gopi.

Zapped back.

I felt a stake pierce me and stood bolt upright, dropping Poppy's hand as if it were a priceless piece of china.

"Hi Aunt Gopi. No, it's all over with Greg."

The relief. I felt like flopping into a crumpled heap. I was a skittle unwilling to ready myself for more bashings.

"Come down to have a chat, yes?"

"I want to have a lie down," I said. "So maybe later."

"I'll follow you down, Gopi," said Poppy. "I'll come back up in a bit, Ollie, if that's okay? Maybe bring you some food?"

"I'd like that."

"Yes, please do take him food," Gopi said, "What a skinny thing he's turned into."

I don't know if I dived or crawled there, but I was very quickly and thankfully on my bed. I fell into a deep sleep.

CHAPTER TWENTY-SIX

It happened that moving to Grandma's for a while was good for everyone. I was persuaded by Mam to transfer to a school in Leeds. The summer term of Year Eleven was like a bad movie you're forced to sit through, the kind where you feel compelled to check your watch every ten minutes. There were three things that were definite—school couldn't end quick enough, Kamal and I were firm friends again and some magic had started to happen between me and Poppy.

I slept in the big bedroom at the back of the house. It had two single beds, neither of which were very comfortable, so I kept switching trying to discern if one of them was a tiny bit less ratty than the other. I say 'ratty' because once when Nathan and I were staying in that room, he said the mattress felt like it was full of dead rats. It stayed with me—one of those sentences which carries such powerful imagery that you can never unhear it. I could not figure it out why they didn't upgrade anything in that house, you know buy new things. They were very generous with other people but tight with themselves. Actually, there were in fact two new duvet covers (though it turned out they weren't new as Grandma got them from a charity shop and told me they were 'perfectly good'). They were bright stripey things which clashed spectacularly with the drab greeny grey floweriness of the rest of the room. Yes, they were definitely frugal with their money—as I say, with themselves anyway. Maybe it's because of all that war stuff. They say everything was rationed. You had to be careful not to waste anything and make do with what you had and feel grateful for even having a roof over your head. That reminds me, Grandma told me that during a wartime raid when the sirens went off, her auntie and uncle and cousins all dashed out of their house as they were one of the lucky families who had an Anderson Shelter. I looked it up after she told me the story and it turns out that it was an air raid shelter to protect people from attacks from the air. Anyway, their shelter took a direct hit and they all died. So, they were so scared to die that they made sure they had a safe place to go to if their area was ever bombed and it *was* bombed, so they sought haven under their special roof, and all got killed. Just think, if they'd said, "Ah, there goes the danger siren! Now that we're well warned, let's go and play cricket in the street," they'd probably all have lived.

Everyone thought it was perfect timing, me going to live with Grandma. Well everyone apart from Poppy. It was verging on unsavoury in my opinion just how thrilled everyone seemed with the idea of me going away. Nathan had mentioned it to so many people that by the time I'd emerged form my room late at night on the day of the funeral, my mum was telling me how thrilled Grandma was at the prospect of her having me as company 'for the foreseeable future'. The fact that Kamal and Poppy were back in my life didn't seem to occur to anyone. All I knew was that I couldn't rescind my 'offer' to live with Grandma. I can't remember who it was, but someone was saying it would be beneficiual for both Grandma and me. Can you believe they even said, "It kills two birds with one stone." I dislike that phrase immensely even when it's used in the right context. It seemed inappropriate to me to use such a phrase in relation to people's lives, loved-ones' lives.

Once the idea of me living at Grandma's had been put into action, I was the least enamoured of anyone. Poppy was nowhere and Grandpa was everywhere. I hadn't bargained for that. It would be like someone saying, "Mum, I really need to get away now that my best friend's died," and for the mother to say, "Well, good news son, I've arranged for you to stay for two weeks in your dead friend's bedroom!"

One day Grandma asked me to help her sort through some of his clothes. I swear I felt a sort of stabbing pain in my heart. Did you know that washed clothes still smell like the person they belong to? I didn't realise that. Unless of course they weren't washed. I wanted to make a huge pile in the garden of all his clothes, set fire to them, watch them go up to heaven in smoke and say some prayers. Grandma had other ideas—three piles which she (seriously!) made labels for. They said, 'Trash', 'Stash' and 'Cash'. The trash section meant charity shops though some of the clothes were so tatty, they should have been trash as in thrown away or put in one of those recycling containers. The cash section, well, you won't be shocked to find out that literally nothing made its way there. And the stash pile consisted of things to be kept—three tee shirts Grandma said she would wear, a few vests that she insisted would make great dusters, several scarves and a coat she said the local priest would want as he had always commented on how much he liked it. Oh, and a pair of sandals that caused quite a discussion—too 'new' to give away, but not new enough to sell. So pretty much everything was going to a charity shop. I kept a few things like his cap. That really really REALLY smelled of Grandpa. Grandma admitted after the not wholly successful three-section-sort method, that it was a system she'd learned about in Girl Guides... about seventy years previously.

I saw a programme about decluttering which suggested a simpler more modern method which was holding every item to decide if it brought you joy. If it didn't, it had to be put in a box to get rid of (after you'd said, "Thank you" to it). The cap did that for me—brought me joy I mean. Grandma went for a nap after the sorting activity and I sat at the kitchen table with my cap. I had made a cup of tea in Grandpa's 'I asked for half a cup' mug which I'd remembered to take back to his house. I then engaged in something which was like accidental meditation. I put the cap in front of me and stared at it for quite a long time, not thinking of anything. When I finally raised my eyes, they were drawn to a parched plant on the windowsill. I had noticed a row of the poor things when I'd first got to the house. But this one had produced flowers. And I mean since the day before, from being dry as a bone, looking like cardboard, the soil recoiling from the sides of the pot. It had bright red flowers. A geranium. It was an impossibility. A miracle. Then I remembered with a gentle but sudden intake of breath—"Don't forget to give me a sign." I was freaked out then and started telling myself that I must have been mistaken about the plant and got up to distract myself with the radio. I switched it on. It was 'Theme for Ernie' by John Coltrane, one of Grandpa's favourite songs, the one I'd played on my saxophone at his funeral. "No," I heard myself saying as I fell back against the wall and slid down it so that I was sitting on the floor. And that's when it happened. I can't imagine how you could hold that much in, over several months, and especially when I had thought it had already come out in the funeral car and in my bedroom, but even more came out. Music to the heart is like a starter gun to athletes in a race. I think I was supposed to be overjoyed that it was true, that there was something like a soul which carried on living when you died, and my lovely dear Grandpa was still 'there', but the pain, the poignancy was too much. So, when I calmed down, I asked in my head not to be sent any more signs. I sent a text to Poppy telling her of these inexplicable happenings and she made it worse by writing, "Ah Ollie, it's so so sad but proof that your grandpa is still around you, watching over you." As if I hadn't had enough of my life being observed and monitored, never mind by a dead person. I couldn't wait for her to come and visit. I was desperate to see her. I yearned for her. I longed for her to take some of my love and some of my pain. Would grandma let her share my bedroom? After all, there were two beds...

Of course, as soon as I'd asked to not notice any more signs, I was looking for them everywhere! Ooh that's the number of his birthday, ah that's the second time I've heard that place mentioned where he went to University, blimey, that cap in the window is the same as his, gosh I swear that penny wasn't there before, that bird's acting strange, I don't believe it, that's his favourite cathedral on the tv. And the songs... the songs. Hardly a few days could go by without hearing one of his/one of 'our' songs. Grandma got fed up with me—"Is there any way we could just go one day without a sign? I miss him enough as it is without you reckoning he's only just hiding behind the wallpaper." Of course, she apologised for her comment, but I did lay off with the sign-gazing. That is until the sign was too bold to ignore.

The letter was addressed to Grandpa. It was upsetting for Grandma—"God, you think you've informed everyone and it still keeps coming!" She went to throw it in the bin, saying it was junk mail, but I insisted on opening it, to sort of honour him I think in a way. Grandma looked over my shoulder, probably waiting to be right about it being rubbish, but she said,

"Look it's about that course. The one about plants. How odd that you've opened it because he asked about it in the library yonks ago especially for you. He told you, didn't he? He thought it sounded like something you might like. Said they'd send some information when it came through."

'The Healing Garden. A practical course in plants for physical and emotional wellbeing.'

"No, he didn't tell me. Sounds pretty amazing..."

I took the leaflet into the living room (what they called the 'lounge') and sat on the vast squidgy green sofa which ran along the back wall, facing the garden. Grandma settled next to me very close, like she was giving me support as I opened my exam results.

"Eden Project," I said. "The course is held at The Eden Project. I've heard of that. I know where it is. What a shame it's miles away."

"Can't be that far, love?"

"Yeah, 'fraid so, it's in Cornwall, way way down the south west of England. Poldark country—you know that show you loved?" I said.

"Sweetie, I know where Cornwall is and it's not too far at all. I thought you were going to say Brazil or something!"

I put the leaflet next to me on the sofa, to my left away from Grandma, but she leant over me and grabbed it back again.

"It's only one year and you come out with a diploma in herbal medicine. You could even go on to do a degree. Sounds perfect, Ollie. You don't think?"

"Yes, it does sound really good, but how do I know if I have enough qualifications? Plus, I couldn't afford it. Anyway, I wouldn't dream of it. I want to stay with you. I'm staying here aren't I?"

Grandma then put the leaflet on the sofa to her right and put her arm round me. With her right hand she tamed some unruly wisps of hair behind her ears, smiled and told me to stay there while she went and got something. I looked across at Grandpa's chair, empty of him. It looked partly out onto the garden and partly towards the tv. Two aging foam pads had extruded at one end from their synthetic covers. Well-fondled wooden arms stretched out waiting. Four spindly Scandinavian legs, back in fashion after fifty years, perched themselves on the floor, eager for the familiar form of my grandpa to press down like a crushing hug. Perhaps no one had told his chair that he wasn't coming back. I was about to actually say out loud, "He's not coming back, you know?" but Grandma came back in.

She had special eyes that were never as brimming with joy as when they knew they were about to see someone pleased.

"He wanted you to have this," Grandma said, managing to stroke my hair while handing me a piece of paper. She sat back down next to me, a bit further away this time.

Thirty Thousand Pounds.

My grandpa had written me a cheque for £30,000.

Grandma said it should pay for the course fees and accommodation, though I'd have to get a part-time job to pay for living expenses.

A stream of sentences whizzed in front of me on an electronic board—"I couldn't possibly." "It's too much." "What if I don't get on the course?" "What if I don't like it?" "What if I fail?"

I said, "Wow. Wow. Thank you." And we hugged for longer than is normal, rocking from side to side.

"He had so much faith in you, you know, Ollie?" she said as we pulled apart. "But he wanted nothing more than for you to have faith in yourself."

I remembered him saying to me, "You must take, courage, Ollie. Do you hear me?" It sounds strange but it stuck in my head more because he'd added, 'Do you hear me?'. The words brought a lump to my throat. That second the phone rang and Grandma, who still had a landline, ran to the hallway and sat in her little chair, shouting, "It's your mam." She embarked on a conversation which I knew would last ages. I got up and walked over to Grandpa's chair and sat on it. It really wasn't comfy at all to me, the original cushions having long since been replaced by the squares of covered (only partially now) yellow foam. I thought back to Grandpa bent over the chair, replacing, for the umpteenth time, one or two of the stretchy straps which supported the bottom cushion. "Bloody things," I could hear him say as they'd snap back on him as he tried to secure them into the grooves at either end of the chair's base. The dying sun spread gold light through the French Windows. The dust on the television seemed to dance. I spread myself onto the arms of the chair and grabbed the smooth wood as if to brace it for what I was about to say.

"He's not coming back. Just in case you didn't know. Grandpa's not coming back, I'm afraid. But I'm here."

I looked out to the garden and a robin had come right up to the window. So still. It started to sing. I'm sure the spindly arm chair spoke to me—"Yes he *is* coming back. There he is."

When Grandma eventually came back into the living room, I realised I must have dropped off as I woke with a start.

"No one's been in that chair."

"Oh. Oh, I'm so sorry. I wasn't thinking," I said.

"No," she said sitting back down on the sofa. "It's fine, love. It's good. I have to get used to things. I'm glad. Who were you talking to?"

"I wasn't talking to anyone. *You* were though."

"You don't miss a trick."

"What she say? Did you tell her about my amazing gift from Grandpa?"

"I did. I tried to get you on the phone, but you'd nodded off. Must be that chair—it's the main activity that took place in it. She knew already, but not about the course. Which she thinks is a great idea by the way. She agrees it's perfectly timed. She knows I want to go and live back there in Newcastle with her so it would all work out."

"Oh," I said, rubbing the smooth wood of the arm. "That's new. You didn't tell me that."

"Well are you interested in that course? Or maybe another one? Something."

"I'm grateful, you know? For the gift. I can barely believe it, that's all. It's a bit sudden. Isn't it?"

"Yes, sweetie. Yes, it is. I'm pushing things. Sorry."

She sighed a huge sigh. The breath took about seven seconds to release itself. I walked back over to the sofa and flopped back onto it, leaning right back.

"I keep waiting for the front door to open," Grandma said. "Or something'll happen, something daft or trivial like a neighbour's dog's doing a poo in our garden, and I'll think, "I must tell Dad." She called Grandpa, her own husband, 'Dad' for some reason. Maybe she only called him that when she was with young members of the family. I could tell she wanted to continue talking, so I didn't say anything, just made the right noises.

She stroked her hand across the green velvety sofa and sighed again to prepare for the next outlet.

"People keep thinking they've got to invite me to things. I usually go because I don't have the energy or even insight enough into my own psyche to know why I never want go."

She folded her arms now, like she was resolving to say no from now on. I said,

"Do you think you just maybe don't want to go by yourself?"

"It must be mustn't it? You go everywhere with your husband—walks, concerts, parties, holidays, weddings, funerals...and then there's just you. I'd regularly cry with joy or with pain at those events, sensing the unspoken empathy from my husband. But now...It's all fake smiles and trying *not* to cry out of self-pity or perhaps because of that gut-wrenching awareness of the empty space where he should be."

I sat up and looked back at Grandma next to me. I knew something of what she was feeling. I missed Grandpa terribly. I missed Lily terribly. I missed Poppy. I missed Kamal. The people I missed were piling up (so to speak).

"You will be happy again, you know? I mean some of the time." I put my hand on hers. "It'll just be a different happy."

She unfolded her arms.

"Oh Ollie, dear dear Oliver, what a great notion to embrace—a different happy. I'm self-indulging here."

She put her other hand on top of mine, so we had three there in the bundle. "You know what it's like to be left, don't you?"

I didn't need to answer.

"Shall I make some tea?" I said.

We both breath-laughed and I got up and left her to sit for a bit. I thought she could do with a moment to feel the release, that small letting go, saying stuff out loud that had only been in her head up till then. Kamal would have said it was 'cathartic'.

When I got back to her, she had perked up no end. She had an idea. She hadn't been to any of her 'Arts Society' lectures in ages and there was one that night entitled, 'Two Women Impressionists' and did I want to go she'd asked me. I swear it didn't occur to me that it could be anything other than fun, informative, and distracting, so I agreed with enthusiasm. I texted Poppy, thrilled that I had something other than mope-city to convey. She said she was really pleased for me and that she wished she could come with me. She was so lovely like that. It actually made her happy to think of me being happy. I bet some people never ever meet anyone who is truly genuinely happy *for* them. Gets bandied about a lot, you know, "I'm so happy for you!" "I'm proud of you." Don't think they really are mostly. Not that it's not a nice thing to say. I used to think it was awful people writing stuff like, "I'm jealous, you lucky bastard!" and things like that, but maybe that's more honest.

'Mary Cassatt and Berthe Morisot'—the sub-heading of the lecture was up on the screen. Grandma and I had got there early and were in the third row on the right, near the middle. It was a hall which I'm guessing was used for all kinds of events. There was a raked seating section at the very back, but no one was up there. There were normal chairs set out in rows in the main part of the hall, and a stage where the screen was. A woman was shuffling in her seat next to Grandma, trying to push her bag under the chair and hanging her coat on the chair in front. Turned out Grandma knew her. It wasn't till I heard this woman say, "I hadn't even heard of Mary Cassatt…" that I sat up. Mary Cassatt. The name was hugely familiar. Jasvandi's poster. Huntington. My mind took me back to the passageway in Kamal's house. I was listening to Jasvandi and Poppy talking. I looked up at the screen and the name seemed to throb and judder there.

"It's called 'Summertime'. That's how the light is so amazing on the water," Jasvandi had said as she was showing her poster to Poppy. Now I would learn more and could tell the others all about it.

I must say, I learned a lot from the lecture and surprised myself by really paying attention.

"Painting was not thought suitable for women in the nineteenth century, but she was as great as any other impressionist—Monet, Manet, Renoir, Sisley," he said as he discussed one of Berthe Morisot's paintings.

"Her lightness of touch and loose brush work made her work somehow feminine, unique and exceptional. Truly, it was revolutionary painting—the faces were fine, yet the background was loose."

I thought of Jasvandi saying of Cassatt, "Femin*ist*, not femin*ine*."

Eduard Manet fell in love with Morisot, the lecturer told us. He apparently assured Berthe Morisot that she would only be successful if she married a male artist. He adored her (painted her seventeen times we were informed), so he must have hoped she'd marry him. There was an interesting turn of fate, though he didn't go into it in any depth, but can you believe, she did marry Manet, but... wait for it... Eduard's *brother*, Eugene Manet?!

At regular intervals, Grandma and I turned to look at each other with raised eyebrows, reacting in tandem to surprise facts.

"Cassatt's 'Breakfast in bed' was painted in 1897 and is at the Huntington Library, California."

My head whipped round to face Grandma, but she hadn't reacted. Why would she of course? It was my memory, my truth, not hers.

"She was very close to the painter Degas, and it is thought that he tried to help her have her work accepted, which must have added to her exasperation when it was repeatedly rejected."

"Sexist dipshits on the selection panel," Jasvandi had said. I laughed when I remembered that and grandma looked at me like I was responding inappropriately. I felt like shouting out what Jaz had said, but I just shook my head.

My gaze wandered up to the curtain bit above the stage. I thought of Jaz and the lovely Huntington Gardens. How we had kissed in the damp heavy heat of the glass house, protected, surrounded by sensuous plants. I missed that moment and yearned to feel that again. Lust like a dense sweating pulsing mass. Yet I wished it had never happened. How messed up is that? Emotion Library— 'This is a dark, thin-aired cavernous corner. Take a torch and breathing apparatus.' I wondered if I'd ever see her again. What had happened to her...? I wished I could give her a hug and let her cry on my shoulder. I missed her. I wondered if Poppy was still in touch with her. I wondered if we would all meet again as friends one day. I mingled lust and Poppy Teasdale now and had to push back in my chair to make room for all the air filling me full of pleasure promises. Then my thoughts swiftly switched to sadness.

As I gazed back at the painting, at the young girl with her mother, I thought of my sister, Lily. I hoped Lily too was lying like that, peaceful and angelic, somewhere unseen in this realm of existence. I missed her more than anyone. I remembered my plants and how Lily told me to look after them, to not let them die. I missed them too. I imagined lying amongst them with my sister, grounded, in a state of bliss. I decided in that instant, that though I could never be with Lily again, at least not in this world, I could be with my plants, with others' plants, with any plants. I would do that course. I would go to Cornwall and be by myself. I would not look to anyone to make me happy but find it in myself and the earth. I prayed I'd find a new way there, a fresh way. Grandpa had arranged this for me. I loved him so much. I missed him so much. I had to do this. I would make him proud as in truly genuinely proud. He was another one of those people who could be happy for someone else. I could do this.

As the clapping started and folk began to gather their belongings, Grandma and I turned to each other again, nodding and smiling, I think probably for very different reasons.

I rang Poppy directly on arrival back at Grandma's to tell her all about the lecture. She said, "Tell me tomorrow when I see you." She was coming the next day!

CHAPTER TWENTY-SEVEN

Amazingly, Billy-Grace, Roo and Devon, with whom I was to share accommodation, were on the same train as me, though we didn't find out till
later. I was kind of glad because I enjoyed the journey so much. Part of it
was right by the sea, and I mean totally next to it. You half close your eyes
and you could be on a speed boat, though certainly nothing felt fast; there
was a cosy slowness about my journey. No one was waiting for me. No one
expected anything of me. Time ceased to exist.

Earlier that year, when Poppy had come to stay, it didn't work out
as I'd expected. Grandma made it clear that she was to sleep in 'the shoe
room' which was a little bunk room with quite a few boxes of...shoes. And
a shoe rack too. Most of the shoes looked like they dated from 1920ish.

I had planned to sneak in there but when I told Poppy about the
course in Cornwall and asked if she would come with me she said no. I
totally understood but I couldn't bear the cold truth that things were not
going to be perfect with her. On paper, I felt that things really really *could*
be perfect. I knew that if we had got together in Grandma's house I would
have fallen so in love with her that I wouldn't have been able to leave her.
I also understand that she probably took that as a rebuff and was deeply
disappointed. It was as if there was all this longing and love and lust floating in the air but it was trapped in bubbles that burst on the dirty walls,
spilling their contents onto the greedy carpet. I can't tell you how many

times we told each other, "I love you," but there was no getting away from the fact that the words seemed flat and fearful. I think that's why we said it so ridiculously often—in the hope that the scariness would go and that it would finally feel like it was enough to secure our future together.

I nearly missed my stop as I dozed off in my timelessness.

In the taxi, on the way to my rented accommodation, I read my texts of which I had three. Well I had received plenty from Poppy (our new mantra was, "I miss you" and one text simply said, "I think about you all the time" which touched me profoundly) but I had three I hadn't read.

Nathan: 'I'm told the surfing and camping opportunities down there are awesome. I'll be down, bro. Hope you come back all chilled and clever with your degree or whatever it is, man.'

Sam: 'Good on you. You made the right choice (for once in your life :o)!) No but seriously, get your shit together and untangle that sweet head of yours. Looking forward to seeing you when I bring your sax down next month. Mucho amor, Sam x'

Mam: 'Darling boy [it wasn't often she called me anything like that], I miss you so much. I miss our old life and I look forward to our new life. I know you've lost your sister and now your grandpa, and that there's still patching up to do with your friends [thanks, Mam], but you have us and most importantly, you have yourself. You're seventeen now, and the world awaits you. Reconnect with your essence through those beautiful plants and trees. Send me photos and send a snap of you with your fave, Blue Rain, as I bet there's one at The Eden Project. Write to me to tell me what Cornwall's like! I've heard it's heaven on earth! Love you, Mam xxx'

Good, I hadn't started crying. I'd have looked like a right wimp in the back of the taxi. It all made sense—what everyone had written. I thought of the first time I saw Blue Rain at Kew Gardens, then the second time when I saw it properly, as in inspected it close up. It had been in London, at Jessica's house. It was the most stunning thing I'd seen in my life... and yet I wished I'd never seen it.

I pulled out the postcard from my backpack—the one with the Aechmea del Mar on it. Blue Rain. The one Poppy had sent me. I don't think I'd fully taken in what she'd written when I read it all those millions of times. This time was different. I read it for the last time before my new life in Cornwall began and after we had said to each other 'I love you'.

'Thought of you, of course, when I saw this. I'm sorry I said 'Blue Rain' reminded me of you. I wanted you to know that I didn't just mean the 'old' you or the blue you. I can see why you love this flower. It does remind me of you. It is exceptionally beautiful with that brilliant pink spike in the middle ending with purply-blue 'bracts.' I think the description said they were called that. It is very unusual. It is tender but tough. It is perfectly smooth but leathery. You'll be amazed to know that I looked up the word aechmea and it comes from the Greek and it means 'spear tip'. I read that is because there are very sharp spines on the outside of the leaves. But inside, the plant is incredibly soft, and though a Blue Rain blooms for a very very long time, it is easy to care for. Plus even though it's easy to care for, so you don't have to give it much, it gives a hell of a lot back. Blue rain's loveliness is always there even if it hides behind spikey leaves and it never gives up. I think that's the main reason I love it.'

Now I did look like a right wimp in the back of the taxi.

Ivy Wigmore, one of our tutors, took us all out on a walk on the first day of the course, up along a path outside the actual Eden Project land. By the way, The Eden Project is a visitor attraction, I suppose what people might call an eco attraction, near St Austell, Cornwall, in the south west of England. The site used to be a china clay pit but now huge domed enclosures called biomes nestle there; thousands of plant species are grown and cared for. It houses the largest indoor 'rainforest' in the world. I couldn't wait to go in as I'd heard it was boiling hot and everyone strips off. That sounds wrong. To be clear, I was excited to experience the dramatic sudden temperature change from cool England countryside to heady tropical forest. As we walked along the high path, I wondered when we'd get to go in. Then I thought of The Huntington San Marino, LA and felt a pang of longing mixed with regret.

On the Eden Project website, it says that the place connects us with each other and the living world, exploring how we can work to create a better future. What promise in a sentence, I thought. My brother told me that they run loads of events there and even have concerts in the summer.

I must also look up Sir Tim Smit who founded The Eden Project because Sam also told me that he used to be a musical composer and producer, so maybe we have stuff in common. I'm not being old fashioned saying, 'Sir'—that is actually his proper title because get this—he was given an award called a KBE which he can put after his name and which means (don't laugh) 'Knight Commander of the Most Excellent Order of the Great British Empire'.

My Huntington reverie was swiftly followed by the thought of music and whether I might one day compose music like Tim Smit. I remembered Grandpa saying I should practise my sax every day like Sonny Rollins. I was ashamed that I had hardly managed once a week at that time. Having zoned out somewhat to Ivy's voice, it was like someone turned up the volume and I heard her saying that she played the guitar in a band called 'Swirling Makerel' and asked if anyone knew a sax player as they were looking for one to join them. Was this it then? Were things shifting and turning their face to the sun? I felt Grandpa nudging me. Then he was prodding me with a stick. I heard myself telling her I could play. She asked if she could drop by to hear me in my room (a 'sort of audition' she called it) as she had to deliver some compost to another student who lived in the same complex. The girl was apparently experimenting with some exotic plants in her room. I said yes. It made me think that I needed something to brighten up my room too.

When three little raps at the door woke me from a doze, I screwed my face up. It felt odd, my teacher being at my bedroom door. But more to the point, why had I admitted to playing the saxophone?

The shock of my life. The most beautiful shock of my life.

Poppy Teasdale! Not a word of a lie!

Standing like a sensual floaty but hardy white cosmos flower.

With a rucksack.

And a plant in a cloth bag.

It jumped into my mind that white flowers are supposed to represent new beginnings and budding love. I hoped it was true.

I wanted to fling myself around her, all over her, but she said,

"Surprise!" accompanied by the biggest eyes and the biggest smile I've ever seen. "Can you help me off with this?"

I reckon my jaw stayed dropped open the whole time I took the plant from her and freed her rucksack and placed it against the bathroom wall and closed the door and stood in front of her to look at her.

Then it was like a movie.

"You came," I said.

The precise same urge came over us both in smooth synchronicity and we leant into each other so that our mouths could meet. I saw the raw truth in her eyes. I couldn't look, so mine fell shut as she kissed me, well as we both went to kiss each other.

Neither of us had time to think about what was happening, but I can tell you that what *was* happening was the most wonderful wonderful thing ever. Her mouth was perfect and soft and firm and smooth. Inside, it was like the wet pudginess of a prunus persica (Latin for a peach). We were fleshy fruit pressing against each other.

When we separated, I opened my eyes. If someone had told me to draw the most beautiful face, this is what it would have looked like—

Poppy's (if I could draw that is.) Our bodies boldly mirrored each others—quivers, clamminess, eager air from the mouth, joint hearts beating through breath. We slow-danced to the bed and sat on the end. She turned away from me for a second to look round the room.

"I'm surprised a student room has a double bed," Poppy said faintly. I didn't need to say, "But aren't you glad?" because my shaky breath and my eyes said it for me. I glanced round the room myself—not much in it apart from a few photos and four posters, actually five. I realised I had photos of all the people I loved apart from Kamal. I thought at that moment that I ought to find one of him and me and get it printed. The posters gave a bit of life to to the room. One poster was 'Ophelia' by John Everett Millais, one was an abstract jazz painting which included an image of a girl with hair made of saxophones, one was of Sonny Rollins, and one was just words with a painted wave saying, 'Rise up before the sea does'. The last one, which I put on the back of the door, had been sent by Jasvandi. I wasn't sure about it, but I knew she'd be cross (to say the least) if I threw it out or whatever. She had sent it to Mam who then forwarded it on. It consisted of brightly coloured swirls with words over them; the top half said 'Feminism: my second favorite F-word' and the bottom half said 'Feminist: a person who believes in the social, political, and economic equality of the sexes, Chimamanda Ngozi Adichie'

Apart from the bed, there was a too short built-in wardrobe with no doors which morphed into a wide desk made from the same pale wood, and a very good quality chair which must have been delivered to the wrong place as you had the sense that everything else had been done on the cheap. I didn't have a TV. You could say the room was on the dull side. Yet it surely had witnessed much passion and conjoinings. And here it was now being gifted with yet another meeting. Surely this was different though. Surely it would be later boasting to all its room friends about its outstanding day and how the incredible connection and depth of love it had beheld had heated up its walls and blistered the low-cost paint.

Poppy pushed me back on the bed, all playful, but her laugh sounded full of apprehension. I remember thinking, "Why is she so nervous? It's not like it's her first time" and then an unfamiliar rush of intense jealousy sickened me. It literally hurt my throat when I imagined her with someone else. I never thought I was a jealous person. I don't think I *am*, but I can't tell you how my heart and my head throbbed with almost hate at the thought of someone else touching her or pretending to love her. I say 'pretending' because I know absolutely that nobody could ever have felt the power of my attraction to her and the insanely intense love or even adoration that I was experiencing.

We wriggled up the bed grabbing and tickling each other, in fun mode, but when our heads reached the pillows, it was like the director of the movie had said through a loud hailer, "Okay guys, move it up a notch now, this is serious stuff."

I swear Poppy had prepared for this encounter because she had no socks and no bra. She whipped off her dress with swift artistry and there she was, naked next to me. By contrast, I was utterly unprepared with thick socks, walking boots, jeans... Yes, I realise that I should have taken the time to undress, but I couldn't bear to 'waste' Poppy as she waited for me. This time might never come again, I thought.

I remembered being in her mum's flower shop years ago, where she worked on Saturdays, and her reading me an article in a magazine which mentioned that the whole of a person's skin was an 'erogenous zone' and that people particularly loved having their necks kissed. She had said, "Boys tend to forget that and rush to do other 'obvious' things." She had laughed so sweetly when I said, "What things?" And then we exchanged a look so heavy with promise it might have crushed the bouquet she was tying. Anyway, no rushing for me that day in my student room.

The noise she made when I bent over her, pushed back her hair and let my breath fall on her neck sent tingling ripples through me. I slowly moved my mouth and tongue over as big an area as I could reach. I saw that her mouth had dropped open and she panted ever so quietly. I had been with other girls, but I had never felt this before—felt so aroused by someone else's pleasure. It was amazing to me that something like that could even happen. Her gratification changed my own panting to gasping.

I realised it must be true about the whole of the skin being a sensitive organ and highly responsive, so I continued my journey round her body. She was like a snake slow-jiggling under my lips and hands. The moans of delight made me shudder with lust. I was inching down her body when she levered me off so that I was on my back next to her. She began to journey round me with her mouth and hands just as I had done with her. I let myself be taken to a level of satisfaction never before experienced. I think she said, "I love you" as she wriggled over my chest. It didn't matter if she had or not because I could really tell that she really did.

When I reached my hand low down, I remembered a conversation from Los Angeles. Jasvandi talked about girls all looking different 'down there'. She showed us an article which had lots of photographs and showed an artwork by someone called Jamie McCartney called 'The Great Wall of Vaginas'. It was quite shocking to me but very educational and even necessary, I thought. If you look it up, you'll see. I remember I had been staggered that we never learnt that sort of thing at school, I mean no drawings or diagrams ever showed what actual women really looked like, you know, all the different variations. How misleading it was to deprive us of this knowledge. Jaz said that because girls never really saw each other yet often saw unrealistic images of 'the perfect vagina' which seemed to be basically what a little girl looked like before puberty, it made some girls think that they were not normal. She said that they could get bad hangups about this, look online at 'before' and 'after' photos, and that some then wanted to get an operation to change themselves. I remember Jaz laughing at my reaction to this—"You look like you've seen a ghost." I remember also wondering if it was Jaz's deafness that allowed her to talk this boldly in front us, in front of her brother. Maybe deaf people were more open or honest or something? Or maybe Jasvandi was just pretty daring and amazing. I have to say it did appeal to me wildly that she so easily talked about such things and that nothing seemed to faze her.

Anyway, I loved Poppy and she was beautiful to me and I didn't care one bit how she looked 'down there'. She certainly felt absolutely sublime and the reaction on her face made my trousers painful on me. As if she read my mind, she undid my belt and the button and the zip herself. She went to touch me but then I remembered another article which had led to a conversation (okay, I know this is getting mental, but I swear it's what came to mind at the time.) I think it was because Poppy and I used to read these articles together in a sort of flirty way and now here we were, putting the articles into practice so to speak. The title was, 'Time to come' and it was about females reaching orgasm much more easily from stimulation with hand or mouth than from actual intercourse. They seem to show and therefore teach in pornography and even regular films that women mainly have a 'climax' from intercourse which is apparently actually totally wrong—misinformation. Poppy said it's because it is mostly men who make films so they skip the bits where women get pleasure. I remember Poppy got angry and said, "It's so sexist. And how is a boy supposed to learn that even if they do the right thing it can take ages for a girl, you know?"

This is what I remembered after Poppy had unfastened my jeans, so I stopped her and instead gave attention to her so that she could relax and feel wonderful. I will confess that I hadn't done this before but let me tell you, the time was soooo worth it. It gave me such keen joy to watch her in raptures. This sounds weird again but it was like it was happening to me. I kissed her in between loud breaths and then thought she might want to sleep but she conveyed, without saying anything, that she wanted me to carry on. It was too complicated to get my socks and boots off so I somehow managed it leaving them on which made the whole experience magnificently filled with mixed expressions of emotions—laughing, groaning, bleating, swooning, and finally crying. I don't think the emotion library could keep a jar for how we felt at the end—there would a be an empty section of shelf with a note saying, 'still undergoing research.'

We lay looking at each other for about ten hours before I said, "What's in the bag?"

Poppy said really quietly,

"What do you think?"

When I said, "Blue Rain" without a questioning voice, fireworks came out of her eyes and she smiled in a way that showed me we would be together forever.

JASVANDI'S JOURNAL 8

Dear Journal,

I thank God for beautiful Joelle. She made me get more therapy and everything is so much better now. She has given me the courage to report the rape again. She told me that I was brave even though I have felt the opposite about it for a very long time. I started looking up what I might expect and how I might deal with it. I came across a staggering statistic worked out from many data sources: in the United States, for every 1,000 rapes, 384 are reported to police, 57 result in an arrest, 11 are referred for prosecution, 7 result in a felony conviction, and 6 result in incarceration. It makes you understand why women don't even tell anyone. But I will try to help break the trend, starting with me.

I never believed I could commit to this level. She's the one—I can sense it. I've never felt like this before. That's how I know. A person is a person, the gender doesn't matter. If that intense magnetic attraction is there, well hey, it's there! It's magic and you can't ignore it. You *shouldn't* ignore it. She told me she thought I was her 'Twin Flame'. I must look up what that means. Maybe Ollie and Poppy are 'Twin Flames' too?

I was sooooooo happy to hear that it worked out between them. He did love her after all. Apparently Poppy has moved to Cornwall to be with Ollie and has enrolled on some sort of flower course. I wish I could visit them. I sent him something to put on his wall in his student room but I know he won't put it up. I did it more to make him think of me I guess.

Good news! Kamal got back in touch. He told me how much he missed Ollie and that he made an excuse so that he didn't have to say goodbye but that he'd given something for Poppy to take down to Cornwall to give to Ollie; he said he framed two photos—one of him and Ollie by the pool in LA and one of just him in the Shakespeare garden at The Huntington Library, Art Museum, and Botanical Gardens. On the back of the pool photo, he wrote, 'Oliver Campbell—first person ticked on my 'To Forgive' list.

It all moved real quick with Kamal and me, and we made the decision to search for our brother together. All we knew is that he was taken to Canada but it turned out to be enough. Kamal said something touching and surprising when we were due to meet him—"I'll never love him as much as Ollibags, you know, Jasvandi?" It did certainly seem like the split with Ollie had been like the end of the world for him. Geez, maybe he had feelings for Ollie too, you know, just powerful feelings. Imagine if all three of us secretly loved the bones of that guy?

Ravi is a real cool person and looks very like Kamal though they are not identical. Even their movements are similar and they keep saying the same things at the same time. I might be wrong but I'd say Kamal is finding the whole thing a bit disturbing. These things will take time I guess. One of the first questions Kamal asked his brother was about his name; he wondered if it was derived from a plant or flower. He said, "Our mother called me after the musician Ravi Shankar". It was intriguing to me that Kamal's response was, "I must tell Oliver."

I must admit I had been kinda obsessed with Ollie myself, but mainly because he wouldn't contact me. Everything feels pretty settled now that he wrote me.

Anyways, like I say, it seems like Ollie has real nice new systems in place. I so wish him the best. He's such a precious soul. I know that I'm the only one who wrote him after his 'letter' telling us three how precious *we* all were, but I don't think I used those words in my email. I hope I get the chance to tell him in person one day.

We've all affected each other so much. Maybe the effects will be life-long.

I sure hope so.

Goodnight, dear Journal.

Pray for us all that we might be courageous, compassionate, accepting, and proud enough to be the best versions of ourselves without hurting anyone else.

Amen.

Printed in Great Britain
by Amazon

63870014R00188